MORNING OF ETERNITY

MORNING OF ETERNITY

or

THE MAGIC BATHROOM

JAMES ERVINE

First published in Great Britain in 2024

Copyright © James Ervine 2024

James Ervine has asserted his right under the Copyright, Designs and Patents Act 1988 to be identified as the author of this work.

All rights reserved. No part of this publication may be reproduced, stored in a retrieval system or transmitted, in any form or by any means, without the publisher's prior permission in writing.

This book is sold subject to the condition that it shall not, by way of trade or otherwise, be lent, resold, hired out or otherwise circulated without the publisher's prior consent in any form of binding or cover other than that in which it is published and without a similar condition, including this condition, being imposed on the subsequent purchaser.

Every reasonable effort has been made to trace copyright holders of material reproduced in this book, but if any have been inadvertently overlooked the publishers would be glad to hear from them.

This is a work of fiction. Unless otherwise indicated, all the names, characters, businesses, places, events and incidents in this book are either the product of the author's imagination or used in a fictitious manner. Any resemblance to actual persons, living or dead, or actual events is purely coincidental.

Edited, designed and produced by Tandem Publishing
https://tandempublishing.yolasite.com/

ISBN: 979-8-3239-8150-2

10 9 8 7 6 5 4 3 2 1

A CIP catalogue record for this book is available from the British Library.

Darkness more clear than noonday holdeth her,
Silence more musical than any song;
Even her very heart has ceased to stir:
Until the morning of Eternity
Her rest shall not begin nor end, but be;
And when she wakes she will not think it long.

– Christina Georgina Rossetti

The hero… in order to interest us, should be neither wholly guilty nor wholly innocent. All weakness and all contradictions are unhappily in the heart of man.

– Napoleon

INTRODUCTION

"The past is a foreign country; they do things differently there." – L. P. Hartley

I wrote this book half a century ago when I was a Major in a Foot Guards Regiment stationed in Chelsea Barracks. (Not the 'Musketeers', who are of course fictional.) By the time I had finished it I had left the army and the manuscript lay forgotten in a drawer. It was only when I retired many years later and moved house that the manuscript came to light.

I read it and was surprised to find that I enjoyed it. (I hope, dear reader, that you will too.) When I wrote it I was a young man and the tale is told by a young man – James. I felt then that it was James's story. Now I see that it is really the story of the woman he loves. She is lovely and, all these years later, I confess I am moved by the events that James describes.

I contemplated trying to rewrite it so that it became an up-to-date story. I found that I could not. Too much has changed.

The words of command from the Captain of the Queen's Guard would not be quite the same. It is of course now called the King's Guard. The soldiers have a different rifle now and rifle drill has changed.

Readers will of course understand that the attitudes, the behaviour and the language used were very different then and will, I hope, accept my apology for anything now found offensive.

The Sixties are a foreign country when we look back on them nearly seventy years later; they are now called The Swinging Sixties. They were very different from today. There was no internet, mobile phones or email. Almost everyone smoked. Most people drank too much and had no compunction about drinking and driving.

The army is very different today. It is now smaller than it has been at any time since World War II. The second battalions of Foot Guards Regiments are now no more. When James joined the army in the 1950s there were ten battalions of Foot Guards. Now there are five. Almost all army officers now have university degrees; then almost none did. Chelsea Barracks was a two-battalion barracks. It has since been sold and rebuilt as expensive flats.

The contraceptive pill was in its infancy (no pun intended) and was initially available only for married women. There was no morning-after pill. The pill made all the difference to the sex lives of both genders and it certainly contributed to the attitudes and behaviour of those living at that time.

Money was different. Before the huge inflation of the 1970s one could have dinner for two with a bottle of wine in a decent restaurant for £5. The same dinner today costs well over £100, as would the £5 tip that James gives the porter. Peter Pershore's inheritance of £40,000 would today be about £800,000.

Parking in London was easy and, in most places, free. James's car, a new 3.4 litre MKII Jaguar, was my car at the time. I have "lent" it to James. It cost £1,200. It was a fine car which when I could I drove at over 100mph. In those times the de-restricted sign, which nowadays means 70mph, in those days permitted any safe speed. One had to put distilled water in the battery from time to time!

I think all the shops and restaurants I mention have

ceased to exist or have moved. The old Guards Club in Charles Street was wound up years ago. Most of the members moved in with the Cavalry Club in Piccadilly whose members kindly accepted them and renamed the premises the Cavalry and Guards Club.

– J.E.
2024

PROLOGUE

Wellington Barracks
The late twentieth century

I pushed the window up as high as it would go and leaning on the window sill I looked out. I had an idea that one wasn't supposed to lean out of the window, but I was confident that I was far too senior for anyone to take any great exception. I wanted to enjoy the view.

The broad expanse of tarmac which is The Square of Wellington Barracks stretched emptily away on either side, except that to my right at the far end of The Square some cars were parked outside the Guards' Chapel. Beyond the railings in front of me across The Square the trees of St James's Park still showed the fresh pale greens of spring. The golden figure on top of the Victoria Memorial was visible above the treetops. It shone brightly in the June sunshine. I couldn't actually see the great bulk of Buckingham Palace because the trees were too thick, but I could see part of the huge crowd outside the Palace and I could hear the Band playing from the Forecourt. It was *my* Band and it reminded me with special poignancy that today was my last day in my Regiment.

I had joined as a recruit thirty years before. Now I was a Full Colonel and in command of the whole Regiment. I was the Regimental Lieutenant Colonel commanding the Musketeer Guards, a Regiment of great antiquity and legendary distinction. Though a Full Colonel I was called a Lieutenant because in the Household Division these officers stand in for their Colonel of the Regiment who are Princes or Princesses or retired Guards Generals.

As it was my last day there wasn't very much for me to do. I had done all that I could to ease my successor's path. We had had many long sessions together discussing everything from the appointment of officers to command the Battalions of the Regiment, to the Regimental Band's forthcoming tour of America. Now he had gone away on leave and would arrive tomorrow morning as the new Lieutenant Colonel. I had almost finished clearing out my desk, though I had a few more letters to write. After lunch I proposed to walk all round my Headquarters and those of the other Foot Guards Regiments in Wellington Barracks to say my farewells. It was a sad thought that shortly after that I should walk out of Barracks for the last time as a serving Musketeer. I comforted myself with the old saying "Once a Musketeer, always a Musketeer."

My gloomy musings were interrupted by the Regimental Adjutant who came into my office and put some papers on my blotter.

"There's a candidate for a commission to see you, sir," he told me. I shut the window. The sound of the Band disappeared.

"Ought I to see him, Michael?" I wondered aloud. "It's my last day."

Major Michael English nodded understandingly. "I know sir. But there's no problem. He's here now. He's just arrived from Australia and his appointment to see the Lieutenant Colonel was made before we knew on what date Colonel David was going to take over from you. Besides, sir, I've talked to him and I don't think there's any doubt that your decision and Colonel David's would be the same."

"I see. This is just a formality, is it?"

My Adjutant grinned at me. "Certainly not, sir."

"Is he an Australian?"

He laughed. "No, sir. Not at all. Shall I bring him in?"

"Very well, Michael. Wheel him in and I'll have a look at him."

"Sir."* He left the room, leaving the door ajar, and I heard him say in a friendly way, "Come on in and meet the Lieutenant Colonel, Tim."

The door opened wide and he ushered in a fair, good-looking young man in a well-cut suit with Huntsman buttons. "Sir, this is the Earl of Coniston who would like to be considered as a candidate for a commission in the Regiment," announced Major English.

I held out my hand. "How do you do," I said. He took my hand with a firm grip and looked me in the eye. His eyes were green, I noticed.

"Come and sit down. Thank you, Michael." I nodded at my Adjutant.

"Sir," he said. He left the room, shutting the door behind him. I gestured to a chair opposite my desk and sat down myself in my own chair beneath a portrait of the Queen wearing the full dress uniform of the Colonel-in-Chief of the Musketeer Guards. I looked at the papers on my blotter. The top one was a form I had to fill in during the course of the interview. Some of the details had already been entered by my staff. The young man's title had been written on the top line. 'The Earl of Coniston'. It rang a faint bell. Had I known his father? I must find out.

The second thing that struck me was his age. "You're almost twenty-one," I observed, glancing up at him. "You're quite a bit older than most candidates."

"Yes, sir. I know. I hope it won't matter too much. You

---

*   In the Musketeers when you want to say yes you say "sir".

see sir, I have some property in Australia and although I've always wanted to be a Musketeer I felt I ought to spend some time in Australia before I joined the Army. I've been out there for the past eighteen months."

"Sheep?"

"No, sir. Cattle." He smiled. He sat easily in his chair managing somehow to look relaxed, confident and respectful all at the same time. He was much more mature than most of the seventeen-year-old applicants whom I had seen in the past two years or so.

"The fact that you're a bit older than most and have seen a bit of the world should make your path an easier one. The Regular Commissions Board is the big hurdle. I can't give you a commission. All I can do is to accept you as a candidate for one, and we can give you some training as a recruit at the Guards Depot. But whether you ever become an officer in this Regiment will depend upon you. You've got to pass the RCB. Nobody can pull any strings there. Many of the young men who fail the RCB – and an awful lot do – fail simply because they are immature." He nodded his understanding and I had a feeling that he would simply walk through the four days of tests at the RCB, as he would effortlessly surmount any other obstacles placed in his path. I made a note on the form in front of me that his appearance was satisfactory. He certainly looked like a Guards Officer. He seemed to be a fit and physically strong man wrapped in a most pleasing and gentlemanly exterior. He looked like a leader of men. His Guardsmen would like him and would follow him. Guardsmen like being officered by gentlemen and the fact that he was an Earl would do him no harm. The solders like to have a sprinkling of noblemen amongst their officers. "Why do you want to join *this* Regiment?" I asked him. It was an inevitable question; one which I asked every candidate.

"I've never thought of any other Regiment, sir. I've always wanted to be a Musketeer ever since I was a small boy. One of my earliest memories is of my mother telling me what a fine Regiment this is. She gave me a toy Musketeer."

I laughed. "Why was that? Was your father in the Regiment?"

"No, sir. My father wasn't a soldier. He was a politician."

I had another look at the form. "Your father died three years ago, I see."

"Yes, sir. He was killed in a helicopter crash. I was still at school at the time."

I decided to change the subject. "Who do you know in the Regiment?"

"Well, sir, there are a couple of chaps who were at school with me who came straight in." He mentioned two names. They were now Ensigns in the Battalion in Germany.

While we talked about them I found myself wondering and worrying about his father: a politician Earl of Coniston who had been killed in a helicopter crash three years ago. The bell that had rung in my mind when I heard the name Coniston was now shriller than before, but there was something wrong, something that didn't fit. I couldn't think what it was. There was also something familiar about the young man opposite me. Had I seen him before somewhere?

"Then there's Major Pershore, sir. I know he's retired but I've known him for as long as I can remember."

I brightened. "Peter Pershore? Of course. He's one of my oldest friends."

"He told me, sir. I stayed with them last weekend."

"Did you then? How extraordinary. I'm going to stay with

them next week on my way to Germany." The Pershores had lived in France for tax reasons since he had retired ten years earlier.

"They told me that too, sir. They're very much looking forward to seeing you."

"How do you know them?"

"Anne is my godmother, sir."

I stared at him as the penny dropped. Anne probably had dozens of godsons but only one who looked like this one and whose father had been a politician. I had a strange feeling in my chest and I felt sweat break out on my back though the office was cool. I needed the answer to one question to confirm what already I realised I knew with something close to certainty.

"What was your name?" I asked him. "What was your name before you inherited your father's earldom?"

"Frensham, sir," he said brightly. "Timothy Frensham. In fact my father never used the title, he renounced it when my grandfather died."

That, I thought, was why the name Coniston had not meant much to me when Major English had introduced us.

It came as no surprise. His looks were the masculine equivalent of his mother's. The colouring was the same: golden hair, green eyes, skin which tanned easily in the sun. "Ah, yes," I said quietly. "I used to know your parents a long time ago."

He leaned forward in his chair, no doubt wanting to hear more, but I couldn't say anything further then. A wound deep down inside me which I had thought to be so covered in scar tissue that it was impervious to any stimulus had suddenly burst open at the mention of his name. Years and years fell away in an instant. How many? Twenty? No, not quite so many. I had met this young man as a little boy of three. Now he was almost twenty-one. That made it seventeen or eighteen years ago; back in the sixties. The Swinging Sixties they were called now though at the time, they seemed no different to the late fifties. They had made little difference to my life. I had been abroad for most of that decade, first in Germany and then in Aden.

When in London I went to the King's Road only to Andrews, the butchers, and to the greengrocer on the corner of Smith Street.

I once entered a shop called 'I was Lord Kitchener's Valet'. I decided it wasn't my cup of tea. I preferred to stick to my usual people in Savile Row.

I stood up and walked back to the window. I couldn't sit still. The memories were too insistent.

It had been a fine June morning exactly like this one when I had first seen his mother. Indeed, looking out of my window now I could easily picture her in my mind standing amongst the crowd outside the railings of Buckingham Palace. I could see the crowd now. It might have been the same crowd as today. The time was just right too. As I watched, my Band came marching into my view from the centre gates of the Palace. I spotted the golden plumes in their bearskins. The Drum Major led the way. A moment later over the tops of the bearskin caps I saw the Colour and I knew that the Old Guard had swung into place behind the Band and the Corps of Drums. That had been the moment. I recalled it vividly. The scene was identical. It might have been yesterday, although I supposed the trees must now be somewhat taller with almost twenty years' growth. But though I remembered that long-ago summer of my greatest happiness with clarity, there was no denying that however similar the view might be, I was no longer the same man. Now I was a middle-aged Colonel burdened with a large overdraft and an inability to cope with more than one late night at a time. My thickening waistline was not compensated by my thinning hair. Then, all those years ago, I had been a Temporary Major, aged thirty, with money in the bank and so fit and full of energy that I could go for days without sleep if I had to.

I opened the window slightly so that I could hear the sound of the Band. As the music drifted into the room young Timothy Frensham, Lord Coniston, got up from his chair and came to stand beside me at the window. "Do you know this march?" I asked him.

He listened for a moment. "Yes, sir. That's *Figaro*. The Coldstream Slow March. They're the dismounting Guard today."

I nodded without looking at him. "It's a great march," I said. "But then so it should be. Mozart." I paused. "They'll break into quick time in a second."

"What will the Band play then, sir?" he asked eagerly.

"I don't know. The quick marches are chosen by the Captain. There's only time for one when they come back to this Barracks. You have to choose three for the march back to Chelsea."

"I see. I didn't know that."

The Band cut out and marched in silence towards us. We were too far away to hear the words of command of the Captain of the Old Guard, but I knew them so well I didn't have to hear them. 'Break-into-quick-time,' he would be shouting, over four paces, as the feet struck the ground, left, right, left, right. Then four more silent paces, left, right, left, right. And then 'Quick' on the next left foot and 'March' on the right foot. I had guessed it exactly right, I saw, as the Drum Major and the leading rank of trombonists started to quick march as the drums rolled. What seemed like a long time later the new quick march tune reached us at the window. It was of course just a coincidence, and not very much of a coincidence at that. The march that the Musketeers Band now played was a popular one, as it had been for a very long time. But it was nevertheless an odd little occurrence, albeit that its oddity was known only to me. The Captain of the Coldstream Old Guard had chosen the same march that I had chosen on that particular morning all those years ago. The Military Band music, which has a special meaning for all soldiers, old and not so old, floating in on the warm morning air and carrying that particular tune was the final ingredient needed to feed my memory. As though a button in a lift had been touched I travelled back through the years.

"I expect you know this march," I said.

"Yes, sir," said the young man at my side. "It's 'Soldiers of the Queen'."

ONE

Eighteen years earlier – Buckingham Palace
Guard Mounting, often known as
Changing the Guard

They're changing the Guard at Buckingham Palace...

A thousand people were hanging on my lips. Outside the railings the crowd waited expectantly in the hot June sunshine, their cameras at the ready. Between the open centre gates the Musicians of the Grenadier Guards Band and the Drummers of my own Battalion were poised and alert. Behind me and to my left the forty-one officers and men of my own Old Guard of Musketeers stood like statues awaiting the next order. Facing the Old Guard, about twenty-five yards away, were the scarlet ranks of the New Guard, their red plumes and buttons in pairs showing that they were of the Coldstream Guards. To their left, between them and the railings, was placed their own Corps of Drums. All told, there must have been about one hundred and eighty soldiers on parade. And everyone was waiting for me. I drew a deep breath: "THE OLD GUARD WILL ADVANCE," I bellowed. "BY THE RIGHT. SLOOOOOW... MARCH." The forty-two left feet of the Old Guard sprang forward, mine among them, and crunched satisfyingly into the pink Forecourt at Buckingham Palace. As they did so the bass drum boomed once, and then again, as the right feet followed the left. As it struck for the third time the whole Band joined in, playing the sonorous but, to me at least, stirring tune which was the Slow March of my Regiment.

The New Guard of Coldstreamers presented arms and I saw the sun flash on their swords and bayonets as they did so, but the shouted commands and the crash of their right feet were drowned for me by the music of the Grenadiers' Band. A second later it was time for me to give my next word of command.

"DETACHMENTS!" I yelled, turning my head slightly to the left as I did so. As Captain of the Guard I was positioned in front of the second file from the right of my Guard and the majority of my men were therefore behind me and to my left. I had to shout even louder than before, so that I should be heard above the noise of the Band. "INTO COLUMN, RIGHT FORM." As soon as I said "Form" I started to wheel round to my right and, having swung round through ninety degrees, I marched forward so that I was six paces in front of where the front rank of the leading Detachment would stop. Then I carefully brought my right foot in beside my left and, raising my left knee first, I started to mark time. I knew that I should have a few seconds to wait. The Band and the Corps of Drums which followed it had not marked time, but had marched straight out through the centre gates and had wheeled to the right on the road in front of the Palace. The rear rank of the Corps of Drums was just turning the corner and disappearing from my sight behind the tightly-packed crowd on the pavements.

Thousands of eyes and lenses turned their attention now to me. The crowd was solid on the pavement on both sides of the gate and opposite me the faces rose in tiers from the gutter to the highest accessible levels of the Victoria Memorial. The faces of those crouching in the gutter belonged, for the most part, to serious-looking young men who wore T-shirts and jeans and all manner of expensive photographic gadgetry. I supposed that they were intent upon taking their films from unusual angles and I wondered momentarily how I should look eleven feet tall with enormous shiny boots and a tiny pointed furry head. I concentrated on the angle of my sword, which I held balanced in my right hand. My fingers and thumb were stiffly pointed forward, not clenched round the handle. That is the only way to keep the blade perfectly vertical. I made sure that my face was set in a suitable expression for the photograph albums of the world and I waited, still marking time.

Through the fronds of black fur which completely hid my eyes but which in no way prevented me from seeing out, I saw a pretty blonde woman standing at the front of the crowd. She was a mere ten or twelve feet away from me, and she seemed to be the only person in the crowd who had no camera. She was looking straight at me and I thought that she smiled slightly. Her eyes were wide-set and her hair was gold and she wore a green summer frock and, perhaps because she seemed to be smiling at me, I wondered if I had met her before somewhere. But if I had I could not for the moment think where it had been.

"Right, sir." The voice of the Drill Sergeant, coming from behind me told me that we were ready to go. I had, I suppose, marked time no more than a dozen paces; just long enough for the two Detachments of the Guard to settle down in their positions for the march back to Barracks. Three paces behind me the Ensign carried the Queen's Colour; three paces behind him was the St James's Palace Detachment and behind them the Subaltern commanding the Buckingham Palace Detachment leading his half of the

Guard. I waited two more slow mark-time paces so that everyone would be ready; then, as my right knee reached its highest point, I shouted: "FORWARD." Our right feet slammed to the ground together and we thrust out our left feet to start matching forward through the big gates. At once I started my salute to the left; my farewell to the New Guard, who from that moment became the Queen's Guard for the next twenty-four hours. The salute to the left with the sword in slow time is the most difficult movement in sword exercises. The head and eyes look sharply to the left and the sword is put through a series of movements collectively known as the 'flourish'. It is bad luck for the Captain that he must perform this exercise in full view of the public, some member of which may well know if he makes a mistake. Worse still, perhaps, is the knowledge that the officers of the New Guard are watching and counting to see that the exercise is properly done and that the Subaltern of the Buckingham Palace Detachment synchronises his movements to those of his Captain. However, I had done the salute so many times before that I was able on this occasion to do it quite without thinking or, probably it would be more accurate to say, without worrying whether I would make a mistake. The complete movement is done over nine paces and these nine paces take the Captain out through the centre gates and into the street outside. To anyone who did not know what it was all about it might well seem that the Captain was saluting those members of the general public lucky enough to be standing on the pavement. On that day they would have been right. I saluted the blonde girl in the green dress. I saluted her beautifully, for she was worth saluting, and I looked straight at her and I was so near that as I passed I saw that her eyes were green too, almost as green as her dress, and her lips were red and full and she smiled directly at me. It was a smile of such promise that it was an agony to turn my head away as I brought my sword to the recover and strode smoothly towards the Victoria Memorial. I felt I must have met her before and deep down I thought, or imagined I thought, that there was something familiar about her. It was infuriating to have forgotten such an amazingly beautiful girl.

I wheeled to the right and automatically aligned myself with the centre file of the Band which was now some twenty yards or more in front of me. I knew that we should catch up as soon as we started to march in quick time. A moment later I heard the double beat on the bass drum and the music stopped. The Band, the Corps of Drums and the Guard crunched slowly onward in almost complete silence for four paces. Through the ranks of the Band I could see the Bass Drummer – the Time Keeper – waiting for me to shout the next and final words. "QUICK... MARCH." Bang... Bang... Bang... Bang... Bang... went the Bass Drum as the Drummer beat out a steady one hundred and twelve paces to the minute, and the side Drummers were with him at once with a rattling five-pace roll. "Out the Escort," I heard the Drill Sergeant scream, and two Corporals rushed past me, one to each side, to cover the gap between me and the Drummers. To my right I saw again the girl in the green dress. She had moved to a new position in front of the crowd to the south of the gates.

And then we had settled down to the march back to Chelsea Barracks. Our iron-shod heels cracked firmly on the pink tarmac in time to the music. Our arms swung strongly to the front and to the rear. The sun shone fiercely down and I saw it flashing on the brass instruments in the Band and on the swinging bugles hanging behind the flautists at the rear of the Corps of Drums. The plane trees were full and green; the sky was superbly blue; the pavements were packed with people from all over the world, their cameras clicking and whirring, and at one point a group of people started to clap us as we passed. I could feel the sweat running down the sides of my face and the back of my neck and I knew that under my tunic my shirt was already sodden. We marched on as only Guardsmen can, and the Band thumped out my first request; 'We are Soldiers of the Queen, my lads,' they played. 'We are Soldiers of the Queen'.

We marched the full length of Buckingham Palace Road. The Band and the Corps of Drums took it in turns to play for us. It was a pleasant march. We passed the Royal Mews and then Victoria Station and the Grosvenor Hotel on our left. Later we passed Victoria Coach Station on our right. I saw its clock showing that we were right on time.

When we reached the end of the road we wheeled to our right and then turned into Ranelagh Grove which led to the back gate of Chelsea Barracks.

TWO

Chelsea Barracks

"I feel sure that you have earned an excessively large glass of champagne, dear boy," said Peter Pershore, and he thrust into my hands a silver tankard which must have contained at least three-quarters of a pint of the stuff. It was a most welcome sight and I gratefully gulped down a good deal of it.

"Is somebody engaged?" I asked him. "I didn't see anything in the paper this morning."

"No, dear boy. At least not that I know of – but one can't be too careful these days." He shook his head, as though infinitely saddened by the foolish ways of man and maid and he drank copiously from the tankard he held. "Today," he said with conviction, "is my birthday."

I laughed. "You had a birthday," I pointed out reasonably, "in March, or was it April? When that aunt or cousin or whatever died and left you all that money you could so easily afford to do without."

"I know, my dear," he drawled. "But it's so boring having only one birthday each year. I like to have several. It's the only way I can buy champagne in the Officers' Mess for all my chums without being thought flashy or taking the ludicrous step of becoming engaged to be married." He drank some more champagne and beamed at me in a friendly way. He was perfectly steady on his feet and his words were distinct but he had a slightly glassy unfocused look in his eyes and I guessed that he had been drinking hard for quite some time.

I had found him in the Ante Room in the Officers' Mess at Chelsea Barracks. After the long hot march from Buckingham Palace I had been glad to get out of my soggy uniform and stand under a shower for five minutes. Then I had put on a clean shirt and a plain blue uniform and walked down to the first floor where the Ante Room is.

It was a large long room often criticised by its conventional users as more like an airport lounge than an Officers' Mess Ante Room. The windows were large and the furniture was modern. The chairs and sofas were upholstered in pale coloured leathers – greens and browns for the most part – and, in short, the place did not look much like the popular image of an Officers' Mess and, were it not for the military pictures on the walls, the room might have been found in any modern hotel.

On that particular day – a Friday at the end of June – there were about forty men in the Ante Room. Most of them stood in groups drinking and smoking; some sat in armchairs reading newspapers and magazines; there was a foursome playing cards in one corner.

Some of the officers in uniform wore their caps. This is an odd custom peculiar, I think, to the Foot Guards. I know that most visitors were amazed when they first saw a Guards Officer eating his breakfast or his lunch with his hat on.

I had found Peter Pershore standing under Terence Cuneo's large oil painting of the 3rd Grenadiers farewell parade in the garden of Buckingham Palace. He wore a beautifully-cut biscuit-coloured tropical suit, and during the past ten days, which I knew he had spent in Jamaica, he had acquired a deep suntan. He looked exactly like the jet-set millionaire which he was and is. He was also a soldier, a very competent officer and the second-in-command of my

Company. Most of the people in the room seemed to be drinking his champagne and he was surrounded by a group of seven or eight officers who appeared to be fascinated by something he was telling them about an air hostess. He finished whatever it was that he was saying as I approached and, giving me the tankard of champagne, he led me off to one side of the room where we could talk without being overheard. We leant out of the open window overlooking Chelsea Bridge Road while we talked. I was glad to see him again. At twenty-nine he was almost two years younger than me, but he was my greatest friend, and it was particularly pleasant that we were serving together, and especially nice to have him in my Company.

"There's no reason why you shouldn't get engaged two or three times a year, is there?" I said. "It would make a change from birthdays, and you could always break off the engagements and celebrate that too."

He looked at me in horror. "Actually put it in the paper, you mean? And then break it off? Dear boy, think of the breach of promise actions. I'd be ruined in no time."

It would have taken a great many breach of promise actions to ruin Peter but like many very rich men he was scared witless by gold-digging women. One day, I supposed, he would marry. He was entirely heterosexual. He was also very intelligent and mature for his age, though those who did not know him well were frequently fooled by the very upper-class playboy exterior that he chose to display to most of the people most of the time.

Two or three months before, he had inherited from a female relation who had lived in Jamaica what was to him a very small fortune. After the Queen's Birthday Parade earlier in the month he had taken ten days' leave to fly out there to talk to the lawyers and inspect his inheritance. I asked him about it.

"My dear James," he said cosily and almost as though he was about to dictate a letter addressed to me. "It's quite splendid, and I've had an absolutely marvellous time. First of all there was the most adorably cuddly air hostess on my flight out there. By some lucky chance she wasn't involved with the Captain."

"Perhaps he was happily married," I said.

"Happily married." He stared at me. "What makes you say that?"

"No reason really."

"Do *you* want to be happily married?"

"Yes. Perhaps one day."

Peter was deep in thought, while continuing to stare at me. Suddenly he looked completely sober. He then said, "May I tell you something I've never told anyone? It's a secret really."

"I won't tell anyone."

He paused. Then, "Do you remember my parents?"

"Very well. They were lovely people."

"They were happily married."

"I suppose they were."

"Very much so. They met in the First War, you know. He was badly wounded and she was a nurse. They fell for each other."

"I believe wounded soldiers often fall for their nurses."

"And do the nurses also fall for their patients?"

"I don't know. Maybe."

"Anyway they did. Madly and permanently. They were very happily married for the rest of their lives. They died almost at the same time. I'm sure they went off to heaven hand-in-hand."

"A nice thought," I said. "But Peter, why are you telling me this?"

"Because… Look, James. You must promise never to tell anyone this."

"I promise. I said so."

"That's what *I* want."

"What?"

"I want to be as happily married as my parents were. That is my only real ambition in life."

I was amazed. I said nothing.

"I know this doesn't really fit my image, but in fact it's the only thing I really want."

I stared in amazement. "Are you marrying the nice air hostess?"

"No, I'm not. That's all over."

"Are you serious about your only ambition being as happily married as your parents?" I asked him.

"Quite sure."

"I imagined you'd like to be a General. You are certainly capable of promotion to the highest ranks."

"Thank you. But I shan't be staying in the Army long enough to be anything much more than a Major."

"So how are you going to achieve your aim?"

"Well," he paused. "The pursuit of happiness. That's what the founders of America thought was important."

"And how are you going to do that?"

"By marrying the right girl and being a devoted husband and father and living happily ever after."

"You can do that and stay in the Army."

"For a while I suppose. But I don't want to spend the whole of my marriage moving house every couple of years. And often living in pretty grotty quarters. We know lots of officers who have had to move house more than twenty times during their marriage. Not good for wives or children I think."

I nodded. "Well, you are a dark horse. I thought you were a very good soldier, who plays the fool for fun."

He grinned at me and took a huge mouthful of his champagne.

"Anyway. Old Aunt Matilda – I never met her you know, she was older than God, but I was her only nephew, which was cosy – she only had her house and a bit of cash."

"How much?"

"Oh – not a lot." His eyes flickered at mine and he looked away out of the window at a passing 137 bus. "I think it'll add up to about forty grand when all the lawyers and accountants and people have finished doing their sums."

"To him that hath shall be given," I muttered, mock-bitterly.

He laughed, slightly guiltily I fancied, and turning away from the window he waved at a passing waiter. "You must have a lot more champagne, dear James, and then you won't feel the pain so much."

In a moment a waiter came over to us carrying a full bottle wrapped in a napkin. He emptied the bottle into our tankards, and I drank some. It was non-vintage but it was Bollinger and quite drinkable.

"What's the house like?" I asked him.

"Superb. I stayed there for the rest of my time on the island. It's not very big but it's in a marvellous position on the north coast, which is where anyone who is anyone lives. It's in its own grounds, surrounded by trees on three sides and open to the sea on the fourth. It has its own private beach and there's a terrace in front of the house and a small swimming pool. The house is only about ten years old and it's extremely well-appointed…" He broke off to drink some more champagne.

"You sound exactly like an estate agent."

"I do rather, don't I? How ghastly. But really it is bliss. There's a car there, which is useful; a large American heap filled with air conditioning devices which trundles along in the most comfy way. And best of all there's a staff of three: there's a sort of butler/chauffeur fellow. He's only about forty and extremely Jeeves-like. There's a cook. She's young and absolutely coal-black and cooks like an angel. I suspect that the butler chap, who's called Jackson incidentally, knocks her off. He'd be a fool if he didn't because they both live in a sort of little servants' wing behind the green baize door, as it were, and she's got the most fantastic body you've ever seen." He waved his hands about a good deal trying to indicate the cook's amazing curvature but succeeded only in slopping some champagne down the front of his trousers. He mopped at it with a vivid silk handkerchief. "I saw her having a swim one morning," he went on. "It was the most electrifying sight."

"Who's the third member of the staff?" I asked.

"What? Oh… the gardener. He comes up from the village every day and does a spot of gentle weeding." The gardener obviously had a rotten figure for I heard no more about him. "No," said Peter firmly. "I must tell you all. I spent last weekend and all this week at the house. It's called Sea View, I'm afraid. Aunt Matilda must have been a rather suburban old dear, don't you think? I took my air hostess along to begin with; somehow or other she managed to get some extra time off and she stayed until yesterday… or was it the day before… I've quite lost track of the time and the day of the week and all." He looked at his watch. "It's not really oh seven hundred hours is it? Far too early for luncheon. Let's have some more champagne."

"Not for me, thank you. I have plans to stay awake this afternoon. And now that you're back you can put your watch right. It's one o'clock."

"Heigh-ho." He sighed and fiddled with his gold Patek Philippe watch. "Perhaps you're right. Maybe I could toy with a little light something. Let's just finish these," he waved his tankard, more gently this time. "We must drink something more distinguished with our luncheon. Anyway," he went on, "I woke up very early one morning and thought I'd go for a swim in the sea. So I left my little air hostess to continue to sleep off our amazing sexual gymnastics of the night before and I pulled on some bum-bags and headed for the beach. There are some steps leading to the cove down the cliff side, and I was half-way when I spotted the cook emerging absolutely starkers from the sea; a sort of black Venus you might say."

"Might you?" I grinned. "How poetic of you, Peter my dear lad. Did she see you?"

"Lord, yes. She spotted me even before I saw her I think, but she just walked straight out of the sea and towards the bottom of the steps where she'd left her towel. I got to the towel before her so, in the thoroughly genty way for which I am renowned far and wide, I picked the thing up and handed it to her as she came over to me."

"And of course, in your thoroughly genty way you turned your back so as not to embarrass the poor girl until she was decently covered?"

"Most certainly I did not," Peter said forcefully. "I had a jolly good eyeful. After all I do employ the girl. And anyway she didn't seem to be a bit embarrassed. She thought the whole thing frightfully funny. She made absolutely no attempt to cover herself up. She thanked me and said good-morning and took the towel and put it round her neck and walked on up the steps, waggling her arse at me and giggling like a maniac. She might have been fully dressed and walking down Bond Street or somewhere for all she cared. And my God," he said with real enthusiasm, "you've never seen such a body. Most marvellous pair of tits in the world," he added coarsely.

"And did you feel like exercising your *droit du seigneur*?"

"I certainly felt like it, dear boy. But I had my air hostess and I didn't want to interfere with Jackson's rights. He runs the place absolutely immaculately and he might sugar off and leave me in the lurch if I started mucking about with his little bit of crumpet. And, do you know," he added confidentially, "I've never had a black girl."

"I have, she was superb."

He looked at me for a moment without saying anything. Then he smiled. "You're rather an experienced old thing in your quiet way, aren't you Jimmy?"

"I get about."

"What have you been up to while I've been away? And how's the sexy Miss Knowle?"

"Not much, and she's fine. What makes you think she's so sexy? You've only met her once."

"Once was enough, my dear. She absolutely radiates randiness. Most extraordinary girl. Not bad-looking either. Her eyes are truly beautiful. You might let me know when you get sick of her." He swallowed the last of his champagne and put his tankard down. "Did you have a good Guard otherwise?"

"Not bad, quiet, alcoholic. I saw a stunningly pretty girl outside the railings during Guard Mounting this morning."

Peter was not interested. "Come on. Let's have some scoff before it all goes." I put down my empty tankard and we walked towards the Dining Room. "Anyone I know?" he added as an afterthought.

"No. No one I know either; unfortunately. But I rather think that I should like to."

"Cheer up," Peter said as we pushed through the double swing doors which led to the Dining Room. "You'll certainly never see her again."

And, of course, I thought he was right.

THREE

After luncheon I went home. I didn't feel guilty about taking the afternoon off. This was to be the first free weekend I had had for three weeks, and, as both I and the seventy-odd men in my Company were clear of duty until Monday, I had taken the opportunity to send all of us away on leave until eight o'clock on Monday morning.

Peter volunteered to go to the Company lines to see that everything went smoothly. I talked to my Company Sergeant Major for a few minutes, but there was nothing for me to do so I left Peter to make sure that everyone had a leave pass and his pay and I got into my car and drove out of Barracks.

In those days I had a flat at the top of a house on Chelsea Embankment and it took me less than five minutes to get there. I parked in the road near the front door and let myself in. It was an old house – about a hundred years old – and the hall was high-ceilinged and satisfyingly cool. In the well of the staircase was the lift. I suspect that it was almost as old as the house and it had the sort of double gates in which one's fingers invariably become entangled. My fingers duly became entangled; but I managed to drive the contraption to the top of the house and disembark without maiming myself. I had had plenty of practice.

My flat was spacious and comfortable though, I suppose, somewhat seedy and bachelor-like, but it suited me splendidly. The drawing room was magnificent and the real reason why I had bought the place; though there were two subsidiary reasons which I will explain later. It was over thirty feet long and it boasted continuous windows along one side. From these windows there was a breathtaking view, both up and down the river and across it to the trees of Battersea Park on the other bank. To my right was Albert Bridge; to my left Chelsea Bridge. At night both were lit up like Christmas trees.

My furniture was functional but not unattractive. It was not valuable except for a rather splendid Sheraton sofa table which I had been given by an aunt. There was a French window which opened onto a roof garden. It was the second reason why I had bought the flat. It had the same view as the drawing room and it caught such sunshine as there was from about seven o'clock in the morning until sunset. It was protected on two sides by the drawing room and the bedroom, and on the third side by the house next door. As the house next door had one storey less than my house there was no window there high enough to give onto my balcony. It therefore enjoyed privacy infringed only by the helicopters which fly up and down the line of the river. My current girlfriend, Anne Knowle, was much given to sunbathing naked there, not so much because she wanted an all-over tan, but more for the benefit of the helicopter pilots in general and the Duke of Edinburgh in particular. His bright red helicopter used often to fly directly over my roof, and though I explained to Anne that that was because we were on a direct route to Buckingham Palace, she fancied otherwise.

The bedroom was next to the roof garden and looked onto it. When I lay in bed I could see only the sky, but sometimes at night I heard the horns and sirens of the boats on the river.

***

This is a story about a girl. She was called Sally, and I first heard her name on that hot Friday afternoon in June after I had returned to my flat. It was Anne Knowle who first mentioned Sally's name and she did so less than twenty-four hours before I spoke to Sally for the first time.

It was late in the afternoon and she was lying beside me on my bed. The sunshine was streaming in through the open windows and we were both luxuriating in the feel of the warmth on our naked bodies.

"They're called Frensham," she said sleepily, "Freddie and Sally Frensham."

When I had gone home after lunch I had stripped off my clothes and stretched out on the balcony on a long chair to work on my tan and read an improving book. The book had been sent to me by the Royal Military College of Science at Shrivenham. They were keen that I should read, learn and no doubt inwardly digest its contents. I was to present myself there, for the start of fifteen months' training as a Staff Officer, at the beginning of October. It was a fairly simple paperback book and its seemingly unpretentious aim was to teach the rudiments of scientific knowledge to empty-headed officers of Foot Guards who were unable to tell an ohm from a volt or one end of a test-tube from another, but who were nevertheless required to spend three months of their Staff Course fitting themselves for senior positions in an Army increasingly concerned with all matters scientific.

The sun was very hot. There was the faint but soothing noise of the traffic swishing past on the Embankment far below. My little book for some reason failed to grip and after a while I fell asleep.

The ringing of the front doorbell awoke me an hour or so later. I felt so drugged and stupid from sleeping in the sun that at first I didn't realise what it was that had woken me. Then the doorbell rang again, twice – one short ring followed by one long one, Di-Da – A in the morse code, and I know it was Anne Knowle. It was typical of her to have developed her own ring, but convenient for me to know when it was her.

Without bothering to put anything on I walked through the drawing room and down the short passage to the front door. The sudden coolness made me almost black out and I stopped and leant against the wall for a moment to recover. As I did so I caught a glimpse of my reflection in a looking glass. I looked awful. I was bright pink and my face and body were pouring with sweat. As I eyed myself without satisfaction in the glass the doorbell rang again.

I had my hand on the door handle when it occurred to me that Anne might not be on her own so I called through the door to her.

"Anne?"

"Who else?"

"Are you on your own?"

"Certainly." She laughed. "What makes you think I want an audience?"

I opened the door and she swept in.

"Wow. What a meaty sight." She ran a cool dry hand down the front of my body and enclosed me with her long slender fingers.

She smiled up at me, her thin red lips drawn back from her small white teeth. Then she put her face up and kissed me on the mouth. She tasted of wine and cigarettes.

"He's all fat and sweaty," she said throatily, teasing me with the tips of her fingers. "And believe it or not he seems to be getting even fatter," she added without looking down. "I've been looking forward to seeing him again so much.

And you too Jimmy darling, of course."

Abruptly she released me and turned away and walked into the drawing room. "But before we do anything else," she turned her head slightly and looked at me out of the corners of her eyes in what I am sure she imagined was an excitingly attractive manner, "I've simply got to get out of these clothes and under the shower. London is hellishly hot today. I'm absolutely dripping."

She led the way through the drawing room and the bedroom and into the bathroom where she stood and inspected herself from all angles in the looking glasses.

I followed her, sat on the edge of the bath and fiddled with the controls until an energetic fountain of warm water spurted from the upper cornucopia. I stood under it and enjoyed the refreshing feeling of the spray drumming on my face and chest. In a moment the ill-effects of sleeping in the sun were washed away and I felt alert, tingling with health and ready for anything – even Anne. I moved from the shower and sat on the edge of the bath again and watched Anne take her clothes off.

She did not seem to be in a hurry. I had often noticed before that once she knew that soon she would get the sexual release she so badly needed, she seemed to enjoy putting the moment off. I have never met anyone quite like her – either before or since. She truly had to have regular, efficient sexual intercourse or she became morose, scratchy and thoroughly unpleasant company. I didn't think she would ever actually be happy in the most conventional sense, but, like a veteran car, when she was thoroughly serviced and cared for she was as smooth as silk and amusing and flattering to own. I have, I suppose, as much sexual pride as the next man and praise from Anne, who would have been a natural selection to fornicate for England, was extremely gratifying. When I had done my job properly and produced in her the four or five orgasms which were her usual form, she would curl up beside me obviously sated. I always felt as though she had just awarded me some particularly coveted decoration.

She was extraordinarily expensive. Unless she was to pay for herself she would eat only in the most expensive restaurants and she had a penchant for the finest wines and the most highly-priced dishes on the menu. To be fair to her this was not from sheer greed or from wanton extravagance, but because over the years she had had a number of rich boyfriends who had encouraged her to develop a sophisticated palate. She also enjoyed little weekend jaunts abroad and I had taken her twice to Paris and once to the South of France. On each occasion I had been several hundred pounds poorer by the time I had returned to London but I had learned a great deal about how to spend my money with style, and, perhaps not surprisingly, I had found this a satisfying experience.

She was in no sense an expensive tart. For one thing she was I think more or less faithful to me. For another, money, as such, seemed to be of no great importance to her. She had never asked me for any and she expected no presents. All that she required was that I should spray money like a fountain whenever I was with her. Any sort of petty meanness with money she found intolerable.

She was extremely keen on sex. So was I. We got on very well together in bed, and she loved that. I was fortunately very well trained by my last lover – who really knew what it was all about – so it was easy for me to assess and satisfy her needs right from the start. Anne reckoned she was an expert too so our first night together was a spectacular success.

She was about twenty-five at that time but I imagine she

had been hard at it since puberty and there wasn't very much that she didn't know about men and women. She had a job as a PA to a director of a large theatrical agency, and through him she had met all manner of the internationally famous and infamous. She had often told me fascinatingly horrible stories about the sexual tastes of famous actors and actresses.

Oddly enough, in spite of her broad experience and racy way of talking she looked demure, quiet and rather uninteresting. Her face was long, her eyes were too close together and her long thin nose was sharply pointed. She would have looked almost ferret-like had her eyes not been large and brown and placid. She had a figure which would never have found its way into the pages of Playboy. She dressed conservatively (on the surface at least) and often wore hats.

I shall never forget the night I first met her. It was in March of that year and I was invited to a cocktail party given by some old friends. I knew most of the people there and there was plenty to drink, so for me it was an excellent party. Just as I was beginning to think that it was time to go I noticed Anne. She was standing by herself, looking out of the window and holding an empty glass. I had had a lovely time, but she seemed to be pretty miserable and I felt sorry for her. I grabbed a glass of champagne from a passing tray and took it over to her. She smiled at me and thanked me and when she smiled I saw that she looked quite attractive and I found that I liked looking into her brown eyes. I found her amusing to talk to, so asked her out to dinner. She accepted with alacrity, and thinking to impress her I swept her off to the Coq d'Or where I suffered the humiliating experience of realising within minutes of our arrival that she was much better known than I was. To her credit she appeared not to notice this and she continued to be amusing to be with. As the evening wore on I found myself becoming more and more attracted to her and three hours later, still reeling at the size of the bill, I found myself in bed with her. By first light next morning I was well and truly hooked.

***

Anne stood in the middle of my bathroom, so that she could admire her reflection from all angles, and took off her dress. "I had lunch at La Speranza today," she told me. "It was extraordinary."

"Why extraordinary?"

"I talked about you all the time."

I wasn't surprised to see that under her dress she wore nothing. She rarely wore underclothes.

"Who did you have lunch with?"

"A girlfriend. The one I'm taking you to stay with tomorrow."

"Why did you talk about me?"

"It was her idea. She wanted to know all about you. She's never shown such an interest in anyone else I've taken down to stay with her."

"My fame must have spread."

"Through me, I think." She climbed into the bath and stood under the shower. I watched as the water coursed down her hard, thin body. "I told her all about you when I first met you back in March."

"Oh? What did you tell her?"

She twisted and turned under the shower for a moment without answering. Then she turned off the taps.

"Absolutely everything. I went down to stay with her the day after the night we met. You remember?"

"I shall never forget it."

"I've always told her all about the men I've had it off with. I think she gets a bit of a charge out of it. Anyway I keep hoping that one of these days she'll feel encouraged to have a boyfriend of her own. She doesn't have any sex life. When I saw her that day you and I had had such a fantastic night the night before that I couldn't think of anything else. I think I was a bit in love with you then – the nearest I've ever got to it anyway – with anyone." She paused for a moment as though remembering. "I described you and everything we'd done in the greatest detail."

I felt rather shocked at this revelation, but before I could say anything about it Anne went on, "Just thinking about it makes me feel randy. Come on, James, let's go to bed."

And obediently I followed her to the bedroom to do my duty so that it was sometime later, when we were lying on the bed, that I raised the subject again. "What are these people called that we're going to stay with tomorrow?"

"They're called Frensham. Freddie and Sally Frensham."

I savoured the name in my mind for a few seconds. Then I tried it aloud. "And it was Sally Frensham you had lunch with today?"

"That's right. She's expecting us at about teatime tomorrow. We can drive down after lunch."

She reached across me for the packet of cigarettes on the bedside table, lit two and placed one between my lips. It was slightly wet so I took it out of my mouth and rubbed the filter tip with my thumb. Anne raised herself on one elbow and looked down at me.

"You'll like Sally. She's a very nice girl and she's outstandingly beautiful. I think she's the most beautiful girl I've ever seen. And she's got a stunning figure. I expect you'll fall for her. Most men do."

She inhaled her cigarette deeply and blew out a cloud of pale blue smoke which flowed gently ceiling-wards. I watched it swirling in the sunbeams. I felt relaxed and content as I always did after having sex with Anne. I wasn't happy exactly, but I was comfortable in mind and body. Nothing seemed to matter very much. I wondered vaguely if I should fall for the beautiful Sally Frensham but as far as I can remember it did not unduly exercise my mind.

"Why doesn't she have any sex life?" I wanted to know.

"Because Freddie's no good."

I wanted to follow that up but before I could do so Anne picked up the large glass ashtray from the bedside table and placed it on my stomach. It was cold. She tapped the ash from her cigarette into the ashtray. "Perhaps it would be a kindness if I lent you to her, as she seems so interested. It's my own fault for telling her so much about you. Though I must say she'd find it hard to believe if she could see you now."

"My God. I didn't think girls talked to one another about things like that?"

"Don't they?" She looked at me with interest. "I can't think why not. I always do. To Sally particularly. As I said, it might encourage her to have a little walk-out and I'm sure that would be good for her. It must be awfully bad for her not having any sex at all." Anne shuddered at the thought of not having any sex at all.

"What did you mean when you said 'Freddie's no good'?"

Anne said, "No good in the sack, dear," mock-patiently.

"Does that mean he's not very good at it, or he doesn't do it very often? Or what?"

"It means he doesn't do it at all. Period."

"How fascinating." I pondered the matter for a while. "Has he never made love to her, do you know? Or did he just get bored?"

"I assume that he did to begin with. I suspect that he simply wanted an heir and when he got one he lost interest. Sally gave birth to a boy about three years ago – Timmy he's called – a nice child and my godson. They haven't had any sex since."

"Why an heir?"

"It's a fantastically old family," Anne waved her cigarette about as she talked. "Freddie's ancestors came over pretty soon after the Conqueror and they've done extremely well ever since. He'll be an Earl when his father dies. Now he's a courtesy Viscount and sits in the House of Commons. The reason we can't go down to stay with them until tomorrow afternoon is that he spends Friday night and Saturday morning in his constituency while the House is sitting. He's frightfully hard-working and absolutely power-mad, I think. He's certain to be in the Government when the Tories get in again."

"Does he have a mistress?"

"I don't know about that. I've never heard of one, but I very much doubt whether he has any sex life at all."

"Why?"

"I'm pretty sure he's impotent."

"He can't be if he had a baby," I pointed out reasonably.

"Well you never know," said Anne knowledgeably. She puffed at her cigarette, happy now that we were on her favourite subject. "He might have just about managed it once or twice and happened to strike lucky."

"Didn't Sally tell you?"

"Christ, no. Sally's terribly proper really. She never talks about it as a general rule. Not even to me. She likes hearing about my adventures, but she never talks about her own." She dragged deeply at her cigarette. "Her troubles, rather than her adventures," she amended. "But just once – years ago – we had one of our girly lunches together and she was very unhappy and it all – or most of it – came pouring out. That's how I know about Freddie being no use." She paused. "That and my own experiment."

"Your own experiment?"

"Yes, darling," she drawled, smiling at me wickedly. "I conducted an experiment to see why Freddie wasn't having it off with Sally."

She sat bolt upright on the bed, folded her legs under her and stubbed out her cigarette in the ashtray on my stomach. She put it out with vicious little stabs and almost upset the ashtray so I held onto it until she had finished and then replaced it on the bedside table.

"Shall I tell you about it?"

Knowing that the question was rhetorical I settled myself comfortably on the bed and puffed at my cigarette. I had heard Anne tell tales of her sexual adventures before and I knew that there was no stopping her.

"It was a couple of years ago. I was staying with them for the weekend at Highworth – that's Freddie's house and, as you'll see tomorrow, it's absolutely super. Sally had told me something rather fascinating about Freddie when we had lunch in London the week before. It was stinkingly hot on the Saturday and we spent all the time we could in the swimming pool. It's a beautiful pool and it's in an old walled garden a little way from the house and it's completely private. She said that whenever they were at the pool alone she wasn't allowed to wear anything. Freddie positively insisted that she swim and sunbathe absolutely starkers. Apparently he adored looking at her in the nude, though he'd often told her that she was never to tell anyone about it. She absolutely swore me to secrecy."

"Should you be telling me about it then?"

"Oh yes, I think so," said Anne, quite unperturbed. "I've told her a lot about you. It's only fair that you should hear about her too."

There seemed to me to be something the matter with her logic but I couldn't be bothered to pursue it. Instead I asked: "Does Freddie leap about in the buff as well?"

"No, apparently not. He always keeps himself covered up. Sometimes when he comes down from London in the evening he makes her go off to the swimming pool with him and strip off and swim and walk about so that he can look at her and he simply sits in a chair drinking a dry martini or something, still wearing his London suit. And he hardly ever touches her," she said, shaking her head in amazement and disapproval, "and when he does he only touches her with his hands," she added coarsely, grinning down at me.

I took a last drag on my cigarette and crushed it in the ashtray. "I suppose he thinks of her as simply an object of beauty for his eye."

"So she is. But why only his eye? That's what I wanted to know. And that's what I reckon I found out that afternoon by the pool. After lunch Sally disappeared. I think she had to take young Timmy to some tiny tots party. I knew she wouldn't be back for hours so I thought it would be amusing to have a go at seducing Freddie. After all he wasn't doing Sally any good and when he discovered what fun it was with me I thought he might start up with Sally again."

"How altruistic of you."

"On the other hand," Anne went on, as though I hadn't spoken, "for all I knew he had half a dozen mistresses tucked away in flats in London – and he could certainly afford it – and Sally was just a hostess and a mother and something to look at.

"Freddie and I went to the pool together and had a swim and then he put on a sort of dressing gown thing and sat down in a deckchair to read his book. He went into the changing room to put it on and I was pretty sure he'd taken off his wet swimming shorts. I lay down on a towel on the grass near his chair and started to sunbathe and after a while I asked him if he would mind if I took my swimsuit off as it was all so private and I wanted to get an all-over tan.

"At first he pretended to be all against it and he made all sorts of feeble excuses for me not to, but I could see that he was really as keen as anything and eventually he gave in. He got up and went to bolt the door so that no one could come in. When he came back, I did a nice little strip for him which he watched with the greatest interest, then I walked about for a while so that he could admire the merchandise from every angle. He said what a nice figure I had and I said 'Thank you, kind sir' and everything seemed to be going splendidly. After a bit I lay down on my towel again and asked Freddie to put some sun oil on my back. He was all for it. He knelt down beside me on the grass and started rubbing Ambre Solaire all over my back. He hesitated when he got to my bottom but I told him to carry on so he did; right down to my feet. When he got there I rolled over onto my back and said something like, 'Be an angel and do my front too, Freddie darling.' My eyes were almost shut because the sunshine was so bright but I peeped up at him through my eyelashes. He sat back on his heels and just stared down at my body and I felt sure he was pretty excited too and I was dying for him to start on my front. You know what I'm like when anyone rubs me there?" she asked me, and she cupped her hands and rubbed them over her breasts and downward to her thighs.

"I know," I said. "Go on."

"Well. I thought that after a few minutes of rubbing me Freddie would realise what he was doing to me and would be quite unable to resist making love to me straight away. But it didn't work out like that. He just sat there staring at me until finally I couldn't bear it any longer and I said 'Go on Freddie, please. I shall get burned if you don't put some oil on me.' So he picked up the Ambre Solaire and leant forward and started smearing again. After a while he said, 'You've got very beautifully proportioned breasts, Anne. I don't remember when I've seen finer.' I thought of telling him that they weren't a patch on Sally's but he was stroking them all the time he was talking and I could only moan. It did strike me at the time that his voice sounded surprisingly calm but I thought that he was just very self-controlled or a slow starter or something. Anyway, as he went on oiling me I got more and more steamed up, but as he didn't seem to be in a hurry to ravish my defenceless, not to say positively eager, body I tried to excite him by making a bit of a production out of how worked up I was getting. In fact it was only about twenty per cent exaggeration because he was quite good at it. He's got rather silly podgy little hands with delicately pointed little fingers and tiny nails and he handled me as though I were made out of porcelain. I was pretty sure he was enjoying himself because a strange sort of light came into his eye. It was most peculiar. Anyway I was getting highly excited by this time. You know what I'm like?"

"Yes." I knew what she was like.

"I was practically on the brink and I was longing for him

to leap aboard, but as he seemed quite happy to go on stroking I decided to take the initiative."

"Good for you," I told her.

"Be quiet. I'm just coming to the point of the story."

"At last. I'm all ears."

She made a face at me. "I reached out and parted the front of his dressing gown thing – it was hanging half open already – and I was all ready to give him one or two encouraging little strokes and squeezes – at which, though I say it myself, I am extremely good."

"I'll second that."

"When to my absolute horror," she said seriously, her eyes wide, "I saw what he'd got."

I sat up, staring at her. My imagination was boggling furiously. "My God. Tell me at once. I can't bear it."

Anne leant forward towards me. "Nothing."

"WHAT? You can't mean it. He must have had something."

"Well, practically nothing."

"Oh." I sank back on my pillow. Anne was merely exaggerating again. "You mean his development was unimpressive."

"Oh no," said Anne, still deadly serious. "It was horrible, really it was. It was limp and tiny and exactly the same size as a little boy of six or seven." She sat back with the satisfied air of one who has just proved a very difficult point. "What do you make of that?"

I didn't know what to make of it then. (Though several weeks later it all made complete sense.)

"What did *you* make of it?"

"My dear," Anne replied sadly, "absolutely nothing. Freddie gave me no opportunity. He didn't realise I had seen the poverty of the land because he was so busy stroking.

When I reached out a hand to touch the horrible little thing – I had some vague idea that it might be miraculously changed by my mystic touch, I suppose – Freddie leapt about a foot in the air and said, 'No, no. We must stop this at once. I've never been unfaithful to Sally. Let's both have another swim.' Then he trotted off to the changing room to put his swimming shorts on. I got up and dived straight in as I was. Believe me, I needed that cold water."

"Has Freddie ever said anything to you about it since?"

"Not a word. And I've never mentioned it to Sally either. A riveting tale though, don't you think?"

"Fascinating. I look forward to meeting both Freddie and Sally with considerable interest. But there's one thing that puzzles me."

"What's that?"

"You say Sally has no sex at all."

"Yes."

"Why doesn't she have a lover? Or a series of lovers?"

"I'm not sure. But I know she doesn't. Fear of the consequences perhaps. Freddie would certainly divorce her if she had an affair which became generally known about. Maybe she's afraid of losing Timmy if he did divorce her, but I've never discussed it with her. All the best-known womanisers in London have propositioned her at one time or another and one day she's bound to give in and kick over the traces."

"It sounds rather as though you want me to be the one. What would you think if I started having an affair with her?"

She looked at me in silence for a moment or two, an odd expression on her face. At length she said: "I think it would be very good for both of you. But I think it's very unlikely that you would succeed where everyone else has failed – in spite of your many good qualities darling." She laughed. "But, anyway," she went on, "I've not finished with you yet my lad – not by a long chalk. So you can forget about the beautiful unattainable Lady Frensham and come back to the present. All this talk of sex has made me feel quite randy, so why don't you show me what a big strong boy you are and then you can take me out for a super dins at the Mirabelle. I'm feeling absolutely starved."

FOUR

The next day Anne and I had a large and rather drunken luncheon in the Savoy Restaurant at a table in the window, and then we got into my car and drove down to Highworth, the Frenshams' house in Hampshire.

Anne slept most of the way but she woke up in time to direct me for the last few miles.

There was a long, well-made-up drive which ended in an apron of gravel in front of the house. Several cars were parked there. I put my Jaguar next to an obviously brand-new dark-blue Mini. Anne and I got out and stretched.

Almost at once the front door opened and two small figures in white jackets appeared. They hurried over to us.

"Carlo and Franco," Anne explained laconically to me. "They're quite safe. Give them the keys and they'll look after our luggage."

I did as I was told and the two men unlocked the boot and started to pull out our suitcases.

I heard Anne say, "Where is Lady Frensham?" to one of them who said something like, "Meelaidee iz in zee pool," in reply. I looked up at the house. It was smaller than I had expected in view of the Frenshams' grandeur, but it was most handsome. It was – and is – Queen Anne, faced with a soft golden-coloured stone which seemed to glow in the afternoon sunshine.

At one side of the house the drive led round to stables, garages and other outbuildings. At the other, a lawn of some twenty acres ran from the house towards distant parkland and a wood and it was in this direction that Anne led me saying, as she did so, something about going to find Sally. Now that I was on the point of meeting the fascinating and beautiful Lady Frensham I found that I felt distinctly excited. I had the sort of feeling in the pit of my stomach that one has just before going in to bat.

As we rounded the corner of the house I saw a tall blonde girl in some sort of green outfit walking across the lawn towards us. She waved as soon as she saw us and broke into a trot. Anne hurried forward to greet her and they kissed and Anne said, "Sally, darling, how lovely to see you," and Sally said "I'm so sorry I wasn't here when you arrived," and "How super you're looking." Anyone who didn't know that they had had lunch together the day before might have been pardoned for thinking that they had not seen one another for months.

However, it all happened very quickly and I remember that I didn't have time to notice very much about Sally except that she was taller than Anne, even though she wore no shoes. Her feet were brown and her toes were rather on the long side and were very straight and her toenails had nail varnish on them.

After their greetings were completed, Sally turned to me and held out a slim cool hand and said, "You must be James," and I saw that she was the girl who I had seen outside the railings at Buckingham Palace the day before.

I took her hand, wishing as I did so that my own was less large. I said, "How d'you do," and I looked into the green depths of her wide-set eyes and for a moment I wondered whether or not I should say anything about having seen her before. There was no look of recognition in her eyes so I decided to say nothing. I smiled down at her foolishly and tried in vain to think of something to say.

"Anne's told me so much about you that I feel I know

you quite well already," said Sally, retrieving her hand from my grasp, "but she didn't tell me how very tall you are. You must look absolutely gigantic in your bearskin. How tall are you?"

"I'm six foot four."

"That is tall."

As she spoke she smiled up at me and wrinkled her nose in a way that I was to come to know well later. I realised that she had recognised me and I knew, with a sudden feeling of absolute certainty, that she had gone to Buckingham Palace especially to see me. The knowledge gave me such a shock of excitement and pleasure that again I could think of nothing to say.

Anne sniggered coarsely. "Never you mind what he's like in his bare skin, Sally," she said. "You're not to flirt with my boyfriend."

I groaned inwardly. I had heard too many jokes about bearskins and bare skins during my service in the Foot Guards to think any of them funny.

"Anne!" said Sally scandalised, or pretending to be. "You know perfectly well…" Her voice trailed away but she avoided looking at me and she blushed slightly. It was, I thought, a most pleasing effect. "Come on," she said. "Come on into the house and I'll show you your rooms." She slipped an arm through Anne's and we turned in the direction of the house. "Then I expect you'd both like to have a swim. The pool is really marvellous today. I'm afraid we've got some rather dreary people here for the afternoon, but they should be going soon. They're staying with the Headcorns," she added, as though that explained everything.

"Have you got anyone else staying here?" Anne asked her.

"No, thank God. I told old Lady Brendon that I was

having most of the bedrooms redecorated so that I shouldn't have to put up with a lot of debs and their young men. It's more or less true actually. But she persuaded me to give a dinner party tonight for the dance. They'll be sixteen altogether – mostly people I've never heard of."

She walked gingerly across the gravel in front of the house. "The stones are agony on my poor old feet," she said. "Like a fool I left my shoes at the pool. I meant to be here when you arrived but it was so super in the water that I was only just getting dressed when I heard you drive up. Is that your car?" She pointed at my Jaguar.

I nodded.

"It's very pretty," she decided. "That's my new Mini next to it. I've only had it since Wednesday."

"They're exactly the same colour," I told her.

"So they are," Sally agreed. "But mine is so little next to yours. It looks as though your car has had a baby."

She led the way into the house and Anne and I followed. The hall was large and cool and oak-panelled and there were paintings of horses on the walls. In the centre of the hall on a round drum table stood a large vase of flowers and Sally stopped and rearranged one or two of the flowers absent-mindedly so that I knew she had been responsible for their arrangement initially. Then she and Anne led the way up the broad staircase, chattering away to one another. I followed. It gave me an opportunity to have an uninterrupted look at the interesting Lady Frensham.

She was wearing a one-piece outfit made out of pale green towelling; trousers and a short-sleeved top joined at the waist and fastened with a long zip at the front. She was very fond of it, I discovered later, and it was, I suppose, an ideal garment to put on after swimming. It was both attractive and functional. It was very tight-fitting and, as

I followed her up the stairs, I tried to decide if she wore anything underneath it. Her body was slim and firm and, though I couldn't detect any of those unattractive bulges which women's underclothes make, I couldn't be certain one way or the other. She stopped on the broad landing at the top of the stairs and threw open the door of a large feminine-looking bedroom with a four-poster bed.

"This is you, Anne," she announced. "Your usual."

"Bliss," said Anne. She strode into the room and threw her handbag onto the bed. Her suitcase was being unpacked by a neatly-dressed foreign-looking maid who smiled at Anne nervously.

"Maria can do anything you need, darling," Sally said from the doorway. "But don't keep her too long because she's got to help me do something about my dreadful hair before dinner." She put up a hand to touch her hair and as I was standing close behind her I automatically looked down at it. It was long and damp and various shades of gold – dark gold where it was wet and pale gold where it was dry. It was a mess of tangles.

"That's okay," said Anne. She kicked off her shoes and started to unbutton her dress. Knowing how very little she was wearing under her dress and not wishing to embarrass Sally by standing in full view I moved off a few paces down the corridor. I pretended to interest myself in a dingy oil painting of some earlier Frensham who looked as though he might have been a chum of Charles II.

"I can't wait to get my clothes off and get into that swimming pool," I heard Anne say. "Can I put my bikini on here and go straight down?"

"Of course," Sally told her. "You know the way. I'll show James where he's sleeping and point out the pool to him, so you needn't wait."

"Not where he's *sleeping*, my dear," Anne called gaily, "where his room is. It's not the same thing at all."

Sally shut the door firmly without replying and turned and walked past me down the passage. Her face was blazing. I heard Anne laughing behind the closed door, but Sally did not look amused. I followed her in silence.

"That's the bathroom," Sally said coldly. "The loo's next door. And this is your room." She stopped before a door and I quickly opened it for her. She walked in.

It was a small but pleasant room with a comfortable-looking single bed, a built-in clothes cupboard, a chest of drawers with a looking glass standing on it, and a couple of upright chairs. A bedside table bore a carafe of water, surmounted by a tumbler and a pile of magazines. The top one was the *Tatler*. In one corner was a washbasin of an old-fashioned design, which boasted an odd-looking contraption intended to hold my six toothbrushes. The wide bay window had a chintz-covered seat in it and Sally went straight to this and sat down.

"May I have a cigarette, please?" she asked without looking at me.

I took out my case and offered it. As she took a cigarette I noticed that her fingers were long and slim and that her nails were well-shaped and painted red. The femininity of her hands excited me. I flicked my lighter into flame and held it to the end of her cigarette. She inhaled deeply and blew out a cloud of smoke.

"Thank you." Still she wouldn't look at me but instead looked around the room almost as though she had never seen it before.

"I'm sorry it's such a tiny room. All the others are either still being redecorated or stinking of paint. I hope you'll be all right. The bed's a comfortable one anyway."

I suppose she realised too late what she had said because she blushed again and shot a quick look at me from her extraordinary green eyes.

I sat down beside her on the window seat and lit a cigarette for myself. "I'm afraid you're finding this very embarrassing," I said gently. She turned her head and smiled at me.

"It's silly, isn't it? I ought to be used to Anne's outspokenness by now. I've known her most of my life and she's always been the same. But I wish she wouldn't say things like that in front of the servants. Fortunately Maria's English is pretty indifferent."

I sat back and looked at her without saying anything. It wasn't difficult to guess that it was my presence not Maria's that had embarrassed her.

"I'm sorry," she said. "Let's forget it. Would you like to have a swim?"

"I'd love to."

"There's a sort of bathing wrap thing on the door." She nodded at the back of the bedroom door where a white towelling dressing gown was hanging.

"Do borrow that if you'd like to." She stood up. "Just go on down to the pool as soon as you're ready. One of the servants will come up to unpack for you in a little while."

She turned to go and I was afraid she would leave without saying anything about our previous meeting. For some reason I felt that I shouldn't mention the subject first. I cast about for an excuse to keep her in the room for a little longer. I had no idea when, if ever, I should have another opportunity to be alone with her.

"Where is the swimming pool?" I asked her. "Are you going back there? Perhaps I could come with you."

She shook her head. "No, I'm afraid I've got far too

much to do before dinner to have another swim today." She looked out of the window. "But I can point it out to you easily enough."

She knelt on the window seat and leaned out of the open window. As she did so I saw that the soles of her feet were dirty, which seemed somehow rather appealing. I also realised that I could easily make out the line of her backbone for its full length and it was obvious that she wore nothing under her towelling outfit. It was a disturbing discovery.

"You can just see the door from here," she said.

I resisted an impulse to pat her prettily rounded bottom and knelt beside her on the seat.

"Do you see it?" she said. "Through the trees."

I looked. We were above the lawn where we had just met but nearer to the back of the house. A hundred yards away, between the immemorial oaks and elms, I could see an old stone wall with a heavy gothic door with a lot of iron studs in it.

"Yes. I see it. It's a lovely old wall. Does it go all the way round the pool?"

"Yes. It's an old walled garden."

"It must be very private."

"Yes," Sally said softly. "Completely private."

I wondered if she realised that Anne had told me about her nude bathing. I almost said something about the joys of swimming without a swimsuit to see what she would say, but at that moment Anne appeared. She wore a very nearly indecently small black bikini and carried a towel and her handbag. We watched her as she strode cat-like across the lawn and disappeared through the door in the wall.

"She's got a marvellous figure," said Sally.

"Not bad," I said ungallantly. "She's a bit thin."

We remained kneeling side-by-side for a while longer.

Sally did not seem to be in a hurry to move away and I found I was enjoying her nearness. Our shoulders touched lightly. The late afternoon sun poured in through the window and Sally smelt of warm girl and of some faint scent that I couldn't identify. Her long slender fingers gripped the window sill. The paint on the sill was cracked and she picked at a loose flake with a long red nail. I noticed with something of a shock that on the appropriate finger of her left hand she wore a narrow gold wedding ring and a Victorian engagement ring with five huge diamonds. For some reason I had allowed the fact that she was married to slip to the back of my mind. I stood up quickly.

Sally sat back on her heels and looked round at me. "I expect you want to get undressed. I must go."

I thought of making a risqué remark, but something made me hold my tongue. Probably it was the feeling of awe which her beauty gave me which made me behave myself. She was so beautiful that I felt almost frightened of her.

I held the door open for her. She paused in the doorway and looked up at me.

"I'm glad that you could come to stay," she said gently. "I've been looking forward to meeting you."

Her eyes flickered and she looked away down the corridor. I stared entranced at the golden column of her neck. Her zip-fastener had come slightly undone and I could see the top of her cleavage. I longed to pull the zip all the way down and discover the warm brown body beneath the cloth, but I managed to resist this impulse too.

"It was nice of you not to say anything to Anne about yesterday," said Sally without looking at me. "I was on my way to have lunch with her, you see. And I went past Buckingham Palace and saw what was going on and I remembered that she had said that you were on that day, so I stopped my taxi and got out to see if I could see you." She looked at me momentarily and then looked away again. "I was lucky, I arrived at just the right time. I had a very good view."

I looked at her thoughtfully. To have found herself such a good position just outside the railings she must have been there for at least half an hour before the ceremony began. That didn't really tie in with her story of a sudden impulse in a passing taxi.

"You shouldn't have smiled at me so beautifully," I said, feeling very daring and slightly surprised to hear my voice saying the words. "You very nearly made me drop my sword."

She laughed, nervously I thought. "That would have been awful. But I'm sure you never could. You looked very smart."

"Thank you."

"And thank *you* for not saying anything to Anne. I didn't tell her, you see, and now I should feel an awful fool if she knew." She smiled. "I'll see you at dinner. I hope you have a lovely swim." And she turned and walked away down the passage. She walked well. Her hips swayed slightly and she held herself up almost like a Guardsman. Her tangled golden hair bounced on her shoulders. When she reached the end of the corridor she turned the corner without looking back.

FIVE

I liked Freddie Frensham for about thirty minutes. Then I changed my mind. Afterwards I wondered why I had liked him at all. It was true that he was not unpleasant-looking – not exactly handsome, but thoroughly presentable – and that he had very good manners. He also had considerable charm when he chose to use it, which he did that afternoon. That was not enough. In retrospect I concluded that I had been prepared to like him because of the story of his sexual inadequacy which Anne had told me the previous day. I had, in short, felt sorry for the fellow.

There were only four people left at the swimming pool when I arrived. The others had, I gathered, returned to the house at which they were staying. The first person I saw as I rounded the corner of an overgrown summer house, which was just inside the studded door, was a plump redhead who lay sunbathing on a low diving board. She had undone the straps of her green one-piece swimsuit and her generous breasts seemed to be on the point of escape. Sitting beside her on the edge of the pool, dangling his long white legs in the cool blue water, was a painfully thin young man with a mournful poetic face. He wore the smallest, the most ungentlemanly, pair of swimming shorts that I had ever seen. 'Shorts' in fact a hopeless misnomer; they were the merest, the most attenuated of briefs. They were nothing much more than the suggestion of a loincloth. Even from where I stood it was obvious that their wearer was totally unimpressed by the nubile charms of his redheaded companion.

Between the front of the summer house and the edge of

the pool was a flat paved area upon which stood a number of comfortable-looking chairs of various shapes and sizes and a large multi-coloured sun umbrella. Anne was reclining luxuriously in one of the longer chairs. Near her in the shade of the umbrella sat a fair man wearing a pair of long utterly respectable swimming shorts – the antithesis of those worn by the poet by the diving board – and open sandals. He stood up as I approached and Anne introduced us.

We shook hands and sat down and made small talk about the weather and the traffic and he asked me how long it had taken us to drive from London. While we talked we eyed one another with interest. At least I did, for I was truthfully interested. He too appeared to be taking considerable notice of me, but I put that down to a mixture of good manners and a professional politician's trick of making each person to whom he spoke feel that he was deeply interested in him. But even though one part of my mind understood this, the experience was still a flattering one.

After we had talked for a minute or two he suggested that I have my swim while the sun was still hot. Obediently I got up and treated them all to a little display of swimming and diving: a neat running dive followed by a compliment on the splendour of the pool and the warmth of the water, two lengths crawl, two lengths back crawl, two lengths butterfly and a couple of showy pikes from the board completed my repertoire. The bosomy redhead moved smilingly out of my way so that I could dive from the board and took her sullen-faced poet to join Freddie and Anne.

When I emerged Freddie suggested that we should have a drink and led the way into the summer house. Inside the fittings were luxurious. There were changing rooms for both sexes, with showers and plenty of towels. In the hall from which these rooms opened there was a table bearing a tray of drinks and glasses and a refrigerator stuffed with all manner of wines, beers and mineral waters.

Most of us drank lager, ice-cold from the refrigerator, and we sat and talked and smoked until the sun went down behind the trees which surrounded the pool. At some point – I forget when – the redhead and her poet left us to drive back to the house where they were staying. They said a temporary farewell to us as they were, it seemed, returning to Highworth for dinner.

I asked Freddie about the name of his house. I said, "It sounds rather… grandiose."

"It sounds like that," said Freddie. "It isn't. 'Worth' is old English meaning 'Farmstead', and 'High' probably means on higher ground than the surrounding land, which it is. Or it could mean that the produce of the farm was highly regarded by their customers; or just possibly the farmer was called something like High, or Hugh or Hew's Farm."

"How long have you owned it?"

"Since about 1850. It was a shooting box but my great-grandfather turned it into what you see today."

I could see that he was really very proud of it.

And at another point during the hour or more that we sat there I came to the conclusion that I thought Freddie Frensham a frightful shit.

Semi-naked he was an unprepossessing sight. I noticed as soon as he stood up to greet me that he was not tall; at five foot six or seven he was short by modern standards and, as I saw later that evening, he was even an inch or two shorter than his wife. His body was weak-looking. His skin was hairless and had gone slightly pink from exposure to the sun. His shoulders were narrow and sloping and his arms appeared to have been fixed onto his somewhat fleshy little torso more by accident than design and to be held in place by pieces of string like some sort of rag doll. I was amazed that he had the strength even to lift a glass to his mouth. He had of course no discernible pectoral muscles and his protuberant stomach bulged over the top of his voluminous shorts. Thereafter whenever I saw him dressed I never failed to be impressed by the skill of his tailor.

His head was just a little too big for his body and his expression, when his face was in repose, was haughty. His nose was thin and slightly curved, his hair was blond and thinning on top and brushed straight back. He grew it long over his ears and at the back of his neck as though to make up for the sparseness on the top. His eyes were a very pale blue and surprisingly piercing. His mouth was well-shaped but the lips were possibly a trifle fleshy and they were always moist. They reminded me of the inside of a plum. He was I knew in his early forties but his complexion was so soft and his face so unlined that he could have been ten years younger.

"I may not be a thing of beauty myself," he said laughing, and I wondered whether perhaps he could read my thoughts, "but that doesn't mean that I don't appreciate beauty."

We had been talking about pictures and Freddie had been telling us of an exhibition that he had been to in London during the week. Anne had changed the subject to statues and Freddie had enthused about a pair of hands by Rodin that he had just acquired and promised to show us that evening. He was, it seemed, if not exactly a patron of the arts at the least a keen collector of beautiful things. Later I discovered that he cared nothing for music or literature. He sought only what he could see and touch and keep.

"I can appreciate beauty in others," he went on. "Perhaps had things been different I might have been a sculptor. I like beauty in the round."

By things being different I supposed that he meant had he not been born the heir to an earldom. It seemed a non sequitur but, I thought, possibly I had misunderstood him. I looked at his hands. As Anne had said they were small and white and plump with short delicately-tapering fingers and tiny child-like fingernails.

"I should have liked to have made a statue of you, Anne," he said.

"Thank you, darling," Anne drawled mock-sexily, looking down at herself. Her hard lithe body was scarcely concealed by the two damp black strips of material.

"Diana, I think," said Freddie, looking thoughtfully at Anne's body.

"Goddess of the Hunt," agreed Anne. "With a bow and arrow perhaps," and she sprang up and posed before us with her legs astride and her arms in the position of an archer about to loose an arrow. She smiled down at us.

"Something like that," said Freddie.

Perhaps it was the coolness in the evening air, perhaps it was the close inspection that two men were giving to her body, but I noticed that Anne's nipples had suddenly become erect and were jutting obviously through the thin cloth. It was a sight that had excited me in the past. This time, to my surprise, I felt nothing, not even the faintest glimmer of desire for her.

Anne sat down, patting me on the knee as she did so. "What about Jimmy," she said. "What about sculpting him?"

"Yes, indeed." Freddie sounded enthusiastic. "The male body is, in many ways, far more beautiful than the female."

He looked at me and smiled in a peculiar way. "You mustn't think I'm queer. How could I be with a wife like mine?" And he laughed; rather too loud I thought.

I smiled politely, surprised at his coarseness. His remark had been, I realised, an attempt at some kind of sexual bonhomie, an effort to show that he was really one of the boys.

"But apart from any sexual consideration," he went on, "you have a beautiful body; the sort of body that Praxiteles would have delighted to sculpt, the body of an ancient Greek athlete."

"I take a certain amount of exercise," I said, taking a long pull at my lager and feeling thoroughly embarrassed. Anne came to my rescue.

"You'd make a perfectly lovely statue, Jimmy darling," she laughed. "Without a fig-leaf, of course."

I was looking at Freddie as she said this and I noticed a fleeting spasm cross his face; it was nothing more than a momentary constraint of the muscles round his eyes, and if I had not been looking directly at him at that moment I should not have seen it.

"In fact, Freddie," Anne continued without a pause, "you ought to have some statues round this pool. It would be a perfect place for them. Get a dozen assorted nude gods and goddesses and dot them around amongst the shrubbery. Then get rid of this pavilion thing," she waved a hand airily and I half-expected it to disappear, "and put up a Greek temple. It would be the most excellent nobleman's folly and extremely practical too." She leaned forward and talked on persuasively. She adored telling other people how to arrange their houses and gardens.

Freddie looked interested. "That's not at all a bad idea, Anne. I shall have to think about it seriously."

"It would be superb," said Anne. She seemed almost angry with him, as though he had told her the idea was a rotten one.

It was my view that the days of bogus temples in gentlemen's gardens were a thing of the past, but I kept my opinion to myself. A long time later I discovered that Freddie had been convinced by Anne's word picture of the beauty of it all and the following spring he did exactly what she had suggested, so that the next summer the pool and its surroundings inside the walled garden looked like a film set. By that time, however, I was *persona non grata* at Highworth so I have never seen it for myself.

SIX

I slipped an arm round Sally's slender waist and held her body close to mine. Looking down I could see the twin hemispheres of her golden-skinned breasts bulging gently from the top of her dress as they pressed against my chest. It was a most pleasing sensation.

"I've been looking forward to this," I said softly.

She looked up at me and smiled. "Have you? I have been too. But I don't think you ought to hold me so tight. I feel I might faint at any moment."

"I'm sorry." I loosened my hold slightly and we danced on in the half-empty ballroom. It was midnight and we had been at the Brendons' dance for over an hour, but Sally had been so much in demand that I had been unable to dance with her until that moment. It was, however, a moment well worth waiting for.

After drinks with Freddie I had gone to my room and shaved and wallowed for some time in a hot bath in a ruminative way. Then I realised with a start that Sally would almost certainly be in the drawing room before everyone arrived for dinner so I dressed quickly and went down.

One of the Italians was hovering in the hall with a tray of glasses filled with liquids of different colours. I asked him which was the whisky-and-water and he grimaced and wagged a shoulder, seeming to indicate something that could have been gin-and-tonic. I thanked him, helped myself to a glass containing a liquid of approximately the right colour and walked into the drawing room.

Sally stood at the far end of the room in front of the fireplace. Behind her, above the mantel, was a huge painting.

It was a landscape. In the background a slow-moving river meandered amongst comfortable-looking cows before disappearing under a gently curving bridge; in the middle distance a ruined temple stood at the edge of a great forest; in the foreground two shepherds wearing sheet-like outfits were, no doubt, congratulating one another upon the weather forecast. The whole scene was bathed in an ethereal evening glow and there was a distinct touch of shepherd's delight about the sky. Sally wore a white silk dress with a thin gold belt and she looked as though she had just stepped down from the picture. (Weeks later she admitted to me that that had been her intention.)

"What a lovely picture," I said, looking directly at her and smiling.

She smiled back at me as though to acknowledge my heavy-handed compliment.

I found myself feeling suddenly shy of her and quite unable to think of anything to say. When I had last seen her she had been a lovely, rather untidy girl; now she was the most beautiful woman I had ever seen. Her golden hair was no longer lank and tangled from swimming; it had been piled up in a seemingly impossible arrangement on the top of her head and fell in a golden cascade at the back. Her dress was fascinatingly low-cut and her arms and shoulders and the tops of her breasts were warm golden-brown skin. Altogether she was a golden girl. I drank half the contents of my glass in a single gulp and hoped that inspiration would strike. Sally came to my rescue.

"Did you like the swimming pool?" she asked me.

"It's splendid," I said enthusiastically, and for the next five minutes we chattered amiably about nothing very much.

Then Freddie joined us and soon afterwards the first of the people who were coming to dinner were announced and I had no further opportunity to talk to Sally about anything for four hours or more.

As Sally had told Anne and me that afternoon, sixteen people sat down to dinner. Apart from the Frenshams there were two other married couples, one of which was the Headcorns. They were the neighbours who were putting up most of the debutantes and their boyfriends who came to dinner including, of course, the buxom redhead and her anaemic lover. One of the debs was the Headcorns' youngest daughter.

Sir Humphrey Headcorn took the foot of the table and Sally sat on his right. He was a tall distinguished-looking fellow with a huge craggy nose and he spent most of the meal trying to look down the front of Sally's dress. I had, I admit it, some sympathy for him, but as he was a High Court judge I felt he should have made a greater effort to restrain himself. So apparently did his wife who sat at the far end of the table, next to Freddie, from whence she shot furious glances at him throughout dinner and spoke hardly at all. Not that her silence really mattered. Freddie was more than happy to do all the talking at his end of the table and I was grateful that I was far enough away from him not to be forced to listen to all that he had to say. I was convinced that he could have had time to eat almost nothing, so short were the intervals between his speeches.

I was stuck between the redhead, who was sitting next to her poet and took no notice of anyone else, and a very properly brought up but entirely empty-headed little deb. She had been taught at what must have been a very tender age that it was good manners to change your conversational partner with the course. During the soup – a deliciously creamy homemade vichyssoise, ice-cold and well adorned with chives – she told me about the dances she had been to during the past week. As soon as her plate was moved her head swivelled away from me as though controlled by some well-greased piece of machinery and I heard her start to tell the man sitting next to her on the other side about the dances she planned to attend during the following week. I ate my sole meunière in silence and listened to snatches of other people's conversation. Anne was sitting opposite Sally and, though I couldn't see her properly without leaning forward, it was obvious that she was flirting with the judge and doing it so effectively that from time to time he stopped his inspection of Sally's cleavage and turned to Anne instead. Looking to the other end of the table I saw that Lady Headcorn had noticed that and seemed pleased. Had she known Anne as I knew her she would have looked, I felt, considerably less happy.

The main course was beef wellington. The meat was a perfect pink in the middle and a superb filling, in which the main ingredients seemed to be pâté de foie gras and finely chopped mushrooms, had been spread thickly inside the pastry. My enjoyment of this was, however, somewhat marred by the well-mannered deb who turned on me as soon as my plate was filled and started to regale me with a tale of her last days at school, and the delicious feast she and her friends had consumed in their dormitory on their last night. Fortunately she went away with the strawberries and cream and I was ready for her when she returned with the cheese soufflé. Before she could utter a word, I launched into a long story about a very funny incident that had taken place in a small battle I had had with dissident tribesmen in up-country Aden. It carried me neatly through to the end of the meal when Sally caught Lady Headcorn's eye and we all stood up as they led the women out of the dining room.

When they had gone Freddie produced some brandy, but

he seemed unhappy about having it consumed by so many strangers and he himself poured out some surprisingly small measures for those who were brave enough to own up to wanting some. As the wines during dinner had been good and as the Italians had kept them flowing handsomely Freddie's attitude seemed a pointless meanness. Fortunately there was also some port – a Taylor's '27 I was amazed to discover – and as I realised that he could hardly pour that out for me I opted for it. To my surprise Freddie allowed it to go round twice and I drank two generous glasses while the judge told us some very funny tales from the Bench and I smoked a huge Romeo y Julieta and decided that it wasn't a bad dinner at all.

Eventually Freddie announced that it was time we started for the dance and we drifted into the drawing room and drank the cold coffee the women had left. A chaotic conversation about the best route to the dance was being carried on by almost everyone at the same time, and Lady Headcorn and Sally were trying to make plans about who would go in whose car. I slipped quietly away to the loo, thereby hoping to avoid being detailed to give anyone a lift. I knew of old what it could lead to. Mothers and hostesses, reasonably enough, expected one to return to their respective folds at the end of the dance whatever little charmers they had entrusted to one's care. This in my experience always meant that one could never leave the dance when one wanted to. When one did get away one was unerringly misdirected through landmark-less country lanes in vain attempts to find the houses in which the dear girls were staying.

The downstairs loo was a huge room filled with coats, hats, gumboots, sticks and umbrellas. The lavatory itself was a superb ancient instrument which I felt sure the

Victoria and Albert Museum would have been thrilled to get their hands on. It had a massive bench-type seat in beautifully polished mahogany into which the handle for flushing the cistern was set. The handle was shaped like that of a stirrup-pump and it rose proudly from a position a few inches from where the right buttock of a seated user would be. I tried pushing it down at first but it refused to budge so I lifted it. It rose for about twelve inches before anything happened and I was afraid that it would come away in my hand, but at last there was a clanking noise and a gigantic volume of water torrented into the prettily-decorated bowl. I dropped the handle quickly and lowered the great seat and its cover.

Outside I heard youthful voices and one or two car doors slamming but I was in no hurry. I spent several minutes washing my hands and brushing my hair and staring at myself in a fly-specked looking glass. My tie, I was glad to see, was just as it should be, but my whole ensemble was, I realised, hopelessly old-fashioned. I wore an orthodox dinner jacket, a New & Lingwood pale cream silk shirt and a plain black bow tie of a conservative pattern. My hair was about a foot shorter than that of all the young men at the dinner party, and they wore large velvet bow ties in black or blue or even red and their shirts were of amazing colours and designs. The poet, I remember, wore a white shirt with a lace-ruffled front and his lace cuffs hung almost to his fingertips. I wondered if Sally thought me rather a square. I felt excited at the thought that I might soon have a chance to dance with her. I felt sure that she liked me. Apart from her attitude that afternoon and the fact that she had gone to Buckingham Palace to see me the day before, I had caught her eye several times during dinner that evening when I had been stuck with no one to talk to and on each occasion she had smiled at me sympathetically. Once while I was telling my war story, I had glanced up and caught her looking at me in an oddly pensive way. It was all rather intriguing.

I wondered whether my breath smelled and I conducted one or two tests to try to find out but I couldn't be sure one way or the other.

When I emerged almost everyone had gone.

"I thought you were never coming out of there," said Anne, confronting me in the hall.

"Have all those funny little birds gone?" I whispered.

"Yes. You're quite safe. Everyone's left except us and the Frenshams. Come on." And she led the way out of the open front door.

There were only two cars remaining: mine and a large black Rolls-Royce. One of the Italians, wearing what looked like the uniform of the Royal Flying Corps, was standing to attention beside the open rear door of the Rolls and Sally was just about to step in. She wore a full length white fur cloak over her dress and she looked magnificent.

"Are you two going to come with us?" she called.

For a moment I almost said yes. The thought of sitting next to Sally in the back of the Rolls-Royce for fifteen or twenty miles was a temptation. Fortunately good sense prevailed.

"It's very kind of you," I said, "but I think I'll take my car. We might want to leave at different times."

"We'll see you there then," said Sally. "Do you know the way?"

"Anne thinks she does, but I think we'll follow you so that we don't get lost."

Sally smiled and climbed into their car. Freddie waved a

plump paw in our direction and followed. The Italian shut the door and hurried round to the front.

Anne slipped neatly into the passenger seat of my Jaguar while I held the door open for her. As always she put her bottom in first, then swung her legs in together. The silk of her skirt made an expensive swishing noise as she did so. I walked round, climbed in behind the wheel and followed Freddie's Rolls down the drive.

I turned my wireless on and found some gentle music. Anne prattled away about this and that but I paid little attention. From time to time I caught a glimpse of Sally's golden head in the rear window of the car in front of us. I had a warm glow of physical well-being from my head to my feet, but somewhere at the back of my mind was a faint tremor of apprehension. Had it been stronger perhaps I should have made some excuse for returning at once to London and then nothing would have happened.

Anne switched off the wireless and prodded my thigh in an unfriendly way with a long sharp fingernail.

"You haven't listened to a word I've said."

I could think of no excuse. "I'm sorry, Anne. I was thinking. What were you saying?"

"I wanted to know what you thought of the Frenshams."

"They're all right."

Anne sighed. "I really do want to know what you think of Sally. Be honest now, Jimmy. Don't you think she's quite something?"

"She's beautiful."

"Would you like to go to bed with her?" It sounded as though Anne was, in some strange way, in a position to offer Sally to me. It was almost as though if I said yes that would be all that would be required for Sally to be mine. I looked across at her without speaking. She was lounging comfortably in the big seat, her body half-turned towards me. She was smiling wickedly.

"You would like it, wouldn't you, darling?" she drawled.

"It sounds as though you want to get rid of me."

She laughed. "Well, I don't," she said decisively. "Not yet awhile anyway. No doubt the time will come. When it does we shall both be very civilised about it. No tears, no recriminations. A drink perhaps, and a fond farewell and then we shall meet as friends whenever we run into one another again. It will all be very sophisticated."

"Are you sure?"

"Quite sure, my dear." She paused. "As long as you let *me* do the ditching, of course."

I laughed. "Perhaps it would be easier if I found you a suitable replacement."

"That would be nice. Do you know anyone suitable? He must be good-looking, rich and very sexy."

"I'll keep my eye open for someone."

"As soon as I'm suited I'll let you go off after Sally," she promised.

"You keep talking about her as though it were a foregone conclusion," I probed gently, wondering if she knew something that I did not.

"It certainly isn't that," said Anne, and I felt a flicker of disappointment. "Let's face it, duckie, Sally must be one of the most dishy and desirable birds in England. All the most expert womanisers have had a crack at her but none of them has got anywhere at all. There's no real reason why you should do any better than all the others but, as I told you yesterday, it's my not at all humble opinion that you'd be good for her. Now that I've finished training you any woman would be glad to get you." She took a cigarette out of her handbag, lit it and exhaled a cloud of smoke in a satisfied way. "It's possible that Sally doesn't really need sex very much – not like you or me. But if that isn't right then I'm sure that she'd be a very good lover."

"Why? If what you say is right she's had almost no experience at all."

"You could soon teach her all she needs to know. She'd be good because she's a good person. She's a kind and generous friend. She'd be a kind and generous lover." She drew at her cigarette again and the smoke swirled momentarily around the inside of the car before being sucked out of the open windows. "She'd have to fall for you of course. But you never know your luck. In a few months' time, when I've found your successor, I'll see what I can do to arrange for you to see more of her."

***

When we reached the house where the dance was being held I drew up at the front door behind Freddie's Rolls and walked round to help Anne out. She swept into the house with Freddie and Sally, leaving me, like the other chauffeurs, to find somewhere to park. It wasn't too difficult. The dance was an extremely well-organised affair and AA men and squads of the local peasantry were surging about, waving torches and tugging their forelocks. I was guided into a spot on the main drive, facing the way I had come in. I was glad of that; turning round in the dark when you are entirely surrounded by drunks is a hazardous business.

I ran the gauntlet of my host and hostess and their spotty daughter and caught up with the rest of our party in the main ballroom where Freddie had commandeered a large table. I sat down next to Anne and someone gave me a glass of champagne. I drank a mouthful of it and looked round hopefully. The champagne was far too cold and Sally was nowhere to be seen.

I was toying with the idea of asking Anne to dance with me when Freddie beat me to it and led her away onto the floor. This seemed to be a signal for everyone else at our table and in a moment I found myself alone with Lady Headcorn, the judge's wife. She smiled at me cheerfully, apparently quite recovered from her disapproval of her husband's roving eye at the dinner table. (If an eye so firmly fixed on one place can be so described.)

"Bad luck," she said happily. "You should have been a bit quicker off the mark and you wouldn't have got yourself stuck with me."

"On the contrary," I said, grinning at her, "any discerning man would far rather dance with a woman than with a mere girl." I waved a hand vaguely in the direction of the dance floor where dozens of debs were whirling round in the arms of their young men.

"Come on then," she said, standing up. "Now's your chance."

I led her into the throng and steered her gently round the floor, keeping an eye open for Sally. I found her at the far end of the room, dancing with a young man, and I circled round in her general vicinity hoping to catch her eye but meeting no success. I took an instant dislike to the young man. He was ridiculously good-looking, with a profile like Cary Grant; he danced far too well; and, worst of all, he was chattering away non-stop to Sally and making her laugh uproariously. I thought it the most attractive laugh I had ever heard.

"She's a lovely girl, isn't she?" said Lady H unexpectedly.

"I beg your pardon," I said, staring at her.

"I said, 'she's a lovely girl'."

"Who is?"

"Sally Frensham, of course, you idiot," she cried gaily, nodding in the direction of Sally and her escapee from 'Come Dancing'. "I hope you're not going to be so foolish as to pretend you hadn't noticed."

I grinned at her. She was no fool. "Yes," I admitted. "She certainly is a lovely girl."

"You've been staring at her so hard I don't think you've heard a word I've said."

For a moment I contemplated trying to bluff my way, but she was absolutely right. I hadn't listened to a word. Fortunately I was saved by the band. They stopped playing 'Moon River', and a group which replaced them at once struck up something ear-shatteringly noisy and horrifyingly energetic. The under-twenties gave whoops of excitement and started to gyrate furiously.

I made a face at Lady H who smiled back sympathetically. She was quite pretty when she smiled and I had a sudden feeling that she must have been rather a dish in her younger days.

"Shall we go and have a drink?" I bellowed at her above the din.

She nodded and smiled and I looked round for a way of escape. Behind a curtain a few feet away was an open French window and I ushered her through the gap. We found ourselves on a long terrace lit with about a hundred tiny coloured lanterns. There were a number of tables and chairs and a lot of people were sitting out. On the lawn beyond the terrace several couples were strolling arm-in-arm. It was a warm soft night.

"I should love a brandy and soda," said Lady Headcorn. "Then let's sit over there for a while. I want to talk to you." She indicated an unoccupied table at the end of the terrace.

There was a long sheet-covered table at one side, behind which a platoon of waiters was hard at work. I asked for two brandies and soda and wondered why she wanted to talk to me.

I joined her at the table and gave her her drink and a cigarette. I took a cigarette for myself, lit them both and sat quietly, sipping my drink and waiting to see what she would say.

"I wanted to ask you if your father's name was James too."

I had had a feeling that she had not known even what my name was, let alone my father's but then I remembered that Freddie had introduced us before dinner.

"Yes, it was. Why? Did you know him?"

"I felt sure it must be," she said, not answering my question directly. "You're very like him to look at, but perhaps you're not quite as handsome as he was."

I was used to this and was not in the least put out.

"When was it you knew him? Did you know him well?"

She smiled – to herself I supposed as she did not look at me. I thought that perhaps she was remembering, but possibly she was only doing mental arithmetic for she said, "The answer to your first question is 'about thirty-five years ago' and the answer to the second is 'yes, very well indeed'." She laughed happily. Twenty years or more seemed to have dropped off her in the last minute.

"We first met in the early 1930s," she said. "I'd been out about two years, I think, and James – your father, I mean – was an Ensign in the Musketeer Guards. We fell for each other like a ton of bricks and we had a most wonderful affair which lasted almost three years. We very nearly got married."

"Why didn't you?"

"It was my fault. I was too young, I suppose, and an awful

ass. I got all socialist-minded – there were a lot of very poor people in England in those days, you know – hunger marches and all sorts of dreadful things going on – and James was very rich of course. They had to be in those days if they were in the Guards. I expect they still are."

"No," I said. "Not really."

"Are you sure?"

"Yes. Fairly sure. I'm in the Musketeers now you see. There are one or two very rich officers, but most people have very little money."

"You're in the Musketeers? How fascinating."

"Do go on," I encouraged her. "I want to hear why you're not my mother."

She looked startled. "What an extraordinary thought. Though it's a very nice one," she added politely. "I should like to have had a son." She pulled a face. "I've had three daughters." She looked at me for a moment in a speculative way as though seeing me in the unfamiliar role of her son.

"Anyway," she said at last, "what happened was that your father went off to Egypt and stayed there for what seemed like for ever to me – I was only about twenty-two then – and I met Humphrey. He was dreadfully poor, a real struggling barrister – and, my goodness, they had to struggle in those days. He was a terrible socialist, almost a communist, I suppose – though I must say he doesn't think it at all funny when I remind him of it. He's thoroughly respectable and right-wing nowadays," she said, smiling fondly. "Back in the thirties he was totally different and a complete contrast to poor dear James, who wasn't nearly so intelligent, and though he was sweet and gentle and kind he had far too much money and he didn't seem to care at all about poor people unless they were his own soldiers." She paused and took a sip of her drink.

"What happened?"

"Well, James went off to Egypt as I told you and he wrote me lovely long letters. Meanwhile I had a most peculiar courtship from Humphrey. Instead of going to the theatre and Ascot and house parties and so on, I went to political rallies and spent hours in teashops talking about putting the world to rights. I absolutely adored it all. So I wrote to James and told him that we were wrong for one another, or some such rubbish and I married Humphrey. I never saw James again. It was sad." She finished her drink and put the empty glass on the table in front of us.

"Would you like another?" I asked her.

"Your father would never have said 'another' like that," she said, smiling at me. "You make me sound like a dreadful old soak."

"I'm sorry. I'll try again," I said. "Would you like a glass of brandy and soda, Lady Headcorn?"

"Yes please," she said brightly. "And please call me Susan. It will make me feel younger."

I walked to the table where the drinks were being dispensed and replenished our glasses. When I returned she said, "Of course I often heard of him during the next few years until the war started. We had a great many mutual friends. So I heard that he married and, now I come to think of it, I rather think I remember hearing that you had been born, and then later I heard that he had been killed, but I don't remember any details. It was right at the beginning of the war, wasn't it?"

"Just before Dunkirk. He was a Company Commander. Oddly enough he was commanding the same Company that I now command – almost thirty years later."

"I think it's rather wonderful that you're in the Musketeers too. I can remember all sorts of things about it. Some of the time your father was stationed at that Barracks next to Buckingham Palace. But he didn't live there. He had a lovely little house in Clarges Street, I think it was. None of the officers seemed to actually live in the Barracks. Is it still like that?"

"Not really, no. I was stationed at Wellington Barracks a few years ago – that's the one near the Palace, but we're stationed at Chelsea Barracks now. There are any number of rooms for the officers so almost everyone has to live in, or if they do live out they're not allowed to claim the allowances for doing so, and it makes life very expensive."

"I don't think they worried much about allowances in your father's time. They all seemed to have flats or houses and they had lots of leave. It almost seemed as though they were on leave whenever they weren't on Guard. That was great fun, I remember. Sometimes your father used to invite me to St James's Palace for lunch or drinks in the evening when he was on Guard there. Ladies had to leave by 7 o'clock. Does that still happen nowadays?"

"Yes. It certainly does." I made a quick decision. "I'm on Guard next Thursday. Will you and your husband come to lunch with me then?"

She looked at me uncertainly. "I wasn't fishing for an invitation, you know."

"I know you weren't. And I really meant it. It isn't every day one meets someone who was almost one's mother."

There was a pause. The band was playing a selection from 'Fiddler on the Roof'. One or two girlish screams came out of the night from the distant darkness of the garden. I wondered where Sally was and I finished my drink.

"In that case," said Lady Headcorn, "I should love to come. I think I can probably still remember the way. There's a narrow little alleyway and a sentry, isn't there?"

"The alleyway is right, but there's no sentry. He was discontinued some years ago when we were short of soldiers."

"I shall find it, I expect. But I'm afraid Humphrey won't be able to come. He's in Court on Thursday."

"It would be quite proper for you to come on your own."

"Because I'm too decrepit to be compromised?"

"Certainly not," I laughed. "Because there will be several other people there. Would you like to bring your daughter?"

"I'm sure she'd adore it but I'm almost certain that she's busy on Thursday. You did say Thursday, didn't you? Yes, I thought you did. Oh, dear."

"What's the matter?"

"I've just remembered that I'm busy all day on Thursday myself, so I shall have to refuse after all. I *am* disappointed."

"So am I. Is it something you can't wriggle out of?"

"Well – not exactly. I'm spending the day in London – shopping with Sally Frensham."

I felt a warm glow expanding inside my stomach. "Why not bring her with you? After all, you have to have lunch."

She stared at me inquisitively for a moment. "All right," she said firmly. "I'll do that, if she'll come."

"I'll ask her myself before the end of this weekend. Perhaps tonight – if I get a chance," I added ruefully.

"You can take me in now if you like. You've spent far too long talking to me as it is."

"I'm sorry," I said quickly. "That was unpardonably rude of me and, of course, quite unintentional. I simply meant that Sally is so popular that I probably shan't see her again tonight. But be that as it may I've adored meeting you, and talking about my father." I drew a breath. "Susan," I added.

She laughed again. "You're quite forgiven. I was only pulling your leg. But tell me, are you in love with Sally?"

"I beg your pardon?"

"Judging by the way you were looking at her when we were dancing just now, I felt sure you must be."

"I met her for the first time this afternoon. And saw her for the first time yesterday."

She chose not to mention this peculiarity. "That's no answer."

"Isn't it? How can you love someone you don't know?"

"With the greatest of ease. In fact it's much easier to be in love with someone you don't know than with someone you do. Anyway, as you haven't denied it I suppose the answer must be yes. I must tell you that I'm entirely in favour. It's high time Sally had a boyfriend." She looked at me critically. "You should suit her splendidly if you're even half the man your father was."

"She certainly is very beautiful."

"Very. She's also a nice-natured and very affectionate girl. She could be happy with the right man. And Freddie is definitely not the right man." She shook her head and sighed. "Oh dear. I think I must be rather drunk tonight."

It was clear both from her words and from the tone of her voice that Freddie was not her favourite man. I suggested as much to her.

"No," she said frankly. "I detest him. He's a power-mad opinionated bore. He's inordinately pleased with himself and he's unhealthily proud of his many possessions, one of which – but not the most important – is Sally. He's positively antique in his attitudes, particularly about his family. When you get to know him better you'll realise that he regards his ancient lineage as of infinitely greater value than any amount of kind hearts or simple faith. But he's a politician to his fingertips and he's usually extremely careful to keep that view to himself. His ambition is terrifying. He'll probably be Prime Minster one day and I should think it'll be a disastrous day for England when that happens. But happen it surely will. He's young and, in his way, very able. The only thing that cheers me up at all is the thought of the absolute agony he's going to go through when his father dies and he has to renounce his earldom. He'll simply loathe it." She paused and looked at me intently. "You realise I hope, James, that he'd make a very nasty and extremely dangerous enemy."

"Yes, I suppose so," I said mildly, but I felt a little flicker of apprehension as I spoke.

"I expect you're as brave as your father was." I wondered unhappily if she was right.

"Now you really must take me back to our table. Or I shall go on boring you about Freddie for the rest of the night. Perhaps Sally is there now and you can ask her to dance. I shall be seeing you tomorrow because, although you probably don't know it yet, you're coming to lunch with me." She finished her drink and we stood up and walked back into the ballroom. "Sally and I decided to split up the work for this weekend. I'm having all the little monsters to stay and giving everyone lunch tomorrow. And in return Sally gave tonight's dinner – and wasn't it superb – and they're allowing everyone to use their swimming pool. It's an excellent arrangement, don't you think?"

There was still no sign of Sally when we reached our table, but the round redhead had been deserted by her poet so I asked her to dance. She was a cuddlesome little armful.

"Are you coming in for a swim?" she asked me surprisingly, as we circled the floor.

"Where?"

"There's a super swimming pool in the garden here," she told me. "There's a sort of open-air nightclub with a discotheque next to the pool. The nightclub starts at midnight, but some people have already been in for a swim. The water's lovely and warm."

"Have you been in?"

"No, not yet. I just felt it with my hand. I definitely will later."

"Are there any swimming things to be had?"

"No, I don't think so. Some people have brought their own swimsuits with them, but several people have been in in their undies." She giggled and started to massage the front of my trousers with her somewhat protuberant tummy. "It should be great fun later on. You must come down there."

I smiled at her and gave her a little squeeze. The massage was noticeably pleasant. "Perhaps I will. But why did you come back here if it's so marvellous?"

"I really only came back to fetch Hubert. I must get him down there whatever happens. But I don't know where he's got to." She peered hopefully around the room but my massage went on without interruption. I supposed that she did it automatically, without knowing what she was doing.

"There he is," she cried suddenly. "He's just gone back to our table." She looked up at me and batted her obviously false eyelashes at me. "Do you mind awfully if we go back there now? Otherwise he'll only run away again."

"Of course." I led her back to our table and the errant Hubert. I was sorry that the massage had stopped.

Hubert was talking to Lady Headcorn and he looked startled as he saw the redhead bearing down upon him. He glanced around anxiously but there was no escape.

"Where have you been, Hubie? I've been looking for you everywhere."

He gave her a wan smile. "Er," he said, "in the, er, you know… in the loo."

She led him to the nearest French window. They disappeared into the night.

I sank into the chair beside Lady Headcorn that Hubert had just vacated.

"What has he got that I haven't?" I asked her.

"I don't know, my dear. Why don't you ask Sally?"

"Why doesn't he ask me what?" said Sally, suddenly appearing beside me.

I leapt to my feet. "Hello," I said fatuously.

Sally smiled at me and sat in the chair next to mine. She said, "I simply refuse to dance one more dance until I've had a glass of champagne and a cigarette. I'm absolutely exhausted."

There were plenty of clean glasses on the table and several open bottles of champagne. I poured out a glass for each of the three of us and gave Sally a cigarette.

"When you feel sufficiently restored, I want to be the first in the queue."

She nodded and smiled. "What is it that Susan wants you to ask me?"

"He wanted to know what Hubert had got that he had not," Lady Headcorn told her before I could speak.

Greatly to my surprise Sally blushed noticeably. "How on earth should I know?" She looked, almost angrily, at Lady Headcorn.

I stared at the bubbles rising in my glass and pretended not to have noticed her discomfiture.

Lady Headcorn was quite unperturbed. "Don't be so scratchy, Sally," she said cheerfully. "We've been having a lovely time one way and another. We have had a fascinating discussion and discovered that I was very nearly his mother. It's been splendid. And you'll never guess where you and I are going for luncheon next Thursday?"

Sally looked perplexed and I wondered whether she had forgotten that she was spending Thursday in London with Lady Headcorn. She shook her head and the long emerald drops in her ears twinkled greenly. "St James's Palace," said Lady Headcorn. "With James. He's on Guard. Isn't that marvellous?"

Sally turned her head and looked at me. "How very kind of you," she said slowly and in an odd tone, as though she meant much more than she said. "I shall look forward to it."

I smiled at Susan Headcorn, meaning to thank her for making my path easy. She had a strange look in her eye and I remember wondering if she had said what she had from some more complicated motive than I had originally supposed. I ground out my cigarette in an ashtray.

"Will you dance with me now?" I said to Sally.

"Yes," she said gently. "I should like to."

I stood up and buttoned my jacket. At the edge of the floor I slipped an arm around her waist and took her hand.

At last we danced together.

We danced in silence for a moment or two. Sally danced well; so well in fact that she made it seem as though I too was a good dancer. For the first time in years I found I was enjoying dancing for its own sake.

After we had done one circuit of the floor Sally said, "I don't quite understand where it is that Susan and I are lunching with you on Thursday."

"In the Officers' Guardroom at St James's Palace. Have you been there before?"

To my surprise she said "No," so I launched into a long explanation about the Queen's Guard while we floated around the ballroom and Sally looked up at me, her green eyes positively shining with interest. Now and again I made what I suppose were rather feeble little jokes but Sally found them hugely diverting and she laughed prettily at them all. I was enchanted with myself; never, I was certain, had I been so witty and charming. It would have been nice if the dance could have lasted for ever but, for us at least, it ended abruptly.

Suddenly Sally stopped dancing and I felt her body stiffen. I was forced to stop too and I broke off what I was saying in mid-sentence.

"What's the matter?" I asked.

She was staring over my left shoulder and for a few seconds she didn't reply. Then she said, "I've just seen somebody that I particularly don't want to meet. Could we go outside somewhere?"

I glanced quickly around. The French window out of which I had taken Susan Headcorn earlier in the evening was a mere six feet from where we stood.

"Is whoever it is behind me?" I asked her.

"Yes, sitting at a table on the far side of the room." She sounded tense and unhappy.

"There's an open door just behind you. I'll dance you out of it. Come on."

Two seconds later we were on the terrace and I led her to the bar, regretfully taking my arm from around her waist as I did so.

"We both need a proper drink after that little excitement," I said. "Brandy for you?"

She nodded. She still looked unhappy and I wondered if she was going to tell me what it was all about. One of the efficient waiters poured us two large glasses of five-star brandy and we took them to an empty table at the far end of the terrace.

The brandy did us both good; Sally looked less unhappy

and I was positively on top of the world. However, I noticed that from time to time Sally glanced apprehensively at the windows opening from the ballroom and it was clear that she would prefer to be even further removed from danger. I had a bright idea.

"I gather that there's a swimming pool here somewhere with a sort of open-air nightclub. Shall we go and find it and perhaps have a dance there?"

"That's a wonderful idea." We finished our brandies and walked down a broad flight of steps which led from the terrace to the lawn below. Sally slipped an arm through mine.

As we moved away from the lights of the terrace into the moonlit garden a strange euphoric feeling came over me. It was uncanny; as though I had suddenly walked into a different world. I felt an odd light-headed sensation which at first I attributed to alcohol, but which I realised after a while must be caused by something quite different. I had after all been perfectly sober a moment before. We spoke little but each word seemed to have more importance than the same word spoken on any other occasion. The garden smelled of flowers and grass and earth, and the music from the ballroom was a gentle background noise diminishing slowly as we strolled across the springy turf away from the house.

I looked at Sally. Her golden hair shone silver in the moonlight. She held my arm firmly and I could feel the warmth of her body through my sleeve, but when she lifted her face to look at me her skin looked lifeless – like a perfect marble statue.

"I feel so peculiar," she said. "There's a sort of... I don't know... a sort of timeless feeling. I can't really describe it."

I stared intently at her face. Her eyes were black pools.

"How odd," I said. "I have a funny feeling too. Do you

think we're both tight?"

"No," said Sally softly. "I'm sure that's not it."

We walked on in silence for a minute or two. "Are you in love with Anne?"

This seemed to be my evening for being asked if I was in love.

"No."

"Poor Anne. I think she's in love with you."

"I don't."

"Don't you? I expect that's because she tells you she's not. That doesn't really mean anything, you know. Not with Anne anyway. She talks about you practically non-stop when I see her on her own. I've heard so much about you that I feel I've known you for years."

"It's been the same with me," I embroidered the truth a little. "I mean I feel I've known you for years too."

"Has it?" She looked up at me and smiled, somewhat hesitantly I thought. "I hope I'm not too much of a disappointment," she said in a small voice.

"No. No disappointment." It was the understatement of the year.

There was a pause. I thought about asking her if I was a disappointment, but I should only have been fishing, and if I was a disappointment she certainly wouldn't tell me so. I decided to use this opportunity to put her right about Anne and me.

"Anne and I are, as they say, just good friends. We've had a walk-out for a few months and we've both enjoyed it, but now it's almost at an end. I suspect that Anne is looking around for my successor. When she finds him we shall part. Amicably, I hope. With no regrets. And then, I have no doubt, you will hear all about her new man."

"She may be looking for someone new, but I'm pretty

sure that's because she feels you aren't sufficiently interested. I've heard all about her other men over the years. We practically grew up together, you know. It's because I've heard all about all her boyfriends that I'm sure she thinks of you as being different."

I thought about this for a while. We had reached the end of the lawn and now found ourselves in a grassy walk which ran between two tall dark hedges. Somewhere in front of us I could hear music and occasional raised voices. I guessed that we were going in the right direction for the swimming pool and I wanted to clear up this business of Anne before we arrived. I had no idea when, if ever, I should have another opportunity to talk tête-à-tête with Sally and I realised, without any particular feeling of surprise, that it was of great importance to me that she should be under no illusion about the reality of my relationship with Anne. The problem was how to do it without being unpleasant about Anne, to whom Sally was virtually a sister.

"I hope you're wrong about Anne's feelings. We've had a very good time together these last months and I'm fond of her – very fond of her. But I'm not in love with her and I never could be. I can't do anything about that, can I?"

"No," Sally said. "You're quite right. You can't make yourself fall in love… any more than you can make yourself fall out of love. It's just one of those things. Poor Anne."

"Yes," though I didn't feel in the least sorry for her. She would be off, I knew, with the next well-heeled stud who came along.

We rounded a corner and found ourselves at the pool. The scene was bacchanalian. A long bar at the far end of the pool was doing a brisk business; several people were actually swimming. The whole scene was prettily lit by coloured lanterns strung up in the trees surrounding the pool.

Sally was still holding my arm and suddenly I felt her grip tighten and she said, "Oh, no. I can't bear it." She pulled me back into the shadows.

"What is it?"

"It's him again."

"Who?"

"The man who was in the ballroom. He's standing over there by the bar."

I looked in that direction but I couldn't make out to whom she was referring.

"We'd better leave if you don't want him to see you." We turned and walked into the darkness of the garden. "I suppose he came out of the house a different way while we were sitting on the terrace," I said. "If he'd come past us you would have seen him."

"Yes, I suppose so." Sally sounded miserable. "What can we do?"

"Well, we can walk in the garden for a while," I steered her off the path and across a moonlit stretch of lawn between two great banks of shrubbery. "But after a time we shall have to go back to the house and then he'll find you eventually – if he knows you're here and really is looking for you."

Sally said nothing.

"If you like, I could take you home."

She stopped walking and turned to face me. "What a marvellous idea."

Because she had been holding my arm before she turned my hand somehow found itself now resting on her waist. Through the thin silk her body felt warm and firm. It was a pleasing sensation, and as she didn't seem to have noticed I kept my hand there.

"But what about Freddie – and Anne?" she asked.

"I'll take you to my car. If we stay away from the paths we're not likely to run into anyone. You can wait in my car while I find them both and say you're not feeling very well and I'm going to take you home. Freddie can take Anne home at the end of the dance."

"Thank you, James," Sally smiled at me. "That's a wonderful idea. You are clever. But won't you be miserable leaving the dance?"

I smiled back at her and slightly tightened my hold on her waist. "If you're not here it won't be any fun anyway." I pulled her closer to me and kissed her on the lips. Her mouth was soft and warm and I found that I enjoyed kissing her.

This was something of a surprise. I had felt for years – at least since I grew up – that kissing was a vastly overrated occupation. I had concluded that it was really only tolerable for what it might lead to. I thought of it as part of the artillery preparation, or perhaps more accurately as the beginning of the move up to the Start Line. Kissing Sally was different. I felt an unexpected thrill of excitement and pleasure and I would have been delighted to have gone on kissing her for ever. Unhappily the kiss lasted for only a few seconds at most. For a moment I thought she was going to let me kiss her. She allowed me to hold her body hard against mine and I felt her breasts pressing against my chest. Her lips started to open to my tongue. Suddenly she pushed me away and stepped back. We stared at one another.

"No, James. You mustn't."

"I liked it," I said, still surprised at the discovery.

"That's got nothing to do with it."

"I'm sorry. I'm not sorry I kissed you. I liked that awfully. But I'm sorry I've made you angry. Will you put it down to midsummer madness and forgive me? Then we can go on being friends."

She smiled. "All right. Are we friends? We haven't known one another very long."

"We're old friends. I think we probably knew one another in a previous incarnation." I was only half-joking.

"That's a nice idea." She took my arm again and we walked on slowly. "Who do you think we were? Antony and Cleopatra?"

"I hope not. Pretty miserable ending."

"Romeo and Juliet?"

"Fiction. And even more miserable."

"Dante and Beatrix?"

"He never even spoke to her. Dreadfully boring."

Sally giggled. "Abelard and Heloise?"

"No thank you. They did something exceptionally nasty to him."

"Did they? What?"

"I'll tell you when I know you better."

"Who was the man who swam across the Hellespont every night to see his mistress?"

"Leander. And of course he drowned, poor fellow."

"Do you suppose all great love affairs end in tragedy?"

"Or in marriage. Thought by some to be the same thing."

"What a bachelor-like remark." We both laughed.

I thought that it was significant that she assumed that we had been lovers in our previous incarnation, but odd that she didn't want me to kiss her in this one. It was a bit of a puzzle, but I had no time then to think about it because a dinner-jacketed figure suddenly appeared in front of us and Sally abruptly stopped laughing.

"There you are, Sally," said the figure angrily.

For an uncomfortable moment I thought it was Freddie. The man in front of us was the same height and build and his voice sounded similar. As he spoke again he stepped a pace closer to us and I realised that I had never seen him before.

"You've been deliberately avoiding me, haven't you?" he snarled.

Sally took her arm from mine but I could feel her tenseness in the air.

"Of course I haven't, Quintin. What nonsense you talk. I had no idea you were here. How are you?"

"You saw me in the ballroom half an hour ago and you deliberately ran off with your pretty young man. I've been searching for you everywhere. I've been looking under the bushes for the last ten minutes."

"That will be quite enough of that," I said.

I wondered whether he had seen us kissing a minute or two earlier but I told myself that if he had he would undoubtedly have said so.

"Mind your own business," he spat at me. "I'd like to know just what you and your fancy boyfriend have been up to for the past half-hour," he said to Sally.

"You know I don't have a fancy boyfriend – or any sort of boyfriend for that matter." She sounded as though she was about to burst into tears. "Please leave me alone, Quin."

Who on earth was this man? He was behaving like a jealous husband. And why was Sally so upset? I expected her to be angry, but instead she was unhappy and frightened. It was odd.

But if Sally wasn't angry, I was. It made me pompous. "I haven't had the misfortune to be introduced to you," I said evenly, "so I haven't the least idea who you are. You've been very offensive. I suggest that you apologise to Lady Frensham and then go away."

"Lady Frensham!" he almost snorted. "Why don't you mind your own business, you stupid young idiot?"

He came up close to me and peered up at me in the dim light. He smelled strongly of whisky. He was obviously very drunk. His eyes glittered insanely.

"It is my business. Apologise and go away before you get hurt."

"I see," he said menacingly. "You're threatening me, are you?"

"Yes."

"Then you've got a surprise in store for you."

He was quite right as it turned out, but it wasn't the one that he expected.

He said, "If you don't go away and leave us alone you'll regret it. We have things to talk about that are no concern of yours."

He put a hand on my chest and gave me a sharp push.

"Do you want me to go away, Sally?" I asked her. I don't know what I would have done if she had said yes; just pottered off looking foolish, I suppose. But she didn't say anything. She just stood there looking miserable. That was good enough for me.

"Take your hands off me or I'll knock you down." I felt like a character in an old-fashioned melodrama.

"All right," he said thickly, sounding like another character from the same melodrama. "You've asked for it."

He stepped back quickly and took a terrific swing at me. Sally screamed, "No!"

I blocked his swing with my left arm – it was ridiculously easy to do – and hit him as hard as I could in the stomach with my right fist. It was the first time in my adult life that I had struck someone in anger. I am glad to be able to report that it was a great success, though the effectiveness of my blow was a frightening surprise. I felt my fist sink deep into the softness of his belly and he let out a rush of whisky-sodden breath, doubled up and collapsed in a huddled heap on the grass at my feet. His eyeballs seemed to start from his head and he was plainly not breathing. For an awful moment I thought that I had killed him. So did Sally.

"Oh, my God," she said. "Is he dead?" She stood beside me and we looked down at him. I was horrified with my handiwork.

After what seemed an age the man suddenly gasped. He wasn't dead. We stood over him wondering what to do.

"Will he be all right?" Sally asked.

"He'll be okay when he gets his breath back," I said confidently, hoping that I was right. "I'll give him a hand."

He was making the most disgusting gargling noises and he seemed incapable of movement, but with my assistance he got up as far as his knees. Then he leant forward and vomited feebly down the front of his dinner jacket.

Eventually he got to his feet and stood swaying slightly in front of us. He looked at me with hatred in his eyes.

"You bastard," he gasped. "You bastard." He turned on his heel and stumbled away into the darkness.

Sally was shivering. As soon as the man was out of sight I put my arms round her and held her close. She didn't resist. She rested against me, her head on my chest. My face was in her hair. It smelled wonderful.

"That was horrible," she said.

"It's over now." I felt like a father comforting his child. It was a novel sensation for me. "He's gone. Let's sit down somewhere and have a cigarette."

There was a garden seat under a tree a few yards away and I led Sally to it. I kept one arm round her waist.

Her hands were shaking so much that she couldn't hold her cigarette still, so I took it from her and lit both our cigarettes myself. My hands were shaking too I noticed. I gave her a lighted cigarette and we both dragged gratefully.

"Who is he?" I asked. "What was it all about?"

She didn't answer.

"Sally?"

"What?"

I repeated my questions.

"He's called Quintin Frensham," she said dully. "He's a cousin of Freddie's. He thinks he's in love with me." She paused. "I'd rather not talk about it anymore if you don't mind, James." She looked intently at me. "Is that all right?"

I nodded.

"Thank you." She leant forward and kissed me gently on the cheek. "Shall we go back to the house now?"

"Would you still like me to take you home?" I asked hopefully.

"I should like to go home awfully. But the reason for leaving early has now ceased to exist." She waved a hand in the direction in which my erstwhile antagonist had departed.

"That's a pity. I was looking forward to driving you."

"That's very sweet of you."

"No, it's not sweet of me at all. It's entirely selfish of me. As soon as I take you back to the house you'll be whisked away by someone and I shan't see you again."

She looked thoughtful. "Do you want to see me again – after all this?"

"Oh, yes."

She didn't say anything for quite a long time, but sat

motionless, staring into the middle distance. Then she drew deeply on her cigarette and sent a cloud of smoke up towards the moon, before she said, speaking very quietly, "We shall see one another again. Tomorrow. And next Thursday." She paused. "And after that who knows?"

SEVEN

I dreamed the most beautiful dream.
I lay on a beach in the sunshine. Sally knelt on the sand beside me. Her hair was hanging loose and the sunshine caught it and turned it into a blazing halo of gold.

I opened my eyes to find that I was truly lying in the sunshine, and for an instant I had that familiar feeling of not knowing where I was that one so often gets when waking in a strange bed.

At once I remembered that I was in Anne's bed at Highworth and I turned my head and saw her lying on her face with her head buried under the pillow. We seemed to have kicked all the bedclothes off during the night. I found that I was lying spreadeagled nakedly on the bed with the full splendour of my morning erection soaring proudly in the early morning sunshine which was streaming in through the open windows.

I looked at my watch. It was half-past six. I had slept for only three hours but I knew that I shouldn't be able to go to sleep again, and I felt wide awake and exhilarated. I reached over and picked the pillow from Anne's head and shook her shoulder gently. She lifted her head and opened her eyes.

"What is it?" she said thickly. Her eyes were completely unfocused.

"It's a lovely morning. What about a swim?"

"No, thank you," she said politely. She closed her eyes and dropped her head. I replaced the pillow and left her. It was obvious that she would sleep for hours.

I pulled on my dressing gown and crept quietly out of

the room. I was surprised to find the bedroom door slightly ajar. I could have sworn that I had shut it properly the night before. I paused for a few seconds in the passage. All was quiet.

I went to my own room to collect my swimming shorts and a towel and then I went down the stairs and let myself out of the front door. There was no one to be seen. As I walked across the lawn towards the pool I felt the cool dampness of the dew on my bare feet. The air was cold and wonderfully fresh and I breathed deeply. Never, I told myself, had I felt so fit and well. My head was clear and without a trace of hangover. For a moment I thought of tearing off my dressing gown and running naked on the grass for sheer joie de vivre, but I kept my dressing gown on.

The old oak door which led to the pool squeaked slightly and I pulled it shut behind me and shot the bolt. It had occurred to me that there was no reason why I shouldn't follow what seemed to be the prevailing fashion and swim naked. I wasn't too keen on the idea of being caught by anyone.

However, as I walked round the side of the summer house and came into view of the pool itself I realised that I was not the first person to think of having an early morning swim. I froze in my tracks, half-hidden by the corner of the summer house and partially concealed by a large rhododendron which grew beside it. A few yards away from me Sally had just taken off her dressing gown and was walking slowly along the diving board. She was stark naked.

When she reached the end of the board she stopped and looked down at the water for a moment. Then she raised her head and looked over the tops of the trees towards the rising sun. Her whole body was bathed in sunlight. It was the most beautiful body I had ever seen.

My throat felt as though it had swollen up and there was a sharp pain in the pit of my stomach. I was incapable of movement. I just stood and stared.

She stood at the end of the board for perhaps a minute. It seemed like an hour. I had all the time in the world to gaze at her; to feast my eyes on the details of her body; to take a mental photograph of her beauty that is as clear in my mind's eye today as it was that morning.

I suppose a purist might have found her body less than perfect. But then not everyone's idea of beauty is the same. Above all, Sally's body was superbly healthy. She had a golden tan which was the same even colour all over. There was no sign that she had ever worn a swimsuit of any sort and I was reminded of what Anne had told me about Freddie's rule. Her buttocks were small and jutting and possibly a little too muscular; her legs were long and straight and strong-looking; her stomach was flat which made the mound below it, lightly covered with dark yellow curls, look particularly prominent; her breasts were surprisingly big but they were firm and set close together, their pink nipples sharply erect in the cool morning air; her head was held high and her hair was tied away from her face with a pale green ribbon, exposing the lovely lines of her throat and her jaw.

I was afraid that she might see me because my dressing gown was the white towelling one which I had found behind the door of my room. I felt certain that it must show up vividly through my rather scanty cover, but being a well-trained infantryman I knew better than to move.

Eventually Sally raised her arms and prepared to dive in. She looked, I thought, like the High Priestess of some sun-worshipping cult greeting the new day.

She took a deep breath and dived into the pool. Her slim body sliced cleanly into the water with the minimal splash of a perfect dive. I took a deep breath too. I think it was the first breath I had drawn since I saw her. Before she came to the surface I stepped back behind the summer house and walked quickly to the door. I unbolted it, went through, shut it behind me and leaned against it for a moment. I felt weak at the knees. For a moment I toyed with the idea of going back in and pretending that I had just arrived, but I decided that I hadn't the nerve. I needed to sit down somewhere to recover.

EIGHT

I sat at my desk in my Company office in Chelsea Barracks. On the blotter in front of me was a sheet of foolscap paper at the top of which I had written: 'Appreciation of the Situation'. I stared out of the window. Half-way across The Square a small squad of Guardsmen and two young officers were being put through their paces by a bellowing Drill Sergeant. The Guardsmen were learning how to be Corporals, and the young officers were learning what hard work it is for a Guardsman to become a Corporal. It was very hot. I felt sorry for them.

It was the Monday morning following my weekend with the Frenshams. I had dealt with a dozen defaulters, inspected some Barrack rooms, signed a large heap of papers and found gainful employment for such of my Company officers as were available for duty. Now I was alone with nothing to do until Commanding Officer's Orders at noon.

I sucked the cap of my pen and then wrote:

'Aim: To decide whether to attempt to have an affair with Sally.

If the decision is "Yes" to decide how to set about it.'

I sat back and lit a cigarette. It was all so difficult.

Sally was so beautiful and so exciting and I simply longed to go to bed with her. There was no certainty that I should succeed but that was no reason for not trying. If I failed I had nothing to lose but my pride, and that could soon be revived. Anne was not a problem, I decided. It would be the work of a moment – or say thirty minutes over a drink somewhere – to hand her over to my able second-in-command. Then I should be free.

On the other hand, just what would I be getting myself into if I succeeded in seducing Sally? Where on earth might it lead? If Freddie found out he might divorce Sally and make me the co-respondent. On the whole I thought he probably wouldn't want the publicity, but I could think of circumstances in which he might feel that he was forced to do so. And where would that leave me? Almost certainly I should have to resign my commission. Officers who divorced their wives were usually allowed to remain in the Army nowadays, but co-respondents were in a very different category. Stealing another man's wife was still considered to be an extremely serious offence. It would be no defence to say that I hadn't intended to steal her, only to borrow her for a while. I was sure that I would be sent for by the Regimental Lieutenant Colonel and told to hand in my papers before worse befell me. It was a gloomy prospect. I liked being a soldier. I had been in the Army for over twelve years. I knew my way around. In a mild way I was conscious of being tolerably good at my job. I hadn't the smallest idea what I should do with myself if I left. I had no family broad acres to retreat to, no urge to become something in the City. I had sufficient private means to live without working, if need be, though I wasn't so well off that I wasn't glad of my Army pay, which was about £50 per week; but I knew I should become suicidally bored within months unless I had something to do.

I turned my thoughts briefly to Freddie. However I wrapped it up it was still the worst sort of dirty trick to 'borrow' his wife, for even the shortest time. I had been a guest in his house. Was I going to return his hospitality by taking his place in his wife's bed? On the whole I thought I probably was, if I could. From what I had heard and seen for myself there was something seriously wrong with him sexually. It looked as though he had abdicated his sexual role in their marriage years before. In a way I would be doing him a favour. It was a comforting way of looking at it. I suddenly remembered Susan Headcorn warning me that Freddie would make a dangerous enemy. I sighed and dragged at my cigarette. I shut my eyes and saw again her golden body as she stood on the diving board in the early morning sunshine. I wanted her.

Very well, I said to myself, suppose I manage to get her. What then? I have never had an affair with a married woman before. How do I go about it? The difficulties must be enormous. Perhaps she doesn't come to London very much. If she stays at Highworth how can I possibly have an affair with her? But, of course, Freddie was a Member of Parliament. They must have some sort of London residence. She must come to London occasionally, perhaps often.

What was I to do? If I did nothing now I could wait until she came to lunch on Guard on Thursday and play it by ear. That was the sensible course, I thought. But I wanted so badly to do something at once. Thursday was three days away. It seemed an age.

I looked again out of the window. I wanted a sign, something to tell me whether to pursue Sally or to forget her. I stubbed out my cigarette and leaned on the window sill. Perhaps the gods would give me some indication. I waited hopefully for a minute but nothing happened to disturb the tranquillity of the bright June morning. There were no flashes of lightning, no thunderbolts, not even a flight of geese flying from left or right to indicate the wrongness or rightness of my intentions.

I sat down again and picked up the *Times*. At the bottom of page two was the sign I was looking for. It was a short announcement entitled '*PEERS AND MPs TO WATCH NATO EXERCISE*'. It read: '*An all-party group of Members of both Houses of Parliament is to visit West Germany on Thursday next* [it gave the date] *to watch the concluding stages of Exercise LONG STOP.*' There was then a list of names. Amongst them I saw '*Visct. Frensham (C)*' and the name of Freddie's constituency.

A spasm of the purest joy shot through me. I almost hugged myself with excitement. I knew all about Exercise Long Stop. It was a massive NATO exercise involving the armies and air forces of half-a-dozen NATO countries. Practically the whole of the British Army in Germany was involved and a great many soldiers had been flown from England to take part. The Exercise had begun the week before and was scheduled to last almost three weeks. If Freddie and his party were going to Germany on Thursday they were bound to be away at least a week, possibly longer.

It was an opportunity which I simply couldn't miss. If I did I should never forgive myself for the rest of my life. I thought for a moment. What I needed, I now realised, was an evening alone with Sally. If I couldn't arrange that I didn't deserve to go to the Staff College.

I opened the hatch between my office and the Clerk's office next door.

"May I have a telephone book, Jones, please. E to K."

"Sir." He pulled it from a pile beside his typewriter and handed it to me. "Do you want a line, sir?"

"Yes, please."

He fiddled with his telephone and I shut the hatch and sat down. I turned to the Fs, praying that the Frenshams were not ex-directory. I was in luck – another sign, I wondered. There was an address in Westminster. It sounded like a block of flats. I dialled the number.

Freddie himself picked up the receiver on the second ring. I said who I was.

"Oh, yes." He sounded distant, bored. His charm wasn't switched on that morning. I was glad. The more I disliked him the easier it would be to forget my scruples.

"I rang for two reasons. First I wanted to thank you both for the weekend, though of course I shall be writing to Sally about that."

"I'm afraid I'm rather busy," Freddie cut in. "Could you telephone another time?"

I gripped the receiver hard.

"I shan't keep you a moment," I said firmly. I plunged on. "I'm having a small dinner party on Friday night and I should be very pleased if you and Sally would come. Black tie. Eight o'clock."

There was a pause.

"I'm going to be abroad then, I'm afraid. Going to Germany on Thursday."

I breathed a sigh of relief. It would have been ghastly if the *Times* had been misinformed. "That is a pity. I wonder…" I paused as though for thought. "Do you think Sally would like to come on her own? I'm sure I could make the numbers right."

"I'll ask her. Hold on."

There was a clunk as he put the telephone receiver down on some hard surface. I heard him call "Sally" and then a murmur of voices. I strained to hear what was being said but they were too far way. Then there was silence.

"James?" Sally's voice in my ear surprised me.

"Hello," I said happily.

"How are you?"

"Very well. It was a lovely weekend. Thank you so much." I broke off wondering whether to go through the business about the dinner party again. Sally helped me out.

"I should adore to come to your dinner party on Friday. Can you find some suitable man for me to make up the numbers?"

"Yes. I have one in mind."

"How exciting. Shall I wear long?"

"If you like."

"What are the other women going to wear?"

There won't be any other women, I almost said. "I expect they'll wear long," I lied. "I'm going to see you on Thursday, aren't I? For lunch?"

"Yes. I'm looking forward to it."

"I'll give you the details about Friday when I see you."

"All right. Until then. Goodbye."

"Goodbye, Sally." I waited for her to hang up before I put my receiver down. I had been gripping so tightly that my hand and arm were aching. The back of my shirt was wet with sweat.

I lit another cigarette and got up and walked about the room. I was too excited to sit still.

I opened the hatch again and returned the telephone book to Jones.

"Do you know where Captain Pershore is?"

"I think he's in the Company stores, sir."

"Will you send someone to find him, please. Ask him to come and see me when he has a moment."

"Sir." Jones shut the hatch.

Now, I thought, to dispose of Anne. When Peter came in, he halted inside the door and saluted me.

"What can I do for you, dear boy?"

"Come and sit down. I have a couple of little problems that you can help me with."

He perched himself on the corner of a table and fitted a

cigarette into a long holder. "Social or military problems?"

"Very social. Very social indeed. Problem number one concerns a handover-takeover."

He raised an eyebrow. "It sounds rather military. I must warn you that I'm feeling so confused after counting practically everything in the Company stores I'm afraid I shall prove a broken reed."

"The handover-takeover concerns one Anne Knowle."

Peter stood up. "Ah, ha. You interest me strangely. Pray proceed, my dear."

"You said last week that you found her attractive."

"So I did. So I do."

"Well, she and I are just about finished. She's looking round for a replacement and if you appear at just the right moment she's yours for the taking. Very satisfactory taking too," I added vulgarly.

Peter sucked at his cigarette holder. "Are you sure it will be so simple?" He seemed uncharacteristically dubious. "Perhaps she won't fancy me."

"She will when I've told her a bit about you."

"You won't tell her about my money, will you?" He looked quite alarmed.

"No, of course not," I said cheerfully, though in fact I had every intention of at least hinting at it. "I'll tell her what a great lad you are."

"What about the actual handover? When is it to be?"

"On Thursday. I want it to seem as though you met by chance so that she can think she's giving me the air, and not the other way round."

"Good thinking. How are you going to do that?"

"Simple. I'm on Guard on Thursday. I'll invite her to come and have a drink before dinner, but of course she'll have to leave at eight o'clock with any other women there.

You come for a drink too. You meet. You invite her out to dinner. She'll jump at it. If you like, pretend that it's to be kept a secret from me. That may stop her thinking that the whole thing is my idea. Take her somewhere extremely good for dinner. She's mad about good food. After that you're on your own, my boy."

"Sounds easy enough."

"She is. But you'll enjoy it. She's quite an experience."

Peter took a slim diary from his uniform jacket. He pulled out a gold pencil and wrote in the diary. "Thursday," he muttered as he wrote. "Queen's Guard. Seven o'clock. Anne. Dinner Mirabelle. Then on to Annabel's. Do you think she'll be up to climbing the stairs at the end of Curzon Street?"*

"She's very fit, probably better at climbing the steps in heels than you. However, you can forget Annabel's. I shall be very surprised if you don't have an early night."

"Well, well," he drawled. "What an enthusiastic girl." He put away his diary and pencil. "Is there anything that I can do for you in return for this excessively generous gesture?"

"Yes, there is as a matter of fact. It's very simple. At exactly half-past eight on Friday evening I want you to ring me up at my flat. When I answer hang up. But make sure it is me before you do so."

"If it isn't?"

"Ask for me. When I come to the telephone hang up."

Peter nodded and grinned at me evilly. "It shall be done." He straightened his Service Dress Cap and put out his cigarette. "There's just time for a drop of the right stuff

---

*   In those days Curzon Street ended with a high wall and a cul de sac at the eastern end. Those on foot could climb up the flight of steps from the end of the cul de sac into Berkeley Square, emerging between Lansdowne House and the Lansdowne Club.

before you go to watch the Commanding Officer dish out his palm-tree justice. So off we go to the Officers' Mess."

I put on my bowler hat and Peter saluted me as I preceded him from the office and we wandered across The Square towards the Mess.

"You won't say anything to anyone about the Friday telephone call, will you Peter? And you won't let anyone see you do it?"

"My dear lad, of course not. How can you ask me such a thing? I'm really quite hurt. All this hard work that you're putting into caring for my welfare seems to have softened your brain. No one will get anything out of me and I'm not going to ask you any questions about what you're getting up to."

We walked in silence for a while. I took off my hat in acknowledgement of the salutes of some passing Guardsmen.

"But James." He sounded serious. "You won't… er… do anything foolish, will you?"

NINE

"St James's Palace Detachment of the Queen's Guard to the front. Remainder – Right TURN," I shouted.

I was in good voice that morning. It was just after eleven o'clock and a watery sun had broken through the clouds. It lit up the neat scarlet ranks of the New Guard on The Square at Chelsea Barracks as we prepared to set off on our march to Buckingham Palace. "To your duties. QUICK MARCH."

We were off. The St James's Palace Detachment advanced across The Square towards me, the Ensign carrying the Colour leading. The Buckingham Palace Detachment performed two left inclines and fell into position behind it. Judging my moment with the accuracy of long experience, I stepped off in time with the Guard and placed myself three paces in front of the Ensign. I followed the Band and the Corps of Drums out of the back gate of the Barracks.

In less than two hours, I said to myself, I shall see Sally again. "I shall see Sally again." I sang it to myself in time to the music of the Band. It went rather well, I thought.

The ceremony at Buckingham Palace went off without a hitch. My opposite number, the Captain of the Old Guard, was a Major in the Grenadier Guards and an old friend from school and Sandhurst. We sat together in the little room at the front of the Palace where the two Captains go while the Guardrooms are handed over and the sentries are changed. We drank glasses of water, glanced at the (for some reason) airmail edition of the *Times* and I studied a card which I was given which set out for me the appointments and movements of the Royal Family for the next 24 hours. The Queen was due to go out to lunch (I guessed) at 12.45. I made a mental note to see that the sentries would be ready to salute her.

Later, as I marched from Buckingham Palace to St James's Palace behind the Corps of Drums, I ran over in my mind the plans I had made for the next evening. I seemed to have forgotten nothing.

I had splashed out on a 16-ounce jar of Beluga caviar from Fortnum's to start the meal off. There were four bottles left of a dozen Dom Perignon 1959 that my mother had given me as a flat-warming present earlier in the year. It had occurred to me that it would be just the stuff to give to Sally.

I grinned to myself behind my curbchain as we swung from the Mall into Stable Yard Gate. Caviar, champagne and soft lights was a pretty corny seduction set-up, but it was civilised.

I brought my sword up to the carry as we marched past Clarence House where the Queen Mother's standard hung limply in the noontime sunshine and the double sentries on the gates presented arms. Even if I got nowhere with Sally, I reflected, I was going to have a jolly good dinner. I looked forward to the caviar in particular. At £30 a pound the Beluga had cost me more than half-a-week's pay.

We marched into Ambassadors' Court in the centre of the Palace. I halted the Guard, ordered the Colour to be marched off and dismissed the Guard to the Guardroom. A small crowd of onlookers stood silently watching us. They had wandered in through the open gateway from St James's Street. The thrilling thunder of the Drummers playing 'The Point of War' as the Colour was marched off seemed to reverberate in the narrow space long after they had stopped playing.

I returned my sword to its scabbard and walked slowly down the little alleyway labelled 'Engine Court', which leads to the Guardrooms. I went first to the Men's Guardroom to talk to the Senior Sergeant and to sign the Guard Report. The Senior Sergeant was in fact my Company Sergeant Major (and most of the Guard were of my Company). He was an old friend. He had been my Platoon Sergeant when I was commissioned and we had known each other well in the ten years since then, while I had become a Major and he a Warrant Officer. We discussed the times when the Ensign and I would go round the sentries during the night.

There was a board displaying photographs of members of the Royal Family who sentries might see and need to recognise and salute. Some of the photographs looked a bit out of date and I made a mental note to see that they were replaced. I then climbed the stairs to the Officers' Guardroom. The Colour-Sergeant who ran the place greeted me in his avuncular way and produced the menus for the day's meals and the wine list. I looked carefully at both and selected the wines I wanted.

"We managed to get you some gulls' eggs, sir," he told me. "I thought the season was over by now but we found that Fortnum's had some and I bought all they had. It'll give you three each, sir."

"That'll be splendid, Colour-Sarnt, thank you. Everything else all right?"

"Sir."

"I'm going to have a quick bath and change," I told him. "Will you send up a glass of Buck's Fizz, please. I'll have it in one of the silver tankards the HAC gave us."

I put my bearskin cap on one of the wooden stands

provided for the purpose, and climbed another flight of stairs to the floor above where the bedrooms and the bathroom were.

My Orderly had already run a bath for me and now he helped me out of my heavy scarlet tunic and hung it in the wardrobe. I lay in the warm water for ten minutes, sipping my Buck's Fizz and praying that Sally would turn up.

At ten minutes to one I was downstairs again, dressed in my Blue, and as brushed and ready as I could be. I was, I knew, in an extremely nervous state and I lit a cigarette and started on my second tankard of Buck's Fizz. As each tankard contained well over half-a-pint of liquid, and as the drink was composed of four parts champagne to one part orange juice, I realised that when I finished my second drink I should have drunk more than a bottle of champagne all by myself.

I was alone in the large room and I perched on the club fender and waited. The two other officers of the Guard were busy. The Subaltern, who commanded the Buckingham Palace portion of the Guard, had not yet arrived. He spent the day at St James's but slept at Buckingham Palace with his Detachment. He would arrive in time for lunch after he had visited his sentries and seen his men eat their lunch. The third officer – the Ensign – was seeing the lunches of the men at St James's.

The Guardroom was a fine setting, I thought, for my next meeting with Sally. The sun poured in through the large windows and the room seemed to bask in its rays. The luncheon table was laid for five as Susan Headcorn and Sally were to be our only guests. The heavy silver and the wine glasses, all superbly polished, looked comfortable on the dark wood.

I wondered if I should be able to tell from Sally's manner

whether I stood a chance with her. In the past four days I had been over and over in my mind her every word, look and gesture in an attempt to decide what she thought of me. It had been a fruitless exercise, but one in which I couldn't help indulging. It would be so much easier, I told myself, if Sally were like the generality of women, with whom one could tell at once whether or not they were interested. I could tell just by looking into their eyes whether they wanted me. They sent out a signal, loud and clear, which said 'I find you attractive. If you want to do anything about it that's up to you.' If there was no such signal it was usually a waste of time to try; but not always. The lack of a signal could mean one of several things: 'I find you completely repulsive. Don't bother me,' or 'I am in love with someone else,' or, and I prayed that Sally came into this category, 'I think you're super but I'm too inexperienced to let you know.'

The Colour-Sergeant appeared from behind the screen which stood in front of the door.

"Lady Headcorn and Lady Frensham, sir," he announced, and Susan and Sally advanced into the room. Both wore small smart hats. Sally was even more beautiful than I remembered.

"This is fun," said Susan Headcorn. "Quite like old times."

I greeted them both and we all sat down, Susan in an armchair and Sally and I perched on the fender.

"Would you like a glass of Buck's Fizz?" I suggested. "It's just the thing for a hot day. Or would you rather have a champagne cocktail or a glass of sherry or something?"

"What is Buck's Fizz?" Susan asked me.

"It's a mixture of champagne and orange juice," I explained. "I can recommend it."

"I should love to try it," said Susan.

"For you, Sally?" I turned towards her and looked into her green eyes.

"Yes, please." She smiled beatifically, but there was no signal there that I could discern.

I nodded at the Colour-Sergeant who had remained hovering in the background to see what drinks were wanted. He half bowed and left the room.

"We've had the most hectic morning," cried Susan cheerfully, and she started to tell me all about their adventures in Harrods. I sipped my drink and wondered how I was going to talk to Sally on her own.

The two younger officers joined us a few minutes later and were noticeably smitten by Sally and amused by Susan, and at half-past one we sat down to luncheon.

I thought it right to seat my guests according to age rather than precedence and Susan sat on my right, Sally on my left. The Subaltern sat next to Sally and the Ensign was at the foot of the table, his proper place at luncheon and dinner on Guard. (At breakfast and at tea the Ensign sits at the head of the table and pours out tea and coffee for the other officers.)

Lunch went well. The food and wine were perfect: gulls' eggs and oriental salt, lobster with a green salad, a lemon soufflé and a great deal of Pouilly-Fumé. Susan Headcorn got slightly, rather charmingly, drunk. Sally was cool and poised and so good to look at that I had to make a conscious effort not to stare at her throughout the meal.

"There used to be a tradition," said Susan, "that I remember hearing about long ago." She had just been told by the Ensign that it was his first Guard.

"What was that?" he asked her politely.

Susan waved her glass vaguely in the direction of the

Queen's Colour, which stood in its place in the corner by the window.

"I was told that on his first Guard the Ensign was required to prove his manhood on the Colour which was put on this table. A girl was produced from somewhere and everyone else stood round to watch and cheer."

The unfortunate Ensign went scarlet and looked to me for assistance.

"I've heard that too," I said. "Though I've never known it happen in recent times. Certainly I wasn't made to perform on my first Guard."

"How perfectly awful it must have been," said the Subaltern, a sensitive soul. "Where on earth did the woman come from?"

"The Captain… er… sent out for her, I suppose," I said.

"But it doesn't happen at all now?" Susan asked. She sounded most disappointed.

"I'm afraid not."

"Extraordinary. And this is supposed to be the permissive society." She finished her soufflé and the waiters came in to clear the table and bring the coffee and liqueurs. Susan accepted a glass of vintage port. "Well, never mind," she said. "If there's to be no cabaret I must at least have a look at all the things here. I seem to remember that there was a screen somewhere, locked away in a cupboard. It was considered far too risqué for women to see when I was a girl."

I saw my opportunity to get Sally alone for a moment. "Tommy is the great expert on everything in this room," I told her, nodding at the Subaltern. "He can tell you whether the snuff box in the centre of the table really *is* made from one of the hooves of Napoleon's charger Marengo; and I think we might allow you a glimpse of the screen. It isn't very daring by today's standards."

I stood up and held back Susan's chair. Tommy found the key which opened the lock on the screen cupboard and everyone gathered round. I hung back and said quietly to Sally, "Come out onto the roof for a moment."

She smiled and nodded and I took her out of the French window and up the few steps onto the roof. It was a large area, covered with duckboards, and there were a number of tubs filled with geraniums and some deckchairs dotted about.

We walked to the far side and leaned on the parapet and looked down into the little court below, where we could see the door of the Ascot office.

"That was a very good lunch," said Sally as I gave her a cigarette and lit it and one for myself. "You obviously make yourselves very comfortable here."

"We do. It's one of the high points in a soldier's life, as far as comfort is concerned. There are lots of very uncomfortable times to make up for it."

"You must all adore it."

"Not everyone. Some people loathe the ceremonial side of soldiering here in London, and of course in one sense we are simply a tourist attraction. The crowds outside Buckingham Palace these days are vast. I don't think many of them manage to see anything at all. Perhaps we should do the whole thing on Horse Guards. We used to do it there in the eighteenth century."

"Do you enjoy it?"

"Very much."

"Perhaps that's because you're good at it. People usually enjoy doing what they're good at and vice versa. I thought you looked very smart when I watched you the other day. You're very tall and you're the right shape. That must help."

I grinned at her, not knowing quite what to say. I puffed

at my cigarette and looked into her eyes again. Did she fancy me? Even a little bit? I couldn't tell.

"What time do you want me tomorrow night?" she said suddenly.

I thought of saying something silly like 'Every hour on the hour,' but I managed not to. She looked perfectly serious and obviously hadn't realised how badly phrased her question had been. Was it a Freudian slip?

"Eight o'clock. Will that suit you?"

"Yes, of course. How many people are coming?"

"Six, I think. Possibly only four."

"Do you want any help with the cooking? Or have you got that organised already? Does Anne help with your dinner parties?"

"Anne doesn't cook. She just eats."

"I could come at half-past six if you like and do anything that needs doing. I adore cooking."

I thought rapidly. My first reaction was to refuse. My plans were laid. It was too late to change them now. Before I could say anything Sally went on, "I could bring my dress with me in a bag and change in your bathroom before the others arrive. Perhaps you'd let me have a bath too." She smiled at me. "I should tell you that I know all about your bathroom from Anne. I'm dying to see it."

That clinched it. If Sally was going to start taking off her clothes in my flat I wasn't going to stop her. Besides, who could tell what effect my bathroom would have on her. My plan was simple and, I suddenly realised, like all good plans it was flexible.

"That is kind. I don't think there'll be very much to do, but I should be very grateful for some assistance. And of course you can have a bath."

"That's settled then. Expect me at six-thirty."

"I shall be looking forward to it."
We smiled at one another in the sunshine.

TEN

I felt fragile on Friday morning. I had sat up drinking and talking until very late and then I had slept badly and had strange dreams. I cut myself shaving and I felt sick when I lifted the silver cover and saw fried eggs looking at me. I settled for a glass of orange juice and a cup of black coffee poured for me by the Ensign and I buried myself in the *Times*. My Aunt Rosemary's mother had died, I noticed. I wondered if I ought to do anything about it. The announcement said 'no letters', which was a comfort.

***

Aunt Rosemary had been one of the first visitors to my flat. She was in fact no blood relation but the wife of my father's younger brother Henry. They lived in darkest Dorset where Uncle Henry farmed in a desultory fashion and I saw them very rarely. But one day my telephone rang and Aunt Rosemary announced that she was coming to London the next day to do some shopping and, as she had heard that I was back now from Aden and she hadn't seen me for more than two years, she proposed to invite herself for tea. She was an unexceptionable woman but, I thought, too boring to put up with alone for more than about five minutes so I tried to think of an excuse. Unfortunately my wits deserted me and while I was still trying to think of something she pressed me. I found a moment later that I had said that I should look forward to seeing her at 4.30 the next afternoon.

After I had put the telephone down I thought of all manner of magnificently convincing reasons for not giving her tea and I almost rang her back to tell her one of them. However, some sort of filial duty prevented me from doing so and I bit the bullet and bought a packet of Earl Grey tea and some chocolate biscuits. For a moment I even contemplated attempting some cucumber sandwiches but I decided that that would be going too far.

She arrived ten minutes early and bustled in under a huge pile of bags. She looked untidy and harassed.

"I'm afraid I couldn't manage to shut the lift doors behind me," she said breathlessly. "I'm terribly sorry."

"I'll go and do them, Aunt Rosemary. Come in and put your shopping down. You must be exhausted." I waved a hand down the short passage that led to the drawing room and she lurched past gratefully, dropping one or two small bags as she did so. I went out on the landing and shut the lift gates. On my way back I picked up all that Aunt Rosemary had dropped. Most of the bags were pale green and had 'Harrods' printed on them. They were not Harrods' usual bags and I asked Aunt Rosemary what they were.

"It's the sale, my dear," she told me. "Those are just for the sale, I think. I've had the most successful day there today. I always come up to London for their sale. It's the greatest fun." She smiled at me, pleased with her exertions, and she took off her hideous brown felt hat. She looked almost human without it. Her hair was short and wildly disarranged and mouse-coloured thickly flecked with grey. Her eyes were large and very pale blue and her nose shone like a beacon. She had on a shapeless brown tweed coat and she carried a crocodile handbag that looked exactly like the 'before remodelling' examples that you used to see in that shop in Beauchamp Place. All in all she looked a bit potty.

"I'll go and make some tea," I said. "Why don't you take your coat off?"

"Tea would be lovely," she said with enthusiasm. "Go and put the kettle on and then you must show me your flat. This is the most beautiful room," she looked around her. "But you could do with one or two more bits of furniture, don't you think?"

She followed me into the kitchen and exclaimed at the magnificence of the modernity of it all. I remembered that her kitchen in Dorset contained only a scrubbed wooden table, a stained old sink and a hopelessly inefficient Calor cooker.

She decided that the dining room was just what I wanted; she said she could see that the roof garden would be a great boon in the summer, which was quite clever of her as it looked pretty grim at half past four on that damp January afternoon. Then she stole towards the bathroom door.

"What's through here?"

"Just the bathroom. Come on into the drawing room and sit down. I expect the tea will be ready in a moment."

I was reluctant to show her the bathroom. But it was hopeless. "I must just have a peep. I adore bathrooms." And she threw open the door, switched on the lights and walked in. I shut my eyes and held my breath. There was a very long silence. I knew what had made her stop talking. When I first saw it I could scarcely believe my eyes and even after I became more used to it – though I never really recovered completely from my first shock – it amused me intensely each time someone went into it who had not seen it before. Reactions varied; they almost all began with the silence of shock, though once or twice I had heard a low whistle of surprise. After a moment or two men usually bellowed with laughter, women's behaviour varied.

It is not easy to do justice to it in writing because no description can properly explain the feeling that the room gave. That feeling arose in part from the look of the room, in part also from the look that the room gave to the person in it and perhaps, though this may seem fanciful to some, in part from a feeling in the room that its creator had left behind her, some indefinable spiritual quality.

It was a large room and it had no window. The main colour – if colour it be – was black. The only other colour was gold.

A thick black carpet entirely covered the floor, and the washbasin, lavatory and bidet were made of black marble. All the fitments were of gold; not solid, I suppose, but nevertheless distinctly realistic and rich-looking. One side of the room was entirely taken up by the bath, which was of the sunken variety and was reached by walking up four thickly carpeted stairs. The carpet ended at a broad black marble surround which ran round three sides of the bath and joined onto the wall on the fourth.

The bath itself was deep and almost round and, as I had discovered, there was ample room for two; or even, I suppose, if one's tastes lay in such esoteric directions, for three or four. It was made of pale golden marble and had four lights let into the bottom so that the bath water, if soapy or filled with bath salts, had a strange translucent glow. The taps were ornate and golden and the water gushed into the bath from a cornucopia held by two foot-high golden figures; a nude full-breasted goddess and an equally nude and obscenely well-equipped god. Another smaller cornucopia half-way up the wall and above the first, contained an efficient shower which I often used, particularly when I was in a hurry, as the bath took such a huge quantity of water to fill it. There was no need for anything as mundane as a shower curtain.

The walls and the ceiling of this extraordinary room were covered with looking glass which had been treated with some substance that prevented it from steaming up. No lights were visible, but just outside the door were two light switches. One controlled the underwater lights in the bath. A ripple in the water was reflected again and again in the other mirrored surfaces which lined the room. The other switch controlled concealed lights behind the looking glasses. They made the walls and the ceiling glow with a gently pink light which gave a rosy look to the dullest grey English skin.

All of this was of course the work of an earlier tenant, and I can take no credit for it. Although, I should like to have met its creator.

I can, however, take credit for not destroying it. It was in a sense a work of art, and it must have cost a small fortune to install, but at first I found it a deep embarrassment. The blatant sensuality of the room was, I felt, too much to bear. After all it would not have been out of place in the most extravagant of the late Cecil B. DeMille's productions and Peter Pershore had several times offered to corner the market in asses' milk on my behalf. Such an insistence on sensuality was almost literally sickening when I wished to shave on a cold wet Monday morning, and soon after I moved in I very nearly had the room gutted and redecorated regardless of the expense. I think I would have done if I had not been shown quite soon after I moved in what an interesting effect the room had on some women.

"Did you do this, James?" There was an odd tone in Aunt Rosemary's voice, which I could not identify.

"No," I was glad to be able to make an excuse. "It was like

that when I bought it." I followed her into the bathroom. She was standing in the middle of the floor, staring wide-eyed at the black bidet.

"What do you think I ought to do about it?" I asked nervously, but I don't think she can have heard me. She inspected herself in the pink looking glass.

"I didn't realise before what an awful coat this was." She shrugged it off and handed it to me. Underneath it she wore a twin-set and pearls and a baggy tweed skirt. She was a tall woman and a bit on the stringy side but her legs were not bad and her ankles would have been outstanding if she had not worn such dreadfully sensible shoes.

"Good heavens." She had had a long look at herself from several angles. "I do look a sight."

There did not seem to be anything to say to that so I went back into the bedroom and put her coat on my bed. When I went back into the bathroom she was examining the bath.

"How does it work?" I showed her how the lever operated which closed the plug and I turned on the taps. Hot water gushed out of the cornucopia held by the god and goddess. The two figures had never looked more naked and I felt hot with embarrassment.

My aunt gushed too. "It's marvellous. I think it's the most wonderful bathroom in the world. I'm absolutely green with envy."

I was flabbergasted. "You're not shocked?"

"Certainly not."

"You don't think it looks as though it had escaped from a French brothel?"

"That's exactly what it does look like. At least that's what I imagine. I'm sorry to say I've never been inside a French brothel."

I found her attitude hard to credit. "But in spite of that

you think it's all right?" I was incredulous.

"It's absolutely splendid, my dear. You mustn't be so bourgeois, James. Enjoy it. Everyone should have a bathroom like this."

The bath was almost half-full now and I did not want to waste a lot of hot water so I turned the taps off.

"I'm very glad you like it," I said weakly.

"I really do adore it, and, do you know what I should like to do more than anything in the world at this moment?"

"What?"

"Have a bath," she smiled triumphantly. "I've always wanted to know what it felt like to be a luxurious courtesan, and if I get into this fabulous bath I shall feel exactly the part."

"You really want to have a bath now?" I could barely believe my ears.

"Yes," her blue eyes were flashing. "That's exactly what I want. Do you mind?"

"Of course not, Aunt Rosemary. What about tea? Would you like it in the bath?"

"Tea?" She pulled a face. "Good Lord, no. I should like a drink. Have you any champagne?"

"Oddly enough, yes. There's a bottle in the fridge."

She leant forward and turned on the taps again. The she smiled radiantly at me. "How marvellous. Give me five minutes to get in and then you can bring me a glass in here."

I laughed nervously. "All right." I fled to the kitchen.

While I struggled with the champagne cork I wondered what on earth was the matter with my hitherto straitlaced Aunt Rosemary. Had she gone round the bend? I tried to remember whether I had ever heard anything about madness in her family. I put the opened bottle of champagne and two glasses on to a tray and was just about to start back to the bathroom when I had an almost blinding vision. I saw Aunt Rosemary waiting for me, stark naked in my bath; and I knew with absolute certainty that if I went in there she would try to seduce me. The knowledge was at the same time fascinating and horrifying.

I went into the drawing room and sat on the sofa amongst her shopping and drank a glass of champagne. I was deeply shocked. It wasn't until some days later that I realised that really it was all the fault of the bathroom and that poor Aunt Rosemary couldn't help herself.

She emerged about half an hour later looking pink and rather pretty and very much ashamed of herself. "I don't know what you must think of me," she said. "I can't understand what possessed me to behave like that. It was most peculiar. I assure you I've never done anything so extraordinary before in my whole life."

I muttered a few platitudes and gave her a glass of champagne.

Later I helped her gather up her bags and took her down in the lift and put her into a taxi. I gave her a nephewly peck on the cheek and she held on to me for a moment before she climbed into the taxi.

She looked at me intently. "Do you know, I'm awfully grateful to you for not coming into the bathroom when I was in the bath. If you had… Well, I don't know quite what would have happened." And she gave me a look that told me more clearly than any words could have done that she knew exactly what would have happened.

A week later the Sheraton sofa table was delivered. There was a note with it. It read: 'We do hope that you will find a place for this in your flat. It used to belong to your grandfather. Your flat is very nice, but the bathroom is a menace!!!

With love from us both. Uncle Henry and Aunt Rosemary.'

It was all written in Aunt Rosemary's handwriting and I felt sure that Uncle Henry had had nothing whatever to do with it.

The very next week my cleaning woman gave me a similar revelation.

She was a woman of gigantic physique and irreproachable virtue and at first I found her rather frightening. One day I returned to my flat in the middle of the morning to fetch something that I had forgotten. Hearing noises from the bathroom I walked in.

To my amazement I discovered the respectable Mrs Catton wallowing in my bath like a pink hippopotamus. She gave a shriek of horror when she saw me and tried to conceal her monumental breasts behind a very small sponge.

"Ooooh, Major," she cried. "Well I never. What an awful thing."

"I'm most awfully sorry, Mrs Catton. I had no idea."

"Oh, sir. I'm the one to be sorry, I'm sure. I don't know what I can of been thinking of. Using your bath like this. What must you think of me? Of course I'll get out straight away, sir. What a terrible thing." And to my horror she stood up in the bath and started to climb out.

I averted my gaze immediately but of course wherever I looked I saw her colossal reflection.

I backed out rapidly, saying as I went: "No. No. Mrs Catton. You stay in the bath. It doesn't matter at all."

I shut the door behind me and went straight back to Barracks. I couldn't decide whether to be shocked or amused, but every time I shut my eyes for a moment I saw again Mrs Catton's massive pink quivering nakedness. It was most upsetting.

I fully expected that that would be the last I should hear of her and that I should have to look round for a new daily woman, but to my surprise she turned up on time the next day and from then on she became the most efficient maid-of-all-work that I could have wished for.

She never again referred to the bathroom incident. Once or twice I caught her looking at me in an odd sort of way – half coy, half flirtatious – and I supposed that she had got rather a thrill out of exposing her all – and what an all – to the young master. In any event she kept the flat magnificently clean and nothing I asked her to do was ever too much trouble.

These two incidents made me think. It was odd that two such virtuous women should have behaved in such an outlandish way. It could only be attributable to the bathroom itself. I concluded that the room possessed some strange property which almost forced any woman with even a scrap of sensuality in her make-up to take off her clothes and disport herself in the bath.

In the months that followed I discovered how true this was.

***

I had just finished reading the *Times* when the Colour-Sergeant said "You're wanted on the telephone, sir. It's a Miss Knowle."

"Thank you, Colour-Sarnt." I took my cup of coffee with me to the telephone. Anne sounded disgustingly well.

"Good morning, darling," she purred.

"Hello."

"You don't sound too good."

"I feel like death."

"Well, I've got some bad news for you, I'm afraid."
"Oh?"
"About this weekend."
"What about it?"
"I can't see you as we planned."
"Did we plan?"

Anne sniffed. "Don't be so boring, James. You know perfectly well we planned to spend this weekend together."

I had been far too busy with my plans for Sally to think of anything else, but perhaps she was right.

"Of course," I said, trying to put some enthusiasm into my voice.

"Well you can forget it," said Anne firmly. "I'm ditching you and going to Paris for the weekend with your friend Peter."

I drank some of my coffee. I suddenly felt much better.

"So this is the end," I said in a sepulchral voice.

Anne giggled. "You needn't sound so exactly like a B movie. But yes. This is the end."

"Oh."

"Peter is a great success. We're going to have a lovely time together. I gather he has a little money."

"Just a bit."

"That'll be nice. I like him awfully."

"Good."

"Are you unhappy, darling?"

"I'm not sure yet. It's too early in the morning. I'll think about it later."

"You'll recover. I must go now. I must have my hair done and do some shopping before we catch the plane this afternoon. I expect we shall run into one another from time to time. And, James…"

"Yes."

"If you don't find someone else, and if you ever feel like it you can ring me up if you want to and we can have dinner and some lovings for old times' sake."

I thought that was rather nice of her. "Thank you, Anne."

"That's all right, darling. You're still the best, you know."

"I bet you say that to all the boys."

She laughed. "I do, as a matter of fact. But in your case it happens to be true."

I said to myself, 'thank you Louise'.

---

* See Chapter Twenty-Two (but not yet).

ELEVEN

"And let us mind, faint heart ne'er wan A lady fair."
— Robert Burns

Everything was ready. Everything, that is, except me. It was two o'clock in the afternoon. I walked into the bedroom and, stripping off my uniform, I climbed under the bedspread and settled down to sleep. I set my alarm for five o'clock and lay back carefully. Mrs Catton had made up the bed with clean sheets and I didn't want to disturb them, but I must have a few hours' sleep if I was to be in good shape for whatever the evening might bring.

I had lunched well in Barracks and had almost cured my hangover. I had congratulated Peter on his success and discussed with him the slight change in my own plans.

The alarm woke me at five and I was wide awake at once. I eased myself gently from the bed and straightened the bedclothes and turned over my pillow. I pulled up the bedspread and pulled and patted it until it was immaculate.

In the bathroom I shaved carefully and closely and managed to avoid the little cut I had inflicted upon myself that morning. I had a long thorough shower and then spent ten minutes cleaning up after myself so that the room would be tidy and clean for Sally to use. I took from the airing cupboard my largest and fluffiest bath towel and arranged it on the heated towel rail for her. I anointed myself liberally with Chanel's 'Gentleman's Cologne' and I admired myself in the looking glass walls. She can't possibly resist you, dear boy, I told my reflection.

Last I selected my clothes: a cream-coloured heavy slub silk shirt with gold Regimental cuff-links, a blue silk scarf, black trousers almost indecently form-fitting, silk socks and soft leather slip-on (and therefore easily kicked off) shoes, no underclothes.

When the front doorbell rang at 6.25 it made me jump and I almost ran to the door.

Sally stood waiting. She was carrying a small suitcase and she looked marvellous.

"Hello," I said happily. "You look marvellous," and I stepped forward quickly and kissed her lightly on the lips. For a moment she was too surprised to move or resist, and before she could do so I stepped back.

"Come on in." I took her suitcase. It was surprisingly heavy.

She hesitated for a moment and smiled cautiously at me.

"Is anyone here?"

"Not yet. We shall be able to cook undisturbed."

She walked through the doorway and down the short passage that led to the drawing room. I followed feeling pleased with myself. Phase One was successfully accomplished; I had kissed her, and now it shouldn't be too difficult to do it again.

"What a lovely room," cried Sally enthusiastically. She dropped her handbag on the sofa and crossed to the long window. "And what a magnificent view."

"It *is* a good view, isn't it?" I picked up champagne and two glasses. "Come out onto my roof garden and see it from there. It's even better."

The French window was open and we went out. I put a glass into Sally's hand without asking her whether or not she wanted it. She took a sip. Phase Two – champagne and talk phase, the most difficult of all – was off to a good start. Phase Three, when Sally got into my bath and Peter telephoned, was a problem of timings but I didn't anticipate any very great difficulty. I knew I could rely on Peter. Phase Four would begin when Sally emerged from the bathroom and found me waiting for her in the bedroom or, in military parlance, the 'killing ground'. That phase, and Phase Five – 'Reorganisation and Consolidation' – which followed it, would have to be played more or less by ear.

"This is awfully good," she said. "What a prettily shaped bottle. It is something special?"

I told her what it was. "Some people think it's the best. But whether that's right or not the great thing about it is that you can drink lots and lots of it without feeling any ill-effects, either at the time or on the morning after."

"I don't believe a word of it." She laughed. "But it's simply delicious anyway. And now I want to have a complete guided tour of your flat, ending up with the kitchen so that we can cook the dinner. Let's start with the bathroom, please. I've been dying to see it for months."

I nodded. "Bring your glass. I'll lead the way."

We went first to the bedroom where she said she thought everything was magnificent and that the room had a nice feel about it. Looking back now, with the benefit of hindsight, that proves to my satisfaction that there is no such thing as premonition. If ever anyone ought to have had a feeling of that sort about a room, Sally should have had one about my bedroom.

We walked through into the bathroom. Sally gasped and for a moment looked deeply shocked. "Anne told me about it, but even so I had no idea…"

I thought her reaction was predictably respectable. She was a conventional girl who had been brought up to think that a bathroom was a cold room with a white enamel bath it in and linoleum on the floor, a room to which one went once a day as a duty rather than a pleasure and in which one remained for as short a time as possible. My sybaritic dream took a little getting used to and I told her so.

"Shall we do the cooking first?" I asked. "Then you can lock yourself in here for as long as you like. I guarantee you'll adore it when you get used to it. How long will it take you to get dressed?"

"If I'm to be ready by eight I think I'd better be out of the bath by seven-thirty. We don't want people to arrive while I'm half-dressed in your bedroom, do we?" she asked seriously, her great green eyes looking straight into mine.

"No," I said, equally seriously. "That would be most unfortunate."

"Do I know the other people who are coming this evening?"

"Yes, indeed. Anne is one. The other is a friend of mine in the Regiment called Peter Pershore."

"Do he and Anne know one another?"

Do they! I thought. "They've met once or twice. They both came to have a drink on Guard last night and I have an idea that they went out to dinner afterwards. Certainly they left together. No doubt we shall discover this evening."

Sally looked thoughtful but said nothing.

"Shall we start cooking?" I asked her.

"You start. I want to take my dress out of my suitcase and hang it up. I'll join you in a moment."

Two minutes later she walked into the kitchen. She had taken off the jacket of the plain green linen suit she was wearing and she was rolling up the sleeves of her silk shirt. The neck was open wide and I saw two rows of fat pearls at the base of her soft brown throat. She made an enchantingly feminine attempt at halting like a soldier with a stamping of feet that made her breasts bounce and she said with a smile, "Guardsman Sally reporting for duty, sir." She paused. "Do I salute?"

"Not without a hat on. Not in the Musketeers anyway. They do strange things like that in the Household Cavalry."

"What do you want me to do? I think I'd better be your kitchen maid. I'll just obey orders."

"You must have an apron before you do anything," I said, taking down Mrs Catton's from its hook behind the door. "This belongs to my daily woman. She's about three times the size of you but it'll do." I wrapped it round her waist and tied it at the back. "There. Now you're the most beautiful kitchen maid in the business." And I kissed her quickly on the cheek and withdrew before she could resist.

She smiled and said "Thank you," though I didn't know whether it was for the kiss or the compliment. In either event Phase One had obviously worked well, and Phase Two was going along entirely to my satisfaction. Now I must concentrate on the talk. But before that there was the cooking to get started on.

Probably because I was brought up during the war I have a horror of wasting food. The idea of cooking dinner for four and throwing half of it away was anathema. So I decided to make a casserole which needed only two hours in a medium oven and which I could finish eating on another evening. I gave Sally a knife and the mushrooms and set her to work.

"My daily woman is what is known, I think, as a treasure. Her one foible is her penchant for having baths in my bath."

And while we chopped and diced and sautéed and drank our champagne I told Sally the story of my discovery of

Mrs Catton, and I moved on from there to an account of the effect the room had had on my Aunt Rosemary and others.

"How fascinating." I thought she sounded shocked but intrigued.

I placed the lid on the casserole and put it into the oven. "That's it. Thank you for helping me, Sally. We've done everything in half the time or less. Would you like to go and have your bath now?"

Sally took off her apron. "Yes, please. Shout at me when I've been in there long enough."

"You've got plenty of time. Help yourself to bath salts or whatever else you fancy. I hope you won't mind if I come into the bedroom. I must look out something to wear this evening."

"Give me five minutes to get undressed and into the bathroom first."

All this talk of baths and dressing and undressing had built up a most intimate atmosphere between us. It was almost as though we were married. I could scarcely believe that I had known Sally for only a week.

I went out onto the roof garden and sat on a long chair and smoked a cigarette and looked at my watch.

It was just after seven so I had plenty of time. It was a perfect summer evening. Far below the Friday night out-of-London rush was still at its height. Here it was peaceful but my stomach was churning with excitement and I felt slightly sick.

According to the amended plan Peter would telephone me at 7.20 or as soon thereafter as he could get through. Anything more exact would, we felt, be too much to expect from the combined French and British telephone systems. At 7.15 I stubbed out my cigarette and walked into the bedroom. I was surprised to see that the bathroom door was slightly ajar.

"How are you getting on?" I called.

"Beautifully. Is it time for me to get out?"

"Not yet. You've got another ten minutes at least. I've just come in to sort my clothes out."

Sally's black dress was on a hanger. She had unpacked a number of bottles onto the dressing table. It looked as though she had moved in for a longish stay.

I banged about with shoes and a clean shirt, pretending to be busy and praying that nothing would go wrong with the telephone call. For an awful moment I wondered if my telephone was out of order. Being a well-trained officer I had, of course, an alternative plan – a sort of wet weather programme – but I knew that it was not as good as Plan A.

From time to time I peeped at the gap in the bathroom door. It was odd that Sally had left the door slightly open, but lucky for me. From a point near the bedroom chair, upon which Sally's clothes were neatly piled, I could see her reflection in the looking glass wall. I dared not look for more than a second or so at a time for fear that she would see me, but when I did risk a glance I saw her standing up in the bath soaping her breasts and shoulders. The sight made me feel weak with desire and I moved away quickly. I leaned against the wall and breathed deeply for a minute or two. Then I looked at my watch. It was 7.20 exactly.

Abruptly the telephone began to ring.

TWELVE

I let it ring twice before I moved. Then I crossed the room quickly, sat on the edge of the bed and picked up the receiver on the fourth ring.

"Hello," I said.

"Allo, allo."

I gave my number.

"'Old on please. I 'ave a call for you," said a heavy French accent.

There was a click.

"Hello." It was Peter. "Is that you James?"

"Yes."

"Well there you are then. How about that? Exactly twenty past seven, dear boy. Aren't I a wonder?"

"Yes." I kept my voice neutral.

"I suppose you're not alone. Never mind. I'll ring off in just a moment and you can make up whatever nonsense you like, but before I do I thought I'd tell you just how much of a miracle worker I am. Do you realise I've practically had to buy the entire French telephone system to get this call through to you on time."

"I see." I tried to sound hurt and angry. It wasn't easy in two short words, so I added some more. "Where are you now?"

"Do you really want to know, dear boy, or is that part of the act? I'll tell you anyway, I have no secrets from *you*. I'm in a noticeably well-appointed suite at the George Cinq, sitting on a Louis Quinze sofa and drinking a vodka martini. Anne, you will be pleased to hear, is in the bedroom getting dressed and is therefore unable to overhear this telephone call. When she emerges we shall trickle over to the Ritz for a champagne cocktail or two – so soothing – and then on for a good nosh-up at the Tour d'Argent, where I have just reserved a table in the window and where even now the chef is flexing his wrists and preparing to do the decent thing by us. I've ordered the *Canard à la Presse*. So succulent. Any more questions?"

"No."

"Farewell then, my dear. Unless I am overcome by alcoholic poisoning, overeating or acute sexual exhaustion I shall see you in Barracks on Monday morning. What a gloomy prospect." He rang off.

"I think you might have told me before you went," I said to the purring telephone. "It's extremely inconvenient." I paused. "I suppose so." I paused again. "All good things come to an end." I tried to sound resigned. "I hope it will be a great success between you. You both have my good wishes. Give her my love and I'll see you next week some time." I put down the receiver and turned towards the bathroom door. Sally stood there looking at me, the large white bath towel wrapped loosely around her.

"What is it?" she asked. "Is something wrong?"

I smiled at her while doing my best to look rueful. To get the most out of Phase Four I had to be a gallant young officer smiling bravely though his heart was broken; a touch of 'vesti la giubba'.

"That was Peter Pershore. He and Anne have gone to Paris together. Anne has ditched me."

"My poor Jimmy." She walked over and sat down next to me on the bed. She held the towel in place with one hand and reached out and took my hand with the other. She gave it a squeeze. "I am sorry. It must be an awful shock for you."

"It is rather." I looked hungrily at her. It was terribly exciting sitting so close to her when she was wearing so little.

"You poor thing." She shifted slightly on the bed and one corner of her towel fell away, half-exposing one of her breasts. I stared entranced. Sally seemed to be unaware of what had happened. The swelling curve of her breast was a thing of beauty in itself, but I was most fascinated by the nipple. It was round and pink and no bigger than a shilling but the centre was thick and hard and erect and at least half an inch long. It was truly womanly and I felt deeply stirred by it. She released my hand and gave my thigh a reassuring pat. I looked down at her slender hand resting high up on my thigh. I thought suddenly of the almost intolerable sensual pleasure of feeling and seeing her hands, with their long fingers and perfect red nails, touching my naked body. I shivered.

"Poor darling," said Sally, misinterpreting my shiver as a symptom of my misery. "It was beastly of Anne to rush off with someone else without telling you. I'm shocked by her. But you didn't really love her, did you? So you'll soon get over it."

"I suppose so," I said gloomily, staring with growing excitement at her nipple and finding it difficult to keep my voice under control. I found it so fascinating that it was a long time before I realised that Sally had called me 'darling'. I wondered whether it meant anything.

"Of course you will," said Sally softly. "I expect you'll have forgotten all about her by tomorrow."

"So soon?" I grated out. Her reassuring hand had moved slightly on my thigh and her fingertips were frighteningly close to the embarrassingly large bulge in my trousers. I prayed that she wouldn't move her hand any closer or look down and I shifted away from her slightly. I might ruin everything if I wasn't careful now.

"In one way," Sally said, "I'm glad that this has happened."

"You are?"

She leaned slightly towards me and the towel slipped even further. One superb breast was now completely exposed and the fat pink nose of the other nipple peeped over the edge of the towel. I tore my eyes away and looked at her face. It was very close to mine. Her mouth was moist and red and her lips were slightly parted. The smell of her body was heavy in my nostrils.

"Why are you glad?" It seemed rather unkind of her.

She leaned forward even further and kissed me softly on the lips. "I'm glad that Anne is out of the way because it means that now there's nothing between you and me."

She suited her actions to her words by dropping the towel. It fell away, leaving her body beautifully and utterly naked. I was temporarily speechless.

"With Anne out of the way the position is vacant isn't it, darling?"

"What position?"

"As your mistress. And I'm applying for the job." She lay back nude on my bed. "I've wanted it for ages. I'm afraid I'm not very experienced but I'm very willing to learn, and I'm sure you'll be a wonderful teacher." She smiled up at me and held out her arms. "May I have the job, please, Jimmy darling?"

I didn't know what to say. It was such a surprise. I looked into her lovely eyes. She seemed both humble and appealing.

"Please, Jimmy. Please make love to me."

I stared down at her. She was the most beautiful and exciting thing that I had ever seen. I wasn't at all sure that I knew exactly what was going on. Something very peculiar had happened to Phase Four of my magnificent plan, but there was no time to worry about that now. I ripped off my shirt and threw it away and started to struggle out of my trousers. They looked very decorative when they were on but they were infuriatingly difficult to get off in a hurry. When I finally managed to extricate my feet and turned to Sally as naked as she was, she looked at me with wide eyes and said, "Oh, my God," in a frightened voice.

"It's all right," I said, as I stretched myself out beside her on the bed and took her warm body in my arms. "It's all right, darling."

I kissed her mouth and her throat and her shoulders and her breasts and I ran my hands all over her body. She moaned and gasped and called my name and said that she loved me (not that I paid any attention to that) and I was delighted to find that she was even more ready for it than Anne always was.

I was ready too when she said, "Darling Jimmy, you will be gentle with me, won't you? It's been such a long time since…"

"Of course I will, my angel," I said confidently and I tried to enter her.

But I was over-excited and too eager and at first I couldn't, and as I tried again Sally cried out and I felt the strength drain away from me though my desire was as urgent as before. I went on kissing and caressing her feverishly, hoping for the best. Partly to play for time, and partly because I wanted to know anyway, I said, "What about babies? Is it all right?"

"Oh yes, Jimmy. I've been on the pill for months."

"That's all right then," I said feebly.

But *I* wasn't, and after a while I admitted that to myself and gave up and lay back beside Sally.

"What's the matter, darling?" She sounded puzzled and hurt.

"I'm sorry, Sally. I don't know what's wrong with me. I expect it'll be all right in a minute."

But really I didn't know whether it would be or not, and I felt hot with embarrassment and sick with the fear that there might be something wrong with me. At the same time I was literally itching to make love to her. It was the sheerest horror.

"Is it my fault? Did I do something wrong?"

"No," I said miserably. "It's not your fault."

"What is it then?"

"I don't know. It could be one of several things. It might be the champagne, but I don't think so. I've had very little really. Perhaps it's because you're married. I've never made love to a married woman before. Maybe it's because I want you so much and it's the first time."

"You really do want me?"

"Oh yes."

"I was afraid it was because you didn't find me attractive."

"You're the most beautiful and attractive girl I've ever known. You're quite different from everyone else." I paused. A thought had struck me. "I think perhaps I was afraid of hurting you. Though it shouldn't have done. You're not a virgin."

Sally looked as miserable as I felt. "Then it *was* my fault," she said. "I asked you to be gentle with me. That must have put you off. I am so sorry, darling. You see, I was a bit frightened. It's three years since I had my baby and I haven't… er… been made love to since then."

"My God," I said. So Anne was right.

"When you took your trousers off and I saw… well, it… he… what do you call him? He looked so huge I thought it would hurt dreadfully." She raised herself on an elbow and stared down at me. "He looks so little now I can hardly believe he's the same person. What do you call him? He must have a name?"

"Ethelred the Unready," I said bitterly.

Sally laughed and rolled against me and kissed me. Her breasts rested heavily on my chest.

"Whatever else you may have lost, darling, you haven't lost your sense of humour. But what shall we do now? Is there something I can do? You've only got to tell me. I wish I was more experienced."

I thought about it. "Later maybe." I shivered – from cold this time. The evening had come and a cool breeze had started to blow in through the open window. Sally shivered too.

"I'm cold," she said. "And I'm hungry."

"I suppose we'd better put some clothes on," I said sadly. I was quite keen to cover my own inadequacy but it would be a pity not to be able to look at Sally's beautiful body any more.

"I've got a better idea," she said. "I left the water in the bath. We can add some more hot and get in together. That'll warm us up."

"That's a splendid idea. You go and jump in. I'll get us something to eat."

"Super." She leapt off the bed and, with a flash of golden limbs and small hard buttocks, she disappeared into the bathroom.

In two minutes I joined her there, carrying a tray with the bottle of Dom Perignon, two glasses, the jar of caviar, a lemon cut in half and two teaspoons. I put the tray on the marble surround, switched off the wall lights and slid into the bath with Sally. In the time I had been in the kitchen she had pinned up her golden hair into a pile on the top of her head and now she was crouched in the bath with the water up to her neck. With only the underwater lights on she was not exactly concealed.

"How beautiful it is," she said. "The water's like liquid gold." She held up a hand and let fall a palmful of water in a small shower of drops. The reflected surface of the bathwater shimmered in the ceiling and the walls.

She looked straight at me as I struggled to undo the champagne cork. "You're beautiful too, James," she said seriously.

I smiled at her. "I don't feel very beautiful. Specially not at the moment."

"Poor darling. Is it very awful for you?"

"*Very*. I don't seem to be an unqualified success as a lover. What about the risks involved?"

She moved over towards me and put her long wet arms round my neck and kissed me gently.

"It's not up to me, darling," she said seriously. "It's for you to decide. I'm not the possessive sort. If you want me you can have me. There aren't any risks from my point of view – not really." She kissed me again and then released me and sat back. Her beautiful breasts seemed to float on the surface of the water. "We'll talk about that another time. I don't feel I know you quite well enough yet. One day perhaps."

I took the lid off the caviar and dug out a heaped teaspoonful. I squeezed a few drops of lemon juice over the grey mound of eggs and put the spoon into Sally's mouth.

"Delicious," she said. I took a spoonful for myself. "Champagne and caviar in the bath with my lover," she said happily. "How sinful!"

I was acutely conscious that I was not yet her lover and I was puzzled that she said she ran no risk. Surely Freddie wasn't the sort of husband to allow his wife to have affairs. And if he was how was it that Sally hadn't had a lover before?

She took my glass from my hand and put it on the edge of the bath. "You're not allowed to drink any more of that," she said firmly.

"I'm not?"

"No, darling," she put her arms round my neck again. "I'm not going to let you get drunk tonight. I've got other ideas. You just tell me what to do and everything will be perfect."

I lay back in the water, half floating, half leaning against the edge, and I put my arms round Sally's smooth golden body and we kissed long and deeply. At once I realised that there was nothing wrong with me after all and a moment later Sally must have felt me growing against her because she laughed triumphantly. I grinned back at her cheerfully. She wrapped her legs around my waist as we lay there in the water and I penetrated her, slowly but without difficulty.

"Oh, my darling," she gasped, her eyes wide.

"Does it hurt?"

"No darling. Don't stop."

I didn't. It had never felt better. I couldn't believe that half an hour earlier I had been impotent. Now I felt like the most virile man in the world.

"Is that nice?" I asked her.

"Oh, yes," she moaned. "Very nice."

"That's good," I said happily. "I'm glad you like it. We're going to be doing a lot of this in the future."

THIRTEEN

Later that evening we sat in front of the fire in the drawing room and ate some of our stew. It tasted better than it had ever tasted before.

"I'm sure you must have done something brilliant to it," I told Sally.

"Darling, you made it all. I was only your kitchen maid, remember. It is very good though. Can I have some more? For some reason or other," she added laughing, "I feel very hungry this evening."

When we had finished our bath we had dried one another gently and walked through into the bedroom.

I lay on the bed and watched as Sally sat at the dressing table and let her hair down. The sight of Sally doing things to her golden hair was one I was to see often but it never failed to intrigue and excite me. She was so deft and quick and her living hair seemed to know just what she wanted it to do. She was a girl who could never have been heard to say, 'I can't do a thing with my hair.' She could do very nearly anything with it.

When she had finished she squirted some scent from an atomiser bottle onto her throat and between her breasts.

"What's that?" I asked her as she put the bottle down.

"Scent, darling."

"Yes, but what's it called?"

"Chant d'Arômes."

"Come over here and let me smell it."

She walked obediently to the bed and I drew her down beside me and buried my face between her breasts. The light flowery scent mingled with Sally's own warm sweet smell was a heady mixture.

"Wonderful," I breathed.

"You really like it?"

"I love it." I took one of her nipples in my mouth and teased it with my tongue until the centre hardened. Then I rubbed it gently between my thumb and forefinger. Sally made a little noise deep in her throat and closed her eyes.

"Is that a nice feeling?" I asked her, interested. It suddenly came home to me that Sally and I had started an affair. We were lovers. For now and for an unknown and unknowable period of the future she was mine. I had a new body and a new mind to explore and to get to know and, perhaps, to love.

"Oh yes," she whispered. "A wonderful feeling."

She lay back, her head on the pillows and her hair spread out like an outsize halo. I raised myself on an elbow and I inspected her thoroughly, with my eyes and my fingertips, from her forehead to her toes. She was perfect.

"Have I passed?" Sally smiled up at me when I had finished.

"Full marks."

"Really?" She was laughing at me, but I was serious.

"Yes, really. I think you're perfectly beautiful – by which I mean that you're beautiful, as you must have known since you were a little girl, and also that your beauty isn't marred by any imperfection. In my eyes there's nothing about you that's wrong – nothing that I would change if I could. However long you and I may know one another I shall never say to myself, for example, I wish her nose wasn't quite so big or her eyes were further apart. There's nothing that could ever irritate me."

She looked at me for a moment in silence, her eyes dark and deep.

"I feel the same," she said at length. "Lie down. Let me have a look at you."

She knelt beside me on the bed and started to explore me, the thick curtain of her hair falling forward over her shoulders and almost covering her breasts. I watched with growing excitement as her beautiful hands moved down my body.

"You must be very strong," she said.

"I'm fairly fit."

"Your muscles are hard."

"Not all of them," I laughed.

She explored further.

"Dear Ethelred," she said. "Is it all right to touch him?"

"Of course. As often as you like. Whenever you like."

"Anytime at all?"

"Within reason."

"Oh dear." She stroked me cautiously. "I don't know how to do it."

I took her hand and showed her what to do. It was extraordinary how inexperienced she was. She was like a virgin. But she learned quickly. In a few seconds her manipulations had the predictable effect. Sally was enchanted with her handiwork.

"It's amazing," she said. "And simply fascinating to feel him growing in my hands."

"Isn't nature wonderful?" I grinned at her.

She laughed. "Yes. It certainly is."

"Have you never done that to a man before?"

"No. Never." She looked away from me for a moment and I had a feeling that I was treading on difficult ground. "I'm glad that it's with you, Jimmy."

I could feel the pressure mounting. "I don't think you'd better do any more of that, Sally."

She pulled her hands away as though she'd been burned. She stared at me wide-eyed. "Why not?"

I pulled her down beside me and kissed her red mouth. "I'll tell you another time. I don't know why you don't know anything about sex but I'm going to have a lovely time teaching you."

For the next hour I made love to her as I'd never made love to a woman before. I suppose Anne and Louise would have been both proud and envious, though I didn't think of them for an instant. At the end Sally and I were completely exhausted. We supported one another into the bathroom where we stood together under the shower and kissed and laughed in the spray.

"I'm so happy," said Sally, as I gently soaped her body. "I've never been so happy in my life. I had no idea that making love could be so wonderful."

I felt terrific. "I'm glad you liked it."

"Did I make a terrible noise?"

"Yes," I said proudly. "Everyone in Chelsea must have heard you. I expect someone will have thought that I was murdering you and the police will be here in a minute to take me away."

"Darling, how awful of me. But, you know, I simply couldn't help myself. It was such a fantastic feeling I thought I was going to die. The last time I think I fainted for a moment or two."

I turned off the shower and started to dry her. "You really liked it?"

"My God, yes. I thought you were going to stop after the first time, and if you had it would have been the most marvellous thing that ever happened to me. I could hardly believe it when you went on and made it happen again and again and again and again like that."

"Do you mean it was the first time it had happened to you more than once?"

"No, darling. I don't. I mean it was the first time it had happened to me at all."

"I'm amazed."

"Why?"

I wasn't quite sure how to answer that question. Eventually I answered it with one of my own. "Have you enjoyed being made love to in the past?"

"Only quite." She wouldn't meet my eyes.

"How many men have made love to you, Sally? Before tonight, I mean."

"Only one," she answered after a pause.

Freddie, of course. Anne was obviously right about him.

"Well, darling, he wasn't very good at it. You're a very highly-sexed and passionate woman."

She looked at me. Her eyes huge and green. "I *am*?"

"Yes."

"Goodness. I didn't realise."

I took a deep breath. "Sally, have you truly not had sex for three years?"

She nodded. "Four actually. Timmy was three last month but of course before he was born I was pregnant."

"And have you never felt during that time that you wanted it?"

"Yes, I suppose I have. But I couldn't do anything about it."

"But you're doing something about it now."

"Yes. But things are different now." She paused, and again she wouldn't meet my eye. "Jimmy, darling, I can't explain now. Really I can't. Perhaps I will one day. But for now, can't we just enjoy one another without explanations. I still don't know you very well."

"We know one another intimately, as the Sunday papers say."

"Physically we do. Not mentally or emotionally."

"All right, Sally," I knew when I was beaten and didn't bother to reinforce failure. "Let's eat some of that stew. It should be perfect by now."

So we dressed in two of my dressing gowns and I drew the curtains in the drawing room and laid a little table in front of the fire and uncorked an old bottle of Burgundy that I had been keeping for a special occasion. Sally redid her hair and put on a little make-up and we took the stew from the oven and sat side by side on the sofa and ate our dinner.

I shouldn't have worried about wasting food. Sally and I finished the stew without difficulty and swallowed a little of the sorbet. When we had finished we put the dinner things in the kitchen and I put a handful of records on the record-player and we settled down comfortably on the sofa again. I poured out two glasses of brandy and lit a long Romeo y Julieta for myself and a cigarette for Sally.

"How long can you stay?" I asked her.

"As long as you want me to."

"All night?"

"Yes."

"What about tomorrow?"

"Yes. The rest of the weekend, if you like. Till Monday morning."

"That's marvellous."

"I must telephone Highworth this evening and tell Nanny where I am and make sure Timmy is all right."

"What are you going to tell her?"

"Just your telephone number. You mustn't worry. She's a friend. She'll keep it to herself. I shall tell her about you when I see her next. I feel I've got to tell somebody, and she'll be ideal. I know she'll be delighted. She's been trying to persuade me to have a boyfriend for ages."

"It's ten o'clock. Perhaps you should ring her now. I'll go and make some coffee while you're doing it."

Whilst we drank our coffee and brandy and I puffed great clouds of blue smoke at the ceiling Sally asked me questions about myself and I told her all she wanted to know. I was glad to be straightforward with her now. I had a feeling that I wanted always to tell her the truth, so when she said, "How lucky that Peter and Anne went away today and left us alone together this evening," I said, "It wasn't exactly luck."

"How do you mean?" she asked.

"They weren't invited."

"They weren't?"

"No."

"Then why did Peter ring up? Oh, I see, it wasn't Peter at all. You just made it up." She paused, staring at me. "Wait a minute. Does this mean that you and Anne are still… how shall I put it?"

"No, it doesn't. Perhaps I should explain."

Sally burst out laughing. I smiled at her uncertainly, not seeing the joke. "What's so funny?"

"The whole thing." She calmed down. "Darling Jimmy," she said. "I think the time has come for us to tell one another the whole truth."

I was still puzzled. "I'm afraid I'm hopelessly lost."

"I'll explain," said Sally, in the tones of one reasoning with an idiot. "It seems that you've got a confession to make to me about this bogus party of yours. I think I can probably guess most of it. But, darling, what you obviously don't realise is that I've got a confession to make to you too."

"I see." I didn't see, but not to worry.

"If you and I are going to get on well together we must be honest and truthful with one another. Do you agree?"

"Yes, I do."

"Well then. Let's confess. You start."

"Ladies first."

"All right." She paused and looked me straight in the eye. "*I* seduced *you* this evening," she announced coolly.

"Oh no, you didn't, *I* seduced *you*."

Sally looked at me fondly but pityingly. "You're quite wrong, darling. Shall I tell you how I did it? I think I've been awfully clever."

I poured myself some more brandy and put my feet up.

"Yes," I said. "Tell me how you did it."

FOURTEEN

A man chases a girl...?

"I decided to seduce you about three months ago," Sally said, drawing her feet up underneath her on the sofa and lighting a cigarette. "It was when I first heard of your existence."

"From Anne, I suppose."

"Yes, that's right. She came to stay for the weekend, and she'd met you for the first time the night before. She was full of your praises."

"What did she say about me?"

"I don't think I'd better tell you." Sally shook her head. "It would be bad for you. I think you probably have far too good an opinion of yourself already."

"Nonsense."

"Well I'll say this. Anne's always told me about her boyfriends, and I don't know how much you know about her, but she has had the most amazing adventures. I won't deny that I've thoroughly enjoyed hearing about them too. She knew she gave me a vicarious thrill when she told me all the details and, as far as I was concerned, it was a jolly sight better than nothing." She grinned at me ruefully, wrinkling her nose. "But for her you were really something special, and that's what intrigued me. At that time I had just decided that it was time I had a boyfriend and so I made up my mind that you were to be it. Wasn't that scheming of me?"

"I'm riveted. Do go on."

"Well, to start with I bided my time. I knew it was no good trying to take you away from Anne while you were both in the first flush of your… whatever it was. Every time I saw Anne I steered the conversation round to you to see how things were going along. To begin with Anne was really in love with you, you know. After a month or so the feeling wore off or she decided to keep it very much to herself, I'm not sure which. I think now that that was caused by the fact that you didn't love her, but of course never having met you I couldn't tell then what your feelings were for her. At that time I didn't mind particularly what they were because it was quite clear that sooner or later the two of you would split up and then if you didn't love her there would be no complications, but if you did you'd be miserable about being ditched and ripe for the rebound. I'd read lots of books and thought about it all a great deal."

"But suppose when you met me you found you didn't fancy me after all? Did you think about that?"

Sally laughed. "Yes, of course I did. And I suppose it would be more accurate to say that I didn't really make a final decision about seducing you until I saw you in the flesh."

"Buckingham Palace?"

"Oh no. Weeks and weeks ago it was. I came to the conclusion I ought to have a look at you before I did anything else. In fact after the way Anne had gone on about you I couldn't wait to see you for myself. So one day when I was in London and when I knew from Anne that you were spending the night with her I got up early and drove round to her house. I parked in the mews opposite the house and waited for you. After a while the front door opened and you came out. You looked at the sky and pulled your keys out of your pocket. Then you glanced round the mews and saw me sitting in my car staring at you. You looked at me for a moment, then you got into your car and drove away.

Do you remember that morning?"

I thought about it. "No," I confessed, "I don't remember it at all. But what did you do then?"

"I decided you *were* exactly what I wanted so I set out to get you. A few days later I saw Lady Brendon and she was just beginning to work out who she was going to ask to her dance. I asked her to ask you and Anne. I explained that you were already coming to stay that weekend. She knew who you were and was quite agreeable."

"Now you come to mention it I did think it a little odd that I was invited. I know the Brendons vaguely but not well. I thought I was a bit long in the tooth to be a deb's delight. I retired from that scene years ago."

"You're going to be making a comeback this summer then, darling. Susan Headcorn is asking you to her dance next Saturday. Haven't you had the invitation yet?"

"No. But perhaps she sent it to Chelsea Barracks. I don't think she knows this address. I'll have a look in my pigeon-hole tomorrow."

"Well, there you are. I arranged last weekend so that we could meet at last. As you know I had lunch with Anne on the Friday and I couldn't resist going to have a look at you at Buckingham Palace, and I also hoped that you'd spot me and then remember having done so the next day when you met me. I thought that might intrigue you."

"It did."

"And so you and Anne arrived and we met. I was in a high state of excitement."

"So was I."

"I played everything more or less as it came after that. The dance went pretty well, didn't you think?"

"I suppose so."

"It was a great help to me," said Sally.

"In what way?"

"I started to get to know you properly. I found out that you're a kind man, and wonderfully reliable in an emergency. Also I found out just how you felt about Anne... and you did kiss me."

"So I did. Incidentally, what about that fellow I hit?"

"Quintin? What about him?"

"What's his problem?"

"Oh," Sally waved a hand vaguely and answered lightly as though it was of little importance. "He says he's in love with me. He's been nursing a hopeless passion for me for years. He's been abroad in America and the Caribbean for about the last three years but I'm afraid absence has made his heart grow fonder."

There was something about the way she spoke that worried me. I didn't think she was lying, but I had a feeling that she wasn't telling me the whole truth.

"Is that really all, Sally?" I looked at her carefully. "This is the night for truth remember."

She looked at me without replying.

"You can trust me."

"I know I can, darling." She leaned forward and gripped my hand. "You're right. There is more to it than that, but I can't tell you now. I will – one day soon. It's all bound up with everything else. Please trust me for now."

I smiled and nodded. "Of course."

"I'll go on with your seduction. We're getting to the most interesting bit now."

I puffed at my splendid cigar. "Pray proceed," I said expansively. "I am hanging on your cherry-red lips."

"When I woke up on Sunday morning... the morning after the dance... it was still very early..."

"So you decided to go for a swim."

"No, I didn't. Not at first anyway. I knew that you would almost certainly be in bed with Anne and I couldn't resist having a peep at you. I opened the door very quietly and crept in and there you both were – sleeping like babies."

"Did I have my mouth open?"

"No, darling, you looked beautiful. You only had a sheet over you and… I hardly like to admit this… but I thought it was too good an opportunity to miss."

"Oh no." I felt myself blushing. "You didn't pull the sheet down?"

Sally nodded. "It was awful of me wasn't it? I don't know what I should have said if you'd woken up at that moment. But after what Anne had told me about you I simply couldn't resist. I must say it gave me rather a shock when I saw the state you were in, but I was very impressed. Why was he like that when you were asleep?"

"I was dreaming of you."

Her eyes widened. "Were you *really*? How marvellous. Well, I stood there looking at you for a little while and then suddenly you started to wake up. I hid in the shadows near the door. I heard you ask Anne if she wanted to go for a swim and when she said no I slipped quickly and quietly out of the room."

"You left the door open," I said, remembering.

"I know. I wondered if you'd noticed. I daren't shut it in case it made a noise. Did you suspect anything?"

"No," I confessed. "Not a thing."

"Well, I knew you were going for a swim so I thought I might join you at the pool. Then I had a better idea and I decided to get there first. I'd just had a good look at you with no clothes on. I thought it would be only fair if I returned the compliment."

"So it was. I almost died of excitement. Did you see me

standing there?"

"Yes. Just. Out of the corner of my eye. I ran all the way to the pool and then I waited till I heard the door squeak and I went into my act." She sipped at her brandy. "Did you really enjoy it?"

"God, yes. You looked like a goddess. I thought perhaps I was Actaeon catching Diana bathing."

"How sweet. But didn't something rather nasty happen to him?"

"He was turned into a stag and his own hounds scoffed him. I can tell you I kept a pretty sharp look out for hounds all the way back to the house."

Sally laughed. "I enjoyed it too," she said candidly. "I got quite a thrill out of knowing you were watching."

She looked at me seriously. "I've become quite a nudist since I got married, you know. I didn't like it much to begin with – it was all my husband's idea – but now I wouldn't be anything else."

"Do you mean you go to a nudist camp or whatever those places are called?"

"Good Lord, no. I don't think I should enjoy that at all."

"What sort of nudist are you then?"

"The private sort. I swim and sunbathe with nothing on whenever I can. Swimming with a swimsuit on is beastly really – swimming nude is a heavenly sort of free feeling. When I've got a swimsuit on I'm jolly careful not to sit in the sun for too long or I spoil my all-over tan. Not that anyone sees it except me and Freddie – and now you, darling. I think I've been getting it this summer specially for you. I hope you appreciate my efforts."

I grinned. "I can't remember what it's like," I said. "It's such a long time since I saw you with nothing on."

Sally giggled. "I can soon put that right," she said, and

she jumped to her feet and flinging off her (my) dressing gown she adopted a flamboyant pose on the hearthrug.

"Very pretty. I do appreciate your efforts." I stood up too and dropped my dressing gown onto the sofa so that she could see just how much I appreciated them.

"Oh no," Sally stared at me with wide open eyes. "I thought he was called 'Ethelred the Unready'. I shall have to have a new name for him. Was there a Saxon king called 'the ever ready'?"

I held her warm nude body against mine and kissed her mouth. Then I picked her up in my arms and laid her on the rug and stretched myself out on the floor beside her.

"I don't think so. Egbert* perhaps?"

"Yes," she said. "That'll do beautifully. Egbert the Eveready. Bert for short."

"He's not short," I said, and I gently parted her golden thighs, and finding she was quite ready to receive me, I proved to her that I was telling the truth.

"My goodness," she gasped. "He's not, is he?"

I began to move inside her.

"Darling, do you think it's all right to do this again. You won't have a heart attack with all the exertion will you?"

"I'll be very careful, I promise." I kissed her slowly. "You still haven't finished telling me how you seduced me."

"I've almost finished. Keep still for a moment or I can't concentrate."

"You've got to the great revelation last Sunday morning," I reminded her.

"After that you couldn't resist me, could you?"

"Easily, if I'd wanted to," I said ungallantly.

"Ah, but you didn't want to. That's because I'd done

---

* He must have been referring to Ecgberht, King of Wessex (802–839). He was the grandfather of King Alfred.

everything so cleverly. All I had to do was wait until we were alone together and then make everything as easy as possible for you. That's why I suggested coming here at half-past six this evening. If a girl takes her clothes off to have a bath in your bathroom that must be a pretty clear indication, mustn't it?"

"I'm not sure that it would be any more."

I hadn't stopped moving when Sally asked me to, and now I increased the tempo slightly. "It would have been a clear enough indication a few years ago, I suppose. Nice young ladies didn't even go into young men's flats, and if they ever did they certainly didn't take their clothes off or they wouldn't have been nice young ladies. Nowadays it's all very difficult for a young fellow. All girls go into men's flats without the least hesitation and if they take their clothes off to have a bath it's probably because they want to have a bath."

"But I left the bathroom door open so you could see me."

"So you did."

"And I came out with only a towel round me."

"Very pretty."

"And I let it slip so you could see my bosoms."

"Beautiful bosoms."

"Oh, Jimmy," Sally groaned. "That's an awfully nice feeling. You won't stop, will you?"

"Not for ages."

"But I did seduce you, didn't I? Please say I did."

"You seduced me, Sally darling. It was very kind of you. I'm enjoying it enormously."

"So am I. Oh, darling. Yes, yes, yes. Oh, Jimmy darling, I love you. I love you. I love you. Yes. Yes. Oh, darling, I do love you."

FIFTEEN

I woke at dawn with a raging thirst and I knew I shouldn't sleep again unless I did something about it. I climbed out of bed and went to the kitchen for a glass of cold water from the mains. I walked out of the open French window onto the roof garden and leaned on the railing and looked downriver at the dawn.

The sky was a sensational display of the red and orange end of the spectrum with the exception of a large patch in the middle – slightly to the right of Battersea Power Station's belching chimneys – which was the clearest iciest turquoise. Down below me the river was at low tide and it swirled sluggishly between the exposed mudflats, a thin mist hovering over the water.

I was in danger of falling in love with Sally, I realised. After thinking about her constantly for a week, a week that had culminated in the passion of the night before, I accepted that I was probably at least half in love with her already. She had, as far as I could tell, everything that I wanted in a woman. There was nothing about her that would put me off, nothing that would turn off the strong feelings for her that I knew had begun to grow inside me. From past experience I knew that if I continued to see her, and make love to her, very soon I should be truly and deeply in love with her. Only one thing could stop that – an instant, complete and permanent separation. But even if I never saw her again I shouldn't be entirely emotionally unscathed. It would take me weeks, perhaps months to forget her. (Of course 'forget' is not at all the right word, though it is a word often used in love affairs; it would be more accurate to say something like 'to reach a point when the memory of a former lover no longer causes pain.') Did I want to go on? Should I get out now when I was not yet too deeply committed? Should I cut my losses? If we went on – and Sally seemed keen to do so – where was it all going to end? Perhaps it would just burn itself out. Perhaps I was wrong about the danger of falling in love with Sally. Perhaps when we had had one another as often as we could for a month or two we would realise that there was nothing left – that it was just sex. But no, I told myself, it can't be that. That was what my relationship with Anne had been all about. This was different.

But if it was different for me was it different for Sally? True, she called out that she loved me when I held her in my arms, but I knew of old that that meant nothing in itself. Probably she wanted me only for sex. Yes, the more I thought about it the more certain I was that that was the right answer. She was a highly-sexed girl who hadn't made love for four years. It was enough to drive her half round the bend; certainly far enough round it to jump into bed with a man she found attractive. On her own admission she had decided to go to bed with me when she had heard about me from Anne and that had been several weeks before she had even seen me. She could hardly have been in love with my description, however enticing. No, all Sally wanted from me was sex – and more sex. At least that was all she wanted now. Her feelings might change. Apart from wanting me sexually she seemed to like me.

I drank some of the water. It was ice-cold and unusually delicious.

Just suppose, I said to myself, just suppose that Sally and I fell in love with one another – fell for one another really hard, like the proverbial ton of bricks. What then? The future stretched away in front of me, uncertain and slightly menacing, but I knew that I wasn't going to back out now. Perhaps I would have been able to then; I realised that it might be impossible later. But this, I told myself, is what life is all about. I would have to go on, taking things as they came, and worrying about each problem as it arose. Later today I must make plans with Sally. I must find out how often I could see her and when and where. Somehow too I must find out why she didn't consider that her husband constituted a risk. It was rather odd.

But… perhaps I wouldn't be given a choice. Perhaps she had decided that she dare not risk it. I dreaded what she might say. Whatever it was she was a lady to her fingertips and she would be polite, but firm – I reminded myself that it is a woman's prerogative to change her mind. Any minute now she might join me on the roof garden; in a dressing gown so that I wouldn't be tempted further.

She might say something like: "Dear Jimmy. I enjoyed yesterday more than I can say, but sadly I've decided that this must end. In the excitement of the moment I thought I could go on being your mistress for weeks and months to come. But now in this chilling dawn I know that that cannot be. We must look on this as a wonderful fling but one that is too hot not to cool down; and I must now grow up and see sense. I must go back to my marriage and my beloved son. I don't suppose we shall meet again but I shall always be able to remember that I managed to seduce a wonderful man and had the most fantastic sex in my life and was his mistress for a day. Goodbye my darling."

That seemed a likely outcome and a sensible one. So why did I dread it? I knew suddenly that it was the last thing I wanted, that I now realised that it *had* gone too far. I loved her deeply and wholeheartedly and would do so for the rest of my life. My heart would be broken.

I stared gloomily at the river. I knew that I would have to behave like a gent. No tears, no fuss, hurrah for us.

"Good morning, darling," she said.

I turned. Sally stood in the open doorway. She was quite naked.

"You look lovely with nothing on," she said.

"So do you." She looked fantastic. Her unbound goldilocks hung down her back and a stream of sunshine suddenly illuminated her hair and body. She was a vision.

She came over to me and stood facing me. She looked up at me, her wonderful eyes wide and glittering. Did I detect an unshed tear?

"I've got a confession to make," she said slowly. "I hope you won't be angry with me. Please don't be."

Here it comes, I thought. "Try me," I muttered.

"I'm afraid I've fallen in love with you, my darling. I can't help it. I am completely in love with you – and I feel I always will be. It's not just our wonderful sex of yesterday. I hope that was as nice for you as it was for me. I forgot to ask you then. But I was so overwhelmed by the fantastic time I was having that I couldn't think of anything else. That wasn't very nice of me. Please forgive me and say that you're not cross with me for falling in love with you. I just adore you. I can't help it, and I don't want to. So please."

Her tears now started to fall. I stared at her. I could hardly believe my ears. I was speechless. Eventually I managed to say, "Sally, my dearest darling. Of course I'm not cross with you. I'm overjoyed. I think I must be the happiest man in the world. I'm mad about you, you silly girl. I'm desperately in love with you. I'd die for you any day." I grinned down at her. "Though I'd much rather live for you."

"You would?" she smiled suddenly through her tears.

"You really do love me? Really properly."

"Really properly. And also rather improperly, I'm happy to say."

We both laughed. Sally put her slim arms round my neck and pressed her body against mine. "I like the sound of that." She giggled and wrinkled her nose. "I'm now the happiest girl in the world."

"Oh yes. Me too. Though I'm not a girl," I added stupidly.

We both laughed and hugged and then we kissed. We kissed a lot, and when we came up for air Sally said, "I can tell you're not a girl." She wriggled against me. "What are we going to do now?" she asked.

"It's still very early. I think we'd better go back to bed."

"Oh, goody."

"In a moment. I can't bear to leave here." The sun had come up over the Power Station and it warmed us. "This is a wonderful morning. One that we will always remember. I think it might be called our Morning of Eternity." I was thinking of Christina Rossetti, who had lived just round the corner.

"That sounds wonderfully romantic. What does it mean?"

"I'm not sure. But I think it means we're going to love one another for ever."

"Oh yes. I'd like that. My darling Jimmy. I do love you so."

"I adore you Sally, and I always will. I promise."

"I'm glad. I'm so very happy to be with you. And it's going to be a lovely day." She kissed me again. The cold air had hardened her nipples and I could feel them against my chest. "Later on can we go on a picnic somewhere? It would be such fun."

"If you like. Where would you like to go?"

"Anywhere you say. On the river perhaps?"

Of course. Maidenhead. That was easy. "Yes, on the river."

"Are we going back to bed now?"

"We certainly are. It's not five o'clock yet and I need a lot more sleep if we're going on the river. You must remember I'm a Major, and we Majors are an elderly lot."

"Poor old thing," said Sally happily. "If you're very good – and I mean *very* good – I might allow you to have a bit more sleep before breakfast."

***

Before we left the flat I telephoned a boat-hire firm at Maidenhead to reserve a motor boat and we packed up as much of our picnic as we could. There was still half-a-pound of caviar left over from the night before and I packed that and two bottles of cold Moselle.

"Shouldn't we make the bed before we leave," said Sally practically. "It'll be horrid to come back to if we don't."

"You're right," I said, surprised.

"Let's do it together," she proposed, and off to the bedroom we went.

"How domesticated this is," I said, as I attempted to keep up with her as she tugged, tucked and straightened. She smiled at me and wrinkled her nose.

"I never expected to get you making a bed. You're not very good at it."

"I've led a sheltered life. And I rather thought you had too. I'm amazed by your efficiency."

Sally laughed. "It's a lovely bed. Very comfortable but not too soft." She put the finishing touches to the bedspread and stood up. "Now we can go."

First we drove along the Embankment and up Tite Street to the Royal Hospital Road where I left Sally in the car and went into the supermarket on the corner and bought the rest of our picnic from the delicatessen. Then we drove via Chelsea Barracks (where I discovered that Sally was right and that Lady Headcorn *did* request the pleasure of my company on the following Saturday) to Westminster and it was my turn to wait in the car while Sally went into her block of flats to change. She emerged onto the sunlit pavement looking clean, crisp and golden in a yellow and white dress, carrying a white handbag and a green scarf. She smiled at me and trotted across the road on her long legs, glancing vaguely up and down the street as she did so. A passing car had to brake slightly to avoid her and I thought how spectacularly nasty it would be if she was knocked down by a truck and I had a sudden vision of her beautiful body being smashed to a pulp before my eyes. It made me feel sick. Sally opened the passenger door and slid neatly into the seat next to mine.

"I was quick, wasn't I, darling?"

"Amazingly so." I was upset and perhaps for that reason I found that I felt angry with her. "You must look where you're going before you cross the road," I said sharply. "You didn't look at all then. You might easily have been knocked down."

She laughed, not realising that I was angry, and as she did so I felt my anger melt. "You are fierce," she said. "I did look really. But I was in a hurry to get back to you." Her green eyes stared thoughtfully at me for a few seconds. "Were you truthfully worried in case I was run over?"

"Yes, I was, Sally."

"Oh."

"I don't want my beautiful new toy to be broken before I've got bored with playing with it," I said, trying to strike a lighter note.

She leaned over and kissed me. "Is that all I am? Just your toy?"

"No," I said seriously. "Perhaps that's not quite all. But I do enjoy playing with you," I grinned. "Let's go and play on the river."

Practically everyone else in London seemed to have decided that it was a good day to get away and the streets were packed with weekend drivers. I found myself enjoying, with the most basic sort of male pride, the swivelling heads of the men in other cars who spotted Sally sitting regally in the passenger seat of mine. It was a few minutes before twelve when I drove out of the centre of Maidenhead towards the river.

"Until a year or two ago we could have turned right here," I told Sally just before we reached the bridge, "and driven down over there to the Guards' Boat Club. But sadly it's closed now. They had magnificent electric canoes there. They were enormous things filled with cushions."

"I suppose you've taken lots of girls out in them in the past – and done awful things to them."

"There were one or two," I conceded. "But they didn't think the things I did were awful. They seemed to enjoy them."

"Poor little birds. Are you absolutely irresistible, Jimmy?"

"Absolutely." I swung the car into a car park beside a large boat house. "This is it."

We got out of the car and locked it. Taking our picnic and a rug and some cushions which I kept in the boot, and which several times in the past had been useful for al fresco seductions, we walked down to the water's edge. Our motor boat was waiting for us and two minutes after we had arrived we were chugging pleasantly upstream towards Boulter's Lock.

"When are we going to have lunch?" said Sally when we had gone about two hundred yards. "I'm simply ravenous."

"You're just as bad as my soldiers. They eat their picnics – known in the Army as haversack rations – immediately after breakfast if they're not physically prevented from doing so. Can you last till we get above the lock? We can find somewhere suitable up towards Cookham, I expect."

Sally put a long brown hand on my thigh and gave it a squeeze. "Suitable for what, darling?" she laughed.

"For having our picnic, of course," I said innocently.

"Is that all?" She pretended to be disappointed but she left her hand where it was. "Can I drive?" she said after a while.

We were sitting side by side in two bucket seats. Our picnic things were stacked on the well-deck behind us.

"If you like. We should be able to change places without capsizing."

Sally slipped into the driver's seat and took the wheel.

"How do you make it go faster or backwards or whatever?"

I showed her. "Do you know the rule of the road?"

"Oh yes, I think so. Keep to the right and give way to sail. Is that enough?"

"I hope so. It's all I know too."

Sally pulled a pair of dark glasses out of her handbag and put them on. "It's very hot. I hope I shan't get sunburned."

"You can take your clothes off if you like," I said expansively.

"No, thank you. But I think I must take my tights off. They're not at all suitable for this sort of thing."

"Shall I do it for you?"

"Certainly not. You hold the wheel for a moment. I'll do it."

She put both hands under her skirt and leaning forward

she managed to pull her tights down to her knees. It can't have been an easy operation and it was hardly surprising that it was attended by a considerable exposure of her long well-shaped legs. There was a chorus of wolf whistles and we looked up to see that we were being overtaken by a large cabin cruiser which seemed to be entirely covered with muscular young men.

"Oh, my God," moaned Sally, puce in the face and attempting to pull her skirt down over her knees.

I steered sharply away from the cruiser and we escaped between two islands into a quieter patch of river. The young men called after us with coarse suggestions for our future conduct. I reached down and put the gear lever into neutral. Gradually we lost way and stopped, rocking slightly in our own wake.

"That wasn't very sensible of me, was it?" said Sally.

I laughed. "Never mind. It seems quite private here. You should be able to complete your undressing without further interruption. We'll let those young men get well away. We don't want to find ourselves going through the lock at the same time as them."

Sally peeled off her tights and, rolling them into a ball, put them into her handbag. I took out my cigarette case and we both lit up.

"You do look after me well, darling," said Sally, her green eyes smiling.

"I'll try to go on doing so. Sometime we must have a talk about the future."

"All right. But not till after lunch. Quite a long time after lunch." She put a hand on my thigh. "Will you be able to find a nice place?"

"I expect we shall find somewhere."

"You won't take me anywhere you've taken other girls, will you?"

"No, my sweet, we'll find a place of our own."

Sally seemed to notice for the first time where she had placed her hand. To my regret she took it away. "Oh dear," she said. "I am behaving badly. What must you think of me? I can't leave you alone. I'm always touching you. I'm really hopelessly out of control."

I took her hand and replaced it on my thigh and leaned forward and kissed her.

"I think you're beautiful and exciting and wonderful and you're behaving exactly as you should. We're lovers now, Sally. Lovers do touch one another, all the time. It's good and it's natural, but in our peculiar circumstances it's something to be on our guard against when we're with other people. If anyone ever saw you with your hand where it is now they'd know we'd been to bed together. It's easy to tell when two people are lovers simply because they can't keep their hands off one another. It's a feeling that doesn't last for ever. Let's enjoy it while we can."

I knew that I loved her.

SIXTEEN

"What a perfect place, Jimmy. You are clever. Do you promise you've never been here before?"

"I promise. It's my trained eye for country. We Field Officers of Foot Guards are experienced fellows."

"In all sorts of ways." Sally stepped ashore and tied the painter round a tree. We had motored up a little creek-like tributary and I had stopped the boat under a huge old weeping willow. There was just room to make ourselves comfortable on the bank within the privacy of the branches. I handed our belongings to Sally and she started to unpack the picnic.

"What's the water like?" she asked me. "Is it all right to swim in, do you think?"

I looked over the side of the boat at the swirling stream. The water was opaque.

"I expect it's polluted," I said discouragingly.

"It doesn't look it," said Sally. "I'm going to chance it. It's so hot today. I'm dying to get out of my clothes and into some cool water. What about you?"

"If you're going in I shall too."

"It'll give us an appetite for lunch."

"If you take your clothes off I shall have an appetite for more than lunch."

Sally laughed delightedly. "Oh, no. Lunch first. I'm hungry." She stood up and started to unbutton her dress.

"That's not fair. I wanted to undress you."

She looked at me for a moment. "Poor darling. You can if you want to."

I stepped over to her and took her in my arms. I kissed her long and hard on the mouth. Her tongue stroked mine and she pressed her body against me and made a little moaning noise deep in her throat. Carefully I undid the buttons on her dress. I pulled it down from her shoulders and it dropped to the grass. With the finger and thumb of my right hand I snapped open the catches of her bra and I eased it away so that her breasts were free. I kissed her nipples until they were as hard and swollen as they had been on the previous night and then I moved down her body, kneeling before her, and peeled her thin panties from her curving hips and coaxed them down the smooth columns of her thighs.

"Let me undress you," said Sally, and she unbuttoned my shirt and tugged it off and ran her hands over my chest and stomach and I felt my skin crawling with excitement as she fiddled with the fastenings of my trousers.

"Egbert!" she cried happily, making the inevitable discovery. "I swear you've grown in the night. It must be all the exercise you've been having."

I tried to draw her down onto the rug but she wriggled out of my arms, laughing. "Oh no, Jimmy. We must have a swim first."

"I can't wait," I said, grinning at her. I lunged forward and tried to catch hold of her but she dodged and took a running jump into the water and disappeared below the surface.

"You wait till I catch you," I yelled and hurled myself in after her. The water was icily cold as it closed over my head but I hardly noticed that for I was more concerned for my feet. I felt them sinking into cold soft mud and before I could wriggle free I felt the clinging tendrils of water weed entwine my legs. Don't panic, I said to myself. Keep your cool. You'll be all right. I resisted the impulse to kick and struggle and I reached down with my hands and pulled away the weeds. I opened my eyes but I couldn't see very much in the murk of the river bottom. I tore at the weeds. As I did so more of them wrapped themselves round my arms. My chest was bursting. I eased first one foot; then the other. The mud was up to my ankles. I had nothing to push on. When I tried to pull up my right foot my left foot sank deeper. I felt the coldness of fear filling my body. This is the end, I told myself. The end. Shall I see my whole life flashing before my eyes? Don't be silly, my brain said. You haven't been down here long. Probably only a few seconds. You can stay down for a minute if necessary. Suddenly most of the weeds seemed to have gone from my legs and arms. I straightened up. I could see light above me. The mirrored under-surface was only a foot or two above my head. But I was anchored as firmly as ever to the dark ooze below. The blood was pounding in my head. I hadn't long to go. I allowed myself to be pulled in the direction of the current and I started swimming with my arms. I wriggled my toes in the cold slime and tried to ease my feet free. For a moment nothing happened. I worked harder with my arms. Suddenly my left foot was free. I did another stroke with my arms and kicked with my free leg. Half a second later my head broke the surface. I let out my breath with a rush. Feebly but thankfully I drew in some fresh air. At once the stream started to carry me away. I felt too weak and sick to do anything about it. It was enough to stay afloat.

Then I wondered where Sally was and I started to swim towards the bank. I grabbed at a root and hauled myself half out of the water. I looked back up the stream. The weeping willow was about twenty-five yards away.

"Sally," I called. It came out as a croak. I tried again. "Sally." That was better. There was no answer. The surface of the water was flat and unbroken. There was no sign of her.

The fear that had just subsided rose again inside me. It came up hard and fast. It was almost a physical force. I pulled myself to my feet and ran back along the bank. Twice I tripped and fell. Twice I jumped up and ran on.

"Sally. Sally." No answer. No sign.

I plunged through the curtain of our willow and almost fell again, this time over the picnic things. I stopped at the water's edge, searching frantically. It was just about there that she had jumped in. Should I just dive in? I mustn't make a muck of it. I must find her soon.

Her hand broke the surface. It looked limp. The fingers were long and elegant. As though in a film close-up I saw her wedding ring. She's dead, I thought.

I took a deep breath. I bent my knees and flexed my leg muscles. I took as firm a purchase as I could on the soft bank and dived. I threw myself, arms outstretched, as strongly as I could. I aimed upstream, at a point just above her floating lifeless hand.

I hit her body hard with my right shoulder somewhere near her waist. I closed my arms round her body and kicked. There was no struggle. The force of my dive simply tore her from the bottom of the river. She lay limp in my arms as I trod water. I knew I hadn't much time. I remembered a little of what I had been taught at school about life-saving and I turned on my back and pulled her over against me. I must keep her head out of the water. I put my hands under her arms and drew her up so that her head rested on my shoulder. Her wet hair was almost in my mouth. My hands clasped her breasts. Foolishly I remembered how we had laughed at school about this position. It didn't seem funny now.

Half-a-dozen kicks with my legs brought me to the bank. The water was shallow there. I struggled to my feet, picked up Sally in my arms and stumbled ashore. I walked quickly to our picnic spot. Sally's face was white. She didn't seem to be breathing. I remembered some more of what I had been taught at school and wondered about mouth-to mouth resuscitation. When I had been at school nobody had heard of the kiss-of-life stuff. I had often seen it done on Army First Aid classes. It must be sensible to get the water out of her lungs first, I said to myself, and I laid her on the rug, face down, and with her head pointing towards the river. There was a slight downhill slope towards the water. I turned her head to one side and opened her mouth and put my fingers inside to make sure that her tongue wasn't in the way.

I knelt beside her, placed my hands together on her back and keeping my arms stiff I leaned forward. I counted the rhythm to myself – forward one-two-three, back four-five, start again. Out loud I said, "Sally darling, I love you. Please don't die."

There was a rush of water from her mouth on my first forward push. Rather less came out on each successive pressure. After I had done about a dozen no more water came out, but she was still not breathing. Should I go on? I had been taught, as far as I remembered, that one should go on for a quarter of an hour or more. No, I decided. I'll try the mouth-to-mouth routine.

I rolled her over onto her back. Her body, even cold and lifeless as it was, was still the most beautiful I had ever seen. I knew I loved her. I loved her for her goodness, sweetness and gentleness as much as for her beauty. I had been looking for a girl like Sally all my life. It would be too much if she was now to be snatched away from me just when I had found her. Surely we would have more than just one night together. I realised that I was crying, the tears pouring down my cheeks. My throat felt sore and almost closed. I cleared my throat, took a deep breath and holding Sally's wet golden head in one hand and keeping her mouth open with the other I breathed into her body and prayed.

Less than half a minute later she gasped, opened her eyes and started breathing.

"Thank God." The relief was indescribably wonderful. I was filled with liquid gold. "Welcome back, darling," I smiled down at her. "I thought for a while that I'd lost you."

At first her eyes were unfocused, the irises huge, grey-green and dull. After a few seconds they concentrated on my face. I wondered idiotically if she would say, where am I?

"You saved me, Jimmy," she muttered weakly. She gave me an uncertain half-smile and then she turned her head away and vomited. I held her forehead with one hand and put the other on her stomach. I felt her whole body being shaken by her retching. When she stopped at last and lay gasping feebly on the bank I picked her up and laid her on the rug and wrapped it round her. She was shivering uncontrollably.

"Get inside the rug with me, Jimmy," she begged. "It'll be warmer that way."

I did as she asked. My body was warmer than hers and she felt cold and clammy as I pressed myself against her, but after a minute or two we were both much warmer. Every few seconds one of us had a fit of the shakes and I supposed we were suffering from shock. It can't have been very serious because after we had lain there for a little while kissing and talking excitedly I was surprised to feel my manhood swelling against Sally's body. Sally felt it too and said, "My goodness, that was a quick recovery."

She shifted her position slightly and it seemed the most natural thing in the world to enter her. For a moment I met resistance and Sally pulled a face.

"I'm sorry I'm hurting you, darling." I *was* sorry, but I wasn't going to stop on that account. This was no time for gentle loving preliminaries; this was a time for an urgent, almost brutal, taking of her body. I felt an elemental savagery inside me. If necessary I would have raped her. I had almost died; so had she whom I loved. Now it seemed that I had to prove we were both alive.

The resistance melted away.

"Go on, darling. Go on," Sally urged me, her face distorted by desire. "I want you. I want you so much."

She feels just as I do, I thought, and I tore fiercely into her.

"We're alive, Sally darling. We're alive. And I love you."

***

We had a riotous lunch. To complete the celebration of our narrow escape from death we drank both bottles of wine, finished the caviar and ate a whole cold chicken in red wine jelly. We laughed and joked and were entirely happy. The only bad moment came when Sally said, "You don't think that what happened just now was some sort of sign from God that you and I are doing wrong, do you? A sort of 'The Wages of Sin is Death' warning."

"No, I don't. I don't think God works like that."

"I have a feeling my father would have thought that. He was in the Church, you know."

"I didn't know. What was he?"

"He was the vicar of the village near Highworth. He died last winter."

"I'm sorry. Do you miss him very much?"

"In a way."

I looked at her in silence for a moment. She didn't seem inclined to say anything more about her father. I took her hand. "We're going to be happy together. As happy as we possibly can be." I twisted her wedding ring slowly on her finger.

"Never mind about that," she looked down at what I was doing. "Freddie won't be a nuisance."

It was a point I wanted to pursue, but this, I felt, was not the moment. "Darling Sally. Here we are in love with one another, but really we haven't known one another for long. I know almost nothing about you. Tell me the story of your life."

She laughed. "All right. But before I start can we move out into the sunshine. I want to get my hair dry."

We had put some clothes on before we ate our lunch but we had no towel and her hair was still wet.

I picked up the rug and the cushions and moved them out of the shade of the willow and spread the rug on a springy-looking patch of turf in a place where the sun shone down hotly between the trees. Sally sat down and began to comb her hair in long slow strokes and I stared fascinated as it twisted springily in the sunshine.

"My life has been one of unrelieved boredom really," she said. "You're just about the first exciting thing that's ever happened to me, except for my darling Timmy of course. Now that my father's dead," she said thoughtfully, "everyone who was important in my early life is either dead or moribund."

"Who's moribund?"

"Freddie's father. He lives in Cumberland all the time now, and he's a complete recluse. I haven't seen him since Timmy's christening. But he and my father were friends. Really great friends, I mean. They met at Oxford. They were undergraduates at the House together. I think my father was probably rather naughty when he was young, and the two of them got into all the usual scrapes that undergraduates used to in those days. Eventually my father sobered up and decided to go into the Church. I was never quite sure why he made that choice. Perhaps he had some sort of mystic experience. Possibly he just thought it would be a pleasant way of life. Later he became a very good man. Lots of people thought that he was a saint. But I've always suspected that came after he'd been in the Church for some years. He once more or less admitted to me that his first vocation had been to life in the country in general and to shooting in particular. He was a famous shot before he got married. Then he stopped."

"Why?"

"I'm not sure. It was probably my mother, but it may have been because he couldn't get away with it any more. In the twenties and thirties I suspect that he could live just the sort of life he wanted. He had almost no money of his own so Freddie's father gave him the living of the parish at Highworth."

I lit a cigarette and blew a thin cloud of smoke towards the branches above us.

"Anyway," Sally went on, gazing across the smooth peaceful-looking river, "after he'd been a curate somewhere for a while he went to join Freddie's father in Hampshire. There he lived the life of a country gentleman, keeping an occasional eye on the doings of his flock and seeing a lot of his old friend."

"Sounds nice."

"I'm sure it was. There was a beautiful and surprisingly comfortable Rectory where I was brought up, and one or two servants provided from Highworth, which had a huge staff in those days."

"What about your mother?"

"She didn't come on the scene for ages. Long before that Freddie's father got married to the most wonderful woman. My father married them and after a year or two Freddie was born. He was the only child they had. Something went wrong when he was born and she couldn't have any more children. Poor Emily. She was such a nice woman and she obviously would have liked to have had more. She was really a mother to me, so I suppose that was better than nothing for her – after Freddie had gone off to school I mean."

She spread her hair out around her shoulders and it hung down like a waterfall of liquid gold suddenly frozen into immobility. She put her comb away and I gave her a cigarette.

"Freddie's father thought it would be marvellous if my father got married and had a daughter and Freddie and the daughter got married."

"How beastly."

"Is it? I don't know. We didn't have to marry."

"You didn't have to. But I expect you were brought up to think that that was what they all wanted."

"Yes. It was. It almost couldn't happen because my father wouldn't get married for simply ages. They kept producing suitable girls for him but he took absolutely no notice at all. They got desperate – and Freddie got older and older."

"What happened?"

"At last my mother turned up. It was just before the war. She came to stay in the village for some reason and she went to church on her first Sunday. My father didn't see her at first. I expect she was behind a pillar. When he climbed up into the pulpit he saw her sitting there looking up at him and he immediately fell hopelessly in love."

"I expect it ruined his sermon."

"On the contrary, he used to say that it was the greatest sermon he ever preached. The love he felt moved him to such eloquence that he could hardly believe his own ears."

"If she was as beautiful as you I'm not entirely surprised."

"Thank you, Jimmy. As a matter of fact I think she was a bit like me. She had my colouring – or rather I have hers. Anyway, she completely changed his life. Before that Sunday he used to give a five-minute sermon, sometimes made up but usually borrowed from a book of sermons and savagely shortened. But from that Sunday on he used to talk for at least half an hour."

"His parishioners must have been pretty sick."

"Nonsense. People came from miles around to hear him and he used to get invitations to go all over the place."

I took a last drag on my cigarette and flicked it into the river. I watched it bob away on the race. "Go on," I said.

"They met properly after church was over and a month later they were married. Freddie's father was best man and it was a great occasion. My father completely changed after they were married. He began working much harder at his parish duties and my mother helped him."

"What was her name?"

"The same as mine – Sarah. My father always called me Sally because he couldn't bear to say 'Sarah'."

"Why?"

"Because she died when I was born. My father went into a decline for several months after she died and Emily looked after me at Highworth. She was always awfully good to me. Thanks to her I had a wonderfully happy childhood. As I'd never known my mother I didn't miss her, and Emily was always there when I wanted her. I divided my time between Highworth and the Rectory and for a long time I even had two bedrooms – one in each house."

"What about Freddie?"

"Oh, he was always about. Of course to begin with he was so much older than me that I hardly noticed him. He's fourteen – almost fifteen – years older than me. When he left Eton I was just about three and I think I can just remember him then, though I suppose it's more likely that I've seen a photograph of him and think I remember. There's a big difference between a little girl of three and a young man of eighteen, but there's not nearly such a difference between a girl of seventeen and a young man of thirty-two. That's how old we were when we became engaged. We were married a year later, soon after my eighteenth birthday. Emily thought that that was quite soon enough. But she and Freddie's father and my father were all absolutely delighted."

"What about you? Were you delighted?"

Sally shrugged. "I suppose so. I certainly didn't mind. I wasn't pushed into it against my will, if that's what you mean. My father didn't have to drag me screaming down the aisle. I quite liked Freddie and I suppose I respected him. I'd been used to looking up to him all my life. He was always very grand and important and all the servants used to get terrifically excited whenever he came home. As a little girl I knew the servants better than anyone, so it was always rather marvellous when Freddie came home. He was always very kind and polite to me. Looking back, I think he's been a big brother to me, although I always knew I would marry him one day. Freddie knew it too. We used to talk about it when I was only thirteen or fourteen."

"You see," I said. "You never had a chance."

"Perhaps you're right. The odd thing was that it never occurred to me to do anything else."

"Were you never in love with anyone else? Lots of young men must have been mad about you."

Sally smiled down at me and stroked my face with her fingertips. "No, my darling. You're the very first man I've ever been in love with."

"But what about the others? Cousin Quintin can't have been the only one to have been smitten by your fatal beauty."

She laughed. "I do hope it's not fatal."

"You must always have known you were beautiful."

"That was the funny thing about the way I was brought up. I never really knew whether I was good-looking or not. It was my father and Emily who managed that and it was clever and sensible of them."

"What did they do?"

"Well, I used to wonder about myself. I was never fat like so many little girls. I was always slim and my hair was always this colour." She touched her hair momentarily. "Perhaps it was a little paler when I was very young. I went to the village school at first and I remember I had no trouble getting the little boys to do anything I wanted. One or two of the most daring ones used to try to kiss me and sent me notes during school but I was such a little goody-goody that I didn't encourage them."

"You've certainly changed since those days," I grinned up at her.

"Apart from that," said Sally, smiling and wrinkling her nose, "I often overheard things that people said about me. You know the sort of thing. 'What an angelic little girl. Isn't she beautiful?' You know. Whenever I asked Emily or Daddy they used to squash me without being in any way unkind, so I thought that I wasn't anything out of the ordinary."

"What would they say?"

"I can't remember exactly. But, for example, if I said to Emily that old Mrs Smithers who ran the village shop had told me what a beautiful little girl I was Emily would say, 'Well, Sally, you've got a nice friendly little face and I think you're quite pretty but I don't think you could be called beautiful because your eyes are too far apart' or 'you're too skinny' or 'your mouth is a little too big' or something like that. It was always something different so that I never got a complex about anything, but I accepted that I wasn't beautiful and I didn't get a swollen head and spoiled. And she always told me that she loved me so I didn't mind about my imperfections."

"What a sensible woman. Where is she now?"

"Freddie's father gave him Highworth as a wedding present and he and Emily moved out and went to live more or less permanently in Cumberland where his seat is. It's a ghastly place. We used to go and visit them from time to time. I don't much look forward to having to live there myself one day."

"Perhaps you won't have to," I said quietly.

I was beginning to think that I didn't want Sally to be a Countess shivering away in a mouldy old castle, or whatever it was, in the wilds of Cumberland. I thought it would probably be much nicer in every way if she were married to me and living in such comfort as I was able to provide.

"I'm sure I shall one day," said Sally. "Freddie says we shall have to."

My heart didn't exactly sink, but it certainly felt less buoyant. Sally had obviously never had any idea that one day she might walk out on Freddie. I was the mere plaything of an idle hour.

Sally went on, "Poor Emily loathed it there. She used to escape to London and Highworth as often as she could, but she had to spend most of the year up there. In the end she died there."

"When? What of?"

"Of cancer of the womb – about three years ago. I miss her dreadfully."

"Poor Sally, I see what you mean about everyone being dead."

"If it hadn't been for you I should be dead too."

"If it hadn't been for me you wouldn't have come here today. So if you had drowned it would have been all my fault."

"Darling Jimmy. You're very sweet. But really it was my fault, not yours. If I'd done what I was told I shouldn't have jumped in. I should have stayed where I was and let you make love to me."

I got to my feet and pulled her up into my arms. "Let that be a lesson to you," I said, mock-severely. Our narrow escape was too recent. I didn't want to talk or think about it yet. "In future you must obey all my orders to the letter. I want no more insubordination."

"No, sir," said Sally, resting her warm body against me and smiling happily. "I'll be a good girl, I promise I will."

"What we're going on with now," I said, quoting the best

known example of how NOT to begin one's instructions, "is Boating."

"What a pity," said Sally. "I hoped it was going to be Loving."

"That comes later. Before that there's going to be Boating and Drinking and Dining and, I suppose, a certain amount of Driving."

"It sounds lovely."

And so we packed up our picnic and loaded everything into the motor boat and started the engine and chugged gently away downstream, holding hands and talking more nonsense. We didn't look back at the place where we had very nearly found watery graves.

The old weeping willow just stood there silently weeping into the river.

SEVENTEEN

We returned to the boat house at Maidenhead just before six o'clock. We were half-drunk on wine, sunshine and love, and euphorically happy with the simple pleasures of being alive and together.

Because we were not in a hurry we drove across the Thames to Skindles where we sat at a table on the lawn and drank a bottle of champagne. It seemed the proper thing to drink.

Later, as the shades lengthened and the evening came, we returned to the car and drove back to London.

Before we left Sally went inside to find a telephone. "I telephoned Nanny. Everything's all right at home, and I've arranged for you to come and stay with us next weekend for Susan's dance... if you'd like to. Please come if you can, Jimmy. It would be such fun."

I thought for a moment. Now that Sally was my mistress Highworth was the lion's den for me. But what of the lion?

"Will Freddie be there?"

"Yes. He's supposed to return from Germany on Friday. But he needn't get in the way." She put a hand on my knee. "I have my own bedroom, darling. And it has a lock on the door."

No gentleman could refuse. I put my hand over hers. "I should adore it, Sally. The invitation is irresistible."

"Which invitation?"

"Both."

"We shall be able to have a lovely time."

"Won't Freddie think it a bit odd – my being there, I mean?"

"I don't care if he does. But I don't see why he should. We've got a house full of people. If Freddie says anything about you I'll tell him that Anne has deserted you and I've invited you down at her request to cheer you up. How's that?"

"Definitely not out."

She sat back looking pleased and happy. "This is very romantic," said Sally, holding my hand. "Thank you for bringing me here. I always thought that having a boyfriend would be wonderful, but I had no idea that it would be as marvellous as it is."

I glowed. "You say the nicest things, Sally."

"I mean them," she said seriously. "I love you."

"And I love you."

"You will tell me often, won't you. I still can't quite believe it."

I made a silent vow that I would tell her every day, preferably several times. I am glad to remember now that I stuck to that vow.

"What do you think will happen to us, Jimmy? I find the future a bit frightening now."

I looked at her thoughtfully. She was so extraordinarily beautiful across the table that it made my chest hurt.

"We'll be all right, Sally," I said solidly. "You can, with every confidence, rely on me." I grinned, unable to be serious for long.

"I know I can," she said unsmiling. "Oddly enough, although we haven't known one another very long, I find myself trusting you completely. I hope we shall see one another often, darling. Freddie will be away next week so we can see each other whenever you like then. You do want to see me?"

"Of course. Every night."

"You haven't got anything else on?"

"Not a thing. And I'm not on Guard again for ten days."

"The only thing is that I think I ought to sleep in my flat in case Freddie rings me up from Germany in the middle of the night. Would you mind?"

"No. But what about last night and tonight? Suppose he rang your flat last night?"

"He didn't. If he had rung there and got no reply he would have rung Highworth, thinking I had gone down there. And if he'd done that Nanny would have told me."

"I see. I take it that you have no servants at your flat?"

"Only a daily woman."

"Wouldn't the same apply next week?"

"Yes, it would. But when he found I wasn't at either the flat or at Highworth I should have to have an excuse ready, and I'd rather save my excuses for when I really need them. This weekend is special because it's our first and it's worth taking a few chances over. Are you sure you don't mind coming to my flat?"

"Yes, I'm quite sure. I was just fascinated to discover how thoroughly you've thought everything out."

"I've got a very comfortable bed."

"Yours and Freddie's?"

"No. Just mine. But would you have objected to sleeping in his?"

"I don't know. I'm quite used to hopping in and out of strange beds…"

"Disgusting beast!"

"And it would be ludicrous to pretend that all the girls I've had have reserved their beds for my exclusive use. But I've never had an affair with a married woman before and I think I might not like getting into another man's bed to make love to his wife. It's rather bourgeois of me, isn't it?"

"I don't think so. It sounds more like the law of the jungle to me."

"Perhaps you're right. Anyway it doesn't arise."

"Unlike you, darling." She giggled.

"Tell me how we shall manage to see one another after Freddie gets back."

"Well, I'm afraid it'll be mostly afternoons, Jimmy. Monday to Thursday afternoons whenever you're not too busy. And we should be able to have Friday nights most weeks."

"The whole night?"

"Yes. I think so."

"I'm glad of that. It was awfully nice to wake up and find your head on the pillow beside mine this morning. I should be miserable if I thought I should never do that again."

"Darling Jimmy," Sally smiled and touched my hand. "I loved it too. We'll have whole nights together as often as we can."

"What about weekends? And how will you manage Friday nights anyway?"

"Well, you see when the House is sitting Freddie and I spend Saturday and Sunday at Highworth. We come up to London on Monday morning and stay until the end of the week. We go out practically every night and we usually give one dinner party a week ourselves, at the flat. On Friday Freddie goes down to his constituency and he spends the night there and goes on to Highworth on Saturday. Sometimes he gets there in time for lunch, but usually he doesn't get there until teatime. It depends how much he has to do."

"Don't you have to go with him?"

"Not often. I used to go more often than I do now, but

it's pretty grim and there's nothing much for me to do, so I only go if there's some sort of official bean-feast. Normally I go down to Highworth on Friday afternoon. From now on I'll go on Saturday morning, and I'll spend Friday night with you... if you want me," she added hesitantly.

I held her hand across the table. "I want you all right," I said determinedly. "And that's exactly what we'll do. Friday night will be our night. I'll arrange never to be on Guard on Friday in future. If I'm not going to be able to see you on Saturday or Sunday I'll swap Fridays – and any other days – for the weekends. The other officers on the Captains' rota will be delighted to have some clear weekends. And on the other weekdays we'll see each other as often as we can. What about having lunch together?"

"Yes. I should be able to manage that most days. But where?"

"No restaurants?"

"Sometimes perhaps. But it's a bit risky."

"My flat then. I'm becoming quite a good cook now that I'm living in my own flat. I shall enjoy cooking light but delicious luncheons for us."

"I shall look forward to it, Jimmy. But don't you have to work in the afternoons?"

"Not often. I have a second-in-command – Peter. I gave him Anne. The very least he can do in return is to do my work for me. Besides, think what good practice it'll be for him for when he has a Company of his own."

"Then we're all set."

"Yes. I must say, I hadn't guessed how dreadfully complicated everything would be."

"I hope I'm worth it."

"Oh, yes. You're worth it all right. You're worth anything... everything. But even if you weren't it wouldn't make any difference to me now. I'm in love with you, Sally. Nothing can stop that." I held her hand tightly. "You do believe that, don't you?"

"Yes, Jimmy," said Sally softly, her eyes shining. "I really think you are."

Before we left I said "I had thought of going out to dinner near here but I have changed my mind. I think it's too dangerous. But even here is a bit risky. We must be careful not to be seen together in future."

"Oh dear, I suppose you're right."

"I am afraid I am. You're a very noticeable girl. Lots of people know you or have seen your photograph in the *Tatler* or at some House of Commons party." I paused. "So no restaurants for us, I fear. And we'll have to have some supper at my flat tonight."

"Have you got anything to eat? We just about finished last night's dinner."

"I am not sure, eggs I expect."

"Good. I am very good at scrambled. We'll survive." She smiled affectionately. "I shall enjoy being a little housewife to you."

We drove back to my flat. Sally's scrambled eggs were the finest I had ever tasted. We ate them by candlelight, and drank some claret, and we talked… and talked. Eventually I said, "It's bedtime you know."

"Is it?" Sally's eyes sparkled in the candlelight. "How wonderful."

I blew out the candles and we headed for the bedroom.

"Do you know," Sally said, "I've always thought that to be told it was bedtime was dreadfully boring. Now I find it's simply thrilling. That, and to be told 'I love you' are the nicest things I can hear."

"Good. It's bedtime and I love you."

She kissed me and we fell into one another's arms and into bed.

We made love with great gentleness and feeling. An immense sense of the power of our love permeated our minds so that the joining of our bodies was the manifestation of a spiritual experience. It was totally different from the purely sexual congress of the afternoon.

When at last we slowly separated we lay together like two spoons in a drawer.

"That is cosy," said Sally, wriggling her bottom slightly. She sounded sleepy. "Darling Jimmy."

"Yes?"

"I'm the happiest girl in the world."

"I'm glad."

"Are you happy too?"

"Very." It sounded inadequate. "I've never been so happy before."

"Today has been the most wonderful day of my life."

"Yes."

"We love each other."

"Yes. We do."

"Do you think anyone else has ever been as much in love as you and I are with each other?"

I smiled in the darkness.

"No, darling."

"That's nice. This is special, isn't it?"

"Very special."

"Will you love me always? I'll always love you."

"I shall love you for ever. In this world and in the next."

"Is there a next world?"

"Oh, yes."

"We'll have a lovely time there, won't we?"

"We'll have a lovely time here first."

"Good." Her voice was faint. She was almost asleep.

"Goodnight, Sally my angel," I whispered, kissing her shoulder. "Sleep well."

She made a little moaning noise which might just have been interpreted as 'Goodnight', but really she was already asleep.

Just before I followed her into unconsciousness I heard the hooting of a boat on the river. It was a mournful sound.

***

It rained all day on Sunday. Sally and I spent the morning in bed reading the Sunday papers just like an old married couple. We didn't get up until noon. Then we bathed and I shaved and we ate breakfast or lunch. Sally drank coffee and I drank beer, so I don't know which it was.

Afterwards we drove to the Pepper Mill in the Old Brompton Road and while Sally waited in the car, which I parked fifty yards down the road towards Queen's Gate, I went into the shop and bought some food for our dinner and some crumpets for tea. The Pepper Mill was just about the only place in central London where one could buy food on Sunday. It was therefore very popular. It turned out to have been sensible to leave Sally in the car because I saw there three people whom I knew. It was a sobering experience. Sooner or later, it seemed almost a certainty, Freddie would get to hear that she had been seen with me. What would he do then?

I said nothing of this to Sally. We drove back to the flat through the rain and settled ourselves in the drawing room. It was so cold and dank outside that we decided to shut the day out. I drew all the curtains and turned on some lights and we sat in front of the fire and watched an old film on the television and ate the crumpets and drank several cups of Earl Grey tea. We made rather a mess on our chins with the melted butter from the crumpets and we began by licking it off one another and ended naked on the hearthrug.

"That was exciting," said Sally. She was sprawled in the most abandoned position imaginable, all disarranged golden hair and limbs. Her face glowed in the way that I had learned it always did after love.

"Do you think we're making love too much?" she asked me seriously. "Will it be bad for us?"

I lay between her thighs and kissed her pretty tummy. "It's good for us," I told her.

"Are you sure? I have a feeling I shan't be able to walk tomorrow."

"You'll be all right."

"But aren't we making love an awful lot? I thought people were supposed to make love only once or twice a week. I've lost count of the number of times we have since Friday night."

"It always starts like this. After a week or two it cools down a bit. After a year or two it cools down even more. But people aren't supposed to make love any particular number of times. Just whenever they feel like it. But we're not breaking any records about quantity, and I don't want to. It's quality that's the important thing. I hope you like the quality, Milady?"

She kissed me. "It's the best quality in the whole world. I had no idea there was such good quality about."

"It helps that we're made for each other."

"Does it? Are we?"

"Yes. We go together well physically. And you're very passionate, and I'm… how shall I put it? I'm affected by your passion."

"Darling Jimmy. You're very experienced. You must have had a lot of girls."

"Yes," I admitted. "Do you mind?"

"No, oddly enough, I don't mind at all. They were all before I came along. It would be pretty silly of me to mind."

"You wouldn't rather that I was more or less a virgin too?"

"Oh no. Think how awful the quality would be then. I like you being experienced. But do you think of me as being more or less a virgin – at least did you on Friday?"

"Yes, I suppose I did."

"I know what you mean. I didn't know anything about it, did I? I actually felt rather virginal."

I ran a hand over her hard flat tummy and caressed the curve of her tiny waist.

"No one would ever know you'd had a baby, Sally. You haven't any stretch marks. Your body is like an eighteen-year-old's."

"Thank you, darling. Tell me more nice things about myself. No, on second thoughts, don't do that. Tell me about your other girls. How many were there?"

"I don't remember."

"You must have some idea. Twenty? Thirty?"

"Do you mean how many girls have I had sex with?"

"Yes."

"Well… what sort of girls do you mean?"

"What sort?" Sally looked blank. "How many altogether?"

"Two or three hundred."

"My God." Sally opened her eyes very wide. "You have been busy."

"They were mostly when I was much younger. I was… er… rather randy in my late teens and early twenties. I think it was the effect of the public school system."

"Why?"

"Well, you know what it's like. Boys stay at school in a totally monastic environment till they're eighteen. Then suddenly they're released on the world and they really start to meet girls for the first time. Oh, they've met a few girls in the holidays, of course. But they're not the same. Friends of sisters; daughters of parents' friends – you can imagine. One was always on one's best behaviour. Nowadays apparently all those sort of girls can't wait to get laid – though I have my doubts about that. I suspect that things haven't really changed quite as much as the newspapers would have us believe. But anyway, when I was a young fellow they were likely to yell blue murder if you even tried to kiss them, let alone tried to find out what went on inside their knickers."

"Coarse beast," said Sally fondly.

"So think of the excitement – to find yourself amongst real live women – of all sorts – who knew what it was all about – some of them anyway – and enjoyed it. I was in heaven."

"But even so, darling. Three hundred?"

"Between the ages of eighteen and twenty-three or four I thought of nothing but quantity. Three hundred is probably an underestimate. I thought sex had just been invented – and of course for me so it had."

"But surely all the girls you met wouldn't go straight off to bed with you?"

"Good Lord, no. You're quite right. But I wasn't too choosey. After a bit I found out that if you're reasonable-looking and fairly well turned out and don't actually smell or anything, you can do marvellously well at parties by chatting up the plainest girl in the room and taking her out to dinner. She's usually so grateful she'd do anything for you after that. Plain girls are often the best in bed, you know. They're so desperately keen to please that they turn in a really superb performance."

"Cynic."

"It's the truth," I protested.

"Hm. Anyway, you can't have got all the girls you wanted like that."

"No. That's true. Sometimes I paid for it. Paradoxically it's much cheaper that way. A lot of men consider it a matter of pride not to pay for it ever. It really depends, certainly amongst the upper classes, upon whether you prefer pride or sex. I chose to forget my pride and have lots and lots of sex."

"Where did you go when you paid for it?"

"The best place was a brothel in Kensington."

"I had no idea there were such things – not in Kensington, I mean."

"Oh yes." I paused and picked up a packet of cigarettes from the coffee table and, extracting two, lit them and gave one to Sally. "Are you very shocked by these awful revelations?"

"On the contrary, I find them absolutely riveting. Tell me about this brothel. I've always wanted to know what one was like."

"It was somewhere near Queen's Gate. From the outside it looked like a private hotel. In fact that's what it was. The sexual side went on under the cover of the hotel side. It was run by the sweetest old lady. She looked a pillar of respectability. You would no more dream of swearing in front of her than you would in front of your most straitlaced maiden aunt."

"She was the madam? Isn't that what they're called?"

"In France, yes. In England too, I suppose. But this wasn't quite like a French brothel either. It was a sort of splendid

British compromise. None of the girls was a proper professional. They were hairdressers and typists and manicurists and salesgirls. They did it partly for the little bit of money they got out of it – it wasn't an expensive place – and partly for the fun of it. Sometimes there were upper-class girls too, who did it just for the fun of it. One officer in my Regiment is supposed to have met his sister there once. They passed on the stairs; he was going up, she was coming down."

"What did he do?"

"He was furious. 'What on earth are you doing here?' he said to her. 'The same as you, brother dear,' she replied. The place was run in a very respectable way. Whenever I wanted to go I'd telephone in advance and make an appointment. Then when I arrived I'd be introduced to the girl, if we hadn't met before, and after a drink or two we'd go to bed. Sometimes there were parties with several men and an appropriate number of girls and a certain amount of picking and choosing went on."

"Tell me what happened when you got to the bedroom."

I grinned at her. "Do you really want to know?"

"Of course. Nobody ever tells girls these things."

"Well, you'd both undress. Then you'd lie on the bed and have sex."

"That doesn't sound very poetic."

"It wasn't poetic. It was physically satisfying."

"Did the girl enjoy it, do you think? Did she say she loved you? Did she kiss you?"

"Most tarts don't enjoy it, they say they love you if you ask them to, I suppose – I never have – and never never kiss. *These* girls usually enjoyed it, kissed a great deal – all over – and didn't say they loved you – just it. Looking back on it now, we were just a lot of healthy young animals enjoying one another's bodies without complications. The woman who ran that place knew what she was doing. It was a public service really. I shall always be grateful to her."

"What happened in the end?"

"She was closed down by the police. And at about the same time I started to grow up and realise that quality was more important than quantity. And so here I am today with the finest quality of all."

"Am I really?"

"Yes," I said, kissing her. "Really. But that's enough about me. I'm not proud of the way I behaved in those years, but I was never unkind to the girls. I never pretended I loved them and if any of them looked as though she was getting serious I ended it before it got complicated. I was tactful and explained that I was being sent away somewhere and didn't know when I was coming back. It was easy, being in the Army, to make an excuse to fade away." I thought about telling her about Louise but decided against it. "Now, tell me about you?"

"About my sex life, do you mean? There hasn't been any. I was a virgin when I married and after that… well, perhaps I'll tell you another time."

And so again I got no closer to what I was beginning to think was something of a mystery. It was tantalising, but I felt it wiser not to bully her.

That night, after dinner, we drove to Sally's flat in Westminster. Fortunately there was no porter on duty in the hall and Sally told me later that the porterage arrangements were erratic. It made things much easier for us.

The flat was more or less what I had expected. There was a large drawing room and a dining room and two bedrooms, each with its own bathroom. One was Sally's; the other was Freddie's. The furniture and pictures were mouth-wateringly beautiful. The whole place, with the exception of Sally's bedroom, reeked of Freddie and his ambition. I guessed that it was designed to impress yet flatter those who were invited there. It was a perfect setting in which Freddie could entertain those who mattered to him.

Sally's bedroom was soft, feminine and smelled of her scent. The bed was a double one, "so that people who come in here think that Freddie and I sleep together," Sally told me. "He calls his bedroom his 'dressing room'."

"You even have separate bathrooms," I said.

"Oh yes. Freddie couldn't bear to share one, with me or anyone. He's terribly tidy and almost infuriatingly fastidious. He could never use a towel or a face flannel that I might have used. He often walks in here when I'm in the bath," said Sally as we went together into her bathroom. "When he's in his bathroom he locks the door. Do you know…?"

"Do I know what?"

"Nothing," she said vaguely. "I was just thinking of something. Do you want to go to bed now?"

I did. For the first time in my life I got into a married woman's bed. It was very comfortable.

EIGHTEEN

I spent every night of the next week with Sally in her flat. We never went out. I arrived each evening between seven and eight o'clock and we spent the evening cooking and eating dinner and talking and making love. It was perfect.

I wondered whether, if we were married, it would go on like that for year after year. Married friends had told me that that sort of feeling soon wore off, but we seemed so right together – and the better we knew one another the righter we seemed – that I couldn't believe that we should not be perfectly happy together always.

Thursday night was to have been our last night together. On Friday Freddie was expected to return and Sally was going down to Highworth with him.

However, half-way through the evening Freddie telephoned from Germany to say that he was staying on for a few more days and he instructed Sally to detail one of the male guests to act as host in his absence. After he had rung off Sally and I put it to the vote and I was elected unanimously.

The next morning I got through my work in Barracks as quickly as I could. Sally had talked a lot about her son Timothy and she was obviously devoted to him. Seeking to ingratiate myself with her I went to Hamleys in Regent Street to find a suitable toy for him. I was successful. I found some excellent toy soldiers and I selected one – a Guardsman in full dress – because he had a golden plume in his bearskin which made him a Musketeer. Then I picked up Sally from her flat and we drove down to Highworth.

When we arrived I presented him to Timmy. I told him about his gold plume, Sally told him I was a soldier who had a uniform just like it. He looked doubtful. "You haven't got a uniform," he said.

"I only wear it when I'm guarding the Queen."

"What do you do when you meet her?" He looked interested.

"I salute her."

"Like this?" He had a go.

"Not quite. I'll show you."

I demonstrated and showed him how to hold his hand and move his arm. "Up the longer way, down the shorter way," I taught him.

He had a go and was soon saying "up" and "down." He became quite good at it. Both he and Sally were thrilled.

It had been a funny feeling going back. It was less than a fortnight after my first visit, but the circumstances were so very different that I felt almost as though I owned the place. Soon after three o'clock Sally and I were in the swimming pool. We bolted the door firmly behind us and took off all our clothes. At first Sally was frightened of the water. She hesitated on the edge.

"What's the matter, darling?" I called. I had dived in, swum a length and a half, and stopped to float, somewhat obscenely, on my back.

"I can't help thinking of last Saturday. I suppose I'm frightened of drowning."

"But this is quite different. The water's clear and safe. There's no mud."

"I know it's silly. I just can't help it."

"Then don't dive in. Go round to the shallow end." I swam to that end to meet her.

Sally sat on the edge and dangled her legs in the water.

"It's cold."

"No, it's not. It's very warm. And you're going to come in for a swim to get your confidence back."

I slipped an arm round her waist and picked her up. I held her against me and let her body slide down until she was up to her loins in the water. I kissed her.

"You see, darling. It's very easy. You're almost in now. It's very shallow here. Let's just bend down gradually until the water is up to our necks – then we'll push off and swim together to the far end. If you get frightened I'll be right beside you."

"You're so good to me, Jimmy. I know I'm being awfully silly."

"No, you're not. It's absolutely natural. But you'll be all right in a moment. Let's swim."

She looked a bit green. She took a deep breath and started to swim cautiously towards the deep water. I pushed off quickly and swam alongside her, smiling and talking cheerfully, as we both performed a leisurely breast stroke. When we reached the far end Sally grabbed at the end and gave a sigh of relief.

"Thank heavens that's over."

"Are you cured now?"

She smiled at me. Her colour was back. "Almost. All I need now is the same treatment you gave me after you rescued me and I shall be a new woman."

I grinned at her. "I think that might be arranged."

I gave a thrust with my hands on the concrete side of the pool and heaved myself out of the water. I stood on the edge, dripping, and looked down at Sally still in the pool. Her submerged breasts looked enormous, partly I suppose because of the refraction of the light, partly because of the buoyancy of the water. The cool water had hardened her thick pink nipples. Altogether it was a stirring sight, a fact which Sally could hardly fail to notice.

"Good old Egbert. He's so reliable."

I bent down and gripped her wrists. "Out you come," and I gave a heave and pulled her straight up out of the pool and set her down on the edge.

"That was very impressive, darling. But do you think you ought to? You might strain something."

"I'm a strong lad. A fact which I am about to demonstrate yet again."

"Over there on the grass," said Sally, pointing.

The turf was fairly springy, but the ground underneath was hard. Being a perfect gentleman, I lay on my back. Sally straddled me on hands and knees, her hair and breasts hanging over my face. I caressed the insides of her wet thighs.

"This was just a ruse to seduce me, wasn't it?" I said.

She wrinkled her nose at me. "I'm always having to seduce you, darling. It's terribly hard work for me."

"You dreadful girl!" I laughed and heaved her off me and she grabbed hold of me and we rolled over and over on the grass until we were stopped by a small tree. I found myself lying on top of Sally and she was laughing up at me. I entered her strongly. It felt right.

"That's good," she moaned.

"Sally," called a female voice from the other side of wall. "Sally. Are you there?"

We froze.

"Sally? Are you in the pool?" The voice sounded familiar, but I couldn't identify it at first.

"Who is it?" I whispered.

"Susan Headcorn," Sally whispered back.

"If we keep quiet perhaps she'll go away."

"It's no good. She must know I'm here." She raised her voice. "I'm just coming, Susan," she called.

"No, you're not," I muttered miserably. "And neither am I." Sally giggled and we separated and stood up.

"Oh, dear," she said looking down at me. "Poor Egbert. What on earth shall we do about him?"

"He'll survive," I said bitterly.

"I won't be a moment, Susan," Sally cried. "I was just changing." She lowered her voice. "Come on," she whispered to me. We ran to the summer house. Sally picked up a bathing robe and slipped it on. There was a small towel on a hook. She pointed at it. "Put that round your waist. You haven't got time to dress."

"Shall I hide in the loo?"

"No, darling. She may have heard us talking. She's bound to guess about us, but it won't matter." She rushed out of the door and a few seconds later I heard the noise of the bolt being drawn.

"My dear," cried Susan Headcorn.

I pulled the towel from its hook and wrapped it round my waist. It was a small towel but it just served. I stepped out of the door as Sally and Susan came round the corner. Susan stopped when she saw me.

"Oh," she said. "Oh, dear. I had no idea you weren't alone, Sally. I am sorry. Hello James. How nice to see you again."

She was confused and spoke very quickly. "I was just passing and they told me you were here and I thought I'd ask you if you'd like to have dinner with us this evening. Not at home. At a restaurant, I mean. Everything's in absolute chaos at home. The house has been turned upside down. Humphrey's coming down on the 5.30 and he said he'd take me out to dinner somewhere and he suggested we ask you and Freddie to join us."

"How sweet of you," said Sally calmly. "Unfortunately Freddie's still in Germany. He won't be back in time for your dance either. He asked me to make his apologies to you. I was going to telephone you later to tell you and to ask if there's anything I can do to help. Is there?"

"My dear, how kind. I can't think of anything at the moment. It's wonderful of you to have so many of the little monsters to stay."

"James has come to stay too, to help me out."

"Oh, I see," said Susan. She looked from Sally to me and then back again at Sally. I could see that at last she took in the details of our costume – or the lack of it. I hung onto my towel. "Oh, I see," she said again. "You and James are…" Her voice trailed away.

"Yes, we are," said Sally brightly. I looked at her. She looked proud and happy. Our eyes met and we smiled. She reached out and took my hand.

"Oh, my dears," said Susan. "That is good news." She turned to me. "You're a very lucky young man."

"I know I am."

"And as a matter of fact you haven't done badly, Sally, either."

"I know too," said Sally.

"Did I tell you I used to know James's father?"

"Yes, you did."

"He was… well, never mind that now. I'm so glad for both of you."

Rationally I had known that she would approve of our relationship ever since our conversation at the Brendons' dance, but I was still old-fashioned enough to feel surprised that she so readily condoned, even approved, what was in fact nothing more or less than adultery. It was obvious that she had no scruples about it.

"He is very handsome, isn't he, Sally?" she said, beaming at me. "You might just as well drop that towel, James. It conceals absolutely nothing."

"You're incorrigible, Susan," Sally laughed. "Don't you dare take your towel off, Jimmy. And behave yourself, Susan. He's all mine, aren't you darling?"

"Well, anyway," said Susan. "You obviously won't want to come out to dinner with us. You'll be much happier on your own."

"As a matter of fact we'd love to come with you," said Sally politely. "But don't you think it would be awfully difficult and embarrassing for Humphrey?"

"I expect you're right," Susan nodded. "I'll be on my way now and leave you two to go on with your swimming."

Sally and I looked at one another and grinned. Susan noticed.

"Oh, my dears. I do hope I didn't interrupt anything. I did, didn't I? How perfectly dreadful of me." To my amazement she blushed.

"It doesn't matter, Susan," Sally patted her on the arm. "It's our own fault. Don't worry about it."

"I'm terribly sorry. I'll go now. I'll see you both tomorrow night." She turned and started towards the door. Sally and I followed. When we reached the door Susan turned and smiled at us. "I hope you'll both be very happy – for as long as you want to be. And do remember that if there's anything I can do to help you have only to let me know." She went through the gate and wandered away between the trees.

"And don't worry," she called back to us. "Don't worry. I won't tell a soul. Not a soul." She trudged off across the lawn and left us to our own devices.

NINETEEN

The weekend passed in a sort of dream. Looking back upon it now, I can hardly believe that it really happened. But of course it did; and for forty-eight hours I was to all intents the master of Highworth. I sat at the head of the table at meals; I helped to look after the rest of the house party; I was generous with Freddie's cigars and port and brandy and, best of all, I slept with the mistress of the house in her superb four-poster bed. I was even allowed to read Timmy a bedtime story. I chose Christopher Robin and in particular his visit to Changing the Guard.

"Is a soldier's life very hard?"

"Yes, quite hard, but you always have your friends with you."

He was pleased.

He was a dear little boy and I liked him. I had a feeling that if I ever managed to take Sally away from Freddie and marry her I would enjoy being his stepfather. I thought I might be quite good at it. Sally adored Timmy. She found it difficult to stop hugging him. He was a very huggable little boy. Fortunately his wonderful nanny saw to it that he occasionally escaped Sally's clutches.

On Saturday night I escorted Sally to the Headcorns' dance and we walked into the house together and shook hands with our host and hostess and their daughter just as though we were a married couple. The judge eyed me doubtfully but Sally told me later that Susan would have kept her word not to talk. "There's quite a lot that Humphrey doesn't get told. If he looked oddly at you I expect it was only jealousy. He's one of my most ardent admirers."

The youngest Miss Headcorn was a pretty little thing and I had a dance with her after her father had stolen Sally from me. When the music stopped a young man with flowing hair and a green shirt rescued Miss Headcorn from my senile clasp and I found myself alone. I looked round to see if I could see Sally and found Susan bearing down on me.

"My dear James," she gushed. "How lovely to find you on your own."

I grinned at her. "Would you like to dance with me?"

"I should love to, James. But unfortunately, as you don't seem to have noticed, the band have gone off to have their supper and the only dancing is in the discotheque in the marquee, which – as they say nowadays – is hardly my scene. However, it gives me a splendid opportunity to have a word in your ear. Follow me."

She led the way out of the drawing room and down the hall to a door at the far end. I opened it for her and she swept in. It was a small sitting room containing a sofa and two or three chairs. One of the chairs had a needlework basket beside it. There was a television set in one corner near the fire.

A young couple lay on the sofa apparently glued together from their mouths to their knees, but they separated briskly enough when they saw who had come in and they jumped to their feet muttering apologies and hurried from the room fiddling with their clothing as they went.

Susan took not the slightest notice of them. They might have been invisible.

"This is my little sitting room. We shan't be disturbed here. Have a drink. And will you pour one for me too please – a brandy and soda is just what I feel like. Everything's over there." She pointed at a tray on a little table in a corner and settled herself comfortably in the armchair by the needlework basket. I poured two strong brandies and soda, gave her one and sat down facing her.

"Here's to you and Sally," she said brightly and we both drank. "I'm sorry I interrupted you yesterday afternoon, but I'm glad that I discovered about you two. It makes it easier for me."

I wondered what she was going to say.

"As you know, I loathe Freddie. He's a sanctimonious ass on the surface, but something very much nastier underneath. On the other hand I adore Sally. She's an angel. And I'm quite certain that being married to *him* is extremely bad for her. That's why I was so very pleased when you came along and seemed so smitten. You're the best thing that could possibly have happened to her – so far. The point is what's going to happen in the future? Have the two of you thought about it yet?" I looked at her in silence, wondering what I was going to say to her. My first reaction was to tell her, as politely as I could, that it was none of her business. However, she had so far proved a good friend and I knew that Sally trusted her. She might be useful to us in the future. I suppose she guessed my problem for she said, "You probably think I'm a frightful interfering old busybody and I shan't be offended if you tell me to mind my own business. But in fact I can keep my mouth shut if I want to, and there is one way at least in which I can help you both."

"Oh?" I clutched at this passing straw. "What's that?"

"I can give you the opportunity to go off together on your own for several weeks – that is, if you can get away in August or September."

"I was planning to take some leave in September. How

can you manage it?"

"Simple. I'll tell you how in a moment. First I want to know if you're serious about Sally. She needs someone to be serious about her. If you *are* serious I'll help you. If you're not I want you to give her up at once before she gets too badly hurt."

I drank some of my brandy. I had a slight boat-burning feeling. "I'm serious, Susan." I hoped I sounded sincere. I felt it. "If I could persuade Sally to leave Freddie there is nothing I should like more than to marry her."

"It would cost you your commission, wouldn't it?"

"I expect so. That can't be helped."

"You really love her?"

"Yes."

She paused. So far she had looked intense and rather hard-faced. Now she relaxed and smiled at me. "That's very good news. I feel rather like a mother to Sally, you know. My own eldest daughter is a year or two older than she is, so it's not so strange." She finished the remains of her drink. "Let's have some more," she commanded me, and I refilled our glasses.

"What do you expect Freddie to do when he finds out?" she asked.

"Sally says he won't be any trouble."

"Why?"

"I don't know. There's quite a lot about Sally I don't know. She doesn't seem to want to talk about her marriage."

"Have you talked about the future? Have you made any plans?"

"No. None at all. I've come up against a brick wall. She says she may tell me about her marriage – one day. For the moment she simply says that Freddie won't be any trouble if he finds out that we're having an affair. What he'd say if he were asked for a divorce I've no idea. And if Sally has she hasn't told me."

Susan appeared to be thinking. "How odd. Do you suppose he's given her permission to have affairs provided she's discreet about them? Lots of husbands do, I'm told. Humphrey brings me back some fantastic tales from the Divorce division. Usually the quid pro quo is that the husband shall be allowed all the mistresses he wants."

"I don't think Freddie has mistresses."

"How do you know? Did Sally tell you?"

"No." I wished I hadn't spoken. "As I told you, she won't talk about her marriage at all. It's just a feeling I have," I added lamely.

"Oh." Susan seemed unimpressed. "Maybe you're right. But perhaps Sally has some sort of hold on him."

I was shocked. "Blackmail, you mean? I don't see Sally going in for something like that."

Susan laughed. "You are loyal. She's very lucky. Never mind, we won't pursue it. But it might not be as simple as blackmail. You'll probably find out eventually."

"Do you think Sally would marry me?"

"Why shouldn't she?"

"Well, for a start she'd risk losing her child. She'd certainly lose Highworth and, as I'm sure you know, she really loves that house. And she wouldn't be a rich Viscountess any more, just a fairly hard-up Mrs with a husband without a job and with no training for anything."

"I don't think you're being entirely fair to her. She wouldn't care at all about her change of status – no proper woman would. She almost certainly wouldn't lose Timmy. A mother almost always keeps a young child in those sort of circumstances. The worst that could happen would be that Freddie would get custody, so that he would have the say about schools and things, and Sally would have what's called 'care and control' and Timmy would live with her. Freddie would have access."

"I see."

"I haven't been a lawyer's wife all these years for nothing. As for Highworth, you're quite right. She does love the place. But no one puts a house before a human being and happiness."

"I hope you're right. I expect you are."

"Anyway the whole point of talking to you tonight was to find out if you are serious. As I can see that you are I'll do all I can to help you. I really do want Sally to get away from Freddie. He's evil."

"What about September?"

"Ah, yes. September. Well, you see I have a sister who lives in Corsica. She has a large house there by the sea and she lives there all the year round. Her husband writes. Humphrey and I go there every summer for the whole of the vacation – that's August and September – and we take our children and grandchildren and their friends. It's pretty chaotic, but great fun. For the last two years Sally has come too, bringing her nanny and Timmy. Freddie came the first year but he left after two days saying that he had special work to do. Really it was because he found the place so uncomfortable. It's not at all his sort of place. Last year he went off on some Parliamentary mission to somewhere or other and, though of course he's been invited again this year, I have no doubt that he'll find some jolly good excuse not to come."

"So I can come to stay too?"

"Certainly not. Everyone would know then. No, this is what you do. Sally comes to stay for a few days. Then she leaves Timmy and Nanny with me and goes off and meets you somewhere. It doesn't matter where you go as long as I know where it is and can send you a telegram if something crops up." She sat back looking pleased with herself. "How's that for a scheme?"

"Marvellous. Simply marvellous. You're a wonder, Susan." A sudden thought struck me. "Suppose for some reason Freddie rings up, and Sally and I are miles away?"

"Rings up!" Susan snorted. "There isn't a telephone for miles. The place is fantastically primitive."

"Suppose..."

"Suppose nothing. I agree all sorts of things might go wrong, but the odds are that they won't. If they do, the worst thing that can happen is that Freddie will find out about you – and you're going to tell him one day anyway."

I stood up and smiled at her. "I think it's a marvellous idea and I'm very grateful. I'll go and find Sally and tell her all about it and we'll make a plan. I'll tell you the details when we've worked them out. You're awfully kind."

"Not really. I want Sally to be happy, that's all. Now off you go and find her."

I finished my drink and put the glass down.

"You will be good to Sally won't you, James. You'll never let her down?"

"No," I said. "I'll never let her down."

And I meant it.

***

I told Sally of Susan's suggestion when we were back at Highworth and tucked up comfortably in her four-poster. I lay on my back with Sally's head resting on my shoulder and watched the gradually increasing light penetrate the curtains.

"I think it's a splendid idea," said Sally. "If everything works out all right."

"Do you think it will?"

"I don't see why not. Provided Freddie shows no sign of wanting to go to Corsica I don't think it matters whether he stays in England or goes where he goes. The only other thing is your leave. Will you be able to get away?"

"I think so. I'll see about it next week."

"I'd already planned to take Timmy and Nanny to Corsica. We were going to go for the last week in August and the first three weeks in September. Timmy loves it there. Susan has several grandchildren about his age and they all run wild together."

"You could take them out there when you planned to – then make some excuse to leave and we'll go off together, or meet somewhere, at the beginning of September. Let's try to have three weeks together."

"Oh, yes. Do let's. It would be so wonderful." Sally looked up at me in the half-light and I kissed her. "Where shall we go?"

"I don't know yet. I'll think about it. Have you any ideas?"

"No, darling. I don't mind where we go. But I don't think we dare risk a hotel, do you? We ought to rent a house or a villa or something. And can we find somewhere where we can be very lazy? Somewhere with lots of sunshine and privacy, so we can run around with no clothes on."

"That would be very pleasant," I said drowsily. "I'll make all the arrangements. You try to persuade Freddie to go away somewhere so he won't be able to rush out to Corsica even if he wants to."

"All right, darling."

There was silence. I wondered if Sally had fallen asleep. "Sally?" I whispered.

"Yes, Jimmy?"

"What will Freddie do when he finds out about us?"

"It'll be all right, I think. He won't be very nice, but I think I shall be able to control him."

"Will he divorce you?"

"Darling you're not to think about it. Let's enjoy the present and let the future look after itself."

And though I tried to make her discuss it further she would not, and eventually we fell asleep in one another's arms.

***

At lunchtime on Sunday, Freddie rang up from Germany and announced that he would arrive at Heathrow on Monday morning. He wanted Sally to meet him. It gave us one more complete night together, and though we were saddened by the realisation that in the morning we should have to part, probably for some time, we made the most of it. With the gentlest persuasion we managed to get rid of the entire house party long before dinner. We had a last swim together, dined à deux at one end of the long dining room table and went early to our separate rooms. Choosing my moment with care I made the short journey from my bedroom to Sally's and we spent the night romping happily in her large bed.

When the daylight started to trickle through the curtains we were lying limbs intertwined in a post-coital cosiness when Sally said: "Shall I tell you when I knew I was going to love you for ever?"

"Yes, please."

"It was that morning on your terrace. When you called it our eternal morning."

"I remember."

"You called me a silly girl."

"Oh. How rude of me."

"It wasn't. It was wonderful. No one has ever called me that before. It made me feel that I was the luckiest girl in the world to have found a lovely man who really loved me. I just knew that you would look after me – a silly girl who needed a proper man." She paused. "I was proved right that afternoon. I was a silly girl to have jumped into that river and almost drowned. You saved my life then. And I've felt completely safe with you ever since. Do you understand?"

"I think so."

"That made me sure that I would love you for ever. I'm very lucky."

"So am I, Sally, my love. So am I."

I left her at six, breakfasted on coffee and orange juice in the dining room at seven, and prepared to leave the house a few minutes later.

I was tipping Carlo who had brought my car to the door and put my suitcase in the boot, when Sally descended the stairs to say goodbye. Her hair was loose and she wore a green silk dressing gown tightly belted at the waist.

"I've come to say goodbye," she announced, holding out a hand. Her face was white, her green eyes were enormous.

I took her hand. It was like a block of ice. For a moment I thought of kissing it, but Carlo was still hovering around. We stood silently together for a few seconds, her hand in mine. Then she took it back.

"I must be off." I tried to sound natural but my voice came out cracked and peculiar-sounding. "I should be able to beat the rush hour in to London if I get going now."

She turned to Carlo. "Thank you," she said. "There's nothing else. You can go now."

He bowed and withdrew in the direction of the green baize door.

"I'll come and see you off," said Sally, without enthusiasm. We walked out of the front door and crossed the gravel to the car. Our feet crunched on the gravel. I noticed that Sally wore open-toed slippers. Her toenails were painted. She put a hand on my arm. "You look very smart. That's a lovely suit."

"Thank you, darling." I tried to think of some light-hearted quip about my tailor, but nothing came to mind. It was too early in the morning. I opened the car door.

"I won't kiss you goodbye," said Sally. "Somebody may be watching."

I nodded. "When shall I see you again?"

"Soon, I hope. Wednesday. Perhaps even tomorrow. It depends on what Freddie has arranged. I'll ring you up when I know what's going on this week. Will you be in?"

"Yes. I'll be in. Try to have lunch at my flat tomorrow. We can spend the afternoon together."

"I'll try. Oh, darling, I am going to miss you terribly. I'm so miserable. Please drive carefully. I couldn't bear it if…"

"I will. And don't be miserable, Sally. I love you with all my heart. We've been very lucky to have had ten days together like this. And there'll be other times. You'll see."

"I long for them. Goodbye now, my darling. I love you."

As I drove away, in the rear-view mirror I saw Sally's green gold-topped figure standing forlornly outside the front door of Highworth. She was still standing there when I turned the corner.

TWENTY

I was in Barracks by ten o'clock. I parked my car outside my Company office and went in. There had been, I discovered, an inexplicable outbreak of peaceableness and obedience amongst the men of my Company during the weekend and there was not a single case of crime for my attention. My Company Sergeant Major seemed torn between a feeling of pleasure at the good order and discipline of the Company and a nagging suspicion that the Non-Commissioned Officers were not doing their jobs properly.

I left him to shout at the Company Clerk about some overdue returns and walked along the pavement at the edge of The Square towards Battalion Headquarters. As I approached I looked in through the large windows of the Orderly Room and saw, as I had hoped I should, that the Commanding Officer was at his desk. He was alone in the large room. The Adjutant, whose desk adjoins that of his Commanding Officer (a custom peculiar to the Foot Guards, I think) was out somewhere.

I opened the door, walked in, shut the door behind me and, turning to face the room, I took off my bowler hat and stood to attention for a moment. The Commanding Officer was engrossed in a letter. I walked slowly across the room and stood in front of his desk. I looked about me at the familiar room. On one side, behind the two desks, were the long windows which gave onto The Square. In the middle distance I could see the railings and beyond them Chelsea Bridge Road and the trees of Ranelagh Gardens. It was the same view that I had from my own office. Opposite the desks two large charts hung on the wall; one gave the name and rank of every Warrant and Non-Commissioned Officer in the Battalion. The Sergeant Major was at the top, then the RQMS, followed by the two Drill Sergeants: not sergeants at all but senior Warrant Officers whose job was to assist the Sergeant Major with ceremonial. The other was a calendar showing what was planned for each day for the next six months. A line was drawn down the entire length of September. Next to the line was the legend: 'Battalion Training – Salisbury Plain'. On the other walls there were prints of Musketeers in the uniforms of earlier days, and above the Commanding Officer's head was his personal Colour, fixed in a wall bracket.

He looked up as I stopped in front of his desk. He smiled and put down the letter he had been reading. "Good morning, James. What can I do for you?"

I looked down at him and smiled back. He wore a superb suit, his linen was faultless and a fat pearl gleamed in his silk tie. With his prematurely iron-grey hair and strong regular features he looked like everyone's beau ideal of a Guards' Colonel. He sat comfortably in his chair, both physically and mentally. He was good at his job and he knew it. Soon he would be a General and another officer would take his place. In a few years' time – perhaps as short as seven or eight years – I might find myself in his chair. It was a possibility that I welcomed. It was in fact much more than a possibility; because of my record to date, and because I had obtained the very necessary nomination to attend the Staff College before anyone else of my age in my Regiment, it was more or less a certainty. There were one or two things that might prevent it: illness of a serious nature might be one; a clash of personalities with a senior officer might be another – that was something that I would have to guard against most particularly when I was on the Staff, where I might find myself in a subordinate position to an officer of another Regiment who, for reasons of his own (insecurity or envy perhaps) purported to dislike all Guards Officers; making a fool of myself over another man's wife might well prove the most damning thing to my prospects of promotion.

"Good morning, sir," I said. "I hope this isn't an inconvenient moment, but I wanted to talk to you about my departure and about handing over my Company and – incidentally – about some leave."

"And the greatest of these is leave," said my Colonel cheerfully.

"Sir," I grinned.

"As a matter of fact you couldn't have come to see me at a more opportune moment, James. I've just had a letter from the Lieutenant Colonel." He waved a hand negligently at the letter he had been reading when I entered the room. It lay now on his pristine blotter and even upside down I could see that it was typed on the writing paper of our Regimental Headquarters in Birdcage Walk.

"It gives me all the latest information about officer postings. The part that concerns you is about George. As you know he was supposed to rejoin us next month and I intended to give him your Company. It would have worked out very neatly. Now of course they want to keep him on the Staff for another six months so I'm back to square one. It's absolutely typical of the way this Army of ours is run. The teeth always suffer – the tail never."

I smiled sympathetically. I knew as well as he did that what he said was true.

"So I've decided to give your Company to Peter Pershore.

He's the senior Captain in the Battalion and there's no likelihood of anyone else coming to us in the foreseeable future. I think it's right that he should be given a try. Do you think he's up to it?"

"Sir," I nodded. "He'll do it very well."

"Will you tell him then? Ask him to come and talk to me about it some time." He took a slim cigarette case from his pocket. It looked plain and rather dull. I knew it of old. It was made of platinum. He offered me a cigarette. I shook my head. He lit one for himself.

"I don't suppose you want to come to Salisbury Plain much, do you?"

"Not in the least," I said honestly.

"In that case how would it suit you to have three or four weeks' leave in September? You go to Shrivenham in the first week in October, don't you?"

"Sir." A warm glow of excitement spread itself generously inside my stomach. "That would suit me splendidly."

"That's settled then. Hand over to Peter at the end of August. Then you can go on leave in September, more or less until you go to the Staff College. Running about on Salisbury Plain will be an ideal opportunity for Peter to get a grip on his Company."

"I'll come back for a few days at the end of September if I may. I shall have all sorts of last-minute things to do, and I should like to do one last Guard. It may be years before I do another." It may even be the very last Guard I ever do, I thought.

"Of course, James. You can even invite me to dinner if you're good."

"I will, sir." I walked to the door, turned and stood to attention for two seconds, put on my bowler hat and left the room.

When I got back to my own office I found Peter sitting at my desk, reading my copy of the *Times* and smoking a cigarette in his long holder. He unfolded himself elegantly as I walked in and saluted me.

"Dear boy," he said. "How nice to see you."

"What's going on this morning?" I asked, taking his place at the desk.

"Everything and nothing. It's all too frustrating. Today looked like a fairly clear day according to the programme – no Guard Mounting or Drill Parades. 'What we're getting on with on Monday morning,' I told the Company Sergeant Major last Friday, 'is a lesson in controlling Mortar and Artillery fire.' It's just what every young Guardsman should know, and also as you are well aware it's something I'm rather good at." Peter had been the Battalion Mortar Officer until a year or so before. "When I arrived at the Puff Range sharp at oh nine hundred hours this morning, I expected to find thirty or forty clear-eyed keen young soldiers simply bursting to learn all about Oscar Tango lines and other recondite parts of the military art."

"What *did* you find?"

"My dear, can't you guess. There was one elderly Lance Corporal, whom I swear I've never seen before. Believe it or not he had both arms in slings and was therefore quite unable to salute. He gave me a friendly nod instead and said, 'Company Sergeant Major sends his compliments, sir, and everyone's on fatigues.' I asked him if he'd like me to teach him about controlling Mortar and Artillery fire and he looked most offended and said he was excused all duties. Who on earth is he?"

"It must be Corporal Wallace. He's just come out of hospital."

"Well I think he ought to go straight back again. Apart from the fact that he looks like a ghost, how in the world do you suppose he manages to attend to what I believe are called the normal bodily functions with both arms trussed up?"

"I suppose the doctors know what they're doing."

"I can't think why you should suppose that." Peter had once had a nasty experience at the hands of an Army dentist and had never forgotten it. "But never mind about the sawbones – talking of ghosts, you don't look too marvellous yourself."

"Don't I?"

"No, dear lad. You have a distinctly unhealthy pallor. What seems to be the trouble?"

"I think it's just lack of sleep." I grinned at him.

"Ah-ha, so that's what you're up to." He raised a hand, palm towards me. "It's all right, James, my dear. I'm not going to ask you any embarrassing questions. That natural delicacy for which I am world-renowned prevents me from encroaching upon your private life. That and the certain knowledge that you wouldn't answer my questions anyway."

"Splendid. However, as I am not similarly hindered tell me about you and Anne."

"Everything is going merrily. Which reminds me that I want to have some leave so we can go away somewhere. Can I have a bit of time off?"

"I don't see why not. Where are you planning to go?"

"I was thinking of going to Jamaica to stay in my new house, but sadly Anne has vetoed that on the grounds that the food isn't particularly good there and it's out of season now. She's persuaded me to take a house in the South of France. It's a pity in a way because I don't like to leave the house in Jamaica empty for too long. I suppose you wouldn't be an angel and go and stay there for a bit? You'd be doing me a great favour."

I thought for a moment. It was the very place for Sally and me. It had privacy. It would be out of season in September. Admittedly it was rather a long way from Corsica, but that didn't really matter.

"I rather think that I should like that," I said at length. "I think that would probably suit me very well. Can I go in September? I'm going on leave then."

"Go any time you like, dear boy. I couldn't be more pleased. I'll write to Jackson – the butler feller – and tell him you're coming. When you decide exactly when you're going to fly we can make a signal to him so that he can meet you at the airport. I'm sure you'll adore the place."

"So am I. That's very kind of you Peter. And now I've got some good news for you. I've just been talking to the Commanding Officer. You are to take over this Company from me before I go to the Staff College."

"For how long? Isn't old George coming back from the Staff?"

"Apparently not. They're keeping him on for a bit. So you'll be the proper Company Commander and you'll be a Major."

"Well, well." Peter tried to look as though he didn't care particularly, but I knew he was pleased. "Field rank, no less. How extraordinary."

"So if you wouldn't mind fitting in your leave between now and the end of August I shall hand over to you before I go away."

"Certainly, my dear. I'm sure I can manage that. I'll totter along and see our young and efficient Adjutant about suitable dates in a little while, but first I think you and I should repair to the Officers' Mess for a little mid-morning restorative. All this excitement fair tuckers a fellow out."

***

During July, Sally and I saw one another whenever we could. We managed lunch or an afternoon several times each week and on two Fridays we were able to spend all night together. Taken all in all it was very much better than nothing, but each time we said goodbye – not knowing when we would meet again – it was a torment. We longed to be able to get away by ourselves and I prayed nightly that nothing would prevent our holiday in Jamaica. By mutual tacit consent we neither of us spoke about what we would do after we returned from Jamaica. We were content – or almost content – to live in the present, looking no further ahead than our planned holiday.

As the weeks went by I knew that I was growing more and more deeply in love and I realised that what I had told Susan about my wish to marry Sally was the simple truth. I was certain that Sally loved me too, quite as much as I loved her. Ours was never one of those relationships in which there is one who loves and one who allows himself or herself to *be* loved. Sally was in love for the first time in her life, she told me. And I, though I didn't pretend that I had never loved before, felt that this time I was in love as never before; that she was the great love of my life. Looking back upon it now, with that well-known benefit of hindsight, I know I was right; Sally was the great love of my life.

But though we loved, and knew that the other loved, and though we felt deep inside us that this was something special, we never spoke of marriage. Perhaps Sally didn't raise the subject because she thought that it was not for her to do so. For my part I said nothing because I knew that she loved her child, and wanted what she thought was best for him, even if necessary at the expense of her own happiness. It was partially because of this that I behaved as I did when something particularly nasty happened to us one evening.

It was a Thursday and Sally and I hadn't managed to see one another for two days. I was in my bedroom at about half-past six, dressing to go to a cocktail party, when Sally telephoned me.

"I've got the most wonderful news."

"Tell me."

"Not on the telephone, darling. Are you busy? Can you come round here?"

"I could. I was planning to go to a party, but I'd much rather see you."

"I don't want to spoil your fun. Go to your party and then call in here later. The news will keep."

"I'd much rather see you. I expect the party will be awfully boring anyway."

"Why will it? You go. You'll have a lovely time."

"It's bound to be boring because you won't be there."

"You are sweet."

"What about Freddie?"

"He's gone to the House. There's a three-line whip and he's making a speech and he's having dinner there with someone. He won't be home till all hours. Come over here and I'll cook us some dinner."

It was irresistible. "I'll be with you in ten minutes."

Sally opened the door to me wearing only a towel. I kissed her and picked her up in my arms and carried her to her bedroom.

"How ardent you are, darling."

"It's been over forty-eight hours since I've seen you," I

said as I pulled off her towel.

"It's not seeing me that's so important, is it?"

She calmly unzipped my trousers and put a cool hand in through the opening. She had learned a lot in a month. "Just as I thought," she announced. "Seeing is not at all the right word."

"It's one of the words." I gasped at the thrilling things she was doing with her fingers.

"Don't you want to hear my news?" said Sally slyly.

"I suppose so," I groaned. "But later on perhaps."

"Can't you wait, sweetheart?" Sally teased me.

"No."

"You're not thinking of making love to me with all your clothes on? I don't think I can allow that. Let me help you off with everything. Let's get rid of your jacket. Put it on the chair there. Now for your tie. Perhaps you'd better do that. I shall only get it knotted. I'll do your shirt buttons. What else is there? Cuff-links? There we are. Now off with your shirt. My goodness, you are a large man, aren't you? Now how do I undo the top of your trousers? Oh, I see. Down they come. What smart striped pants! Do they come down easily? Something seems to be in the way… Oh, yes. There! Egbert! How lovely to see you again. I think you've put on weight since I saw you last. But it doesn't feel like fat. It's all muscle. I hope you haven't been taking exercise with anyone else. No? That's all right then. You can be specially nice to me this evening. Lie down here, Jimmy. Ah, that's nice, darling. Oooh, yes. I like that very much. Oh, Jimmy, I do love you. I really do, you know. Oh, darling, that's nice…"

Suddenly a bell shrilled stridently outside the bedroom door. I thought it was the front doorbell at first, but it didn't stop ringing.

231

"What on earth's that?"

"Division Bell. Freddie must have left it switched on yesterday. I'll turn it off." She stood up. "Don't go away. You too, Egbert."

She opened the door and went out into the hallway. Two seconds later the bell stopped ringing. I opened my mouth to call to Sally to tell her to hurry back, but before I could speak I heard the distinctive noise of a key being placed in the lock of the front door. A moment later I heard Freddie's voice.

"Well, well," he said, in his odd, slightly-too-high-pitched voice. "It's a good thing I'm on my own."

"Oh." She sounded startled and frightened. "Hello, Freddie. I didn't expect you back for hours."

"I'm paired. So I thought I'd come back here and have some dinner and an early night. What a lovely surprise to walk in here and find my beautiful wife with no clothes on."

Sally gave what sounded to me like a very nervous laugh. "I was in the bathroom when the Division Bell went. I just came out to turn it off."

"Well, you can leave it off tonight, thank God. Come on into the drawing room and pour me a drink."

"All right, Freddie. I'll just go and put something on."

"No, no. You stay as you are. You know I like to see you walking around with no clothes on."

"Please, Freddie. I feel a bit cold."

There was a momentary pause.

"You don't feel cold to me. You're as warm as toast."

I shivered at the knowledge that his small plump hands were touching her body.

"Come on. No more argument. Pour me a whisky and soda and I'll tell you how I managed to get away from the

House. It was rather peculiar really..."

His voice faded away to a murmur and I guessed that they had gone into the drawing room. I got up as quietly as I could and started to put my clothes on. That seemed to me to have the first priority.

When I was dressed I had a quick look round the room to make sure that I had left nothing behind. Fortunately Sally hadn't given me time to empty my pockets so there was no evidence of my presence. The bedspread was rumpled and I tugged it straight. Sally's towel lay on the carpet. I picked it up, thought for a second, and took it into the bathroom and hung it neatly over the rail.

I was rather proud that I was acting so coolly. I told myself that I must think carefully and make no mistakes if I were to escape undetected.

I crossed to the open bedroom door and listened. I could hear Freddie's voice from the direction of the drawing room but I couldn't hear what he was saying. I looked round the side of the door and down the passage. The front door looked invitingly back at me from the far end, but I was in the worst possible place for an escape.

Sally's bedroom was at the extreme end of the passage-shaped hall from the front door. To my right was the door of Freddie's room and beyond it the door of the loo. To my left were three doors – the kitchen, the dining room and the drawing room. The last was nearest to the front door and it was half-open. While it remained like that I knew I should not be able to get out. Even if I should be lucky enough to pass the open door without Freddie seeing me, I couldn't open the front door without making a noise.

A moment's thought told me that Sally would realise that and, presumably, she would do her best to shut the drawing room door as soon as she could. I waited, ready to take my chance when it presented itself, and prepared to step back into the safety of the bedroom if Freddie came out.

A few seconds later I thought my opportunity had come. There was silence. As I watched I saw the pool of light which came through the drawing room door start to narrow as the door was pushed to. I was just about to step forward when I heard Freddie's voice. It was raised and I heard each word distinctly.

"It's such a hot evening, Sally. Don't shut the door. I like the through draught, don't you?"

"It's all right, I suppose." Sally's voice come from just inside the door.

"Or are you shutting the door so that your lover can get away unobserved?"

Instinctively I shrank back inside the room and froze. I'm going to be caught, I told myself. He knows. Terror gripped me. I wondered if I should hide under the bed; or perhaps somewhere in the bathroom would be better.

"What on earth are you talking about?" Sally sounded calm and untroubled. You magnificent girl, I said to myself.

Freddie laughed. It was an odd sort of laugh. "Just a joke."

"It's not very funny." It sounded as though she had moved away from the door now, but when I risked another peep I saw it was still open. There was no escape that way. What could I do?

The only course that seemed to be open to me was to remain hidden in Sally's bedroom until Freddie had gone to bed. It might be a very long wait. And there was the danger that he might come into the room and find me. The shame of being discovered skulking in a woman's bedroom was too much for me. It would be better to walk straight into the drawing room to confront Freddie now. That course had several advantages. I should have the initiative. Unless

Freddie really suspected that I was hiding in the flat he would be very surprised when I walked in. I should also discover Sally's attitude towards me. Would she agree to a divorce so that she and I could marry? Would she have any choice? Or would Freddie forgive her if she promised never to see me again? That seemed a real danger. I might lose what little I had. Wouldn't it be better not to risk it? After all I couldn't tell how Sally might react to a confrontation between Freddie and me. There was a possibility that I might find myself out on my ear. The status quo wasn't perfect, but I daren't take the chance of losing Sally altogether. Half-a-loaf perhaps; but a very beautifully wrapped half-a-loaf. Three weeks in Jamaica alone with Sally. That was worth something, wasn't it?

Suddenly I thought of the kitchen. What a fool I was. Surely there was a back door in there. I shut my eyes and tried to picture the room. Yes, there was a door, I was certain of it. It was at the far end of the kitchen. It had a towel hanging on a hook and a number of carrier bags on the door handle. It must lead to some back stairs. I was crazy not to have thought of it before.

I peered out into the hall again. Freddie was talking in the drawing room. Silently I crossed the gap to the kitchen door. I opened it carefully, entered and shut it behind me. Surprisingly Freddie's voice was now much louder, and I could hear what he was saying.

"… two weeks in Tokyo. I shall fly over the Pole. I'll stay with the Sandfords some of the time there. Then a week in Singapore with the Maxwells before I go on to Australia…"

I looked around me and at once saw the explanation. There was a hatch into the dining room next door and the hatch doors were open. I bent and looked through. I found that I was looking straight across the polished surface of the dining room table and through open double-doors into the drawing room beyond. Freddie was sitting in an armchair, his back half-turned towards me. Sally stood on the hearthrug facing him. The late evening sunshine slanted in through the window and bathed her body in gold. I felt slightly sick that Freddie was looking at her nakedness but I couldn't help seeing his point of view; she was an object of great beauty. If all he wanted to do was look at her I supposed I shouldn't object too strongly.

"When will you be back?"

"Well I can't be too exact about that. As my itinerary is planned at the moment, I get back to London on September the 26th. But of course that may have to be changed. It certainly won't be any earlier than that. It might be later. But I shall try to be back by the 1st of October."

Of course, I said to myself. This is the good news that Sally didn't have a chance to tell me. Freddie is going to go away. Where had he said he was going? Tokyo, Singapore, Australia. It could hardly be bettered. Far away from both Corsica and Jamaica.

"We should be back from Corsica a day or two before you."

Freddie laughed. "Corsica!" he snorted. "I wish you joy of it."

"I suppose that's why you're doing this trip."

"Not entirely. It'll be a very useful trip in lots of ways. But I shan't be sorry not to be able to go with you to Corsica. It's not really my sort of holiday. All that sun and discomfort. You won't go and spoil your tan there, Sally, will you? I don't want to see you all mottled when I get back."

"You needn't worry. I was all right last year wasn't I?

Antonia and I found a very private little cove where we could sunbathe in the nude."

I looked at the door at the end of the kitchen. It was just as I had remembered it. I thought it was time to go. I tiptoed over to it. There was a bolt at the top of the door and I eased it gently back. I held my breath as I did it. There was no sound. There was a key in the lock. I tried to turn it. At once there was a scraping noise. I stopped. Freddie was talking. He seemed to have noticed nothing. It had been, I realised, a very little noise, but I knew that I daren't try again until there was something to distract his attention. The door itself might easily make a loud noise as I opened it.

I stood by the door with my fingers on the key and waited for my opportunity. While I waited I listened to the conversation in the drawing room. I was horrified to hear Freddie say, "Are you going to take your boyfriend to Corsica with you, now you know I won't be there?"

"I haven't got a boyfriend, Freddie. Go and have a look round if you don't believe me."

I prayed that he wouldn't call her bluff. If he made a move, I told myself, I should be out of the door in a flash. He might hear me go, but he wouldn't know who I was. That, I supposed, would be something.

"I wasn't serious about his being here now," said Freddie evenly. "But I do know that you have a boyfriend. And what is more I know who he is."

At that moment I admired Sally more than ever before. The adrenaline was pumping round my body in such quantities that I could have lowered the Olympic record for any athletic achievement in the book, but I couldn't have spoken to have saved my life.

Sally's voice was calm and clear. She might have been discussing the weather.

"I haven't got a boyfriend, Freddie. I've never had one."

There was a moment of silence. How sensible of her, I thought, not to ask him who the boyfriend was. It must have been dreadfully difficult to resist the urge to say "Who do you think it is?" Freddie obviously thought so too.

"Don't you want to know who I think he is?"

"Why should I?" she said coolly. "As I haven't got a lover you're either making the whole thing up or you've been listening to unfounded gossip."

I cheered silently.

"If you did have a lover," said Freddie slowly, "you'd want to know who I thought he was, because if I'd got it wrong you'd know you were in the clear."

"Very clever. So that proves I haven't got a lover, doesn't it?"

"I'm not sure."

Sally laughed. "You can't have it both ways, Freddie."

"I'll tell you anyway." He sounded much less certain now. "It's that idiotic Guards Officer. Anne Knowle's pretty boyfriend. What's his name?"

"James. And, as you say, he's Anne's boyfriend, not mine." Her voice sounded quite steely.

"You were seen in his car a few weeks ago. It was when I was away in Germany."

"Oh, yes?" Sally couldn't have cared less.

"Yes." He sounded even less happy now but I guessed that he was resolved to plod on to the end. "A friend of mine was driving somewhere in London and he stopped at some traffic lights side-by-side with the car you were in. He told me that he knew both of you and he smiled across at you and waved. You didn't notice him. You were too busy talking to one another. He said it looked as though you were in love."

Sally laughed. "How on earth could he tell that?"

"It was an impression he got. He could have been mistaken, I suppose. He also told me that you had been seen together at the Brendons' dance last month."

"Ah. I know who your friend is."

"You do?"

"Yes. It's Quintin, isn't it?"

"How did you know? Did you see him?"

"In the car? Oh, no. But I saw him at the dance all right. He came up and insulted me and James. He even tried to attack James, and James had to knock him down. Did he tell you that?"

"No, he didn't."

"I think he's mad. I didn't tell you about it myself because I'm really quite sorry for him. I expect he made up some rubbish about what he saw me and James doing. What was it? Making love in the long grass? Really he is impossible. If you remember, Anne brought James to stay with us that weekend. The wretched man can hardly be blamed for having a duty dance with his hostess."

Freddie said nothing for a moment. I heard the clink of glass and I realised that he was pouring himself a drink.

"I should like one of those," said Sally firmly. She knew she was winning. "You can be pouring it out while I go and put a dressing gown on. I've had enough of standing around like this for one evening."

"Don't go for a moment, Sally." He sounded stern. "I just want to get this quite clear. Here's your drink."

"Thank you."

239

"First, I accept what you say about the dance. Quintin is a bit unbalanced about you. We both know why. But what about the car?"

"What about it?"

"Quintin said he saw you in that young man's car in London – somewhere in Kensington I gathered – on the Friday before I came back from Germany." He must believe her, I thought. He'd never have given that point away if he hadn't.

"I remember very well," said Sally confidently. "That was the day before Susan's dance. Do you remember you rang me up from Germany to say you wouldn't be back? Well, I got James to drive me down to Highworth. He was invited to the dance too. It was as simple as that. We must have been on our way to Highworth when Quintin saw us."

"I see."

There was a long pause. "All right," said Freddie eventually. "I'll accept that too."

"So I should hope. It happens to be the truth."

"All right. All right. I've said I accept it. I won't mention it again. I can understand why Quintin behaves as he does. I know he can be pretty awful, he was very unpopular at school and still is. I've never liked him, but he is my closest blood relation and that's important to me. But nevertheless… well, let me put it like this… this is an opportunity for me to give you a warning. I've been meaning to talk to about this for some time. There'll be a general election in a year or two. It may come sooner than we think. When it comes my party will almost certainly get in, probably with a large majority. Barring accidents we should stay in power for ten years at least, after the mess that the present Government have made of it. When we get in I shall be given a job. Not in the Cabinet at first. I'm a bit too young and I haven't had the experience. I might be made a Minister of State at the Defence Ministry. That's one of the reasons for this trip of mine. However, with at least ten years ahead of me in power the sky's the limit. Do you understand?"

"I think so. But what will you do when your father dies?"

"I shall renounce my peerage immediately. I shall have to if I'm going to remain an MP. My constituents will be happy."

"What about when you die. How will that affect Timmy?"

"He will have to decide whether he wants the earldom. That'll be up to him."

"If he's still very young will that present a problem?"

"I don't think so. Peers can be any age. However, I'm not planning to die young. Timmy might be quite old before I pop off. Anyway, that is my plan for my future. It closely involves you. Most people think we have an ideal marriage."

"Ha, ha."

"Please don't interrupt, Sally. I intend that people should go on thinking that. It can do me nothing but good. Therefore I don't want you to allow even the smallest breath of scandal to touch your good name. Do you understand that too?"

"Yes."

"I suppose there must be times when you feel the need for sex. I don't know what you feel about that, and I don't want to know. If there are then you must just do without. Have a cold shower or something. You've managed so far. Now it's more important than ever that you should continue to do so in the future. Is that clear?"

"Perfectly." Sally's voice was cold now. "But just for the sake of interest, what would you do if you ever found out that I was having an affair?"

"Shall I tell you? Yes, it might help. I've thought about it very carefully, you know. Just, as you say, for the sake of interest, suppose I discovered that you were having an affair with that boy James."

"What would you do to me?"

"To you, Sally. At first nothing. My aim would be to keep you out of it. The minimum amount of scandal, you understand? I should start with him. I should begin by warning him off. If that didn't work I should do my best to ruin him. And I should tell you what I was doing so that you wouldn't feel inclined to run off with him. If you did, of course, I should divorce you and take Timmy away from you. I should have no choice by then."

"Oh," said Sally in a small voice. "Tell me. How would you ruin James?"

"Well, perhaps ruin is rather a strong word. I should just make life very difficult for him. In his case there are two or three people I could get to help me. People who would keep quiet. One would be the Lieutenant Colonel of the Musketeers. He was at Eton with me. I could easily persuade him either to make the young man resign from the Army or send him away somewhere. How would he like to go to Saigon, do you think?"

"There aren't any British troops in Vietnam."

"There are Australians. He could be attached to them, perhaps. It doesn't matter, does it? This is just an example we're taking, isn't it, Sally?"

"Yes."

"Perhaps it would be better if he was made to hand his papers in. When he left the Army I could make it very difficult for him to get a job. And as you may know, Infantry Majors aren't exactly selling like hot cakes in the commercial world at present."

"I see. But you wouldn't divorce me?"

"Why not? If you became a public scandal I should have no choice."

"You know what I should say if you tried it?"

"What about?"

"About Timmy."

"If you think that would stop me, Sally, you're a fool. Nobody would believe you for an instant. They'd all think you were mad. I should simply deny it."

There was another long silence.

"I suppose you're right," Sally said at last. "Nobody would believe me. It would sound too grotesque." Her voice was low now. She sounded unhappy. I longed to put my arms round her to comfort her. What *was* it all about?

"I'll go and get dressed and cook us some dinner."

"Yes. All right. I'll let you go now. I'll have another drink and watch the news on BBC2."

A moment later I heard the television volume come on. There was a band playing. It was my opportunity. I turned the key, pulled open the door and escaped. I shut the door behind me and hoped that Sally would guess that I had gone that way and would lock the door. As I ran quickly down the stone stairs that led to the street below I looked at my watch. To my surprise it was not yet a quarter-to-eight. If I hurried I should be able to get to my cocktail party before it was over. I needed a drink. I needed a lot of drinks.

I hurried.

TWENTY-ONE

"How much did you hear?" Sally asked me. "Most of it, I suppose. I left when Freddie turned the television on."

We sat on my balcony over the remains of our lunch. It was the day following my narrow escape.

Sally had telephoned me early that morning. She had been very brief.

"Can you give me lunch at your flat?"

"Yes."

"I'll be there at one."

"I'll look forward to seeing you," I had started to say, but she had rung off.

I poured the last of the vin rosé – a very good Tavel – into our glasses, gave Sally a cigarette and lit a cigar for myself.

"What are we going to do?" she asked.

"Do you still love me?"

She nodded.

"I love you more than ever," I told her.

She smiled. It was the first smile she had managed since she arrived. It made me feel happier. So far I had had a nasty feeling that this was the end, that this was the last time I should see her.

"There are three things we can do," I said. "Either we can stop seeing one another and say goodbye now, and never see one another again." I hammered it in hard. "Or we can go on as before."

"What's the third thing?"

"You can leave Freddie and come and live with me. We could be very comfortable here."

"But, darling, what about the things he'll do? What about you? What about the Army?"

"I don't think he can do as much as he makes out. I've been thinking about that overnight. I don't think he could force me out of the Army unless he divorced you."

"But he would divorce me if I came and lived with you," Sally almost wailed. "What would you do then?"

"I've no idea, darling. But don't worry about it. I could find something. I've got quite a bit of money of my own. My father was killed in the war, you know, so we didn't pay death duties. My mother has most of the money during her lifetime, but one day I'll have quite a bit more."

"Could you live on what you've got now?"

"Not for ever. Besides I should get pretty bored doing nothing all day. I'll get a job all right." I attempted to exude a confidence I was far from feeling.

"Oh dear. I really would love to be married to you, Jimmy my darling. I should be so happy with you. You're such a nice person. But I should be miserable always if I lost Timmy."

"You might not lose him. Young children usually go to their mothers, when there's a divorce."

"But not always. He's three now anyway. He's not a baby. One day he'll be an Earl. The court might think that Freddie should bring him up."

"I suppose they might."

"There's a chance. I daren't take it."

I thought about it. "Then this is the end?" I said gloomily.

"Oh, no, darling. I couldn't bear never to see you again. Please don't say that."

"You want to go on as we've been doing?"

"Yes, please, Jimmy. If you'll take the risk, I will."

"Oh, I will, of course. I'm much too mad about you to

let you go now. I'll take you on any terms I can get you."

"Thank you, sweetheart." She kissed me.

She was being hopelessly illogical, but I didn't care.

"There's just one thing," I said.

"What is it?"

"Last night, when Freddie said he'd divorce you, you said that if he tried to you'd say something about Timmy, and he said nobody would believe you."

"Yes."

"What was all that about?"

"I'm sorry, Jimmy. I can't tell you."

"It's part of whatever it was that you couldn't tell me before, is it?"

"Yes, darling."

"Was that what you were relying on when you said to me that you could stop him from divorcing you?"

"Yes. And although he said nobody would believe me I still think it might do the trick if it ever came to it. I'd rather not tell you about it until the worst happens."

"All right, darling. I'll leave it at that."

"Can I have a glass of brandy, Jimmy, please? I've finished my wine."

I went inside and fetched a bottle and we both drank some. Now that we had made a decision we felt happier.

"You heard what Freddie said about his trip to the Far East, didn't you? It means that everything is all right for our holiday in Jamaica. It'll be lovely there, won't it, darling?"

"It'll be lovely here too," I said coarsely. "If you remember we were interrupted last night at a particularly interesting moment. Shall we go to the bedroom and go on where we left off?"

Sally laughed and stood up. "What a good idea. I was seducing you, wasn't I? But you were saved by the bell."

***

"Ladies and gentlemen, we shall be landing at Palisadoes Airport in ten minutes. Will you please extinguish your cigarettes and fasten your seat belts."

The lighted panels above the aisle read, less politely, 'No Smoking. Fasten Seat Belts.'

I reached over and took Sally's hand. "We're almost there, darling."

She smiled contentedly. "We're going to have a lovely holiday, aren't we, Jimmy?"

"Yes, Sally. A lovely holiday." And then what, I wondered?

It was a month later and the end of August. We had been able to see one another much less during that month. When the House of Commons had risen for the summer recess, Freddie and Sally had gone down to Highworth and I had been able to see her only when she had invented an excuse to come to London to shop or see her dentist or have her hair done. A week before we flew to Jamaica she had gone to Corsica with Timmy and his nanny, and she had flown back alone the day before. I had met her at the airport and had driven her straight to my flat. She wore a large pair of sunglasses and a Hermès scarf more or less covering her face. It would, we realised, be very difficult to explain her presence in London at that time, if it were reported to Freddie. It was a Saturday evening at the end of August and it was unlikely that there would be anyone about who knew us, but we had resolved to take as few chances as possible.

We stayed in my flat until it was time to go back to the airport. We drank my penultimate bottle of Dom Perignon and we made love with the sharpened desire of ten days' separation. We were very excited.

Very early the next morning we drove out to the airport. I had left my car in Chelsea Barracks for safety and we went in a mini-cab. We had agreed to keep our distance from each other until we took our seats on the aircraft. It would have been easy for either of us to explain our presence at the airport but virtually impossible if we were seen together. Sally wore her scarf and sunglasses again. We sat separately at the departure gate and were the last to board. We looked carefully at the other passengers but thankfully there was no one we knew.

The flight was long but uneventful. My watch said it was half-past nine in the evening when the stewardess made her announcement, but I knew that in Jamaica it was only half-past three in the afternoon.

"It looks as though we're going to land in the sea," said Sally, who sat next to the window and was looking out.

I glanced past her head and saw what she meant. Our Boeing was skimming along what seemed only a few feet above the water. We flew lower and lower. At the last moment when disaster seemed imminent, dry land appeared below us and at once we crossed the overgrown pedestrian crossing that was the threshold of the runway and our wheels thumped down on the concrete.

"We're in Jamaica," said Sally. "And I love you."

A wonderfully handsome policeman asked us how long we wished to stay in Jamaica and wrote in our passports that we had permission to remain for twenty-eight days. We walked out into the main hall of the airport building.

"Good afternoon, Major," said a slightly-built man in a black suit. "I am Jackson, sir. I received Captain Pershore's cable. The car is outside. If you give me your baggage checks, sir, I'll collect your baggage and take it to the car. Did you wish to go straight home now, sir? Or did you wish to stay in Kingston tonight?"

I gave him our tickets. "We hadn't really thought about it, Jackson. What do you recommend? Have we far to go?"

"Not very far, sir. It's a slow drive to the north coast, but we can be there by dinner time if you like."

I turned to Sally. She was looking round anxiously.

"What do you want to do, darling?"

"Let's go straight to the house, Jimmy. It'll be quiet there."

"Of course," I said. "We'd like to go to the house please, Jackson."

"Very well, sir. I'll show you and your lady the car, sir." He had large brown eyes and a soft deep voice. I decided I was going to like him.

The car, as I remembered Peter had told me, was an enormous old Buick. A massive air-conditioner fixed under the dashboard made the inside as cold as a refrigerator.

"That's better," said Sally, as we sank onto the back seat. "I thought I was going to pass out from the heat as we walked across the tarmac. It's much hotter here than it was in Corsica."

"What a globe-trotting girl you are. Corsica on Friday; London on Saturday; Jamaica on Sunday."

"And, thank heavens, no more travelling for at least three weeks. Whoever it was who said it was better to travel than to arrive didn't know about modern air travel."

While we were talking, Jackson and a porter appeared with our luggage and put it into the boot of the car and a minute later we were on our way.

Sally and I sat happily together, holding hands, and watching the strange scenery slip past as the big car drove round the narrow strip of land that encompasses Kingston's natural harbour and into the city itself.

I said to Sally, "I'm afraid this is our only opportunity to see anything very much of Jamaica. It would be too great a risk to do any exploring. It's low season but there is still that awful small-world chance that we could see, or be seen by, somebody who knows either of us."

Jackson had to drive slowly because the streets were crowded with cars, pedestrians, occasional tourists with cameras slung round their necks, young men selling juices from brightly-coloured carts and women carrying baskets of produce on their heads. But when we drove up the hill and out along the winding road which runs across the centre of the great island, our progress was not much quicker. Jackson was a slow and cautious driver and on one occasion we were held up by a horse and cart filled with waving girls in their school uniforms. We waved back.

When we saw the sea again at the north coast Jackson turned to the west, and we drove through Port Maria and along the coast road towards Oracabessa. It grew dark as we drove and when at last we reached the house we could see very little of the grounds. Jackson turned the car to the right through what looked like banana trees. The headlights lit up the house as the car swung round to stop at the front door and I saw the house was small and low-built and had a large roof with widely overhanging eaves. Jackson sounded the horn and got out of the car and held open the back door for Sally and me. As we climbed out, the hot night closed round us like a damp blanket. There was a loud noise of insects.

The front door opened and a girl in a white overall stood ready to greet us.

"This is Magnolia, sir and lady," said Jackson. "She is the cook and the maid."

Magnolia smiled at us, revealing a mouth seemingly overfull of dazzling white teeth. Her black eyes darted between me and Sally, taking in every detail. She was bold and very pretty. To my surprise she gave a little curtsey. Peter's aunt had obviously had old-fashioned ideas.

"Magnolia will show you the house while I bring in the bags, sir," said Jackson gently.

I nodded. "Thank you. We should like some dinner soon, if you can manage it. Then we shall go to bed. We're very tired."

He bowed, and I left him and followed Sally and Magnolia into the house. In the lighted hall I saw that Magnolia had the blackest skin that I had ever seen. It was so black that it was almost blue; not a shade of dark brown like most of the other people I had seen on our drive across the island. Why such a very black-skinned girl should have been called Magnolia I couldn't imagine. It seemed rather a poor joke. As she led us round the house I couldn't help watching the swaying of her curving hips and I remembered all that Peter had told me of his encounter with her on the beach. It gave me ideas. She showed us all the rooms, talking all the while in a sing-song voice impossible to reproduce on paper.

There were three bedrooms, each with its own bathroom. We saw ours last. It was obviously the 'master suite'. The rooms were cool with efficient silent-running air-conditioning. Peter's aunt had done herself well.

The drawing room was next to our bedroom and it faced the sea. The wall on the seaward side was made completely of glass and all the chairs and sofas were centred on this wall in the same sort of way that they might have centred on the fireplace in an English drawing room. The view was spectacular, even at night. The moon was full and high and it made the sea shine like a Household Cavalryman's cuirass.

We walked out of a French window onto a broad terrace which was bounded on the clifftop side by a low wall. There was a gap in the wall at one side and a steep flight of steps led down the cliff to the beach below. We went to the edge and looked down. The house was built so that it was at a slight angle to the shoreline and it faced roughly north-east. From the terrace we looked not only out to sea towards Cuba, a hundred miles away to the north, but also eastwards along the dark irregular coastline towards Port Antonio. The beach was shaped like a crescent moon, and it was too symmetrical to be entirely natural. I discovered later that someone had blasted the cliffs at various points to enlarge the area of the beach. The sand shone white in the moonlight. In the centre of the curve of the bay and right at the water's edge was a big black rock. It must have stood ten or twelve feet high and there seemed to be some sort of vegetation growing on top of it. The bay faced due north and it was easy to see that the beach would provide perfect privacy. There were no waves.

"The pool is here," said Magnolia, pointing along the terrace. She switched on some lights and the terrace was lit up by a number of concealed bulbs and we saw that a few yards away and up two shallow steps there was a small swimming pool. It was immediately outside our bedroom window. Magnolia pressed another switch and several underwater lights came on.

"It's just like your bath, darling," Sally laughed. "A bit bigger, that's all. It's going to be quite like home here."

We followed Magnolia back into the house and she showed us the dining room where the table was already laid for dinner. A door from the dining room led to the kitchen and the servants' quarters, which were not invited to inspect.

"Why is there a swimming pool when the sea is so close?" Sally wanted to know.

Magnolia beamed. "Old Mrs Pershore like to swim, man. But she no good at climbing stairs to beach. So she have pool put in. Is very nice pool. You want to swim before supper? Supper in thirty, forty minutes. Whatever you say."

"It would be rather nice, wouldn't it, Jimmy? I must have either a swim or a bath. A swim would wake me up. I feel as though I've been traveling for weeks."

I said, "A drink would help us too."

"All drinks in the drawing room," said Magnolia. "You like me to fetch you some drinks to the swimming pool?"

"No thank you, Magnolia. We'll help ourselves. Dinner in three-quarters of an hour?"

"Yessir." She bobbed and beamed and swayed off towards the kitchen. "Three-quarters of an hour," she sang to herself.

"We can undress in the bedroom," said Sally.

"I'll get us some drinks and join you there."

I met Jackson in the drawing room. He showed me a cupboard lavishly stocked with drinks of all sorts and I selected some scotch whisky and poured two generous rations into large tumblers half-filled with ice cubes.

Sally was walking around the bedroom in her underclothes. I gave her a glass.

"Darling, this is the most blissful place. We can have a wonderful time here without going anywhere. You are clever. It's absolutely perfect."

I stripped off my clothes and perched on the edge of the bed and sipped my drink and watched her as she moved about the room.

"The air-conditioning in here is terribly efficient," she went on. "There's a dial on the wall over there. You just set it to whatever temperature you want. It says 70 now, but it feels icy compared with outside."

"We're well inside the tropics. But the climate here is supposed to be very good. It never gets too hot."

"I'm dying for a swim. Do you think it would be safe to go in with nothing on? I have packed a couple of bikinis but I think they must be at the bottom of my suitcase."

"And you wouldn't want to wear one anyway," I grinned.

"Of course."

"I'll turn the outside lights off. Then I'm sure it'll be all right."

We found some bathing wraps in a wardrobe and put them on and walked out of the door which led directly from our bedroom onto the terrace by the pool. I found the light switches and turned them all off. Almost at once there was a splash as Sally dived in. A moment later she called out, "It's very warm, but just cool enough to be refreshing. Come on in."

I went to the edge of the pool. As my eyes grew accustomed to the darkness I made out Sally's pale skin in the centre of the pool. The moonlight was so bright that within a few seconds of switching off the lights I could see almost as clearly as if it were daylight.

I took off my bathing wrap and dropped it on a wooden seat which was just outside our bedroom window. I walked round the pool. The warm night was magnificently sensual on my body. The feeling of freedom which nudity gives, allied to the caress of the soft warm air, and combined with the controlled fire of the good whisky in my stomach made me feel tough, fit and randy.

I braced myself on the edge of the pool, sucked in my stomach muscles and raised my arms. Sally looked at me from the far end of the pool. She was exposed from the waist up and she looked like a perfectly-made marble statue.

"Come on, Apollo," she called. "Don't stand there all night."

I bent my knees and dived in. As I did so I heard, or thought I heard, a noise coming from the darkness of the garden at the end of the terrace. It sounded like a feminine giggle.

***

Magnolia proved to be the most excellent cook and Jackson was a deft and obviously well-trained butler. Our dinner was superb and we went to bed tired but happy, and full of good food.

"Anne was a fool to spurn this place because of the food," said Sally as we undressed. "I don't suppose she and Peter ate any better in France. I shall get as fat as butter with three weeks of this food."

"Nonsense," I said, patting her flat, almost concave, stomach. "Lots of exercise will keep you fit."

"What sort of exercise had you in mind, darling?"

"There are several possibilities. Two spring to my mind at once."

"Really? How fascinating. What can the second one be?"

"Swimming, of course. I've found a cupboard filled with skin-diving equipment – everything one could want. We can go out and explore the reef. There'll be all sorts of fishes to see, and masses of beautiful coral. It'll be great fun."

"It sounds all right." Sally sounded a little doubtful. "And skin-diving sounds particularly sexy. But don't you think we might be eaten by a shark or barracuda?"

"I don't think so."

"Will you look after me, Jimmy?"

"Of course, darling." I kissed her. I should like to look after you for ever, I thought.

When we were ready to go to bed I turned off the lights and drew back the curtains and we lay in bed staring out at the beauty of the night.

"We're going to be happy here, Jimmy, I know we are. Whatever happens in the future this is going to be a time that I shall always look back upon with happiness. It will be my own private fairy tale."

"Yes, darling," I said, kissing her lips. "Three weeks of heaven. It's more than most people have."

TWENTY-TWO

I woke early, soon after first light. Sally slept like an angel, her long eyelashes lying fan-like on her cheeks, her hair spilling all over the pillow. In the uncertain light her skin looked pale, with no trace of tan, and the disarranged bedclothes exposed one superb alabaster breast. I propped myself up on one elbow and watched her. As the light grew stronger her skin tone changed, first to a delicate pink and then to the soft golden-brown that I knew so well. At the same time her fat soft nipple turned from a dull brown to a rosy pink so that it looked like a cherry on an ice-cream.

It was still very early and I felt that it would be sensible to go back to sleep, but I was so wide awake that I knew that it would be a waste of time to try. I remembered when I had woken on my first morning at Highworth. Then I had known that I could not sleep again and I had got up and gone for a swim and I had seen Sally. Perhaps it would be a good idea to go for a swim now. Of course I shouldn't see Sally. But never mind. I could still have a swim.

It was then that I remembered Magnolia. Peter had found her swimming in the early morning. Perhaps she went every morning. It would be fun to catch her as he had. It would be only fair too. It must have been her who I had heard laughing in the garden as I stood naked on the edge of the pool the night before.

I swung quickly out of bed and pulled on my bathing wrap. Sally didn't stir. I quietly drew the curtains together so that the light wouldn't disturb her and let myself out onto the terrace.

It was a perfect morning. It was already warm, though

of course not nearly as hot as it would be later. There were masses of flowers at the ends of the terrace and tiny hummingbirds hovered round them. I walked to the top of the steps and looked down. The beach was deserted. There was not even a towel at the bottom of the steps. I was half-relieved, half-disappointed.

Oh well, I said to myself, I'll have a swim anyway. I went down the steps to the beach. The sand was cool under my feet. I had a careful look round at the clifftop. There was no one to be seen, so I took off my wrap and hung it on the end of the handrail at the bottom of the steps and walked down to the water's edge. To my right the sun had just risen over the Blue Mountains and it bathed the little cove in golden light. The sand was bright yellow.

I stopped when I reached the water and stood still while the tiny ripples washed my toes. There were no waves and the sea stretched away from my feet to the horizon without a blemish. At the edge the water was clear and translucent. As the water deepened so did the colour. It started with a pale aquamarine and ended with a strong vivid blue.

It was a great morning to be alive and a great place to be alive in. I drew a deep breath.

"Oh, man," said a soft sing-song voice from a few feet away. "Oh, man. That is good."

I turned my head to the left and saw Magnolia. She was stretched out on a flat rock less than a dozen feet away from me. I was not surprised to see that she was as naked as I was. She was smiling up at me, her white teeth shining.

She lay on the seaward side of the large rock which stood in the centre of the beach which was why I had not seen her before.

My first reaction was that I ought to cover myself up, but I had nothing but my hands with which to do so and that seemed too coy and maidenly. I stood still, my arms hanging loosely at my sides, and I looked with genuine appreciation at Magnolia. She looked as though she was made of India rubber and she had the earthy body of a young peasant. She was quite unlike Sally, who had a tiny waist and long beautiful legs; Magnolia's legs were short but strong and well-shaped. Her stomach was flat and muscular; her hips were broad and comfortable; her mound wore a sprinkling of what looked like wire wool; her breasts were high and full. They were her best feature I decided, as I inspected them. Later I learned that though she appeared fully mature, and probably was, she was still only seventeen years old at the time. Her extreme youth may have accounted for their outstanding qualities.

"You like me?" she asked, stirring slightly on her rock.

"You're a very pretty girl, Magnolia."

She beamed. "You're very pretty too, man. Very pretty. Would you like to do it with me, man? I'd sure like to do it with you."

"It's very kind of you," I said graciously. "But I'm afraid I have a previous engagement."

Magnolia smiled at me and let her eyes travel slowly down my body. She licked her lips. It wasn't difficult to guess what she was staring at, and the knowledge had a strange and unexpected effect on me. I had never been inside a nudist colony in my life, but I had read about them and talked to people who were prepared to admit that they had. Everyone said that men didn't get erections. They said it was impossible. The weird thing was that here I stood in a sort of nudist colony for two and there was absolutely no mistaking what was happening to me. I could feel my manhood swelling with every second that Magnolia stared at it. It just grew and grew.

At first I tried to resist. I told myself that I ought not to allow myself to behave like this, particularly not in front of a servant.

It was no good. I realised after a moment that I was enjoying it. An elemental feeling shot through me. I was a man; she was a woman. It seemed somehow right and proper that my body should salute hers in this way. She was a beautiful and very sexy-looking girl. The phrase 'Black is beautiful' kept running through my mind. It made a lot of sense.

It made a lot of sense also that Magnolia should stare with such obvious respect at my obvious maleness. Her look was almost one of worship. It was, I remembered, the earliest sort of religion.

She sat forward on the edge of her rock, her thighs pressed tightly together, her huge dark eyes staring, her large breasts heaving as her breathing quickened. Her pink tongue slowly licked her lips.

"Man," she gasped. "He is big."

I looked down. She was right. He seemed even bigger than usual as he pointed up at the sky like a mortar adjusted to maximum elevation. I was delighted with myself and the effect I was having on the nubile Magnolia.

She moaned. "Please, man. Come here. I want him."

The temptation to cross the few yards of sand which separated us was very nearly irresistible. Somehow I resisted it. I told myself later that it was my love for Sally which strengthened me, but if so I was quite unconscious of it at the time. I didn't even think about Sally.

We remained like a tableau for perhaps a minute. I felt like a god. Suddenly Magnolia started to move towards me. Although my body wanted to remain my brain came to life at last. I walked forward into the sea. When the water was up to my thighs I threw myself forward and swam vigorously towards the reef. When I had gone a fair distance I stopped swimming, turned on my back and looked at the beach. There was no sign of Magnolia.

***

After that I kept away from the beach in the early morning. Whenever I woke up feeling that I wanted a swim I contented myself with the swimming pool. Sally slept so deeply in the mornings that I always did so on my own. Once I went to the edge of the terrace and looked down. Sure enough, there was Magnolia splashing about in the shallows, her magnificent body shining wetly in the early morning sunshine. She saw me standing there and waved and beckoned to me to come down. I smiled and shook my head and turned away. I didn't trust myself.

I said nothing to Sally. It seemed unfair to tell her that I had been tempted to be unfaithful to her, and with the cook of all people. It would only make her unhappy, and I didn't think it would improve her feelings about me. She loved me and she trusted me. I was happy to leave it at that. After all, I told myself, I hadn't been unfaithful. On the contrary, I had been very faithful indeed; I had resisted a very powerful and attractive temptation. Yet somehow I failed to convince myself.

Our days were uneventful but deeply satisfying and fell into a comfortable routine. It sounds an almost ridiculous thing to say, but they were in fact the happiest days of my life. Sally and I were continually in one another's company and we grew to know one another better and to love one another more than I would ever have dreamed possible a few months earlier.

We didn't leave the house and its grounds. The weather was consistently superb and we were content to stay where we were. We had breakfast on the terrace and spent the morning on the beach and in the sea. The reef was close to the beach and we could swim to it in a couple of minutes. We spent hours exploring it and looking at the fishes.

After luncheon we went to bed for an hour or two before swimming again. In the early evening we dressed and sat on the terrace and drank and talked and watched the sun go down, and then we had dinner and went back to bed.

We made love whenever we felt like it – mostly in bed; often on a towel on the beach; once in the sea; once under the shower in our bathroom. But basically it is true to say that during those days sex ceased to be the prime reason for our relationship. It diminished in importance until it became simply a part of us. Sally summed it up when she said, "When we first met I wanted terribly to go to bed with you. I couldn't really think beyond that. I was horribly frustrated and I wanted a man. Before I even saw you I decided you were the man I wanted, just on the basis of what Anne had told me about you. When I actually met you it was almost unbearable. Then we became lovers – in the physical sense I mean. It was even more wonderful than I thought it was going to be, but at the same time I was surprised to find that I liked you too. I hadn't really thought of you as a person before that. You were just a big attractive man who was going to go to bed with me, if I could possibly manage it. Then practically at once I discovered that you were a real person and that I liked you. Soon after that I realised that I loved you. I don't know why it happened so quickly. I suppose it was a combination of things – partly because I liked you, partly because I thought you were attractive, partly because I found I rather respected you, partly because the sex was so good. The sex part was very important to begin with. I couldn't really think of anything except when you were going to make love to me next. I thought of it all the time, of how exciting and messy and super it all was. I was in a permanent state of sexual arousal. I was just besotted by sex. Now it's all different. Sex is still marvellous and I adore it, but it's not the only thing in our lives. It seems to be that you only worry about sex either when you aren't getting any or if there's something wrong with it. When it's perfect, as it is with us, it doesn't seem to be so important. I just accept it now as a part – a very nice part – of our love for one another."

We both wished that we could stay on for ever, but we accepted tacitly that we could not. As we entered the third week of our stay the days seemed to be racing by, no sooner had the sun come up in the morning than it was evening again.

One morning we had spent an hour swimming on the reef and had come back to flop onto the huge towel that we used for sunbathing. We took off our goggles and flippers and stretched out on our backs to let the sun dry us.

"That was splendid." Sally lay back on the towel and threw her arms out wide. "This is the life all right. I've never been so happy. I never dreamed it was possible to be so happy. And it's all thanks to you, Jimmy."

I poured a generous dollop of Ambre Solaire into my right palm and began to anoint Sally's body. I did every bit of her from her neck to her ankles. She lay back making happy little noises from time to time.

"Oh darling," she almost whispered. "You have very clever fingers."

"I've been very well taught," I replied, foolishly. I was

befuddled by sun and the feel of her lovely body under my hand.

"By all your girlfriends?"

"No. Just one."

"Anne?"

"Before Anne."

"Then who?"

"I don't want to tell you."

"Why on earth not?"

I paused, wondering how much I would have to tell her, while wishing I hadn't said what I had in the first place. "You will be shocked if I tell you."

"No, I won't."

"She was older than me."

Sally, whose eyes had been closed so far, now opened them wide and stared up at me. "How much older?"

"About twenty-five years, maybe more."

Sally raised herself on one elbow and said, "I *am* shocked."

"You said you wouldn't be," I pointed out, futilely.

Sally looked very serious. "Tell me more. Much more, I think. Who was she?"

"A very smart middle-aged woman who picked me up in a picture gallery."

"Tell me all about it. About her," Sally said firmly.

"All?"

"Oh, yes, absolutely all," she insisted. "I love hearing about your past. You know that."

"You're a most unusual girl."

"Good. Then you won't forget me." She smiled happily up at me. "When did it happen?"

"Two years ago. I was at a loose end one day so I went in to look at the pictures. There were very few people there. I found myself looking at portraits of the Emperor Napoleon and his first wife, Josephine.

"'Do you think she's attractive?' asked a woman standing next to me. I looked round to see who she was talking to. There was no one else around. She looked at me. She had a twinkle in her eyes that I had come across many times in the past. I smiled at her.

"'She's not pretty.' I nodded at Josephine.

"'No, she's not – but attractive perhaps?'

"'If she smiled. But her mouth is shut.'

"'That's because she had no teeth. Just black stumps, caused by chewing sugar cane when she was a girl in Martinique.'

"'What a pity,' I said.

"'But she was very good in bed. Napoleon was besotted by her, but she was flagrantly unfaithful to him. She didn't really love him, I don't think. She had lots of lovers who said how good she was. She had a particular trick which she called her zig-zags.'

"'What were they?'

"'Nobody knows. History doesn't record that. But I think I've worked it out. Would you like me to show you what she did?'

"I turned to have a proper look at her. She was beautifully turned out. She wore a pretty suit – Chanel I thought; crocodile shoes and handbag, pearls and a small diamond brooch. She was quite tall and lean, rather than thin. She was obviously middle-aged but I saw that she must have been very pretty when young. Her face now was handsome and amused-looking. Her eyes were large and deep brown. She was almost laughing.

"All this I took in in a moment. I decided to take a chance.

"'Yes please,' I said, smiling at her.

"She nodded. 'Good. Shall we go? We'll get a taxi. It isn't very far.'

"We walked together, but not touching, towards the exit.

"'You're a soldier, aren't you?' she said.

"'Yes. But how can you tell?' I wasn't wearing a Regimental tie.

"'Your bearing and your highly-polished shoes. It's obvious. My first husband was a soldier and you walk just like him and he had lots of lovely shoes. What sort of soldier are you?'

"'I'm a Captain in the Foot Guards,' I told her. She looked pleased.

"We left the building and hailed a taxi. She told the cabbie where to go and we climbed in. I didn't hear the address she gave but she was right. It wasn't far. We stopped outside a block of flats in Curzon Street. I paid the taxi and we went in and took a lift up a few floors. She opened the door of her flat and led the way in. I followed. The flat looked nice. She went into the bedroom.

"'What is your name?' she asked. I told her. 'I shall call you Jamie,' she said. 'It's my favourite name.' I'd never been called Jamie before but I didn't mind. 'I'm Louise.'

"She took off the jacket of her suit. She had a cream silk shirt underneath. 'It's such a hot day that I think we ought to have a shower. Take all your clothes off and go to the bathroom.' She pointed at a door. 'I'll join you in a moment. I'll just undress too.' She disappeared through an arch into what I later discovered was her dressing room.

"Five minutes later we were both in the shower together. There was plenty of room for two. She produced some soaps and she started to wash me. She made a thorough job of it. 'You can wash me too,' she said. I was hesitant. 'It's all right. I shall enjoy it.'

"I got going. Her body was slender, her stomach was flat, her breasts small but firm and high. She was completely hairless. It was the first time I had come across a woman with no pubic hair.

"When we decided we were clean we got out and she gave me a towel. You won't be surprised to hear that I had an erection."

Sally giggled. "No. I'm not. But go on."

"Well, she looked me up and down.

"'You have a nice body,' she said.

"'So have you,' I told her. 'You look and feel very fit.'

"'I swim every day,' she said.

"She looked at my penis. She said nothing. After a bit I said, 'Is it all right?'

"'Oh, yes.'

"'Is it… er?'

"'Big enough you mean? Certainly. I've seen many erections over the years, some bigger, some smaller, but size isn't important, you know. Men always worry about it, but you're *all* wrong. It isn't the size that's important. It's what you do with it that's the interesting thing. Anyway, lips and tongue and fingers are much more important. Let's go to bed and you can show me what you do with your willie.'

"We did – and I did. I thought it went rather well but I was in for a shock.

"'That wasn't too bad,' she said. She was lying back with her head on a large pillow. 'You were too quick. You'll have to learn to slow down. And I didn't come, you know.' She smiled quite cheerfully. 'You've got a lot to learn, but I shall enjoy teaching you.'"

"That's what you said to me," said Sally. "And you have," she added happily. "But go on. Tell me more. I'm still rather shocked."

"Well, that was the beginning. It lasted about three months and she taught me well. First she told me that her first husband had said that when dealing with a machine gun he was taught 'stripping and assembling and names of parts.'

"'Well,' Louise said, 'I've stripped you and now I shall start to assemble you.'

"'What about names of parts?'

"She laughed. 'Perhaps later, when I know you better.'"

Sally said, "Did she give Egbert a name?"

"She did, but I'm not going to tell you what it was."

"You must. We tell one another everything. Well, almost everything," she added quietly.

"All right. She called me her 'Toy'. She said she liked playing with her Toy."

Sally screamed with laughter. "Of course," she said. "You were her toyboy, weren't you?"

"She told me that almost all girls who really like sex are fascinated by their lover's willies and usually give them a nickname."

"That seems to be right," said Sally. "I felt I needed to name Egbert. I'd got to know him as a sort of person and I've become very fond of him." She stretched out a hand and gave him a soft sensual squeeze of appreciation. "Did you have any other girlfriends at the same time as Louise?"

"No. I didn't. I'd just come back from Germany when I met her and I hadn't found anyone interesting. 'Why did you pick me up?' I asked Louise one day when we were lying on her bed, dozing after a most enjoyable bout of love-making. 'What attracted you?'

"'Well Jamie, if you want honesty…'

"'I do.'

"She thought for a moment. 'You're not beautiful, but

you have a nice face. I thought you looked as though you were a good man. You were big and strong-looking and you were very well-dressed. You wore a beautiful suit. All your suits are very well cut, very smart. I'd been following you around that gallery for a while and you seemed to like the sort of pictures I like. I decided you were just what I wanted.'"

"Just like me," Sally interjected. "You said it lasted for three months. How did it end?" she asked.

"We got to know one another well. We didn't spend all our time in bed. Several times we went to the cinema which was almost next door. There was a nice little restaurant in Shepherd Market where we often had dinner and we talked about all sorts of things; current affairs mostly. She loved politics. Also history. She read masses, she had lots of books. But also lots of erogenous zones. She found those fascinating."

"What are they?" Sally asked.

"They're parts of the body which are particularly sexually stimulating."

"How many are there? Have I got any?"

"Darling Sally, you certainly have, your whole body is thoroughly erogenous."

"Really? How lovely. I like that." She stroked my chest. "I'm sure you have lots too."

"I guess so. You certainly stimulate me."

"Go on with your story. What ended it?"

"One day we were in her drawing room drinking gin and tonic before we went out to dinner. She suddenly said, 'Jamie, do you love me?'

"I liked her very much but I wasn't actually in love with her. I didn't want to hurt her feelings so I said 'Yes, I do.'

"She looked at me thoughtfully. She looked rather sad.

After a while she said, 'I don't believe you. I've known real love several times, though not for ages now.'

"I'd learnt that her first husband had been killed in the war – in Italy in 1943 – and she'd loved him very much. After that she had two other marriages and countless lovers. She adored sex.

"'I'd be able to tell if you were,' she went on. 'But you're not. However, I could put up with our friendly sexy relationship for quite a long time. Unfortunately I've fallen in love with you, and that presents a difficulty.'

"I didn't know what to say.

"She went on, 'I'll explain it to you. Because I love you – and I love you very much and I've adored our time together – I want to keep you to myself for the rest of my life and that would be wrong. It would be terribly unfair to you. We never talk about our respective ages and I'm not going to tell you even now how old I am. Your age and your life are what is important now. You must find a nice girl to marry. You must love her and she must love you. The only lesson I haven't been able to show you is that when two people – of any sex – truly love one another their sexual congress, let's call it, moves onto a higher, more rarefied plane. It becomes a spiritual as well as a physical thing. It is heavenly. Truly wonderful. That's what you must go for and I wish you all the luck in the world in finding that. You and I can never experience that together. So we must part. I love you dearly and my love is proved by my letting you go.' I was dumbfounded."

I told Sally, "I didn't know what to say. 'Must I go? I don't want to,' I eventually told her.

"'Tomorrow morning,' Louise said firmly. 'We'll go out to dinner now – our last dinner, and we'll have all our favourite things to eat and drink. Then we'll go to bed for a last long night of wonderful sex and in the morning I shall pour you into your clothes and say goodbye. I expect I shall cry a bit but you mustn't try to persuade me to change my mind. You're going to be a brave soldier.' And that's exactly what happened," I told Sally.

"Oh, dear," she said. "What a sad story. I feel like crying myself. Poor Louise. Did you ever see her again?"

"No, I didn't. I was sent abroad a few months later – to Aden. When I came back the following year I thought I would look her up – not for sex – but because I wondered how she was getting on. I rang her number but got an unobtainable noise so I went round to her flat. There was no answer at her door so I found the hall porter who recognised me. I asked about Louise. 'Hello, sir,' he said. 'I remember you very well. You had that big blue Jaguar. The lady left at the end of last year. She sold her flat and she went.'

"'Where to?'

"'She wouldn't tell me or give me a forwarding address. She just said she had decided to live abroad.'

"And that was that," I told Sally.

"She didn't want to see you again because she wasn't sure she could trust herself," said Sally sensibly. "I suppose you could put a detective onto it. But that would be wrong."

"I agree. There was no merit in doing anything about her.

"A few months later I met Anne and you know the rest." I paused. "But that's all in the past, just part of my history. What she taught me has helped me to be the good lover that you deserve in view of your peculiar life so far."

"It has been peculiar," she agreed. "Now everything is different and wonderful and I'm so very happy. But I don't agree with one thing she said to you." She raised a hand and stroked my cheek. "She said you weren't beautiful.

She's wrong. You are."

I smiled down at her. "That's love talking. Louise later said that she'd had several beautiful lovers but they were all really mostly in love with themselves. They couldn't resist looking at their reflections in any mirror or shop window that was available."

"You don't seem to be too pleased with yourself," said Sally. "Did you tell Anne about Louise?"

"No. I never told anyone – until now."

"Why not?"

"I was sort of ashamed of myself. Although I'd had a wonderful time with her I was sure that I didn't want anyone to know about her."

"Why not?" she repeated.

"Well. I suppose I was afraid I would be a laughing stock if it was known that I, a twenty-eight-year-old Captain in the Infantry and a pretty big and tough one at that, had been the toyboy of an old lady."

"Ouch," Sally winced. "I understand. I won't tell anyone. I promise. But I'm truly glad you told me about her. I don't think any the less of you for it. It makes you an even more rounded person, and the fact that she taught you so much about sex has been a boon for me." She beamed up at me. "Now I know where the zig-zags come from. Clever Josephine. I adore them."

I felt a sweeping sense of relief. I had got all that off my chest. I was content. My love for Sally was now total and uncomplicated and pure and I knew it would last for ever.

I said, "Sally, darling. Let's go on being happy. Let's stay together always. Let's get married."

There was a pause. I had a strong feeling that I had done it badly, been too abrupt. I should have led up to it gently. I had had long enough to prepare a proper speech. I had in fact done so, I had been thinking about it for days and I had thought of all sorts of attractive and convincing things to say to her. Now I could remember none of them. There was just one thing I knew I ought to add.

"I love you, Sally. I'll *always* love you."

There was another pause. Sally lay back on the towel, her green eyes shining up at me.

"Darling Jimmy," she said at last. "You're very good and I should love to marry you."

"You *will?*"

"Yes, darling. I will."

I could scarcely believe my good fortune. I tried to speak, but found that I couldn't. I bent over and kissed her instead. Later I said, "I really will do my best to make you happy."

"I know you will, Jimmy. And I'll do my best to make you happy too, darling."

"You'll do that just by marrying me. How soon do you think we can arrange it?"

"I don't know. Freddie and I will have to get divorced. I'll try to persuade him to let *me* divorce *him*, but I don't care awfully. If he divorces me I suppose he'll cite you as co-respondent. Will that mean you'll have to leave the Army?"

"I expect so. But we won't worry about that now. It'll take months to get the divorce through, won't it?"

"Yes. But I'll come and live with you straightaway – if you'll have me."

"You bet. I don't think I could bear to be separated from you now. We will try never to be apart, won't we?"

"Yes, darling. We will."

Sally jumped to her feet and pulled me up after her. "Let's have another swim," she said. "I'm so excited and happy I think I need to cool off. Thank you for asking me to marry you, Jimmy. I'll try to be a good wife to you."

"You'll be the best wife in the world." I took her hand and we walked together down to the sea.

When we were half-way between the cliff and the water a yacht appeared round the little headland to our right and moved across our little bay. It was just beyond the reef and no more than a hundred and fifty yards from us. It was a three-masted yacht, but it had no sail set and I could hear its engine. There was almost no breeze that morning.

It was a smart and expensive-looking boat, with lots of fresh white paint and well-polished brass, and four or five well-dressed people on the deck at the stern. It was obvious that they had seen us.

"How very embarrassing," I said to Sally. "Shall we lie down or run straight into the sea?"

"It's too late now," said Sally calmly. "They've seen everything there is to see." She waved at the yacht and one of the men waved back. We seemed to be causing considerable amusement on board.

We walked casually forward into the water as though there was nothing peculiar about our nudity, and then we dived forward and swam. Just before we reached the sea I saw that one of the men had found a large pair of field-glasses and had trained them on us. It was unpleasant knowing that we were being so closely examined and I was glad to get under the water. I stayed under for as long as I could and when I surfaced the white yacht was some distance away. The man with the field-glasses was still watching us. I scowled at him.

"Don't worry, darling," said Sally, swimming beside me. "We love one another, and we're going to be together always. Let him look at us. Nothing can harm us now."

But she was wrong.

TWENTY-THREE

The next twenty-four hours were the happiest hours of the happiest days of my life. Looking back upon them now, it seems like a dream. I know that I was happy. I knew at the time that I was happy. Both Sally and I remarked upon it frequently.

We had a marvellous time. We talked incessantly, making plans for the future. We ate and drank and made love. We were drunk with excitement as much as with all the champagne that we drank. It was superb. We felt god-like.

That afternoon we drove along the coast to Dunn's River and climbed the Falls. It was exhilarating. There were very few people about, but of course we had put on bathing things. It was the first time I had seen Sally in a bikini and I was so excited that when we returned to the car we got into the back and were there for quite a long time…

We spent the next morning on the beach. It was to be our last morning in Jamaica, and we wanted to make the most of it. As we came ashore after our swim Sally said, "Let's come back here for our honeymoon, darling. There can't be anywhere in the world that would be better for us than this."

I agreed. "It is perfect."

"Egbert likes it here too," said Sally, playfully running a hand down the front of my body and taking a prisoner. "He's put on weight, I'm sure," she said, laughing up at me. "I think he needs more exercise."

I smiled down at her. My chest was bursting with happiness and love. It was the greatest joy that I had ever known.

In a sense our love reached its apogee at that instant.

"Darling Sally," I said, smiling into her heartbreakingly beautiful green eyes. "Egbert and I love you very much."

And then everything went wrong.

Click.

Click. Click.

"What's that?" she said.

We turned our heads.

A few feet away from us stood a man in a gaily-patterned shirt and yellow trousers. He was holding an expensive-looking camera in front of his face.

Click.

He took the camera away from his face and wound on the film with a quick experienced movement. For a moment I thought it was Freddie. Then I realised that it was his cousin, Quintin.

"Very pretty," he said. "Very pretty pix, my dears."

I started forward towards him. He held up a hand.

"No rough stuff," he said. "For your own benefit."

He was standing in the lee of the great rock. It was obvious that he had been hiding behind it while we swam. He could hardly have chosen his moment better.

I said "Give me that camera," in what I hoped was a menacing tone.

He stepped back a pace, made a small adjustment to the camera and raised it to his face again.

Click.

I realised that he had aimed it past me at Sally. I turned and looked at her.

"Quintin," she almost wailed. "No. Please don't."

Even in her misery she looked supremely beautiful. She had made no effort to cover her naked body.

"Give me the camera," I said again. I felt the anger

rising inside me. The disgusting little brute was spoiling everything. The love that Sally and I had for one another was sacred. We should have remained alone and undisturbed in our paradise. Now this horrible creature had come blundering in to make it dirty.

The first thing to do was to get the film. Later I could sort out the repulsive Quintin.

I jumped forward. Quintin jumped back.

"Toby," he called urgently. "Toby."

Another figure emerged from behind the rock and stood next to Quintin. He was a gigantic black man. He must have topped me by at least four inches and he was about three yards wide. I hesitated. It would be like attacking a London bus.

Toby grinned unpleasantly. He wore a white shirt and black trousers, both of which looked to be several sizes too small. His size sixteen feet were encased in highly-polished black leather shoes.

"Come on, man," he said. "Come and get me." He looked past me at Sally and licked his lips.

"I thought you might want to get rough," said Quintin. "So I brought Toby along. He can teach you a lesson. I hope you'll be unwise enough to attack him."

He produced a camera case, which was hanging from his shoulder by a strap, and put his camera away.

"I could have taken these pictures with a telephoto lens," he said, "but I couldn't resist seeing your faces when you knew you'd been caught." He laughed. "I'll be on my way now," he went on. "I must get these developed and printed. I'll bring some prints for you to see this evening. I think I should be able to be with you at about sevenish. We can all have a friendly drink together and I'll tell you what I've got planned."

He turned and started to walk up the beach towards the steps. When he had gone a few yards he turned and said, "You won't try anything silly this evening, will you? You'd regret it dreadfully if you did." He gave a little wave and resumed his journey.

I hadn't much time. If he got away with those photographs Sally and I were in trouble.

"Wait a minute," I called. "Let's talk about this. Don't go yet."

"We'll talk this evening." He kept walking.

I looked at Toby. He crouched, waiting for me, his two huge fists looking like the hams which hang in the window of Paxton and Whitfield's shop in Jermyn Street. "Come on, man," he breathed. "Come on."

I advanced quickly towards him. I hadn't the time to be devious.

Toby telegraphed a gigantic blow with his right and I swayed back out of range. I felt pleased with myself. This was going to be easier than I had thought. He was too big to be quick.

The handful of sand which he must have concealed in his left hit me straight in the eyes. It hurt. I put up my hands to rub it from my eyes. I was almost blinded.

I heard Sally scream from behind me and then I felt a searing agony tear through my body as Toby's hard leather shoe caught me squarely in the naked testicles. I doubled up and crashed to the ground unable to speak, unable to move, as wave upon wave of the most excruciating pain I had ever felt wracked my twisted body.

As though from a great distance I heard Quintin laughing.

"I think that makes us quits, old boy," he called. "Come on, Toby. That'll be all."

They went away.

I knew that Sally was somewhere near me. I could hear her crying but I couldn't think of anything except the pain. I wanted to lose consciousness. Infuriatingly I couldn't.

Eventually I got a grip on myself and I tried to open my eyes. I dared not move. The pain was too much. It had become just bearable if I didn't move. I lay quite still.

I felt water being splashed on my face. Sally was washing the sand from my eyes. I was grateful for that. It wasn't the pain in my eyes that I was worried about. That was quite submerged in the greater pain in my stomach. I was afraid that the agony of the kick had brought tears to my eyes, and I didn't want Sally to think that I was weeping. I know that it was a foolish thing to worry about, but that didn't seem to matter.

Sally was being very sensible and keeping her head. She was talking to me gently. After a while I could make out the words.

"...Just lie here quietly, darling. You just lie here until you feel better. I'll stay with you. When you're well enough to walk I'll get you up the steps. Then you must go to bed. You're not to worry about Quintin. You're not to worry about anything. We'll sort everything out later. You'll see."

I looked up at her. She was squatting beside me on the sand. She looked abject.

"Are you all right now, darling?" she asked.

"I think so."

"Can you move?"

"I'll have a try."

"Does it hurt awfully?"

I nodded.

There was a clatter of feet on the steps. We looked round. Magnolia and Jackson were hurrying down.

"They locked us in the broom cupboard, man," called

Magnolia. "Jackson broke the door down."

Sally stood up, walked quickly to our towel and put on her bathing wrap. She picked up mine and returned to me. Magnolia and Jackson reached me at the same time. They were panting from their exertions.

"I'm so very sorry, sir and lady," said Jackson. "They just took us by surprise. First the English gentleman said you were expecting him, and when I said I'd announce him he got nasty and that big bad man put us in the cupboard and locked the door. What did they do here, sir?"

Sally replied, "They attacked us. They kicked my husband. Will you help him up to the house, please, Jackson. I don't think he can walk very well."

They fussed round, helping me into my bathing wrap, and then I managed to walk slowly up the steps, leaning heavily on Jackson as I did so. In the midst of the pain in my body and the torment in my mind was one small gem of pleasure. Sally had called me her husband. It had sounded good, and I was determined that nothing should be allowed to interfere with our future. Somehow I should have to find a way to silence Quintin.

***

"How do you feel now, darling?"

"Not too bad."

"Do you think the codeine are starting to work?"

"I expect so. Do you think I could have a drink?"

"I suppose it would be all right. What would you like?"

"Something long and cool with a lot of rum in it. Not the dark rum, the pale stuff."

"All right, Jimmy. I'll get it for you. You stay there. Do you think we ought to get a doctor to have a look at you?"

"No thank you, darling. I'll be all right."

Sally managed a smile. "Oh, darling. I do hope you will be. It would be the last straw if you weren't."

She left me lying on the bed and went through into the drawing room.

I lay back on the pillows and thought of what I would like to do to Quintin. The pain was much less acute now.

Sally returned with a long glass of liquid in a few minutes. "I've invented a special sort of Planter's Punch for you," she said, presenting it to me. "It's got everything in it."

I drank some. "It's delicious. Two of these will put me on my feet."

"Two of those will put you on your back for the afternoon, which is the best place for you. I've been doing some thinking and I've decided what I'm going to do."

"What?"

"Well. You remember that man with the field-glasses on the yacht yesterday. It's obvious that must have been Quintin. I had a feeling at the time that there was something familiar about him. He didn't know we were here before that or we should have had a visit earlier. It was just our bad luck that he happened to come past when he did. It's the most grotesque coincidence. Anyway, there it is. He's caught us, and he'll be back this evening to show us those photographs and to tell us what he wants in exchange for the negatives."

"He wants *you*."

Sally nodded. "Yes. He's wanted me for ages. I expect he wants me to be his mistress."

"You don't think he wants you on a more permanent basis?"

"Marriage, you mean? Oh, no. He's far too attached to Freddie to want to break up our marriage."

"He has a pretty strange set of values, if you ask me."

Sally said nothing for a moment. Then she said, "Jackson is going to drive me out in the car to go along the coast to look for that yacht. It shouldn't be hard to find."

"What's the point?" I asked.

"I've known Quintin for years. I might be able to talk some sense into him if you're not there. He *hates* you."

"Shall I come with you? I could wait in the car."

"No. You stay here and rest. Then you'll be in good form for this evening if I can't deal with him this afternoon."

"What do you suppose he proposes to do with the photographs? He is going to say in effect: 'Go to bed with me or I'll do something with these photographs.' But what?"

"I suppose he'll send them to Freddie."

I smiled at her. "Do we care? The worst thing that can happen will be that Freddie will divorce you. We want him to do that anyway."

"I'd rather that he allow me to divorce him."

"That might still be possible." I laughed. Poor Quintin. I was going to have a lovely time that evening. "Don't bother to look for the yacht, Sally. When he threatens to send the photographs to Freddie we'll just laugh in his face."

Sally was silent for a while. "You're probably right, darling," she said eventually. "I'll think about it. On the whole I think it would be better if I got the negatives back. It makes me feel quite peculiar to think of Quintin looking at those pictures. Do you understand, Jimmy?"

"Yes of course. You go if you want to. Take care of yourself."

"Quintin's quite harmless. He really does love me in his way, you know."

She kissed me and left and I finished my drink and eased my body down in the bed. The mixture of codeine and rum had almost taken away the pain and I felt sleepy. My last thought as I drifted off to sleep was that I had told Sally that I was going to be all right. But suppose that I wasn't. Suppose that never again could I hold Sally in my arms and…

I slept.

***

When I woke up I was pouring with sweat, though I was covered only by a sheet. I kicked it off and lay there panting. The sun had moved round a bit and the terrace looked different. I glanced at my watch which was all I wore. I had been asleep an hour.

The bedroom door opened and shut. I turned my head. Sally was here, I told myself. But no. It was only Magnolia. She swayed over to the bed and stood looking down at me. She had a big inviting smile on her sexy face and a dark green medicine bottle in her hand. I knew I ought to cover myself up but my legs and arms didn't want to move and, anyway, I told myself, she's seen it all before.

"How're you feeling, man?" she sang softly.

"All right, thank you Magnolia," I grinned at her. "Where's my wife?"

"She and Mr Jackson has gone in the motor. They left about thirty minutes ago. They're not coming back for a long time. We is all alone here."

"Oh."

Magnolia sat down on the edge of the bed. She licked her thick lips and looked with interest at my exposed body.

"That bad man do very bad thing to you. I hear the pain is very big."

"That's right, Magnolia. It's not pleasant." As I had on the beach on my first morning in Jamaica I found that I was enjoying having Magnolia looking at me. The white dress she wore made her look like a nurse; and nurses are sexy.

"And now you's worried to know if you's still a man?"

I didn't know what to say to that, so I said nothing.

She held up the green bottle. "This lotion is very soothing. It make you well soon."

I wondered what it was. My over-excited imagination conjured up a picture of a witch doctor in full regalia stirring something in a cauldron. "I suppose you got it from your local obeah man?"

"No, man," Magnolia looked a bit puzzled. "It come from Boots the Chemists."

"Well, I suppose that's all right then. Do I drink it or what?"

"You put it on and rub it in. I show you what to do."

It was tempting. It wasn't every day that beautiful girls offered to massage me in the most intimate way imaginable.

"I don't think you'd better, Magnolia. It might have an… er… unfortunate result."

"What unfortunate result?"

"Er… it might… er… excite me too much."

"Like on the beach that morning, you mean," she sang excitedly. "But that would be good, man. That was a beautiful thing to see, man. I do it now, and if that happened to you again you would know you is well. Lotion is good for you anyway."

She uncorked the bottle and poured a little of the lotion into the palm of her left hand. She put the bottle on the bedside table and dipping the tips of her long fingers into the liquid she leaned forward and started to anoint me.

My stomach muscles tightened in apprehension of pain but Magnolia's touch was so gentle that I felt nothing but pleasure. Almost at once a delicious warm feeling started to spread through the lower part of my body.

The top buttons of Magnolia's dress were undone, and as she leaned forward to perform her ministrations my eyes were drawn to the deep cleavage between her breasts. Magnolia looked into my eyes, no doubt to find out how I was enjoying my massage, and saw where I was looking. She sat back and smiled at me.

"Would you like to do it with me, man? I is excited now. It would be good. I know you is a good lover."

I stared at her. I stopped looking at her cleavage but the material of her dress was very thin and I could see that her nipples were thickly erect. Why did she think I was a good lover? She must have seen Sally and me making love on the beach. We had been sure that we could not be overlooked there, but Magnolia knew the place better than we did and we had often enjoyed prolonged periods of love-making in the sunshine.

"Magnolia. I would love to make love to you. I am sure you would be a wonderful lover too. But, you see, I am very much in love with my wife and I simply cannot be unfaithful to her. I hope you understand."

She looked at me for a long moment. "I do understand. I am sorry, man." She looked down at her handiwork which she had not released. Then she bent down and gently kissed it, stood up, took her bottle and her leave.

I watched her go. She closed the door quietly behind her. I stared out of the window. I felt half-pleased with myself and half-sorry that I had missed a wonderful sexual adventure. It seemed I was growing up. But what about Magnolia? What a girl she was! I knew somehow that she was one of nature's ladies. I felt sure she wouldn't tell, and I turned out to be right. I liked her and I respected her. She was really something: beautiful to look at; a cordon bleu in the kitchen; and probably a beatific lover in the bedroom. What a girl indeed! Whoever got her in the end would be the luckiest man on Jamaica.

TWENTY-FOUR

I was asleep when Sally returned. I woke to find her sitting on the bed beside me. She looked sad.

"How do you feel, darling?" she asked me.

"Much better, thank goodness. How did you get on?"

She shook her head sadly. "It was no use, Jimmy. We couldn't find the yacht. We looked as far as we could. He'd never get there and back in time if he was as far away as Montego Bay."

"He may have left the yacht."

"Yes. I suppose so. Anyway that's that. Now we'll just have to wait and see what he says this evening."

"Don't worry, Sally. It'll be all right. We'll play it by ear, but I think we just tell him to go ahead and send the horrible things to Freddie, don't you?"

"I don't know, darling. I don't know anything any more. Except that he's taken away a part of our love for each other and I'd like to get it back."

"I'll get it back for you, darling. I expect he'll have made careful arrangements so that we don't beat him up when he comes here. It'll probably be impossible to achieve anything then. But perhaps I can follow him when he leaves and get the photographs later."

"It would be marvellous if you could."

"Let's go and have a swim," I suggested. "It'll make us both feel better. Then we'll be in good form when the dreaded Quintin turns up."

***

He arrived punctually at seven o'clock.

Sally and I were dressed and waiting in the drawing room and Jackson showed him in. He wore the same shirt and trousers that he had worn that morning. He carried a small briefcase which he dropped on the coffee table.

"Good evening, Sally." He nodded coldly in my direction. Neither of us spoke.

"Aren't you going to offer me a drink?" he said at last.

"No," I said rudely. "Tell us what you want. Then go away."

"How uncivilised you are. I've been to such trouble to be here on time this evening too. I assure you this will all be much less unpleasant if we behave like gentlemen."

"You wouldn't know how," I said.

"Oh, I'll give you a drink," said Sally unexpectedly, and she crossed to the table where the drinks were and poured him some whisky.

"Thank you, my dear," said Quintin, taking the glass and giving me a triumphant glance. "That's much better. Now we can get down to business. I think it would be better, Sally, if our young friend here were to leave us. He's not really concerned in this."

I looked at Sally. I suspected that she would have preferred me to have left the room, but she said nothing.

"I'm staying," I said. "I'm in the photographs too, am I not?"

"Indeed you are. They wouldn't be at all the same without you. Would you like to see the prints now? Help yourself. They're in the briefcase." He gestured towards it with his glass.

Sally touched the briefcase but seemed to be unable to bring herself to open it. I took it from the table, undid the zip fastener which ran round the side and extracted the contents. There was an envelope which contained a dozen coloured prints. They were about three inches square. There was also a buff-coloured file cover. Quintin took that from my hand before I could open it.

"You can look at that last," he said smoothly. "It's my pièce de résistance."

I glanced through the photographs and passed them to Sally. Quintin had arranged them in chronological order. The first showed us beginning to emerge from the sea; the last, taken I guessed from somewhere half-way up the steps, showed me curled up on the sand with my hands between my legs and Sally kneeling beside me. They were good photographs. The colour and clarity were startling. I felt sick. I glanced at Sally. She looked a bit green.

"What are you going to do with them?" she asked Quintin in a small voice.

"With those?" he said cheerfully. "Absolutely nothing, my dear. Keep them as mementoes of your holiday if you like." He brandished the buff file cover. "This is what I'm going to do things with. But only if you make it necessary. And I very much hope that you won't."

"What is it?" Sally asked.

"It's the best photograph of the whole bunch, and I've blown it up so that you can see all the detail. It's quite a work of art, I'm sure you'll agree."

He handed the file to Sally and she opened it and gasped. I looked over her shoulder at the single glossy print. Quintin was right. It was a superb photograph. Sally and I stood at the edge of the sea. Our heads were slightly turned and we were smiling at one another, but our bodies were fully exposed to the camera, and never have I seen two people look more naked. Sally's face and body were at their most strikingly beautiful, and the colour print did the fullest justice to her tan, but you could see every pore of her skin, every hair, every drop of water. The same was true of me, but the thing that gave the photograph its immediacy, its shock value, was the fact that Sally's beautiful right hand was clasping my swollen partially erect penis.

I had forgotten that that was what she had been doing immediately before we realised that Quintin was taking photographs. The realisation hit me in the pit of the stomach like a blow. Sally was right. Quintin had taken away something that was very much our own. He had invaded our privacy in an unforgivable way, and might be on the point of destroying our love in a most cruel and effective way. A slow anger started to burn inside me. I looked at Quintin. He was a nasty little insect and he needed squashing.

"You've made a great mistake taking those photographs," I said to him.

Something of the hate I was beginning to feel for him must have come across because he looked slightly scared and fidgeted nervously with his whisky glass. He cleared his throat and said, "There's nothing to worry about if you just do as I want. But don't try anything now. I've taken certain safety precautions to prevent you trying anything this evening."

"What are they?"

"Never mind the details. But if I'm not back... where I'm staying... by nine o'clock, a friend of mine will take certain actions with this photograph that you will both regret."

"I see." I poured myself a drink and sat on the sofa. Sally was still staring at the photograph. "Tell us what your conditions are. What have we got to do to get the negatives of those photographs… and all the existing prints?"

Quintin sat down in an armchair. "There's nothing for you to do," he said to me. "It only concerns Sally."

Sally lifted her head and stared at him. She looked ill. "What do you want?" she said tonelessly.

"Can't you guess?" said Quintin. He shifted uncomfortably in his seat. I suppose there was some faint trace of decency left in him. When it came to actually spelling out his loathsome proposition even he baulked at the repulsive melodrama of it all. This must have been one of the reasons why he wanted me out of the way.

"You tell me." Sally's voice would have frozen the sea outside if the windows hadn't been shut. She sat beside me on the sofa and took my hand in hers.

"You don't get the photographs back," he said. Realising that he was forced to explain he seemed to have taken the bull by the horns. He rushed on, telling us what he must have rehearsed a hundred times that afternoon. "At least you don't get the photographs back until I'm tired of you Sally. And I doubt if I ever shall be. But if and when I no longer want you I'll let you go and give you the negatives."

"And in the meantime?"

"In the meantime you become my mistress."

There was a silence. Sally and I stared at him. We must have looked frighteningly full of hate. He knocked back the last of his drink and got up and walked to the table to refill his glass.

"It won't be too awful for you," he said, managing what I am sure he intended to sound like a light laugh. "I shan't be too demanding. You must spend one night a week with me at my flat in London. That's all. I'm not greedy. You can do whatever you like on the other six nights."

He laughed again. He seemed to be getting his confidence

back now that he had managed to get up the courage actually to name his conditions.

"What about Freddie?" I said. "He's bound to find out."

As I spoke Sally gripped my hand tightly. She was too late. Quintin roared with laughter. "Freddie?" he laughed. "Oh, dear me. Freddie won't mind. I should think he'd be delighted. Do you mean to say you don't know about Freddie? Haven't you told him, Sally?"

"Never mind about Freddie," said Sally. "That's none of your business."

"Isn't it? Oh, well, if you insist." He looked at me. "You are living in a dream world, old boy. Don't you know about Freddie and me and your beautiful mistress here? I really am surprised."

"There's one thing you haven't told me," said Sally quickly. It was clear that she didn't want him to go on in this vein.

"What's that? When do we start, do you mean? When you come back to London, my dear. I can last a few more days. Next month, shall we say?"

"No," said Sally. "That's not it."

"What then?"

"You haven't told me what you intend to do if I refuse."

"I haven't, have I? How remiss of me. In a way that's the best part. I do hope you won't force me to do it, because I really would hate it. It would ruin everything. I expect you'd kill yourself, and I shouldn't like that at all. Believe it or not I'm really very fond of you, Sally. In my way I love you. I've loved you for years, you know. I don't want to do you any harm, but I've got to such a stage now that I can't think of anything except getting that beautiful body of yours onto a bed. Forgive my vulgarity but I really can't help it."

"So what will you do if I refuse?" Sally asked him again.

"I'll tell you. And then I really must be on my way." He glanced at his wristwatch. "You can give me your answer when you're back in London and have had a chance to think it over. Honestly I don't think you've any choice. After I've gone you may wonder if I really would carry out my threat. The answer is that I most certainly would if you did refuse to co-operate. But as you'll see in a moment you daren't risk it."

"Are you ever going to tell me?"

"Yes, now." He was enjoying himself hugely. "Have another good look at the large photograph."

Sally picked it up and we both stared at it.

"It's a good one, isn't it? I'm very proud of it. The focus is perfect and the timing was exactly right. It's good enough to win a competition. I thought that as soon as I'd finished developing it. That's what gave me the idea. I expect you'd find it difficult to hold your head up in the sort of world you move in, Sally, if that photograph was on public exhibition. Isn't that right?"

Sally didn't speak. She was white behind her tan.

"I thought so," Quintin went on. "Imagine how you'd feel when you arrived at a party – or what about a Government reception, if the Tories get in next time? As you walked in you wouldn't know how many of the people there had seen this photograph. Just think how you'd feel. Think of the sniggers, the off-colour jokes, the respectable hostesses who would never speak to you again. Life wouldn't be very easy, would it? Or very pleasant."

"You couldn't put that picture on public exhibition," I said. "No one would accept it. It's obscene." I felt Sally shudder as I spoke and I wished I had phrased it in some other way.

"You're quite right," said Quintin. "But I've thought of a way round that. I shall make a large number of copies. Not too many though. I wouldn't want to flood the market. It would be best if the prints had a certain scarcity value. I think a limited edition of, say, a hundred should do the trick. I shall make a list of a hundred people who know Sally well. Then I shall put the hundred prints into a hundred envelopes and address them to the people on my list. I shall then arrange for them to be posted all together if one of two things happens – either if you won't do as I want, Sally, or if anything ever happens to me. Think of the excitement at a hundred breakfast tables the next morning. It would be the scandal of the decade."

He finished his second drink and stood up. "I'm glad that's all over," he said. "I'll be off now. I'll leave you to finish your holiday and I'll see you in London in October, Sally. I'll ring you up when you get back and you can tell me whether I shall have the pleasure of your company in my flat once a week, or whether I must post the photographs." He walked towards the door. "I hope you'll decide to do the sensible thing. Of course you will. I shall look forward to our first night together with the keenest anticipation."

He took a small brown object from his trouser pocket and held it up for me to see for a moment before returning it. "That's the rotor arm of your car, old boy. I don't think it would be a very good idea if you knew where I was staying, so I thought I'd take it out so that you wouldn't be tempted to follow me when I leave. I'll put it on the top of the gatepost at the end of the drive. Goodbye now."

***

"I'll tell you all about it now," said Sally. "I should have told you before, but I couldn't bring myself to. I was afraid you wouldn't love me any more, and I couldn't bear that. Now I must tell you. I only hope you'll understand." She smiled feebly across the table at me.

"I'll see if we can have some more coffee and some brandy," I said, signalling to our waiter.

We were sitting at a table for two in the huge dining room of a hotel a few miles along the coast from our house. It was our last night in Jamaica and there seemed to be nothing to lose now so, soon after Quintin left us, I suggested we go out to dinner. I can't pretend that we really enjoyed our evening out, but it made a change of scenery and looking at the other diners tended to take our minds off our problems.

Sally looked so beautiful in a white silk dress that I knew that nothing she could tell me would make the slightest difference to my love for her. I told her so.

"If you have ever done anything of which you're ashamed," I went on, "it won't make any difference to me. Everyone does something they regret and are ashamed of at some time in their lives."

A waiter refilled our coffee cups and another waiter brought two over-large brandy balloons and a third offered me some cigars. I selected one and the waiter rolled it gently in his fingers, smiled his approval at me, and producing a cutter snipped a neat incision at the end. The hotel was American in almost every respect, the most noticeable of which were the prices. The service was magnificent.

When all the waiters had withdrawn and my cigar was glowing satisfactorily I smiled across at Sally.

I said, "Tell me the worst. I can stand it."

"I do hope you can, darling." She looked a bit doubtful. "Here goes..." She drank some of her brandy. "The worst…" She hesitated again. "The worst is that Quintin is the father of my son Timothy."

I stared at her. "Oh."

"I was afraid it would be rather a shock for you, darling." I pulled at my cigar. I didn't know what to think.

"Tell me the whole story," I said at last.

"Oh, darling," said Sally miserably, "I will tell you of course. But have you stopped loving me? I love you so much that I can't bear the thought that you might not love me any more."

I took her hand across the table top. "I'll love you for ever," I said. "Tell me all about it. Then we'll decide what to do about Quintin. We can't make a sensible plan until I know everything."

"You're quite right, Jimmy. Give me a cigarette and I'll try to explain. I'll have to go back to my wedding day really," Sally began through a cloud of smoke. "Otherwise nothing makes sense. I've told you before about how I grew up and how I married Freddie more or less because it was expected of me. I was looking forward to being married and now, with the benefit of hindsight, I can see that I was looking forward to the physical side of it particularly. Imagine my disappointment when Freddie told me on our wedding night that he didn't like sex, that it was all rather disgusting and unpleasant and that we wouldn't be having any. I'm not sure he didn't quote Lord Chesterfield at me. You know: 'The position is ridiculous, the pleasure momentary and the expense damnable.' Sex was ugly, he said. Man ought to aspire to beauty. And he was glad that he had married me because I was beautiful and he loved to look at beautiful things. That was when I started being a nudist. We spent our honeymoon – three very peculiar weeks – in a villa in the South of France. Freddie persuaded me to take all my clothes off to sunbathe and he seemed to like looking at me. I was shy to begin with but he more or less bullied me into it, and eventually I came to like it. At first I hoped that my nudity would excite him and that he'd change his mind about sex, but he never did anything more than look at me and very occasionally pat or stroke me."

"So he's never ever made love to you?" I said. What Anne had told me about him now made sense.

"Never. He's never even kissed me, except for a polite peck on the cheek, usually when there are people about. I suppose that's all part of his happily-married-man act. He'd hate anyone to know there was anything unconventional about him."

"What is wrong with him, do you know?"

"I've no idea. I've tried to discuss it with him once or twice but he refuses to talk about it."

"Have you ever seen him with no clothes on?" I was remembering what Anne had said.

"Never. We've always had separate bedrooms and bathrooms. Physically there is absolutely nothing between us at all, except that he genuinely likes to look at me in the nude."

I shook my head in amazement. I didn't pretend to understand it fully, and I made a mental note to ask the Medical Officer about it when I got back to Chelsea Barracks.

"Didn't you want to have sex?" I asked.

"I did rather. I was curious about it, and after I'd been married a few months I got lots of offers. I almost did have an affair once. It was about a year after my wedding. A young man called Richard asked me to have lunch with him in London. We'd met at a house party and flirted together very enjoyably. We agreed to meet at a little Italian restaurant and I rather hoped he was going to fill me up with Chianti and take me back to his flat and show me what it was all about."

"What happened?" I asked, feeling jealous.

"My goodness, it was terrible. I arrived at the restaurant which was frightfully dark inside. Richard wasn't there so I sat at a table and waited. Five minutes later Freddie walked in."

"What bad luck!"

"It wasn't luck. He knew. He never told me how. He walked straight up to my table and sat down. He said Richard wasn't coming. He'd unexpectedly gone abroad. We had lunch together. He told me he knew all about everything. And he gave me a strong warning about my future behaviour. He said if he ever caught me out in that way again not only would he ruin the man concerned but he would divorce me. He said he hoped I realised the effect that that would have upon my father. He was right about that. It would have killed Daddy. He thought it was the greatest thing that had ever happened when I married Freddie."

"So you didn't think of misbehaving again?"

"No, darling. Not until my father died and I heard about you."

"What about Quintin?"

"Ah. That was very different. Very different indeed. After the Richard episode I suppose Freddie decided he'd have to give me something to do to keep me quiet, so he thought I should have a baby. He was very keen to have an heir anyway. He's half-demented about his family line. He started to ask Quintin down to Highworth for weekends. They both made a big effort to be nice to me, and looking back on it I think the original plan must have been for Quintin to seduce me. But I didn't like him at all and I suppose he didn't dare to make a pass without some sort of encouragement. Eventually Freddie told me his plan. He said he wanted an heir, but that for medical reasons he was unable to father one himself. There could be no question of adoption, he said. I must give birth to the baby myself, and Quintin would be the father. Artificial insemination was also out of the question because it was essential to the family honour of the Frenshams that no one but the three of us should know about it. Quintin was to be the father because he was a Frensham and because Freddie knew he could trust him not to tell anyone."

I was dumbfounded. "I can hardly believe my ears," I said at last. "What did you say to him?"

"I refused, of course. I said I thought it was the most repulsive proposal that I had ever heard. Freddie was ready for that. He said he was sorry I didn't like the idea, but that he thought it probably wouldn't be too awful for me and that if I worked out the dates very carefully I probably wouldn't have to go to bed with Quintin very often. He also said that if I agreed to do it he would buy an annuity for my father so that he could end his days in comfort. On the other hand, if I refused, he said, he would have to get rid of me because he had to have an heir, so he would have to marry someone else who would agree. He said he could divorce me at any time for adultery, naming Richard as the co-respondent. He had bought Richard, he told me. For a very great deal of money Richard was prepared to swear that he had made love to me."

"But you were a virgin," I said. I felt rather proud of my quickness. "You could have fought it and called your doctor to give evidence that you were *virgo intacta*, I think it's called."

"I thought of that too. Though not till later. I told Freddie and he said it made no difference. He'd taken legal advice about it, he told me."

"And you accepted his word for that?"

"Yes. Freddie wouldn't lie about a thing like that."

"I can hardly believe all this, but do go on."

"It's all quite true, I assure you, Jimmy. Anyway, Freddie reminded me of how my father would feel if I were divorced like that. He also said that he would arrange for my father to be deprived of his living if he divorced me."

"My God. He's scarcely human. What did you do?"

"What could I do? I was only twenty-one. I had no one to turn to. No one to go to for advice. I gave in. I persuaded myself that it would be nice to have a little baby to look after, and perhaps sex with Quintin would be fun. I was still keen to find out what it was like."

I felt sick and angry. I drank some more brandy. "It's the most horrible thing I've ever heard. What happened?"

"You don't want all the details, do you? In fact I don't remember it very clearly. It's a long time ago and I've made a big effort to forget it. Now that I'm talking about it, it seems a bit clearer. I don't know if you're still going to love me after this but even if you don't I shall still go on loving you, and in fact it's a great relief to be able to tell someone about it after all this time. Particularly someone I love, someone sympathetic." She stopped talking and smiled at me with such sweetness that I felt a little pain in my heart.

"I'm getting a sore throat with all this talking," Sally said. "But I'd better finish now that I've started. I had sex with Quintin twice, on two successive months. I got hold of a book about sex and I worked out exactly when I would be likely to conceive. I told Freddie the date and Quintin came down for dinner and to stay the night. I had rather a lot to drink at dinner because I was frightened. No one said a word about what was going to happen but Quintin kept looking at me excitedly all through dinner."

"How horrible."

Sally looked hard at me. "I'm going to be absolutely honest with you, darling, because we love one another and because we've got to trust one another from now on." She shook her head as though she were impatient with herself. "I don't mean that exactly. I know you've always been absolutely honest with me, and I trust you completely."

I said nothing. I had a pretty good idea of what she was going to say. The important thing was to be loving and kind to her. I gave her an encouraging smile. "Tell me, darling," I said.

"Well…" she hesitated.

"I suppose you're going to say that you thoroughly enjoyed having sex with Quintin and that you feel you shouldn't have."

Sally looked at me as though I had just discovered penicillin. "Darling, how did you guess?"

"It wasn't difficult."

"In fact it wasn't as marvellous as all that. Nothing like it is with you."

I felt better.

"The first time was simply awful. Absolutely agony. It was because I was a virgin, of course. In a way I'd been quite looking forward to it, so it was a horrible shock when it hurt so much. I'd read books and I knew it was supposed to hurt a bit, but I didn't think it would be quite as painful as it was. I practically screamed the house down. I wasn't at all brave. After it was over I made Quintin go away at once. I hated him because he'd hurt me so much. He was very rough too. He made no attempt to be gentle with me, though he knew it was the first time."

"What about the second time?"

"That was different. I was terribly disappointed when I had the curse a fortnight after the first time, and I realised I'd have to go through it all again. Quintin came down for the night again, but I hated and feared him so much that I couldn't bring myself to sit down to dinner at the same table as him. I had dinner in my bedroom and he and Freddie had theirs in the dining room. Heaven knows what they talked about."

I called for some more brandy for both of us. I knew I needed it, and I suspected Sally did too. "Go on, darling. Get it over."

"He came into my room after dinner and was awfully nice. He said he realised how much it must have hurt the month before but that it wouldn't hurt this time and that he promised he'd be gentle. He told me I was beautiful and he said he'd fallen in love with me. Then he undressed me and made love to me. He was quite good at it, I realise now, though not nearly as good as you, Jimmy. It was a lovely feeling, I found, and I wanted it to go on and on. Unfortunately he finished too quickly for me and I was left high and dry. It was dreadfully frustrating. He went straight off to sleep and I lay there in the darkness, hating him for what he was and for getting me excited without making me come, but at the same time I longed for him to wake up and do it again."

"And did he?"

"Yes. Twice. Once in the middle of the night, and once early the next morning. It was no good for me either time, though I think perhaps it wasn't really Quintin's fault the last time. He managed to keep going for quite a long time, and afterwards I blamed myself. I thought it was because I disliked him so much. I despised him too. He got disgustingly sweaty and he smelt repulsive, which didn't help, but when he was inside me it did give me the most thrilling sensations. That made me despise myself too. I asked myself how I could be such a beast as to actually enjoy having sex with such a monster. Now I'm yours I understand more about it."

I laughed. "Because I'm a monster too?"

Sally smiled. "No, darling. That isn't what I mean at all, and you know it. I mean that I know now that I didn't come with Quintin because he wasn't good enough at it. Anyway he left me before breakfast and I had a cold bath to cool my feelings down a bit. Three weeks later I saw my doctor and had a pregnancy test. When I got the news that it was positive, Freddie was, of course, delighted. I suppose he told Quintin not to bother to come and stay that month. He didn't mention it to me. He behaved exactly as though the baby was to be his own. In his way he's been a good father. When Timothy was about eighteen months old Freddie asked me in a tentative sort of way if I would like to have another baby, but I refused point blank and fortunately he never raised the subject again. I think he was content with one, as it was a boy. And though I should have liked to have had a little sister for Timmy I wasn't prepared to have Quintin slobbering all over me again."

"Was that the end of it?"

"Yes, it was really. Except that Quintin decided that he was in love with me and, to cut a long and tiresome story short, he's been pestering me to go to bed with him ever since."

I looked at her and felt a fleeting moment of sympathy for the loathsome Quintin. A whole night in bed with Sally would be enough to make any man fall hopelessly and irreversibly in love with her. It had been enough for me, I remembered.

"Now I'm telling you about it," Sally went on, "it's all coming back to me very clearly. I just don't know how I can steel myself to go to bed with him again. He's *so* disgusting."

"Don't worry about it, darling," I said, exuding a confidence I was very far from feeling. "I'll fix him. I promise you won't have to go to bed with him."

She smiled at me. She looked relieved, as though she knew I'd manage it somehow. "I do hope I won't, darling. I do dread the idea of people seeing that photograph. I think I'd kill myself if he sent it to everybody. I just couldn't bear it."

"Don't worry," I reassured her. "Incidentally, I imagine this was the piece of information that you thought you could use to make Freddie let you divorce him, rather than the other way around."

"That's right. Surely he'd rather give me what I want than have a scandal like that?"

"You'd think so. I agree." I remembered what I had overheard when I had been hiding in the kitchen. "But Freddie doesn't seem to be too worried about it, does he?"

"No, he doesn't. But he may just be bluffing."

"It's possible. I think we must get lots of good legal advice when we get back to London."

"Perhaps we'd better do that before I leave him." Sally finished her brandy and put down the glass. "I've done so much talking that I've got a really bad sore throat now. I think I'll go to the loo. They may have some sort of lozenge I can suck." She pushed back her chair and stood up. I stood too.

"I'll try not to be too long, darling," she said. "You do still love me, don't you?"

"Oh, yes. More than ever."

She smiled and turned and walked out of the room. A number of heads, both male and female, swivelled after her as she passed. I wasn't surprised. She was the most beautiful woman in the world.

I sat down and sucked at my cigar.

"Hello, James," said a voice beside me. "I thought it was you. I could only see the back of your head from where I was sitting, but I knew it was familiar."

I looked round and stood up quickly. I could hardly believe my eyes.

"Aunt Rosemary! What on earth are you doing here?"

"I won't stay a moment," she said. "Do sit down. Can I sit here?" She slid into Sally's chair. "It's lovely to see you, my dear. And what a beautiful girl you're with. Your father would have approved."

"Is Uncle Henry here?"

"He's here in Jamaica, but he's not here tonight. He stayed at home this evening. Are you having a holiday? You must come and call on us."

"We're going back to London tomorrow."

"What a pity. We're here for another ten days. Then we're going to the States."

"How gay you're being."

Rosemary giggled. I suspected that she was a little drunk.

"My mother died a few weeks ago. She'd been an invalid for years you know, and a terrible lot of work for everyone, so it was a merciful release really."

For her or for you, I wondered?

"Anyway, she left me quite a lot of money and Henry and I thought we'd spend some of it going round the world before we're too old to enjoy ourselves any more. We're doing it very slowly and in lots of comfort. Wherever we can we're staying with friends and friends of friends."

It was amusing to see her, but I wished she'd go away before Sally returned.

"We're staying in the most splendid house party here in Jamaica," Rosemary gushed on. "The house belongs to the most charming American. It's the most comfortable place you could imagine. It's got a beautiful yacht too. We go cruising along the coast in it sometimes."

"It sounds lovely."

"Oh, it is. I can't tell you. They're a fascinating bunch of people in the party. Some of them are over there." She gestured behind me and I turned and looked in the direction she was indicating. It wasn't difficult to identify her table. Five very rich-looking people sat at a table by the window. They were eating strawberries and drinking champagne. One of the five was a very pretty dark girl who stared at me with hot black eyes and smiled slightly. "That's Felicity Fanshawe," said Rosemary. "She's a model. She's with a well-known photographer, but he decided not to come out with us this evening."

"Who is he?"

"Quintin Frensham," she said. "Have you heard of him?"

"Yes, I think so." I tried to sound vague and slightly bored. Inside I was in turmoil. This was too much to be a coincidence. It must be fate. I knew I must be very careful not to put a foot wrong.

"It's a relief Quintin didn't come out tonight. None of the party can stand him. He's terribly pleased with himself. We all think he's odious. Henry and I can't think what Felicity sees in him."

"Where are you staying? Where's the house?"

"You can almost see it from here," she said. "It's on the point beyond this hotel. It has its own private road with the name of the owner on the gate."

"What did you say his name was?"

"I didn't say, James," she said and she told me the name. Of course I had heard it before. Practically everybody had. He was a politician, an unsuccessful presidential candidate a few years earlier.

I nodded. "It sounds very exciting."

"Oh, it is. I'll tell you all about it when we get back to England. You must come down and stay with us. It's sad you're going home tomorrow. I think your girlfriend is perfectly lovely, my dear. Is this serious?"

"Yes. Very serious."

"I'm glad. It's time you settled down. I'll go now before she comes back. I expect you want to be alone." She started to get up.

A sudden thought struck me. "Before you go, Aunt Rosemary…"

"Yes, my dear? What is it?"

"Have you told your friends my name?"

"I don't know. I can't remember. Does it matter?"

"Yes. It does."

"Let me think." She paused. "What I said was, 'I think that's my nephew, James. I must just go over and say hello to him.' Or something like that."

"You didn't mention my surname?"

"I'm sure I didn't. After all it's the same as mine."

"Yes," I said. "But a nephew doesn't have to have the same name as his aunt, does he?"

"No, of course not."

"Well then, I want you to do me a great favour."

"I will if I can." She smiled at me. "What is it?"

"I don't want you to tell anyone in your house party what my name is. It would be better if you didn't even tell Uncle Henry. Make up a name, if you have to say anything about me. Say I'm something in the City. But don't let on to anyone who I am. It's very important."

Aunt Rosemary looked at me in silence for a moment. My urgency seemed to have sobered her. For a nasty moment I thought she was going to refuse. Then she said, "All right, James. I'll do it. It sounds rather thrilling. But there's one condition."

"What's that?"

"That you tell me all about it one day. Will you?"

"Yes, I will. One day."

"You're James... Robinson, if anyone asks me. Are you a stock broker or a merchant banker? Perhaps you're in Lloyd's. I think I'll be vague about you. That'll be easy."

We both stood up.

"Goodbye, my dear," she said. "See you back in England one day."

I kissed her on the cheek. "Goodbye, Aunt Rosemary. Don't give my love to Uncle Henry. At least not until you've left Jamaica."

She smiled and waved a hand vaguely and her bright blue eyes twinkled with excitement. Then she wandered off to her table.

Sally returned a minute or two later. Heads swivelled again.

"Darling," she said, when she was seated. "You'll never guess what the loos are called here."

I wasn't interested. I wanted to tell her the plan I had made.

"The ladies is called 'Gulls' and the gents is called 'Buoys'." She spelled them out. "Would you believe it?"

I smiled. "I'd believe anything after this evening." I told her what had happened. She stared over my shoulder at Aunt Rosemary.

"What are we going to do?" she asked me.

"That's easy. I'm going to take you back to our house. Then I'm going to go and burgle that house and steal back the negatives and any other prints he may have. Then we'll go back to England tomorrow, you can divorce Freddie, and we'll live happily ever after."

I waved at my waiter and indicated that I wanted my bill. Sally looked worried. "Darling, I don't think that's a very good idea. Suppose you get caught?"

"I'll manage, don't worry."

"But suppose you can't find the photographs?"

"If I don't find the photographs we'll be no worse off than we are now. But I expect I shall. I can't believe that I should be given an opportunity like this if the gods weren't on our side. If I don't do something about this I shall never forgive myself. Once Quintin gets back to London and makes his arrangements about those photographs it'll be ten times more difficult to find out where they are. Tonight they're bound to be at this house he's staying at, and they'll probably be in his room."

Sally nodded slowly. "I do hope it goes all right," she said. "Would you like me to go with you?"

"I'll be better on my own. You go to bed."

"I shan't be able to sleep. I shall just lie there worrying about you and thinking what a horrid sore throat I've got."

TWENTY-FIVE

It wasn't difficult to find the house, and it was only a few minutes after eleven o'clock when I walked through the open white gates and started up the long drive.

I had taken Sally home as quickly as I could, and I had changed into a pair of black trousers and a dark blue polo-necked jersey. Sally was gargling in the bathroom when I was ready to go. I kissed her goodbye and told her not to wait up for me and I drove back past the hotel until I identified the gates that I was looking for. I overshot them, turned round and drove back to the hotel. It was just under seven-tenths of a mile by the dashboard mileometer from the open gates to the hotel car park. I swung the big car into a space well away from the road and left it there. It would be dangerous, I knew, to leave the car near the house. Quintin was the only one who knew what it looked like, but anyone might be suspicious of an empty car on a road where there was only one house. I locked up and walked quickly back along the road to the gates. I was prepared to take cover at once if a car approached but I was in luck and I completed the journey without seeing anyone or, so far as I could tell, being seen.

There was a strong and obviously new wire fence on each side of the gates, which I was delighted to see were still open. It was painted black and I hadn't noticed it when I had driven past in the car. It was very high and in the darkness I couldn't see the top. It stretched away on either side and I thought it would be prudent to investigate it further. I paused just inside the white-painted steel gates and pondered the problem. Time spent in reconnaissance is never wasted, I told myself, but on this occasion I had very little time to spend. I knew that if I was to have any idea of the layout of the inside of the house I must get into a position from which I could observe before everyone had gone to bed and all the lights were turned out. Fortunately there had been a large number of cars still outside the hotel when I had parked. I hoped that Aunt Rosemary and her friends had not yet returned. But if they hadn't yet they soon would. I had no time to spare. I decided to push on at once.

I walked silently along the edge of the drive, ready to move quickly into the cover of the trees on either side if anyone came near me.

The night was dark and hot. There was no moon. It was, I thought, a good night for patrolling. After I had walked about a quarter of a mile the trees on my right thinned and then stopped. I moved to the last tree. I could hear the sea.

My night vision was well established now and I soon realised that I was standing within a few yards of the edge of the cliff. The drive curved round to the left and started to slope downward as it disappeared into the trees again. There was a very faint glow of light through the trees and I realised that the house couldn't be very far away.

Half a mile to my right across the smooth black sea I saw the lights of the hotel. I shut one eye to preserve my night vision as I looked. There were lights on everywhere. There was even a bonfire on the beach and I saw people moving about and heard the faint strains of a dance band.

In front of me the cliff was steep and high; more than twice the height of the cliff at the house where Sally and I were staying.

I stood quietly in the deep shadow below my tree and listened for two or three minutes. When I was satisfied that everything was quiet I moved on again on the next leg of my journey. This time I kept off the drive itself. I moved parallel to it through the trees. The ground sloped gently down as I walked, but I was still high above sea level when the trees came to an end and the drive expanded into a broad area in front of a long U-shaped single-storey white house.

I stopped twenty feet inside the cover of the trees and lay down.

The house, I now realised, was built at the end of a long narrow peninsula which pointed like a finger towards Cuba. I could see the sea on both sides of the house. To my left there was a garden which adjoined the house. There wasn't much to it; just a few shrubs and a large oval swimming pool. There was enough light from a window at the left-hand end of the house for me to see that the garden was deserted. No one seemed to be in the mood for midnight swimming.

There were two cars parked near the front door, which was wide open and immediately opposite me in the centre of the house. I could see through the doorway into a large marble-floored hall and I was tempted to get up and walk straight in. It would have taken less than ten seconds.

I resisted the impulse and looked at the right-hand wing. I heard a wireless playing steel band music and some laughter and I decided that I had located the servants' quarters. Left flanking was my best plan.

I stood up and moved back into the deep security of the trees before starting to work my way round to the seaward side of the swimming pool. When I reached the cliff on that side of the peninsula I turned right and slowly moved towards the house. Forty feet below me I heard the sea washing sloppily over the rocks at the bottom of the cliff.

I stopped again when I reached the edge of the garden and took cover behind a bush. I could now see the full length of the left-hand wing. There was a massive picture window and through it I saw half a dozen people in what must have been the principal drawing room of the house. It was a large room, furnished in abominable taste and it jutted out over the sea. The views from the window must have been spectacular.

It was impossible from where I crouched behind my bush to see where the bedrooms were. I guessed that they must be somewhere beyond the drawing room, probably with similar sea views. I could see a narrow terrace in front of the picture window and I prayed that it ran the full length of the wing and gave access to all the bedrooms. If it did, I congratulated myself, all I had to do was find out which was Quintin's and my night's work was as good as done.

Aunt Rosemary and Uncle Henry were amongst the people in the room. Henry, looking slightly sunburnt and prosperous, was standing at one side lighting a large cigar and talking to a tall distinguished-looking man who I recognised from photographs and television as my ignorant host. He might have stepped out of one of those advertisements for an expensive brand of scotch whisky which one used to see in *Esquire* magazine, and if even half of what I had heard about him was true the only fact of importance in the world of which he was ignorant was my presence in his garden.

The other people were the remains of Aunt Rosemary's party at the hotel. There was no sign of the pretty dark girl whose name I had been told but had now forgotten. There was no sign of Quintin either.

I settled back on my haunches and prepared to wait until they had gone to bed. It wouldn't be safe to move any nearer to the house until the drawing room lights were put out.

I had to wait only fifteen minutes in fact, though it seemed like a couple of hours. Every few minutes I peered round the bush to see if any of them had gone and I willed them to feel sleepy and go to bed. Four of them succumbed pretty quickly, but Uncle Henry looked set for a long discussion with our mutual host and I was afraid he'd go on all night. I remembered from my childhood how excessively fond he was of the sound of his own voice.

Fortunately for me, the distinguished American seemed to find him as boring as I always had, and after a while I was glad to see him leading Uncle Henry gently towards the door of the room. A moment later the room and the garden outside were plunged into darkness. I stood up at once and moved towards the house.

Ideally I should have stayed where I was for a long time to get back my night vision and to make sure that everything was quiet. Sadly I had no time for that. I had to get a look at the bedrooms as quickly as possible before everyone had gone to sleep. Only by looking in through the windows could I hope to locate Quintin's room. There was very little time to spare. I might already be too late.

I moved cautiously along the terrace in front of the now dark picture window, ready to drop to the ground if the lights came on again. It was very dark and I kept my left hand on the railing to guide me. At the end of the house the terrace and railing suddenly stopped. My vision was sufficiently restored and peering into the darkness below I made out a tiny artificial harbour formed by an L-shaped jetty. The white yacht I had seen the day before was tied up there, and there was also a powerful-looking motorboat. I lent on the railing and peered round the corner of the wall. All I could see was that the centre section of the house was narrower than the two end sections – the one where I stood and a similar one at the far end of the house – both of which jutted far out over the sea. By leaning as far out as I dared I could see that the centre section consisted of a row of bedrooms, each with its own balcony terrace. The balconies were separated from one another by high dividing walls and it wasn't difficult to guess that this afforded complete privacy to the occupants of each bedroom when they chose to sunbathe on their balcony. The house was built like a young hotel.

I relaxed against the railing and thought for a moment about my next move. The obvious way to have a look into those bedrooms was from their own balconies. There was only one way to get to the balconies other than by walking through the rooms themselves, and that was from the roof. I looked down at the long drop to the sea. It looked singularly uninviting and for a moment I wondered whether it wouldn't be sensible to think up an alternative plan. Perhaps if I were to set fire to the house I should be able to get in and find Quintin's room in the confusion… I decided I didn't think much of that.

I took a deep breath and climbed onto the railing. I turned to face the house, steadying myself on the wall. The gutter was within easy reach. I took hold of it with both hands and pulled down, gently at first, then harder. It didn't even creak. I gave a pull and a heave, got a foot into the gutter and a moment later I was on the roof. I was delighted by my agility. Now what?

I crept up the gentle slope of the roof until I reached the top. It was even easier than I had anticipated. The house was well built; its owner, I had no doubt, being the last person to tolerate shoddy craftsmanship from his builder. From where I sat on the apex of the roof I could count eight bedrooms simply by totalling the dividing walls between their terraces, but I couldn't see whether their lights were on or off. How was I to reach the nearest balcony?

The gutter ran to the corner of the building a few feet away. Then it did a right-angled turn and ran back to the nearest balcony, a distance of about twenty feet. That was the straightforward route. Its only disadvantage, that I could see, was that I should be relying entirely upon the strength of the guttering for the full length of the twenty-foot journey. If the gutter failed me I should fall sixty feet to the rocks below.

The alternative was to climb across this roof to the roof above the bedroom wing. The only snag to that course was that anyone standing below would see me silhouetted against the sky. On balance I decided that this was a risk I should have to take. I walked carefully along the ridge of the roof. It was no more difficult than the simplest balancing obstacle on the assault course at Pirbright; only the darkness made it in the least complicated and by now my night vision was almost perfect again. I reached the conjunction of the two sections of the roof. In a few seconds I was above the first bedroom and its balcony. I could see no light from the bedroom window and I wondered whether I had struck a lucky place to get down by choosing an unoccupied bedroom.

The balcony below me measured about twelve feet square. It was bounded on the left by the wall of the house; on the right by the wall which divided it from the terrace of the adjoining bedroom, which rose to the level of the eaves of the roof; and at the far end by a railing like the one on the drawing room terrace. I spotted the shadowy shapes of several long comfortable-looking armchairs – they were too luxurious to be called deckchairs.

I braced myself and prepared to jump down. As I did so I saw the unmistakable glow of a very large cigar being drawn upon by a man who was really enjoying it. It came from the furthest chair.

I drew back and froze. A moment later I heard a creak which was clearly audible above the sound of the sea and a shadow detached itself from the chair and moved slowly towards the railing. It was my Uncle Henry. No doubt Aunt Rosemary had forbidden him to smoke his cigar in the bedroom so he had come out here to finish it. I wished he would hurry up. I dare not move an inch while he was there. Even with the sound of the sea to cover any noise I might make he would see me at once if he turned. My only hope was to flatten myself in the corner of the roof and pray that he wouldn't look up.

I crouched uncomfortably, counting the number of puffs Uncle Henry took and longing for him to decide he had had enough and throw the stub away. The only merit I could see in my situation was that I now knew that bedroom number one did not contain Quintin. I also thanked God that I hadn't chosen the gutter approach to the bedrooms. I should have walked straight into Uncle Henry if I had come that way.

At last he finished his cigar. He tossed the end over the railing and I watched the lighted end describe a shallow parabola before it disappeared towards the sea. He turned and walked towards me. I held my breath. Without pausing he strode to the door that led into his bedroom and disappeared from my sight as neatly and as silently as his cigar. I paused for a carefully counted thirty seconds then I edged myself to the gutter and looked cautiously down. The wall of the bedroom which gave onto the terrace was made entirely of glass. Thick curtains obscured the room within.

I lowered myself by my arms until I hung only a foot or two above the balcony. I let go and dropped with a soft thud. I moved quickly away towards the railing before I looked back. No sound came from my uncle and aunt's room.

I looked over the railing. The cliff fell away sheer in front of me. Far below I saw the whiteness of the little waves as they broke over the jagged rocks at the cliff bottom.

I held onto the railing and swung myself round the dividing wall onto the next balcony. This bedroom too was occupied. I could see a strip of light an inch wide in the centre of the window between the curtains. Carefully avoiding the chairs, I walked over to the window and peeped through the crack in the curtains.

The pretty dark girl, whose name I now remembered was Felicity something, was unzipping her dress. That took care of bedroom number two. Perhaps Quintin was in number three. I must be getting warmer.

I should of course have moved on at once but, shamingly, the sight of a girl taking her clothes off was too much for me. Come on, James, I said to myself. You have work to do. You have no time to waste watching this sort of thing. A few seconds won't make any difference, my other self replied. She *is* a very pretty girl.

As usual my other self won. I watched her take her dress off and hang it on a hanger and put it away in a cupboard. Then she took off her black petticoat and draped that over the back of a chair. As she straightened up, her back was towards me. It was long and smooth and slender. She wore only black panties and tights. (No one wore stockings in those days, more's the pity.) She had no bra and when she turned in my direction I saw that she didn't need one. She had a figure like the animated clothes horse that she was, and her breasts were small and high and needed no support. She was a really lovely-looking girl with long delicious legs and it seemed a shame that her bosom wasn't rather larger. She appeared to share my opinion. She sat down at her dressing table and after staring hard at her reflection for a while and pulling a number of faces she picked up a jar and, digging her fingers into its contents, started to massage her breasts in a circular motion. Some sort of hormone cream, I supposed. She stared into the glass with a dreamy expression on her face and her little dark nipples became stiffly erect. They weren't the only thing.

That was enough for me, I decided, my better self taking over. Much more of watching that sort of entertainment and I should be in there with her with an offer of assistance. The girl was far too attractive to be allowed to do that sort of thing on her own.

With mixed feelings I backed off and moved to the railing. I put my head round the corner of the dividing wall to see if I could see anything of bedroom number three. It was as well that I did. The curtains were pulled back, the sliding glass doors were open and I could see Quintin lying on the bed. He seemed to be half-undressed and he was looking with great interest at a piece of paper that he held in his left hand.

I pulled my head and shoulders back to safety and wondered what to do. It should be possible with a little caution to get onto his terrace and to find a position behind a chair from which I could observe right into the room. If he heard or saw me then my plan was to take the bull by the horns, go straight in, beat him up and get the photographs by force. It gave me some pleasure to think of it. He deserved a thrashing. But on the whole I thought it would be more prudent to take the photographs without his knowledge… if I could.

I slid over the railing onto the outside, stepped sideways until I had passed the dividing wall and then climbed back over the railing onto Quintin's balcony. Keeping close to the wall, and therefore almost out of Quintin's vision if he should choose this moment to look up, I crept towards the window. There was a large wooden day-bed just outside the window and I lay down and inched my way forward on elbows and toes, in the most professional infantry fashion, until I was safely concealed behind it and could see underneath it into Quintin's room. My field of fire included the whole of the bed on which he lay and half a large chest of drawers on the opposite side of the room. There was a bedside table between the bed and the window. At the back of the room I could see the beginning of a passage which I imagined must lead to the door and to the bathroom.

I looked at Quintin. He had taken off his trousers and he lay on his back on the bed in his shirt and underpants. His knees were raised and I saw that he wore black silk socks and Old Etonian sock suspenders. Now that I was so much nearer I could see that the piece of paper he held in his hand was a photograph. I couldn't see what it portrayed but it had a familiar look about it and I guessed that it was one of those that he had taken that morning.

I lay there staring at him for a while, trying to decide what to do. Should I bound in and attack him? Would it not be better to wait until he had gone to sleep? I didn't want to give him the chance to raise the alarm.

Suddenly I heard a tapping noise.

"Who is it?" Quintin called, and I realised that someone had knocked at his door.

Whoever it was must have replied because Quintin stood up and thrust the photograph into the drawer of his bedside table. He picked up a dressing gown and started to struggle into it.

"Come in," he said.

Felicity appeared in the archway of the passage that led to the door. She wore a tiny black bikini and her long black hair was concealed in a black scarf tied like a turban. She was skinny but very sexy.

"I thought it would be nice to go for a swim, Quin," she said. "It's too hot to sleep at the moment."

Quintin carefully tied the sash of his dressing gown. "That's a very good idea. Is everyone else asleep?"

"I suppose so. There's no noise anywhere."

"I shall go in with nothing on then. How about you?"

"No, thanks."

"I insist."

"Oh, all right then. But do behave yourself."

"I may do. I may not. Come on. I'll undress out there."

A moment later the room was empty. It was the chance I had been waiting for.

I jumped up and walked quickly into the room. I pulled open the drawer of the bedside table expecting to find there all the photographs he had taken that morning. I was out of luck. The drawer contained only a small bottle of aspirin and one photograph. I took it out, shut the drawer and had a close look at it. It was a picture of Sally alone. I was somewhere out of sight to one side. Sally looked very beautiful and very naked. I tore the print into four pieces and was about to stuff them into my pocket when I saw a large glass ashtray on top of the chest of drawers. Beside it, amongst the rubble of money, pocket watch, fountain pen, diary and cigarette case which Quintin had obviously taken from his pockets when he began to undress, I spotted a cigarette lighter. It lit at the second attempt and I held the pieces of photograph in the flame until they caught. Then I dropped them into the ashtray where they burnt prettily.

I looked round the room. Where had he put the rest of the photographs? There was a briefcase – the one he had brought to the house earlier – lying on a desk near the window and I opened it and looked inside. Nothing. I went through the drawers of the desk and drew a blank again. That left only the chest of drawers amongst the most obvious places. Speed was important. I started with the bottom drawer and worked up, leaving the drawer below open. I remembered being told that that was what burglars did when they were in a hurry. Time enough to shut them and conceal any other sign of my presence after I had the negatives.

Quintin didn't seem to have very much in the way of clothes. What he had was distinctly unattractive. His underwear and socks were in the most hideously bad taste, but I didn't even pause to shudder. I was as quick as I could be, but I knew I hadn't missed any possible hiding place. I even went through a pile of handkerchiefs in the top drawer in case he had hidden the negatives between their folds. Nothing.

I stood back, my hands on my hips, and wondered where to look next. Where else could they be? Possibly in the pocket of a suit. There was a fitted cupboard next to the chest of drawers. I had my hand on the handle when a voice said, "I had an idea that I should be having a visit from you."

I turned round.

Quintin stood in the doorway. He wore his dressing gown and a broad smile; a smile of triumph. "How nice of you to place yourself in my hands," he said smoothly. "Burglary's a serious matter here, you know. I don't think you're going to like the inside of a Jamaican prison."

He put out a hand and pressed a bell-push on the wall. Far away I thought I heard the bell ring.

TWENTY-SIX

"I don't believe I'll wait for the police to arrive," I said. "I'll be on my way now."

How long had I, I wondered? How long before someone answered the bell? Had he really been expecting me? Was there time to beat him up and force him to tell me where the negatives were?

The answer to the last question was almost certainly no. If I was to get away I had to get going quickly, yet something held me back. I couldn't bear the thought that I had got so near and yet had failed to achieve my aim.

"You'll have a job getting away," said Quintin happily. "This place is practically a fortress, you know."

I had a sudden bright idea. I smiled cheerfully back at Quintin. "That's too bad," I said. "But it doesn't matter very much. I expect your host will understand, and even if he doesn't I don't care. I've done what I came to do." I waved at the ashtray with its blackened and curled pieces of photograph. "I found the negatives and now they're destroyed."

I watched his eyes very closely as I spoke. I hoped that Quintin would be unable to prevent his eyes looking, just for a moment, in the direction of the hiding place. His eyes didn't even flicker. He just looked straight at me. He was still smiling.

He sneered, "I know you haven't found them. Felicity recognised you in the hotel tonight, so I thought you might come here, though of course I didn't know what your aunt had told you. I was ready for you, just in case. I made sure all the doors were unlocked so that you could walk straight into my trap. In a few seconds you'll be under lock and key. And if you tell anyone what you really came for then I guarantee that I'll do what I promised with those photographs."

I knew then that I had lost. My raid was a fiasco. If I were to salvage anything from the ruins I must get away now – get away so that I could fight again another day.

I turned and ran out of the open French windows on to the balcony.

"Wait a minute," Quintin shouted after me.

"Not me," I called cheerfully. "See you in London."

I climbed onto the railing and started to pull myself onto the wall which divided Quintin's terrace from Felicity's. It was flat at the top and if I took it carefully and kept my balance I could walk along it to the roof.

Out of the corner of my eye I saw Quintin running out of the bedroom window. He rushed towards me.

"You can't get away," he called, but his voice sounded less confident now. "You can't."

"Can't I now?" I was standing upright on the dividing wall. "We'll see about that."

I suppose Quintin must suddenly have decided that there was after all a real possibility that I might escape. But in view of his behaviour a few moments later perhaps that is taking too Christian an attitude. More likely he saw an opportunity to kill me and remove me from the scene even more effectively and permanently than if he had me arrested. If he killed me I should no longer be a rival, and better still I would be unable to tell anyone what he had done.

Whatever the reason he suddenly leapt forward and grabbed my ankles as I stood balanced on my precarious perch only a foot or two from the seaward end of the wall.

There was nothing for my hands to hold on to. I flailed with my arms and I tried to keep my balance. It was hopeless. As I felt myself falling I tried to twist my body so that I would fall inside the railings. I almost made it. Afterwards I wondered whether Quintin had given my ankles a twist to send me over.

"Help," he bellowed as I started to fall. "Help me. He's getting away."

He was very nearly right. Thanks to him I almost got clean away to the next world. As I crashed down towards the sea my right arm brushed the railings. I grabbed instinctively with my hand. I caught one of the uprights. I gripped and held on. The force of the jerk as my body stopped falling nearly dislocated my right shoulder. I reached up with my left arm and grabbed another upright post. I hung by my hands with my face towards the cliff and wondered what would happen next.

"Help, help!" Quintin was yelling. "There's a burglar. He's trying to get away."

I felt a savage pain in the fingers of my left hand and realised that he had kicked my knuckles. I shifted my grip quickly, but he kicked me again and again. I looked up. Surely he must peep over the railings in a moment or two to see how I was getting on. I tightened my shoulders so that I hung not like a sack of potatoes but like a gymnast on a horizontal bar. I swung my legs about trying to get a toehold on the cliff face but this part of the house jutted out from the cliff and I couldn't feel anything. I could hear the sea splashing on the rocks below me.

Quintin stopped kicking my fingers and started climbing over the railings.

"This is the end of you," he said quietly. "You're going to be killed while trying to get away." The quietness of his voice was in sharp contrast to his shouts of a moment before.

He clambered over the railings a few feet from where I hung and started to work his way along the outside towards me. He held on carefully with feet and hands.

Inside the house I could hear people shouting and running about. It sounded as though someone was hammering on Quintin's bedroom door. I had only to hang on long enough and Quintin's attempt to murder me would be a failure.

I wondered how he proposed to finish me off. He would have a job reaching down far enough to aim a kick at my head. I supposed he would try to kick my hands again. I pulled back my left hand – the one nearer him – and waited. I said nothing. I realised with a sort of weird satisfaction that I hated him. I hated him as I had never hated anyone before.

He kicked at my left wrist. I was too quick for him.

"Go on," he whispered hoarsely. "Let go. Die. Get out of my way. Don't you realise Sally is mine? I've loved her for years. I'm the father of her child. She's mine, mine, mine."

His voice rose and he kicked me hard in time with his words. Some of the kicks connected. They hurt. I let go with my left hand and swung back, taking all my weight on my right arm.

For a moment I think he thought he had me. He shuffled towards me a little further and when he saw that I was clinging on with only one hand he let himself down to the full extent of his arms and tried to kick my face. It was stupid of him. He would have done better to kick my right arm, but it was the opportunity I had been waiting for.

I reached up with my left hand and made a grab at him. By chance the front of his dressing gown swung open at that instant and my clutching fingers closed on the soft squashiness of his naked genitals. It gave me a shock and

I almost let go. It was the first time I had touched a man there since I left school. Desperation and hate made me hang on. I squeezed and gave a sharp tug.

"Let me go," he screamed. "Let go, you bastard."

He was hanging on with his hands only now, but he was still a foot or so above me.

I tugged again, harder this time.

"I'm going to tear them off and stuff them down your throat," I told him.

"You wouldn't. Please let go," he pleaded. He was quieter now as he begged me to release him.

I suppose I was momentarily mad. I found that all I could think of was that if I pulled off Quintin's sexual apparatus, he would be unable to go to bed with Sally.

I started a steady downward pressure.

Quintin started screaming. We both stared, horrified and fascinated, at what I was doing.

Suddenly Quintin stopped screaming.

"Oh no," he almost wept. "I can't bear it. It's coming off."

And then perhaps because the pain was too much for him or possibly because he couldn't bear to have his manhood removed he gave up the struggle. He let go of the railing and grabbed at my hand.

For a long instant he seemed to hover in the air in front of me. His tortured face was a foot from mine. In a strange way I suddenly found myself feeling sorry for him. I let go with my left hand and reached for his arm. It was no good. My fingers slipped on the silk of his dressing gown and, just as though he had pressed a button in a lift, he rushed downwards into the darkness. He let out another terrified scream which went on and on until it was abruptly cut off by a dull thud. There was no sound of a splash and peering downward in the gloom I thought I could make out his body, the dressing gown wildly disarranged, spread out on a rock at the water's edge.

In a way I rather admired him. He had decided, albeit in the heat of the moment, that he would rather die than live as a eunuch. I remembered reading somewhere that Frenchmen would rather die than live without sex, but that Englishmen placed self-preservation first. That made Quintin a Frenchman, I supposed.

There was, however, no time to muse on this interesting topic. I pulled myself up and managed to grasp the top of the railing. While I tried to get a foothold on the edge of the terrace I looked over the railing into the bedroom. It was still empty. Though I hadn't realised what was happening at the time I now remembered hearing a series of crashes from the door which led to the passage outside. As I looked there was another one, accompanied by a splintering noise, and a large fully-dressed man came running into the room. Two men in dressing gowns followed him. They looked quickly round the room and then ran straight towards the terrace – and me.

I suppose I was so full of adrenalin at that moment that I could have done almost any feat of strength or agility known to man. Certainly I couldn't have done what I did next in cold blood.

I gave a great sideways leap so that I was protected from sight by the dividing wall from which I had almost plunged to my death a minute before. My hands grabbed and held the railings. I made a rapid heave-to-chest, leapt lightly over the rail and landed on my toes on Felicity's terrace. I paused, breathing as quietly as I could, and waited for the applause. None came. I moved on across the terrace until I was in the dark shadow in the angle between the wall and the house itself.

I heard footsteps on the terrace next door.

"What's going on?" said a voice. "Where are they? Where's Quintin?"

"They may have fallen over the rail," another voice answered. I recognised it as that of my unwilling host. It was a rich deep American voice simply oozing with the huge self-confidence that great power gives to a man. I had seen him on television a few months before when he had been interviewed at London Airport. His voice once heard was unforgettable.

There was a pause. I guessed that they were looking over the railing.

"I think I can see someone on a rock down there," said the first voice after a moment.

"Can you see who it is? I can't see a darned thing without my glasses," said the American cheerfully.

"No. It's too dark. But I'm sure there's only one."

"The other one may be in the sea. If he is he's probably okay. And if that's right it can't be Frensham or he'd be calling out. So I guess that's Frensham you can see on the rock. Is he moving?"

"No. I don't think so. Who do you suppose the other one was?"

"Search me. Some kind of crook. We'll try and catch him. Then we'll see. Right?"

"Yes. What shall we do?"

"Get some of the men and start a complete search of the house and grounds. You, Toby," he said, and I realised that my antagonist of the morning was with them, "you press the button to shut the gates at the end of the drive. Wherever he is now he can't have got that far yet, and when the gate is shut the only way out of this joint is by sea. So get the power boat going, go see what you can do about

Mr Frensham down there, and then cruise around the area and keep your eyes open. And tell everyone there's a thousand-dollar bill for the guy who catches him."

"Yes, sir," said Toby. I heard him run off.

There was a babble of other voices, male and female, as some of the guests came out onto Quintin's terrace. I heard my Aunt Rosemary say, "What's happened? What is it?"

Everyone else chimed in, all speaking at once. Our host silenced them by saying in his comfortable bass voice, "Just one moment, ladies and gentlemen. Just one moment and I'll tell you what's happened."

They fell silent and he went on, "It seems that an intruder broke into Mr Frensham's room a few minutes ago. We don't know who he is or where he is now. Mr Frensham discovered him and rang his bell for assistance. One of my servants answered the bell but couldn't get into the room and hearing noises reported the matter to me. Frank and I came along to the door and found that it was locked on the inside and we couldn't get in. That's not very surprising because, as you all know, these doors lock automatically unless the catch is turned. It would have taken time to have found one of the master keys to open the door from the outside and it sounded as though Frensham was grappling with the intruder. Frank and I could hear him calling for help and saying the man was trying to get away. I had Toby smash the door down but by the time we got out here there was nobody here. It looks as though both men may have gone over the rail. Frank says he can see a body on the rocks down below and I've sent Toby to see what can be done about that. I suspect that it will prove to be Frensham, and that must mean the intruder pushed him over. Maybe the intruder fell over too, maybe he didn't. If he didn't he may be at large somewhere in the house or in the grounds. I intend to catch him."

He paused. I shivered.

"What can we do to help?" asked Aunt Rosemary.

"Go back to your rooms," he told them. "That will make the search easier for my servants, and it'll make it safer for you. This man is very likely a killer."

Somebody gave a horrified gasp. I longed to say, "Don't worry everybody – it's only me."

"That's okay," he went on. "There'll be no danger if you do as I say. I suggest that each lady has somebody check her room before she goes in to make sure this man isn't hiding there. If he isn't in the sea I expect he's got away by now, probably over the roof. But he may be hiding in one of your rooms. When you've checked that he isn't in your room lock yourself in till morning. I'll see you're informed of any developments."

As soon as he stopped talking they all started to chatter again. I caught garbled snatches of what they said as I stood pressed against the wall a few feet away. Almost at once they began to move away from Quintin's bedroom, and their voices faded. I stayed where I was, wondering what my next move ought to be.

If what the owner of the house had said was right – and I could see no reason to doubt it – my only escape route was the sea. The gate at the end of the drive was presumably now shut, and for some good reason was unclimbable. Perhaps it was electrified. There were men in the grounds searching for me, and I could hear the engine of the speedboat as Toby searched the sea at the bottom of the cliff.

My best plan, I decided, would be to get onto the roof and lie low there (or lie high perhaps it ought to be) until the hue and cry had quietened. In a few hours I could have a try at escaping. If the sea it had to be, I preferred the steps from the terrace by the pool to any of the cliff faces I had seen so far that night.

I was just about to move back towards the railing when the French window three feet from where I stood was slid open and the dark-haired model girl, Felicity, stepped out. She wore some sort of dressing gown.

I froze where I stood. She walked straight past me to the railing and leaned over it looking down towards the sea. She stayed like that for several minutes. I wondered whether it would be a good idea to go into her room and hide somewhere there. On balance it seemed a bad idea. There was probably nowhere to conceal myself satisfactorily, and even if I did find somewhere it might be impossible to get out again without being discovered. I was in a very dark corner where I stood. The chances were that she would walk past me again without seeing me. I waited, watching her.

It gave me a shock when she suddenly shouted, "Who is it? Who is it, Toby?"

An unintelligible cry came from below. Felicity repeated her question.

There was another cry. It seemed to satisfy her because she called, "Is he all right?"

Again I couldn't make out the reply.

"Are you sure?" she shouted.

The reply to this question concluded the conversation. She straightened up and, turning away from the railing, walked back towards her bedroom. I pressed my back against the wall and narrowed my eyes lest she see the whites of them in the darkness.

She paused in the open window and looked straight at me. She stared at me in silence for a moment, then she said in a low, almost conversational tone, "He's dead. Quintin's dead. You've killed him."

"I didn't kill him. He tried to kill me. He tried to push me over. In the struggle he was the one who fell."

She didn't say anything. She simply stood and stared at me in silence. In the hot air I could smell the scent she wore.

"Don't you believe me?" I said at last.

"If you want me to." She sounded bored, as though it were of no importance to her. "He's dead. Quintin Frensham is dead." She said it slowly as though trying to comprehend some great truth. "I can't really believe it yet."

I supposed she was in a state of shock. When she realised what had happened she was going to scream the house down. I toyed with the idea of hitting her on the chin and knocking her out while I had the chance, but I couldn't bring myself to do so. I wasn't sufficiently modern to start thumping women, and her chin was a very pretty one.

"You'd better come into my room," she said suddenly. "It'll be the safest place for you to hide. You won't be able to get away for a couple of hours at least."

She smiled at me and walked into her room. Puzzled, I followed her.

"Shut the window and pull the curtains," she ordered. "We don't want anyone to look in and see you."

I did as I was told. I still couldn't believe she was going to help me.

"What's happened to your hand?" she asked. We both looked at my left hand as it gripped the edge of the curtain. It was badly grazed and it was bleeding slightly in two or three places.

"Quintin kicked my hand to try to make me let go of the railings." I spoke slowly. I was glad that the state of my hand corroborated what I had told her before. "He wanted to kill me."

"Why?"

I didn't know how to reply to that. Until I knew whether I could trust this girl the less I told her the better. Even if I found her unexpectedly one hundred per cent on my side I still intended to tell her as little as possible. The old intelligence maxim 'need-to-know' flashed through my mind.

"Never mind," she said quietly. "It's none of my business. Something to do with your girlfriend, I suppose."

I nodded.

She smiled and turned away. "Come into the bathroom and I'll do something about your hand."

Again I followed her. She led the way into the bathroom and made me sit on a stool while she washed the blood from my hand and covered the only really nasty graze with a piece of sticking plaster. I enjoyed her attentions. Her fingers were long and pointed and rather like Sally's. I felt the same thrill of sexual excitement at the feel of them on my skin and the thought of them on my body that I had felt when I had first seen Sally's. I supposed I was kinky for beautiful hands.

"The only way to get away from here now," she told me as she worked, "is by sea. I hope you're a good swimmer. This house is built on a peninsula and when the gates at the end of the drive are shut there's no escape that way. The gates and the fence are built to keep people out, but they'll be just as efficient at keeping you in. The cliffs are high and sheer all round and though there are one or two climbable places you'd never find them in the dark. Your only way out is down the steps to the dock where the yacht is tied up. I expect they'll put a guard on that while they search the house and the grounds but eventually they'll have to give up and I expect they'll think you've drowned. When they've all gone back to bed you'll be safe to go."

She smoothed the sticking plaster over my knuckles. It hurt but I managed to be a good soldier. My nanny would have been proud of me.

"I hope that stays in place properly," Felicity said. "The shark and barracuda are supposed to be able to smell blood in the water, so if you bleed too much while you're swimming I suppose they'll eat you."

"What a jolly thought."

"I'm in a very jolly mood tonight," she said happily. "This is the best night of my life."

"Why?"

"I'll tell you in a moment. Come into the bedroom and take your clothes off."

I stared at her.

"Why?" I repeated.

"You don't want to get them wet, do you? Take them off and I'll give you a plastic bag."

I said nothing.

She laughed at me. "How coy you are. But you needn't be. I know exactly what you look like with no clothes on. I helped Quintin to develop the photographs he took of you and your girlfriend this morning." She looked me slowly up and down, the tip of her pink tongue protruding slightly between her pouting red lips. "I was distinctly impressed."

It took a moment for the penny to drop.

"You helped him to develop the photographs?" I said. "Then you know where they are? Are they here?"

She smiled sweetly. "Do you want them back?"

"Yes please."

I glared at her. I was thrilled by the thought that the photographs were after all almost within my grasp. At the same time there was something about her manner which made me wonder if she was going to be difficult about handing them over. If necessary, I thought, I would have to revise my gentlemanly attitude towards her chin.

Her eyes widened and she stepped back. I realised that I probably looked pretty fierce.

"It's all right," she said quickly. "I'll get them for you."

"Where are they?"

"Here. In the bedroom."

"Let me see."

She led the way back into her bedroom. I followed. She went over to a chest of drawers, opened the top drawer and pulled out a large brown envelope.

In my eagerness I almost snatched it from her. I ripped it open and shook out the contents onto the bedspread. There were half a dozen prints in various sizes and a number of negatives.

"Are they all here?"

She was standing with her back to the wall. She looked very frightened. She nodded.

"Are you sure?"

"I'm sure. Quintin gave that to me this evening. At about half past six. When he'd finished developing and so on. I saw him put everything in there."

That sounded fair enough.

"Did he give you any special instructions?"

She looked blank. "No, not really. He just asked me to keep the envelope for him. He was afraid you might manage to follow him back here and search his room."

"Were there any photographs in his room?"

"Not that I know of."

It was a trick question, but the answer was a reasonable one. Probably Quintin wouldn't want his girlfriend to know that he was keeping a photograph of another woman for his private delectation.

I was satisfied. "Have you a lighter or some matches?"

Without answering she went across to the dressing table and took a small gold Dunhill lighter from a handbag. She held it out to me at arm's length.

"Thank you." I took it from her. She still looked terrified so I smiled at her. "I'm not going to eat you," I said.

She grinned a little shamefacedly. "You're going to burn them?"

"Yes."

"Don't set fire to the bed. There's an ashtray here." She picked up a big glass ashtray – the twin of the one in Quintin's room – and brought it over to me. Even then I didn't trust her completely and I watched her out of the corner of my eyes to see that she didn't steal any of the photographs.

I burned them all, one after another, until there was a substantial heap of charred remains in the ashtray. The last one to go showed Sally standing at the water's edge. Felicity stood at my shoulder and watched as the flame caught the bottom of the picture and I put it down flaming in the ashtray.

"Your girlfriend's very lovely," she said. "She's got the most beautiful breasts I've ever seen. I'm very envious."

I said nothing. The photograph curled and blackened but one could still see the outlines of the picture, the curves of Sally's body.

I picked up the ashtray and carried it through into the bathroom. I prodded at the burned photographs until they were broken into tiny pieces, then I flushed them down the lavatory. I washed out the ashtray and returned to the bedroom. A great weight seemed to have been lifted from me.

For the first time I felt almost happy. I smiled at Felicity.

"Thank you," I said. "That was kind of you."

"They were of no use to me," she said cautiously. She was still a little frightened.

Now that the photographs were destroyed and I could think straight again I realised that I must depend upon this girl if I were to escape. If she turned against me I was sunk. She had only to scream and I should be on the run again.

"I should love a cigarette," I said humbly.

"Of course." She gave me one and lit it for me.

"We've got a bit of a wait now," I said, sitting in the small armchair and dragging gratefully at my cigarette. "Tell me why this is the best night of your life?"

The only other places to sit were the bed and the dressing table stool and she chose the bed. She arranged herself comfortably with a pillow behind her head and lit a cigarette before she answered.

"Because Quintin is dead."

"Oh?"

She looked at me thoughtfully through the smoke of her cigarette and I guess that she was wondering how much she could or should trust me. I didn't blame her. I had done the same.

At last she said, "Quintin was going to blackmail you with those photographs, wasn't he?"

I nodded. I didn't think it was necessary to explain that actually it was poor Sally who was to have been blackmailed.

"Well, he's been blackmailing me for years. That's why I'm here now. It was the sort of foul thing that he liked doing." She paused for a moment and smiled at me. "Now that he's dead it's all over. All over."

I was fascinated to know what it was that he had blackmailed her with, but I couldn't really ask her. In order to be blackmailable one has to do something that one doesn't want everyone to know about.

While I was wondering what to say there was a sudden commotion outside her bedroom door. I heard voices and doors slamming. I stood up. There was a sharp knock on the door.

"Miss Fanshawe?" a voice called.

Felicity raised a long index finger to her lips and then pointed at the bathroom. I had taken two steps towards the bathroom door before I realised that I should be trapped if I went in there and I changed course and went over to the window.

"Yes?" she answered.

"Would you come out here, please. The police are here."

"Very well. I'll be out in a moment."

I opened the window as quietly as I could, walked through and looked back into the room. Felicity had got off her bed and was inspecting her face in the glass. She put some powder on her nose and touched up her lipstick and fiddled with her hair for a moment. Then she walked down the passage to the door, tightening the sash of her dressing gown as she went.

I moved into the dark corner of the terrace where she had found me and prepared for an anxious wait. I discovered that I still had my half-smoked cigarette in my hand and, regretfully deciding that it was too risky to smoke, I dropped it on the floor and ground it underfoot.

I wondered if Felicity would hand me over to the police. On balance I thought that she probably would not. But she might. Perhaps she was still frightened of me and regretting her earlier intention to help me. I moved my position slightly so that I could see into the bedroom through a crack in the curtains. If the police came into the room I should have time to take a running dive into the sea. I didn't much fancy the idea but it was my only hope. I thought that if I dived well clear of the cliff I should have a good chance of avoiding Quintin's fate.

After what seemed like an hour, but was in fact four and a half minutes by my watch, Felicity came back into the room. I waited for a moment to make sure that she was on her own, then I walked back in to join her.

She smiled at me. It was such a beautiful and reassuring smile that the tight knot of anxiety that had been screwing up my guts for the last few minutes immediately dissolved.

I smiled back and was just about to speak when she put her finger to her lips again. Without speaking she beckoned to me to follow and led the way into the bathroom. I followed her. She shut the door.

"I don't think it's safe to talk in the bedroom for a few minutes," she said. "The door is pretty solid, but if anyone was right outside they might hear your voice."

I nodded agreement. "What is going on? What are the police doing?"

"They've searched everywhere and – surprise, surprise – they haven't caught the murderer."

I shuddered.

"We were all asked out into the hall just now to be told that he's got away and that there's no further danger." She giggled.

I breathed a sigh of relief.

"So I can get out through the gate – the way I came in?"

"I'm afraid not. It's been decided that the gate will be kept shut and a further search of the grounds will be done as soon as it gets light." She smiled at me sympathetically. "So it's still the sea for you. Are you a good swimmer?"

"Fair. But what about the motor boat?"

"No good. It's been immobilised."

I thought about it. She was right. There was no other way.

"How soon do you think I can go?"

"Give everyone half an hour to get back to bed. Then I'll go out and see if the coast is clear. If it is you can go down the steps to the sea. I'll give you a plastic bag to put your clothes in."

She went back into the bedroom and I heard her opening and shutting drawers. A minute later she reappeared holding a large plastic bag.

"I think this should do. Put everything in there."

She leaned back against the wall and folded her arms as though waiting for the performance to begin.

I grinned at her. "I never take my clothes off in front of women," I told her, "except when I'm just about to go to bed with them."

She grinned back at me, very prettily.

"Well?" she said. "Why not? There's plenty of time."

"All right," I said. "You asked for it." I jumped forwards and made a grab for her. She dodged and ran out of the room, squealing with laughter. I laughed too and I restrained myself from following and I shut the door.

It was just a bit of fun, I told myself as I undressed; just a joke. But was that really all it was?

I rolled my clothes up into a bundle and put them inside the bag. I contemplated keeping my underpants on to swim in, but I realised that if I did I might have difficulty disposing of them when I got ashore. So everything went in except the belt from my trousers which I used to do up the parcel.

I put the parcel on the loo seat and stood up. Now what?

I caught a glimpse of my reflection in the glass above my washbasin. My tan was as good a camouflage as my dark clothing had been. It was as well that it was all over.

But I certainly couldn't walk out into the bedroom without a stitch on. I found Felicity far too attractive and it worried me a lot. Only a few hours ago I had almost been unfaithful to Sally with Magnolia. I thought I should find it easy to resist any further temptations that came my way. But the ghastly thing that I now realised was that my head didn't rule my body. It was like a badly-disciplined Battalion which wouldn't obey the orders of its Commanding Officer.

If Felicity gave me the smallest encouragement I should certainly fall.

I stared at my reflection.

"You're a useless waster," I told it.

I pulled a face.

Being a waster was one thing, I decided, but being a flasher was something else. There was a limit. I picked up a dark-coloured towel and wrapped it tightly round my waist. Then I opened the door and went into the bedroom.

TWENTY-SEVEN

Carrying my bundle of clothes under my arm, and wearing only Felicity's towel, I tiptoed down the hall outside her room. She stood at the open front door, looking anxiously about her and beckoning me to follow. It had been her idea that she should lead the way to make sure that the coast was clear.

Outside we stood quietly together in the darkness for a moment, looking and listening. When we were sure that there was no one about, we set off round the corner of the house towards the garden. When we were opposite the pool and had completed about half the journey to the steps I suddenly spotted the silhouette of a man. He was standing by the railing. I took Felicity's arm and drew her silently into the shadows at the side of the house.

"What is it?" she whispered.

I pointed.

She nodded. We stood for a while uncertain of our next move. I wondered if he was simply taking a stroll, and if he would wander away after a minute or two. However, it soon became clear from his immobility that he was a sentry, posted to guard the steps.

Felicity pressed herself against me and put her lips close to my ear. "I think it's Toby," she whispered. "We'll have to get him to move. I'll cause a diversion by jumping into the pool. As soon as he moves you slip past him."

On the other hand, I thought, if he doesn't move I don't know what I shall do. But it wasn't a bad plan and I couldn't think of anything better. I nodded.

"Give me my towel now," she whispered.

I hesitated again. I had to leave it somewhere and this was an excellent way of disposing of it. I handed it over. I felt very naked.

She smiled up at me. I could see her teeth gleaming whitely in the starlight.

"Goodbye," she whispered, putting her mouth close to my ear again. "I've enjoyed meeting you. Ring me up in London sometime. I'm in the phone book."

She kissed me gently on the cheek and moved away quickly and silently into the darkness of the garden.

As soon as she had gone I crept forward towards the steps, taking advantage of the shadows. Toby was looking out to sea.

When I was as near to him as I could get without emerging into the open I pressed myself against the wall and awaited further developments. I hadn't long to wait.

There was a loud splash as Felicity jumped into the pool. Toby swung round and looked. He didn't move. 'Oh, God,' I thought. 'He's too well-disciplined. He isn't going to leave his post.'

"Who's that?" he called out.

"Ooooh," squeaked Felicity. "I didn't know there was anyone there."

"Is that you, Miss Fanshawe?"

"Yes, it is. But you're not to come any nearer. I haven't got a stitch on."

Toby laughed. "That's okay, Ma'am. It's too dark to see that."

He obviously didn't believe what he was saying because he took two paces towards the pool as he spoke.

Felicity splashed about in the water.

"I couldn't sleep," she said conversationally. "It's all been too horrible. Poor Mr Frensham. What do you think happened to the other man?"

"I expect he fell in the sea, Ma'am. He didn't have time to get away through the house. I bust that door down quick, you know."

"Do you think he drowned?"

"Maybe." Toby took two more slow paces towards the pool. "There's a strong current round this point. The body would be swept clear round and along the coast. I might easily have missed it in the boat."

Felicity splashed about without saying anything for a moment.

"Suppose he's alive," she said. "Will he get away?"

"I doubt it, Ma'am. Police will be looking all along the beach, waiting for someone to swim in. The boss is a big man. They'll do a lot for him."

I sent a silent message of thanks to Felicity. The more information I had the better.

Toby advanced another pace as he spoke. A couple more and I should be able to slip past behind him.

"I hope they catch him," said Felicity convincingly. "Anyway, I'm going to get out now. You make sure you're looking the other way."

"Don't you worry, Miss Fanshawe. It's too dark to see anything tonight. I can't even see my hand in front of my face."

"That's good," said Felicity.

Toby was a dreadful liar. His night vision must have been much better developed than mine and he was nearer the pool than I was, but *I* could see Felicity quite clearly as she emerged up the steps at the far end of the pool. I could see the long white length of her back and the division between her small buttocks.

On the edge of the pool she turned and posed for us. Toby crept a little nearer, his head jutting forward as he strained to study her nudity.

I detached myself from the shadow of the house and stole silently on my bare feet past his massive back and down the steps. When I was about half-way down I heard Felicity say, "What on earth did I do with my dressing gown?"

And the great idiot spoiled it all for himself by answering, "It's on the chair behind you, Miss Fanshawe."

Felicity gave a shriek of horror. "You brute," she cried. "You could see all along."

It was a nice performance. She should have been an actress, not a model.

The great yacht moved gently against its moorings. I walked quickly along the little quay beside it, praying there would be no other sentry to worry about.

At the seaward end of the quay I sat down and put my feet into the water. It swirled, black and rather frightening around my ankles. I tried not to think about the horrible things that might be swimming or crawling below me. I put my clothes bundle on top of my head and fixed my belt under my chin to hold it in place. It felt awkward but it seemed quite secure.

I lowered myself carefully into the water. It was much colder than the sea off our little beach. I let go of the quay and pushed off. At once the current gripped me and I felt myself being swept out to sea. The current was far too strong to fight against, so I concentrated on staying afloat. If I had ever wondered why the house I had just left had a swimming pool I did so no longer. The sea at this point was most definitely not safe for bathing.

When I had been dragged out about a hundred yards the current began to change direction and I found that I was being carried along roughly parallel to the shore. I could see only one light in the house and that, I realised, came from Felicity's bedroom. By now, I imagined, she would be back in her room, drying herself after her swim and preparing to go to bed. I could picture it all very clearly in my mind.

She had not been in the bedroom when I had emerged from the bathroom and I had waited for her, smoking another of her cigarettes.

When she returned a few minutes later she was in great form, obviously thoroughly enjoying the adventure.

"I've been prowling round the house," she told me. "There's no one about. It's safe for you to leave now, I think." Her eyes were alight with excitement and she looked mouth-wateringly attractive. "Are you ready?"

"Yes," I said. I had mixed feelings. On the one hand, my brain was ordering me to leave at once, partly because I had to go sooner or later anyway and partly to remove my body from the temptations of Felicity's bedroom. On the other, my ill-disciplined body was trying to disobey orders, partly because it didn't fancy the idea of the imminent swim and partly because it did fancy Felicity's. Somewhat to my surprise my brain won. "Let's go," I said.

"I'll lead the way to the front door. You follow me when I wave at you."

And so we had left.

After a while I realised that the current had lost its strength and that I was moving more slowly. I could see some lights in the hotel and I began to swim slowly towards them. They looked a very long way away but I swam on, thinking about Felicity, and Magnolia.

I wanted to be a proper husband to Sally, and had every intention of being so. It had never been necessary for me to be faithful to anyone before and I had always assumed it would be difficult if not impossible. In the last twelve hours two beautiful women had offered themselves to me with no strings attached. Looking back now as I swam in the cold water I was amazed and then rather proud to realise that I had turned them both down. The other extraordinary revelation that now occurred to me was that I found I had no regrets. I had surprised myself.

Of course, we weren't actually married yet, but I had stayed faithful. The silly thing was that sex with any other woman was the palest shadow of the joy and wonder of making love with Sally. The two acts were totally different.

I stopped swimming. I was very tired and the weight of the clothes on my head was already pushing me downward. I floated just above the surface. The hotel was very much closer, I now noticed. I could see the beach and the bonfire and a couple dancing together on the sand.

Exhaustion overwhelmed me and I started to sink. My feet touched the sandy bottom. In some weird way that I couldn't understand I could still see the bonfire and the couple dancing. I wondered if this meant that I was already dead. It was most peculiar. A small wave slapped into my face. I blinked and rubbed the water from my eyes. The scene was the same. The sandy bottom was firm under my feet. At long last the truth struck me. I had been swimming in less than five feet of water.

I was alive and almost ashore. I felt suddenly excited. I wanted to get back to Sally. She must be worrying about me. I could reassure her. I waded slowly towards the beach. Where, I wondered, were the police? How was I going to escape them?

Another dancing couple had joined the first and now that I was closer I could hear the soft strains of Frank Sinatra singing something like 'Songs for Swinging Lovers'. There were a lot of other people lolling on the sand around the bonfire, between twenty and thirty at a rough guess. As I watched, a young man wearing swimming shorts with tight-fitting legs that reached half-way down his thighs stood up and wandered round the fire. He held a bottle of some pale-coloured liquid – rum or whisky – and he seemed to be refilling people's glasses. Judging by the voices I could hear they were all Americans.

I looked round for an escape route. The hotel filled most of the crescent-shaped beach. That meant that there were three possible routes; one to the left of the hotel; one to the right; and one straight through the middle. The beach party was on the right at one end of the beach. The hotel itself was, I decided, far too dangerous. Only the left-flanking route remained.

I waded back into the deeper water and then moved across to the far end of the beach. I was almost at the water's edge when I saw the policeman. If he hadn't chosen that precise moment to light a cigarette I should have walked straight into him a minute later. As it was I sank back down into the little waves and eased myself backwards into the sea again.

There was nothing else to do but return to the beach party and hope to be able to escape to the right as soon as they had gone to bed. I waded across and sat on the bottom of the sea so that my head was just above the surface, and I watched them and longed for them to go to bed. I was so close that I might have been a guest at the party myself except that I didn't have a glass in my hand. I looked enviously at the young man with the funny shorts who held the bottle. I could have used a stiffish shot of whatever it was.

When the record came to an end he jumped up and said,

"This party is moribund."

"Let it die, feller, let it die," said someone in a relaxed drawl.

"Bed is what I want," said a girl's voice.

"And it's just what you're gonna get," a man answered.

Everyone laughed.

"Okay," said the young man whose party I presumed it was. "One more swim, then bed."

"It's three o'clock in the morning, feller," someone told him.

"Right. It's the best time. It's a race now. To the diving stage and back. Last one back buys champagne for everyone here tomorrow."

"Oh no," said several people, but they all seemed to be getting to their feet.

I looked round. At first I couldn't see the diving stage but at last I spotted it. It was some way out in the centre of the bay. I moved off to my right so that I shouldn't be run into by the race.

"The girls can have a five-second start," the young man announced. "No cheating."

They were drawn up in two lines between the bonfire and the sea. The girls were in front, all wearing small bikinis. The men were behind them. They all wore shorts similar in cut to their host, but in different and amazing hues and patterns.

"On your marks. Get set. Go, girls, go!"

The girls, screaming with excitement, rushed into the water. Five seconds later the men followed them.

This was my chance. I pulled my clothes bundle off my head and waded quickly ashore. Once clear of the water I ran past the bonfire and into the shadow of the palm trees at the edge of the beach. I paused and looked back. No one seemed to have noticed me. I could hear splashes and excited cries from the young Americans as they raced back from the diving stage, and a few seconds later the first of them emerged from the sea, laughing and yelling encouragement to their friends.

I turned inland and moved off between the fat boles of the palm trees. The ground sloped steeply upward and I realised that I was at the end of the fault in the cliffs. To my right the ground rose almost sheer. Unless I tried to climb up the cliff face itself this was my only way out. I wondered if there was a policeman on this side too. I prayed that the police – who could not have had an unlimited number of men to spare for what might easily prove to be a completely wasteful exercise – had decided that no stranger would get past the beach party unchallenged and had therefore concentrated their efforts elsewhere. My prayer went unanswered.

At the top of the slope I came to the coast road. I stopped behind the last tree and looked unhappily at the two police cars parked, so far as I was concerned, in exactly the wrong place. Even if I were to climb the cliff there was no way round them. There was no escape this way either.

I walked slowly back down the slope to the beach. There were only two courses open to me now. One was to take to the sea again; the other was to go through the hotel. I didn't think much of the first idea. I felt too tired to swim very far, and even if I managed to reach another bay there was every reason to suppose that the police would be waiting there too. Even if they were not, or if I was able to slip past them, I should still have a long walk back to the car in the hotel car park. I should be at risk all that time. On the other hand, to walk straight into the hotel was to invite instant arrest. I put down my bundle of clothes and sat on it. I couldn't really think straight.

The young people's beach party was breaking up at last. The race was over. No doubt someone had been adjudged the loser. Now they were drying themselves and pulling on wraps and jerseys. It gave me an idea.

I stood up, undid my parcel and started to get dressed. I pulled on my pants and my trousers and put on my shoes. It wasn't easy to do and I got quite a lot of sand inside my pants. It was extremely uncomfortable. I made a little hole in the sand at the foot of a large old palm tree and, screwing my plastic bag into a ball, I buried it in the hole and smoothed the sand over it. I threw my jersey over my back and knotted the arms in a casual way under my chin. I spent a minute threading my belt through the loops on my trousers and patted my hip pocket to make sure the car keys were safe. I was ready.

The beach party had packed up. The boys and girls were strolling back in twos and threes towards the hotel. I waited until the last lot – a group of six or seven – had started to drift off before I emerged from my hiding place. I walked in what I hoped was a casual saunter, pretending to button my fly-buttons as I broke cover. I hoped the policeman at the far end of the beach, supposing he was looking in my direction and hadn't slipped off somewhere to buy some more cigarettes, would draw the obvious conclusion.

I caught up with the last group before they were half-way back to the hotel. The first person to notice that I had joined them was a pretty girl in a very small bikini. She had very blonde hair which fell down her back almost to her waist. It sparkled in the light from the embers of the dying bonfire.

"Hi," she said. She walked close to me and slid a cool plump arm around my waist.

"Er… Hi," I said.

She looked at me inquisitively. "I haven't seen you around before."

"I've been around," I answered vaguely.

"Oh. You're with George, are you?"

I made a noise that could have been interpreted as either an affirmative or a negative. It seemed to satisfy her.

"Great party, wasn't it?" she said.

"Right," I said. I knew that was American, but it seemed a little abrupt. "Great party," I echoed.

We had reached the hotel now and we wandered round a large swimming pool and up a short flight of steps that led to the bar. The dining room, where I had had dinner that evening, was just beyond the bar, I remembered.

The remainder of the party moved on into the hall but my blonde hung back.

"Do you have to leave just yet?"

For a horrible moment I thought that she must know who I was. Then I realised that her question meant that some of the beach party were not staying in the hotel and were about to leave. No doubt that was George and his friends. It was too good an opportunity to miss.

"I guess I do. It's late."

She sighed. "What a pity," she said. She stroked my chest with her fingertips. "You're so pretty and I do want to get laid so badly."

My God, I thought. Are all women sex maniacs? Yet again I was being tested. Yet again I had declined. I was officially a changed man. The gods must be laughing but they weren't going to beat me.

"How about tomorrow?" I said. I didn't want to make an

enemy of her then and there. She was good natural cover and, anyway, I was too much of a gent to turn her down flat.

"Have lunch with me," I went on.

"Great," she said. "You'll pick me up?"

"Right. One o'clock."

"What's your name?"

"Er. Johnny."

"Johnny what?"

"Yes. That's right. Johnny Watt. My ancestor invented the steam engine."

"Say…" she seemed impressed.

We wandered on into the hall. There were two very smart-looking policemen standing near the desk. They eyed us incuriously. We were just tourists to them. Good for the economy, but not what they were looking for. We kept walking.

Under the portico outside the front door everyone was saying goodnight, or good morning. There was another police car there. An officer was sitting at the wheel.

"Night, folks," someone called, and those who were leaving started to walk towards the car park. I heard an engine spring to life. I detached myself from my new girlfriend and gave her a farewell peck on her small, rather engagingly freckled nose.

"Goodnight, honey," I said. "See you tomorrow."

I walked away from the residents. As I did so there was a sudden hush as everyone stopped talking. They all seemed to be staring at me. The police officer in the car looked at me intently. The young man whose party it had been looked at me in amazement. He opened his mouth and said, "Who…?"

I gave everyone a cheerful wave and a beaming smile.

"Goodnight, folks," I called. "Great party."

"Goodnight, Johnny," called my girlfriend. Everyone else joined in, possibly feeling ashamed that they hadn't recognised me before.

"Goodnight, Johnny," they chorused. "Night, Johnny."

I was definitely the popular guy of the moment. I walked quickly off towards my car, pulling the keys out of my pocket as I went. Headlamps were cutting swathes of light across the tarmac. I saw my car, ran over to it, unlocked it, climbed in and started up. A car near me moved off and I followed it.

I was the last to drive out of the car park. The police had a road block on the main road just outside. There were flashing lights and several police cars. A police officer was holding open a portable barrier as our cars drove through. I waved a thank you at him as I drove past. As we accelerated down the road I watched in my rear-view mirror as he swung the barrier closed behind me.

TWENTY-EIGHT

Sally greeted me at the front door. "Darling, I've been so worried about you," she said as I held her tightly in my arms. "I've worked myself up into the most frightful state."

She was right. Her lips were noticeably hot as we kissed. Indeed, her whole face was burning. Her eyes were unnaturally shiny and seemed to be about twice their normal size.

I said, "You've got a temperature."

"I know. I took it an hour ago."

"What was it?"

"102."

"My God. You ought to be in bed."

"I have been, darling. It didn't help. I've lain there ever since you left, wondering what was happening to you. I couldn't sleep. Are you all right? What happened?"

I picked her up in my arms and carried her to the bedroom. "The photographs no longer exist. I burned them all."

"Thank God. But what about Quintin?"

"He's dead."

"Good heavens! How? Why? You didn't kill him?"

"No, darling. I didn't. I'll tell you all about it in a minute." I put her down on the bed and got the codeine bottle from her dressing table. "Have you taken any of these?" I asked her.

"No."

I gave her two and she swallowed them with some water I fetched from the bathroom.

"Have you any other symptoms?"

"Just a sore throat."

"Bad?"

"Rather uncomfortable."

"What do you think is wrong?"

"I don't know, Jimmy. If it wasn't for my throat I'd think I'd brought it all on by worrying about you. But my throat started before."

"So it did. It looks as though you're getting a cold. Or possibly even the flu." I started to undress. "Anyway," I went on. "We're going back to England in a few hours. Do you feel up to travelling?"

"Oh, yes, darling. Please. I want to go home so badly."

"Back to Highworth?"

"No, darling. Back to London. Back to your flat. I'd like to pull the curtains and bolt the door and just be there with you. It'll be lovely."

I climbed into bed with her and switched out the light. I wrapped my body round hers in the position in which we always went to sleep.

"I'll tell you all my adventures," I said quietly in the darkness. "Then we'll try to sleep for a few hours. Tomorrow we go back to London."

And then I told her the whole story, omitting only what I had done to Quintin to make him let go of the railing.

"You are good to me, Jimmy," Sally said when I had finished. "That horrible creature might have killed you. I'm glad he's dead. He deserved it."

"Yes, he did. The law may not believe in hanging people. But he wasn't fit to live."

Exhaustion caught up with me then, and I felt myself sinking into sleep. I hugged Sally tightly to me.

"It's all over now, darling. We can go home and be together always. For as long as we live."

"Yes, Jimmy. For as long as we live. We'll be happy, won't we, darling."

"Very happy," I said, poor fool that I was. "Very happy."

We slept.

***

The return journey to England was unremarkable. After breakfast we packed our bags and said goodbye to Magnolia, who eyed me politely with a twinkle in her eye as she curtseyed. Jackson drove us to the airport. I tipped Jackson generously and thanked him and said goodbye.

"Thank you, sir. I hope that you and your lady will come back to see us one day."

"I hope so too," said Sally, smiling at him.

"We'll be back," I said with confidence. "We'll certainly come back."

We shook hands and walked away.

I was nervous about the police, though I knew they could have no description of me unless Felicity had let me down. I held my breath as the passports were stamped but neither my name nor my face evoked any interest.

"Somehow I have a feeling that we won't come back," Sally said.

"Why not, darling? Haven't you enjoyed it?"

"Oh, yes, Jimmy. It's been the happiest time in the whole of my life. It's just a feeling I have. I just know I shan't be coming back."

I didn't pretend to understand. "Oh, well," I said. "There are lots of other places. Let's have a drink before we go out to the plane. It might help your sore throat."

Sally was putting a brave face on her sufferings, but I was certain by then that she was beginning a really nasty attack of flu. Her temperature had been down to 99 degrees when we awoke and there had been no opportunity to take it since, but I guessed that the fall had been caused by the codeine and the sleep. Her hand, as I held it now, was very hot and dry and I felt sure that her temperature was high again. She needed to be taken home. I wanted to leave Jamaica before the search for Quintin's 'killer' became too thorough.

In the Boeing, Sally tried to sleep and I read and looked out of the window and worried about her. It was a long flight and, so far as we were concerned, it was the middle of the night when we arrived at London Airport. But, of course, Jamaica being six hours behind, that made it morning in England. Sally put on her dark glasses and we escaped into a taxi.

"In a few months," I said cheerfully as we bowled up the M4, "we shan't have to worry about being seen by anyone. We'll be married. It'll be marvellous, won't it?"

"Marvellous, Jimmy." She rested her head on my chest and I put a protective arm round her shoulders and we travelled the last few miles more or less in silence.

We had been away for three weeks. When we had left it had been summer; now it was just beginning to be autumn. I shivered in my tropical light-weight suit and held Sally's hot hand to warm me.

"It's nice to be home," she said. "It's wonderful to see other places, but it's lovely to be back in London."

We both eyed with nostalgia the normally unappetising aspect of the Earl's Court Road at the beginning of the rush hour. "You're right," I said. "But we'll go on lots of other holidays, won't we?"

I made the cab wait when we reached the Embankment. I took Sally and the luggage up in the lift and opened the door for her. Then, ordering her to go straight to bed, I returned to the taxi and went on in it to Chelsea Barracks. I paid it off outside the front door of the Officers' Mess and went inside. There was no one about. There was a large bundle of letters and papers in my pigeon-hole and I glanced through it idly. There appeared to be nothing of great importance. Two officers were getting married. The Regimental Adjutant wanted to know if I intended to contribute to their wedding presents. One was engaged to a Miss Caroline something-or-other; the other had landed the Honourable Katharine something else. I wondered for a moment whether the officers would be circularised in this way when I was married. On the whole it seemed unlikely.

For the rest, my mail consisted of instructions from the Adjutant about the training at Salisbury Plain (all of which I consigned to the waste paper basket) and of the Guard Rota for the month of October. My name appeared once only – on October 1st I was to be Captain of the Queen's Guard. It would be my last Guard.

It wasn't a difficult date to remember so that went into the waste paper basket too.

I left the Mess and walked past the parked cars outside to my Jaguar. It felt odd to sit in the familiar comfort of the driving seat after such a long time. I pumped up some petrol and the engine started at the second attempt. I drove out of the Barracks gate, waving an acknowledgement of the sentry's salute, and I turned up towards Sloane Square. Twenty minutes later I was back at the flat carrying two carrier bags bulging with food I had bought in Gardeners in the King's Road.

Sally was in bed. She looked distinctly unwell.

"How do you feel, darling?"

"Pretty awful. But better since I got into bed. I have just

talked to Franco on the telephone. He had heard from Susan that something had gone wrong with their return flights and Timmy and Nanny will have to stay on there for at least another week. Obviously Timmy is overjoyed. He loves it there. But I'm absolutely longing to see him."

I said, "Right, I'll take you down to Highworth tomorrow morning and I'll go on to my mother's. I'll stay there for a bit. I haven't seen her for far too long, and I can see what needs to be done about her cottage."

I'd told Sally about the cottage after she had agreed to marry me and we were making plans. The Cottage – as we called it – was really quite a nice little three-bedroomed house. It was quite separate from my mother's house and had been empty for several months. Sally and Timmy and Nanny could live there comfortably after she left Freddie.

Sally wasn't very much better the next day. True, her temperature was down, but that was the only improvement. Her throat was much sorer and she complained of feeling worse.

Poor Sally. She didn't really complain at all. She simply seemed very low, and when I asked her how she felt she said something like "not too good."

I fed her on soup and bought her some throat lozenges to suck. We left the flat and I drove her to Highworth.

"How many days will it be before I see you?" I asked her as we drove round Sloane Square.

There were a number of respectable-looking people standing outside Peter Jones waiting for taxis. Sally nervously pulled at her scarf and turned her head away.

"I don't know, darling." Her voice was hoarse. "I'll leave as soon as I've told Freddie. I won't stay a night under the same roof with him. I need to get ready to leave him on the day he gets back. I'm not sure how long I've got and there is a lot to do. I'll ring you when I've seen him."

I said, "I start the Staff Course in less than a fortnight. Or do you think I ought to send my papers in straight away? You and I may cause quite a scandal."

We stopped at traffic lights. Sally put a hand on my knee and said, "Don't send your papers in, darling. And don't tell anyone about us until it's all arranged. Not until I leave Freddie and come to you."

"Why not?"

"Because... I can't explain. But please don't."

"You're not backing out on me, Sally?"

"Oh, no, darling. I'm most certainly not. I love you terribly and I want to be married to you more than anything in the world. I just want to keep it private for a little bit longer. Please trust me."

I looked across at her. She was so beautiful. "I trust you, Sally. I'm going to do my best to make you very happy."

"You already have, Jimmy. The days we've spent together have been the most wonderful in my life."

I smiled at her. "There are going to be many more," I said. She didn't reply.

Sometime later she said, "I shall miss you, Jimmy."

"It's not for very long."

"No. Not too long."

At Highworth I dropped her and her bags. I said, "Goodbye, my darling. I'll be waiting for you to ring."

We kissed one another on the lips.

"Goodbye, Jimmy. Thank you for my lovely holiday."

TWENTY-NINE

Four long days dragged by.

Several times I thought of telephoning Sally at Highworth. Each time I decided against it. Sally had said that it would be better not to and I thought that I had better respect her wishes. Possibly she was still laid low with flu.

My mother woke me at eight o'clock on the fifth morning by shaking my shoulder.

"Wake up, James. Do wake up. You're wanted on the telephone."

I was wide awake in an instant. "Who is it?"

"She just said her name was Sally. I don't know why you young people can't announce yourselves properly. It was all so different when I was young. One gave one's name properly then. I expect you know scores of girls called Sally. How on earth can you know who it is?"

"I know who it is all right," I said, pulling on a dressing gown. "I most certainly know who it is." In accordance with Sally's wish I hadn't told her anything.

"That's nice, dear. Then there's no problem. Take it in the study downstairs. Then you can be private. Why do you think she's telephoned so early in the morning?"

I didn't answer. I was half-way down the stairs by then. I dashed across the hall, slammed the door of the study behind me, and hurled myself at the telephone.

"Sally. Sally. Is that you?"

"Hello, darling," said a small deep voice I could hardly recognise.

"Sally?"

"Yes, Jimmy. It's me."

"You sound rather funny."

She made an odd-sounding noise that I didn't at first identify as a laugh.

"I've almost lost my voice. It's silly isn't it?"

"Are you all right?"

"Not too bad."

"Are you at Highworth? Is Freddie back?"

"Freddie's not due for two more days. And Jimmy..." Her voice faded.

"What is it, Sally?"

"Darling, I'm afraid I've been even more silly."

"What have you done?"

"Well, darling. I've caught some sort of bug. Nobody seems to know quite what's wrong with me, so I've been put into hospital in London. They're doing tests on me to try to find out what's wrong."

"My God."

"It's all right, darling. I feel fairly well. I'm not in pain or anything. I just feel rather tired and sort of feeble all the time."

"What are they doing to you?"

"Well, they've tried all sorts of antibiotics, but none of them seems to make any difference. So now they're doing tests. They took some blood out of my arm last night. A huge great syringe full."

A drop of iced water seemed to run down my spine.

"What else have they done?"

Sally tried to laugh again. "Oh, darling. I can't possibly tell you on the telephone. All sorts of things. But never mind about the tests. I rang because I'm bored and lonely, and though I know this is awfully selfish of me – you haven't seen your mother for ages – but I wondered if there was any chance of your coming back to London."

"I'm on my way."

"You are? Jimmy, you are marvellous."

I did a quick calculation. "I'll be with you at twelve o'clock. Which hospital are you in?"

"I'm in Sister Agnes. I'm very favoured, aren't I?"

"Yes."

"My doctor fixed it. He's got hidden depths."

"Yes. Darling, I'll ring off now. The sooner I start the sooner I'll be with you."

There was a pause.

"All right, Jimmy." Her voice sounded faint. I guessed that talking had tired her. "Take care of yourself, darling. Drive carefully, won't you? And, Jimmy…"

"Yes, Sally?"

"I'm sorry I rang you so early in the morning. I've been awake for ages. I was so longing to hear your voice. Your mother sounds awfully nice. Will you apologise to her for me?"

"Of course." I had a sudden thought. Long years of visiting sick soldiers in hospital made me ask automatically, "Is there anything you want?"

"Only you, Jimmy. I love you so much."

***

Soon after twelve I parked my car on a meter just outside the nurses' home in Beaumont Street. I locked up, fed the meter and walked across the road and up the steps to the front door of the hospital. An unobtrusive brass plate to the right of the door bore the inscription, 'King Edward VII Hospital for Officers,' and underneath the words 'Sister Agnes Founder' gave the explanation for the establishment's world-famous nickname.

I was given directions in the hall and I went up in the lift and reported to the red-belted sister in charge of Sally's floor.

"Lady Frensham?" she said crisply. "I don't think she's having any visitors at the moment."

She looked crisp too; crisp and clean and efficient. But she had kind brown eyes which exactly matched the softly curling brown hair upon which her cap was perched. She seemed to be only about twenty-five years old.

"She telephoned me this morning," I said. "She particularly asked me to come and see her."

"Oh" she said. "Are you a relation?"

"No," I said. I told her my name. "I'm just a friend," I added. For some reason it sounded inadequate, though I couldn't imagine why it should. When I am ill I would much rather be visited by my friends than my relations.

She smiled at me. "So you're the famous James. She's told me about you."

What? I wondered.

Her face fell. She looked at her watch. "But I'm afraid you can't see her now anyway. She's in the theatre."

I was in such a state of anxiety that for a long idiotic moment I thought she meant that Sally had gone to see a play. I was on the point of asking which theatre when the penny dropped.

"What's happening to her?"

"Her doctor's doing a test."

"Doesn't he know what's wrong with her yet?"

A shutter seemed to fall across the back of her eyes. "I don't know what the position is," she said. She was being crisp and efficient again.

"When can I see her?"

"In an hour or so, I expect."

"Oh. Can I wait?"

"I shouldn't. Go and have some lunch and come back this afternoon. Come at half-past two. You'll be able to see her then. I'll tell her you called when she comes out of the theatre."

"All right." I paused. "What do you think is wrong with her?"

"Honestly, I don't know. I shouldn't like to guess. It's probably nothing much." She gave me an encouraging smile. "Come back at half-past two."

***

I drove first to my flat. Mrs Catton had been coming in each day while I had been away and, having nothing else to do except wallow in my bath, she had treated the place to an autumnal clean. Everything that could be polished gleamed and glowed in the September sunshine.

I emptied my suitcase onto the bed and changed into a dark suit. There were eggs and a bottle of champagne in the refrigerator but neither appealed to me at that moment. I felt a need for some human company and I left the flat and drove to the Guards' Club in Charles Street.

The company in the bar there was all too human and I found several chums with whom to drink gin, and much later, to lunch.

Soon after two o'clock, feeling fortified and refreshed, I left the Club and walked down Charles Street to Moyses Stevens in Berkeley Square.

Even at the end of September the summer sun still had some kick in it and I was grateful for the cool sweet-smelling gloom of the big flower shop. I took off my bowler hat and wondered what to buy. I had some idea that it was considered bad luck to take red flowers to a hospital. Or was it mixed red and white flowers that one was supposed to avoid? I wasn't sure. To be on the safe side I bought four dozen yellow roses. They were so expensive that I was glad I had had the foresight to cash a cheque when paying for my lunch at the Club.

Replacing my hat at the proper angle and carrying my large fragile parcel I returned to the meter where I had left my car and drove back to the hospital. As I got nearer the horrible feeling of anxiety which had started with Sally's telephone call that morning, and which had not been entirely dispelled by my drunken lunch, started to grow bigger inside me. It neutralised the alcohol. By the time I walked through the door of the hospital I was ice-cold sober.

There was no sign of the crisp kind sister when I stepped out of the lift on Sally's floor. I found a pretty nurse who relieved me of the flowers and took me straight to Sally's room. Throwing open the door she said brightly, "Here's a visitor for you." Then she gave a winning smile and left us. "I'll put these in water," she said as she shut the door behind her.

I looked at Sally.

Her tan had faded slightly and her face looked thinner, but otherwise she looked just as she had when I had last seen her without the fever. I wasn't quite sure how I expected her to look, but somehow I had thought that she would be noticeably different if there was anything seriously wrong with her. The fact that she was just the same made me feel much better.

"Hello, darling," she said. Her voice was husky but not nearly as bad as it had sounded on the telephone.

"Darling Sally." I sat on the bed and kissed her. "It's marvellous to see you again."

"You too, my love. I've missed you so much."

"How are you feeling?"

"Not too bad. Rather tired, that's all. I'm much better now you're here."

"I came earlier but they sent me away."

"I know, darling." She smiled at me, wrinkling her nose. "Miss Ames – the sister – told me. You made a big impression on her."

"I did?"

"Oh, yes. And she's been awfully good to me. She's an angel."

"She said you were in the theatre this morning. What did they do to you?"

"Oh dear," said Sally. "It was rather horrid really." She pulled open the front of her nightdress. There was a small neat dressing in the middle of her chest between her breasts. I stared at it.

"What happened?"

"They stuck a huge great needle into me."

"My God. Did it hurt?"

Sally smiled. She closed the front of her nightdress. "No, darling. They gave me a local anaesthetic first."

"What's it all about?"

"I don't know yet. They haven't told me a thing."

I took out my cigarette case and offered it to Sally.

"No, thank you, Jimmy. My throat's still too sore for smoking. But you go ahead, then I can smell the smoke. That'll be better than nothing."

I lit a cigarette. "Tell me exactly what's happened since I saw you last."

"Well, let me see. It seems such ages ago now. I felt so

awful when I got to Highworth that I sent for the doctor. He ordered me to bed and gave me some sort of antibiotic and some lozenges for my throat. The next day I felt no better and I had some lumps in my neck and under my arms. Here, you can feel them if you like."

She took my hand and placed the tips of my fingers on her neck. I could feel the little soft lumps under the skin.

"After that Dr Jones tried some different pills and got me to try some gargling, but nothing seemed to do any good. I just felt feeble and rather sort of... panty, you know?"

"Short-winded?"

"That's right. And I felt weaker and weaker all the time. Anyway, yesterday morning he decided that I ought to go into hospital, for 'tests and observation' which I feel sure means that he hasn't the slightest idea what's the matter with me. Anyway, he's called in the most divine specialist who I'm absolutely mad about. He's the one who stuck the needle into me this morning."

I shook my head. "What a puzzle it is. But I'm delighted to see you looking so well. The only thing that worries me is that you look rather thin."

"Darling, I'm afraid I haven't been eating much. I haven't felt like it."

"Is the food nasty?"

"No. It's excellent, I think. It's just that I'm not hungry."

"You must eat. When I leave you this afternoon I'll go to Fortnum's and buy all sorts of delicious things to tempt your appetite with."

"That would be nice, Jimmy. But you won't go yet, will you? I've missed you so much. Please kiss me, darling. I've missed being kissed. We haven't made love for such ages that I've almost forgotten what it's like." She smiled up at me from the pillows. "If you twiddle the knob below the window on the door it stops people seeing through from the other side." I got up and twiddled the knob. Sure enough, the window became opaque. Sally said, "I think that probably all I need is some good James loving. That will make me better again – I hope." I sat down beside her on the bed and, bending down, I kissed her on the lips. "I hope I'm not catching," she said between kisses.

"I caught you weeks ago, darling. We've caught each other for ever."

"Oh, yes," she moaned. "For ever and ever." It sounded like a prayer.

I slipped a hand inside her nightdress and fondled the familiar thickness of her erect nipples. "I love you, Sally," I whispered.

The door opened behind me and I sat up quickly and pulled my hand away. I looked over my shoulder.

A tall, very thin man in his late forties walked into the room. He had a long horse-like face with deep furrows on his forehead. He wore a beautifully-cut double-breasted suit and an Old Etonian tie.

"Darling, this is Professor Dalton. My specialist."

Dalton's long lugubrious face smiled briefly at me. "I'm glad you're back," he said to me. I thought it odd that he knew anything about me at all, but I supposed that Sally had been talking to him too.

He picked up her wrist and permitted himself a second brief smile. "Your pulse is rather fast," he said.

Sally and I laughed. I felt embarrassed.

"I'm afraid I shall have to ask you to go now," he said to me. "I have some work to do."

"Oh, no," said Sally.

"Just for an hour or two." He was firm. "He can come back this evening."

"All right," I said. "I'll go and buy some things for you to eat and come back later. Goodbye Sally."

"Goodbye, darling."

I stood up. I smiled at the doctor and walked over to the door.

"Would you mind waiting outside for a moment," he said. "I should like to have a very quick word with you before you leave."

I nodded and walked out into the corridor where I found a chair and sat down. Was I going to get a rocket for kissing the patient, I wondered? What on earth could the man want with me otherwise?

I didn't have long to wait. Less than a minute later he came out of Sally's room. I stood up.

"Let's go and find somewhere to talk," he said, and he led the way down the corridor to the glass-fronted room where I had seen nurses on my earlier visit. There was no one there now. We went into a narrow office and sat down. I found myself on a bench seat which ran the length of the office. There was a notice board above my head. It was covered in picture postcards. The Professor perched on the edge of the tiny desk. I wondered idly why there were two telephones.

He sat and looked at me for a moment without speaking, as though trying to decide what to say. His eyes were cold and grey and clear and something about the way in which he looked at me sent a cold chill though my veins so that when at last he spoke I was not surprised by what he said.

"I've just received the results of the tests," he told me. "There is no doubt at all, I'm afraid."

"What is it?" I managed to say.

"It's called pan-myeloid leukaemia."

"Oh." I couldn't think of anything else to say.

"I'm going to give her a transfusion now."

"I see." I felt numb. "It's incurable," I said. It was more a statement than a question.

"Yes. At the moment quite incurable I'm afraid. In a few years, who knows… There's some interesting work being done."

"Will it be in time to save Sally?"

He shook his head. "Oh, dear me, no. She has only a *very* short time."

"How short?" I was expecting him to say something like, "six months to a year." When he replied I almost fainted.

"Days at most. Possibly only hours."

"My God. Is that all?"

He nodded. "When it reaches this stage it's very quick."

"Only hours," I muttered. "It's impossible."

He didn't say anything. I sat in silence for a moment, looking out of the window. "Will there be any pain?" I asked him. I felt oddly grateful for his clinically aloof manner. It helped me to keep a grip on myself and to think straight.

"No," he said. "There should be no pain at all. She'll feel very weak. She may feel somewhat short-winded."

I nodded. "She's feeling that already. She's just told me."

"Yes. She'll simply get weaker and weaker. She may die in her sleep."

I sat in silence for a moment.

"Are we going to tell her?" I asked him.

"That's a matter for you. My own view is that she should be told. And in fact it may not come as very much of a surprise to her. I find in these cases that the patient often has a premonition of death."

"Sally hasn't said anything," I said. "Who's going to tell her?"

"I will, if you like."

"When?"

"Later this afternoon. Before you return this evening."

"I'd be grateful if you would."

He smiled a gentle, rather kindly smile. "It'll be easier for me to do it, Lord Frensham." He sighed. "I'm used to it."

I sat absolutely motionless for a moment. Then I drew a deep breath. "I'm not Lord Frensham."

He stared at me coldly. "If you're trying to be funny I'm afraid I must tell you that I don't see the joke."

"It's no joke," I told him my name. "If this hadn't happened she was going to leave Frensham for me."

To his credit he grasped the changed circumstances very quickly. "I see," he said levelly. "In that case I shall have to ask you to forget what I have said and I must proceed as though I had yet to break this news."

"I can hardly forget what you've told me," I pointed out.

"What? Oh, no. Of course not. But I should be grateful if you would keep it to yourself. I've placed myself in a somewhat embarrassing position, you know." He looked at me accusingly. He obviously thought that it was all my fault.

"I knew you – I mean I knew Lord Frensham wasn't due back for a day or two. When I walked into Lady Frensham's room just now and saw you… Well, naturally I assumed…"

"Naturally," I said. I thought of telling him that he should have knocked at the door before walking in, but I realised that the misunderstanding was Sally's fault really. It was caused by this modern slackness about introductions.

I stood up. He had his problems, and I had mine. "You'll still tell her?" I asked him. He nodded. "When you've told her," I went on, "tell her that you've told me too and that

I'll be back in a few hours with some food for her dinner."

"I'll tell her," he said obediently.

I paused in the door. "When do you think she'll die?"

"I can't be accurate."

"An intelligent guess then."

He shrugged. "In her sleep tonight. If not then, sometime tomorrow. Or tomorrow night. It won't be long." He shrugged again.

I nodded. "Thank you." I left the hospital and got into my car and drove to Fortnum & Mason. It seemed the only thing to do.

THIRTY

I put the food in the refrigerator and took a full bottle of whisky to the bathroom. While the bath was filling I undressed and drank some of the whisky straight from the bottle. When the bath was full I climbed in, taking the whisky bottle with me.

I felt numb inside and out, and neither the hot water nor the whisky made the smallest impression on me. There were only two thoughts in my mind: it was bloody unfair; and what on earth was I going to say to Sally?

When the whisky bottle was a third empty the telephone rang.

I got out of the bath and took a bath towel through into the bedroom. I put the towel on the floor and stood on it. It saved the carpet. I found I was still holding the whisky bottle so I took a swallow and picked up the receiver with the other hand.

"Hello."

"Jimmy?" Her voice sounded marginally less husky.

"Yes?"

"It's me. You sounded rather strange."

"It's me all right. I had my mouth full."

"Oh."

There was a pause. I tried to think of something to say.

"The Professor's just left," Sally went on. "He told me."

"I see."

"He said he'd told you too."

"That's right."

"They're sending a telegram to Freddie. I suppose he'll

come straight back. He may be here tomorrow."

"Yes, I should think so."

There was another pause.

"It's a strange feeling, Jimmy."

"It must be."

"I've been lying here looking out of the window since he left. Everything looks just the same outside."

"I suppose so."

"I've made a decision, darling."

"Oh? What is it?"

"Darling, I don't want to die here."

"I see. Where do you want to…" I couldn't say the word. "Where do you want to go? Home to Highworth?"

"No, not Highworth. I want to be with you. At home with you."

I thought for a moment.

"All right, Sally. I'll come and get you."

"How soon will you get here?"

"I'll be as quick as I can. About half an hour, I suppose." It would take all of that in the rush-hour traffic and I had to get dressed first. "Say three-quarters of an hour," I amended.

"All right, Jimmy. I'll be waiting for you."

"Will you be in your room?"

"Yes. I shan't tell them I'm leaving. They'll only think of some reason to stop me."

"Oh. I suppose it's all right?"

"I can discharge myself if I want to. I'm not catching."

I said nothing.

"And, Jimmy," Sally went on after a pause. "You will hurry, darling, won't you. I feel I haven't very much time. And I want to be with you."

"I'll hurry, Sally."

After I had rung off I wished I had told her that I loved her. For some reason it seemed very important that I should tell her that before she died.

Praying that she wouldn't die before I reached her, I dressed and left the flat.

For the third time that day I drove into Beaumont Street. This time I didn't bother with a meter. I parked immediately outside the door of the hospital on a space marked 'Ambulances Only.' I took the keys out of the ignition and got out. I left the doors unlocked.

A porter came down the steps towards me. He looked like an old soldier. He had a nice face and no doubt he found it an unpleasant duty having to tell motorists to move on. I took out my wallet, extracted a five-pound note and folded it into four. As he opened his mouth to speak I forestalled him.

"I've come to collect a patient," I told him. "She may not be able to walk so I shall have to carry her out. I've left the car unlocked. Would you be very kind and keep an eye on it until I come down. I shan't be long."

He tried to refuse the money, but I insisted.

"I didn't know anyone was being discharged this evening, sir. They usually leave in the mornings."

"Didn't you?" I said sympathetically.

"But that's all right, sir. I'll keep an eye on the car. In a way it's an ambulance, isn't it?"

"So it is," I agreed.

I left him standing there and went inside. I felt invincible. Nothing could stop me. I got the lift to Sally's floor.

I saw the red-belted sister in the corridor. She had her back to me and I thought it would be better if she didn't see me, so I tried to sneak past her. It was no good. She turned to face me just as I approached. She looked at me with her sad brown eyes. I noticed that she wore a sort of label on her well-shaped bosom. It read, 'Miss J. Ames'. I wondered what the J stood for.

"How is she?" I asked anxiously. She couldn't be dead yet surely.

"Weak," she said. "She's looking forward to seeing you."

"Good." I paused and made a decision. "I'm taking her away now," I said.

Her eyes widened. She shook her head. "Oh, no. You can't do that."

"Why not?" My temper was just below the surface. If anything caused the surface to erupt I knew I should start breaking things.

"Well, it's against the…" Her voice trailed away. "She's too weak to go anywhere. It'll kill her."

"She's dying anyway. Isn't she?"

She nodded. Her eyes were still very wide. She looked frightened. I realised that I probably looked as though I was on the point of knocking her down.

I managed a horrible sort of smile. "I'm taking her now. I'd be very grateful for your assistance."

She nodded obediently.

I took a deep breath and led the way into Sally's room. She seemed to have shrunk since I saw her last, but she was delighted to see me.

"Darling," she whispered. "You have been quick. Can we go now?"

"The car's at the door. Is there anything you want to take with you?"

"Just my bag. I don't need clothes, do I?"

"No, darling. You can go straight to bed when you get there. Do you think you can walk?"

"I don't know. I expect so. I'll try, shall I?"

"No," I said. "I'll carry you."

"You ought not to leave, Lady Frensham," Miss Ames chimed in. "I don't know what the doctor will say."

"I expect he'll be furious," said Sally, smiling. "Tell him how sorry I am. He's been very kind to me. So have you. You've all been very good to me, and I'm grateful. But there's nothing more you can do for me now, is there? Now I want to be with the man I love."

She said it very simply and I felt the tears pricking at the back of my eyes. No, I said to myself. I shall have plenty of time for crying later. There's to be none of that now.

It was a warm night and Sally was covered only by a sheet and a thin white bedspread. She wore a long plain white cotton nightdress. I pulled back the bedclothes and bent and lifted her up in my arms. She felt unnaturally light. Miss Ames picked up her handbag from the bedside table. She looked miserable.

"What shall I say to your husband if he comes here?"

"I don't mind," said Sally.

"Tell him the truth," I said. "Tell him you don't know where we've gone."

I moved towards the door. "Is there anything else you want, darling?" I asked Sally.

She looked over my shoulder. "Yes," she said. "Your beautiful roses. I can't leave those behind."

I looked inquiringly at Miss Ames who was dithering near the door. "Would you be very kind, Sister?"

"Yes. All right." She pulled the yellow roses out of their vase and started to wrap them in a copy of the *Evening Standard*.

I carried Sally out of the room and down the corridor to the lift. Sally pressed the button and we waited.

"Thank you for coming to get me, darling. Did you buy

something nice for our dinner?"

"Yes, Sally. Lots of delicious things."

Miss Ames caught up with us as the lift arrived. She carried the flowers and the handbag. I smiled cheerfully at her.

We had to stand aside as several people stepped out of the lift. I supposed they were visitors who had come to see other patients. In a strange way I found I could stand outside myself sufficiently to see things as they must see them. I realised how odd it must seem to them to meet a young man carrying a beautiful girl dressed only in a nightdress.

We went down in silence to the ground floor and walked out to the street.

My new friend the porter was standing beside my car. He saw us coming and opened the passenger door. I put Sally in. She looked forlorn and unprotected in her white nightdress and I unlocked the boot and took out my old rug. I wrapped it round her and she stroked it with her fingers.

"This is the rug we took on our picnic on the river, isn't it?" she said.

I nodded. I shut the door and said goodbye to Miss Ames who still clutched Sally's bag and flowers. "Thank you, Sister," I said, taking them from her. "I'll put these on the back seat."

"Goodbye," she said. "Good luck. Ring me up if you need any help."

I smiled and said goodbye again and got into the car and drove away. Miss Ames waved. The porter saluted.

***

I drove home one-handed. My left hand held Sally's right, and she clung to it as though to stop herself drowning. The effort of leaving the hospital had drained away a little more of the tiny store of strength which remained to her.

Now that we were on our way and were together again there seemed to be no particular urgency. I drove slowly and chose a route which would give her a pleasant last look at London. We didn't speak much, but as we drove down the King's Road where the pavements were crowded with young people and the public houses had overflowed into the streets, Sally said in a low voice, "I feel like a little girl at a party who's having a lovely time and enjoying herself enormously, but who's suddenly told that it's time to go home." I didn't speak. There seemed to be nothing to say. "I'm not ready to go home yet," she went on. She sighed and smiled weakly at me. "But I suppose I've got to do what I'm told."

I carried her up to my flat and put her in my bed. Then I went back for the flowers and her handbag. I locked the car and went up in the lift again.

"Give me my bag please, Jimmy. I must do something about my face. I'm afraid I feel too feeble to help with the dinner. Can you manage all right?"

"I can manage," I said. "Would you like something to drink?"

"Yes, please."

"There's some champagne."

"That would be lovely, darling."

I took the flowers to the kitchen and found a vase and tried to arrange them. I found arranging flowers a difficult thing to do at the best of times, but now my eyes kept misting over, making it hard to see what I was doing. After a bit I gave it up. I shoved the rest of the flowers into the vase as best I could and left it at that. I felt terrible. The anger of a half-hour or so before had faded now to be replaced by a feeling of utter hopelessness. I washed my face under the kitchen tap and dried it on a tea cloth.

I took the bottle of champagne out of the refrigerator and opened it. I placed it and two glasses on a tray. I noticed, with no particular feeling of surprise, that the champagne was my last bottle of Dom Perignon. I picked up the tray and carried it through to the bedroom. I went back and fetched the flowers.

Sally had put some lipstick on. She looked quite cheerful.

"Darling Jimmy. What lovely flowers! And what lovely champagne!"

"I haven't been able to arrange the flowers very well, I'm afraid."

"They look marvellous to me."

She took a glass of champagne and we drank, looking at one another over the rims of our glasses.

"I'm sorry I've been such a nuisance, Jimmy. I've only just realised how very inconvenient it's going to be for you after I'm dead. I mean, what on earth are you going to do with my body?"

"I'll think of something," I said vaguely.

She smiled.

"You're very good to me, darling. You've always been very good to me. You're going to make some lucky girl a marvellous husband one of these days. I'm only sorry it can't be me. I was looking forward to it so much. All my girlfriends would have been so envious."

"I don't want to be anyone else's husband, Sally. You're the only girl I've ever wanted to marry. I shan't marry anyone else. Not ever."

"Yes, you will, darling. I want you to. You mustn't get married too soon. I'll come and haunt you if you do that. But in a year or two you'll find someone nice."

"I doubt it. You've spoiled me for all other women."

"You say the sweetest things to me, Jimmy, but you'll find someone to be happy with. And you'll stay in the Army too, won't you? You'd better stick to single girls in future, then you won't jeopardise your career. You're such a beautiful soldier it would be a terrible shame if you left. You'll be a General one day if you stay on and I'll be very proud of you. I shall be watching you all the time from… wherever I get sent. You see I've thought it all out. It wasn't really a surprise when they told me this afternoon. I've had a feeling about this since we were in Jamaica… since that last night when my temperature went up. Something told me that it was more than an attack of the flu. That's why I knew I should never be returning to Jamaica. That's why I didn't want you to tell anyone about us."

She fell silent. After a while I said, "I don't think I can go on without you, Sally. Life will be intolerable if I haven't got you to talk to… to tell everything to. I think I'll shoot myself and come with you."

Her eyes opened wide. For the first time she looked frightened. "No, darling. You absolutely mustn't do that. That's cheating. You've got to go on living."

"It's my life. I can end it whenever I want to."

"Oh, no, Jimmy. That's not right. You really mustn't. I want you to promise me that you won't do anything like that. Please promise me."

At first I would not. But she pressed me, and she seemed so unhappy that in the end I promised. It seemed the easy thing to do. Later it proved a hard promise to keep. Sally relaxed when I had done as she asked, and we talked of other things.

Later I went back to the kitchen and loaded another tray with all the exotic things I had bought at Fortnum's that afternoon. I carried it back to the bedroom and Sally and

I tried to eat our dinner. Neither of us ate very much. I think Sally was too weak to eat. I didn't feel like it. But we finished the champagne and as it was the last bottle it reminded us of the first, and we talked of all the happy times we had had together.

"It has been wonderful, Jimmy darling. Thank you so much. It's sad to think it's all over now."

As the evening wore on she seemed to get weaker and weaker. She was fading away in front of my eyes. She spoke less often and her voice grew huskier and fainter.

"I'd like to sleep for a little now, I think," she said. "It's all right, darling," she added, seeing my sudden look of anxiety. "I'm not going to die just yet."

She closed her eyes. "I love you," she whispered.

I tiptoed from the room, carrying our dinner things. When I returned Sally was sleeping peacefully. I felt her pulse. It was feeble but steady.

I sat in a chair and watched her while she slept. How unfair it all was, I thought. I had found the only woman in the world for me, and now she was leaving the world. The useless anger that I had felt earlier in the evening rose inside me and I couldn't sit still. I got up and walked out of the bedroom and out onto the balcony. I lit a cigarette and looked at the river.

I was so angry that I struck the balcony railing with my fist. It hurt and the pain sobered me. I turned and looked through the bedroom window. I had left the bedside light burning and I could see Sally clearly. Her long golden hair had never looked more beautiful, her face was perfect. If only there was something I could do.

How soon would she go, I wondered. Tonight? Tomorrow?

She may die in her sleep, the doctor had said.

She might have lived for several days in hospital, but the

effort of travelling back to my flat had taken it out of her to such a great extent that I realised that she couldn't last very much longer. I suddenly knew that she would die that night.

I stared at her. Was she dead now? I wanted to be with her at the end. And I hadn't said goodbye to her properly. I had been so overloaded with misery that I hadn't told her all the things that were in my heart. Perhaps now it was too late.

I threw my cigarette away and rushed into the bedroom. Sally was very still. I knelt beside her and felt for her pulse. I couldn't find it.

"Sally," I cried.

She opened her eyes. They were dark green, the darkest I had ever seen them.

"My darling," she whispered.

"Oh, Sally. Can you hear me properly? Can you understand what I'm saying?"

She nodded slowly. She was very weak.

"Thank God for that. Oh, Sally, my darling love. I'm so very unhappy that you're leaving me. I just don't know what I'm going to do without you." Tears started to roll down my cheeks. I made no attempt to stop them. I couldn't have done so even if I had wished to. I went on, speaking painfully slowly. Each word felt as though it was torn from my soul. "I've known so many women, Sally darling. But you've put all the others out of my mind for ever. I spent years looking for you, and now that I've found you you're being taken away from me. It's so unjust."

Sally put out a hand and stroked my face and I could bear it no longer. I threw myself forward on to the bed beside her and took her in my arms. I kissed her lips again and again. Sally kissed me and I felt her hands stroking my hair and after a few minutes I stopped crying and a strong feeling of warmth spread through my body. I felt at peace. In some magical way Sally had given me the last of her strength. We held hands and smiled at one another.

I whispered, "Thank you, Sally. I feel better. What did you do?"

"I prayed for you, darling. You'll be brave now. Remember that we had three months together. Three months of perfect happiness. From that night here in this room when we first became lovers… until tonight. It's a lot more than most people have. And we had our beautiful honeymoon in Jamaica. We've really been very lucky."

I smiled. "You're right. After all we might never have met. But we did, and I shall always thank God for that. We have been very lucky. Thank you for all our wonderful times together. Thank you for loving me." I paused and leaning forward I kissed her for the last time while she lived. "I'll always remember you, Sally. The memory of your goodness and beauty will stay with me all the days of my life. I shall treasure your memory until the day I die, and when that day comes we shall be together once again. I shall love you for ever."

She smiled at me with great sweetness, her eyes shining. Her nose wrinkled in the way I knew and loved so well.

We held hands and looked into one another's eyes. After a while Sally gave a little sigh and her eyelids flickered and closed and I realised that I was alone once again.

EPILOGUE

Headquarters Musketeer Guards,
Wellington Barracks
Eighteen Years Later

For ever wilt thou love, and she be fair.
— Keats

I sat down again in my chair and looked at Sally's son.

"Did you know my parents well, sir?" he asked me.

I stared at him, wondering how to answer. I could hardly say, "I killed your father and your mother died in my arms a week later." Instead I opened the cigarette box on my desk and offered it to him.

"No, thank you, sir. I don't smoke."

"Very sensible," I said, helping myself to one and lighting it. "When I was your age everyone smoked. I've never been able to give it up."

I took a deep drag. "Your parents," I said quietly, still wondering what to say. I was probably the only person in the world who knew that he was no more an Earl than I was, but I wasn't going to tell him that either. "It's a long time ago now but I remember staying at Highworth a couple of times. Do you have the house now?"

"Yes, I do, sir. I was brought up there."

"What about your place in the Lake District?"

"My father had to get rid of it because of death duties when my grandfather died. It's a teacher training college now."

I nodded. "I rather lost touch with your father after your

mother died," I told him. "Your godmother Anne was your mother's best friend and she was a girlfriend of mine before she met her husband Peter, a great chum of mine."

"Anne told me when I was there last weekend," Timothy said. "You introduced her to Peter."

"I suppose I did," I agreed. It sounded quite respectable put like that. It had been the very happy marriage that Peter had hoped for.

"And you were their best man."

"Yes. That's right." I remembered their wedding. Freddie Frensham had been there. It had been the first time I had seen him since Sally's funeral.

The funeral had taken place at the little church in Highworth. I had driven Anne to it and thereby I hoped might be assumed to have a reason for being there.

In the car we had talked of Sally. She wanted to know everything that had happened and I told her most of it. Fortunately Sally had not been able to tell her what had happened on our last day and night in Jamaica.

Anne seemed well-informed. Sally had told her a lot. I wasn't surprised. I knew women told their best friends just about everything.

"I'm very sorry for you," she said. She fished in her bag and produced her cigarette case. She selected two cigarettes, lit them with the lighter on the dashboard and passed one to me. We both puffed for a moment. "You will be sad. Terribly sad," she said. "But you must comfort yourself with the thought that you – and I in a way – gave her the happiest few months of her life. My part was simple. After you and I met and we had become lovers and I had our first night of fantastic passion…" she sniggered at the thought, "I couldn't wait to tell Sally all about it. I always told her about my sex life. She loved hearing about it. She wanted to know all about you and I told her in great detail. I always knew she would find a lover of her own one day and I couldn't understand why she hadn't done so already. As I told you she'd had lots of offers. I later learned the reason."

"It was because of her father," I said.

"Yes, that's right. But once he was dead and was therefore out of reach of Freddie's ability to hurt him – and her – she felt ready. I told her at just the right moment about you and she seemed interested. So several weeks later when she casually – she thought – asked about how we were getting on I indicated that you were wonderful but I was getting a bit bored. I wasn't at all actually," she reassured me with a smile. "So she suggested I come down to stay for that dance… And bring you."

"She had decided to seduce me. And the most wonderful few months of my life had started."

Anne agreed. "Hers too. She knew no more about sex than what I had told her. She'd never had an orgasm, you know."

"Yes. I think I did."

"And she really loved you."

"And I her. With all my heart – and I always will."

"You'll never get over her," she puffed at her cigarette and stared out of the windscreen. She didn't notice that tears fell silently down my cheeks. "But you'll learn to live with it," she went on knowledgeably.

I managed to drive safely, albeit very slowly by my usual standard. I stopped crying and I didn't do so again that day.

The field next to the church was being used as a car park and an AA man showed us where to park. There were lots of cars already there. Sally was going to have a good send-off.

We left the car and walked arm-in-arm across the field and into the road.

"Do you know what Sally's ambition was?" Anne asked me.

"I don't think so." To marry me, I hoped.

"She wanted to love and be loved by a good man."

"Oh."

"She told me that *you* were that man."

"She *made* me a good man."

"She thought you were perfect. She told me that there was no doubt in her mind that the two of you were as truly and wonderfully in love as any human beings could be. She knew that you were special because when you made love to her you always saw to it that her pleasure came first."

"That's true. I'd been taught that that was the proper way for a man to behave." I'd never told Anne about Louise and I didn't intend to do so now.

"As I know well," said Anne. "She said that sometimes – quite often really – the two of you had such a perfect time together that it was almost like being in heaven. She called them the best times of her life."

It was a togetherness thing, I reflected. In one way it was agonising to talk about this, because I knew that anyone who had never experienced such happiness could not possibly understand it. But I couldn't stop her and anyway it was lovely to hear about Sally.

"So, were they the best times in your life too?"

I said "Yes. They certainly were." And so they had been – each had been a prolonged and intensely intimate embrace of mind and body. We experienced exquisite sensations and seemed to float in a sort of quasi-Nirvana of almost unbelievable blissfulness. When we eventually emerged Sally's eyes sparkled with happiness, and her whole body glowed with pleasure, so that she was even more stunningly beautiful than usual. I would never forget it.

Anne and I walked together towards the lychgate.

"*We* had some lovely times, didn't we?" she said.

"We did indeed."

"I loved our time together. Thank you for it. Though I don't think we had any Best Times of the sort Sally described. Do you think I might have them with Peter?"

"I certainly hope so."

"Anyway. That's how I know that you made her happier than at any time before you came along. Both in bed and out of it."

I said nothing more. I felt very sad but I was determined not to start crying again. We reached the lychgate and we walked through it into the churchyard.

I gathered from Susan Headcorn, who we talked to there before we went in, that some consideration had been given to burying her in the family mausoleum in Cumberland. I was glad for Sally's sake that that plan had come to nothing. Highworth was where she would have wished to lie.

Susan was in a state of agony not much less acute than my own. She was saddened at Sally's passing, sorry for me, longing to talk to me about it and find out exactly what had happened but unable to talk in front of Anne. She was obviously constrained by feelings of sympathy. I could understand her point of view.

As we walked into the church she put a hand briefly on my arm and said quietly, "Poor James."

I nodded and smiled vaguely at her.

"I long to have a talk to you," she said.

"I'm on Guard tomorrow," I told her. "Come to lunch. We can talk afterwards."

Her brow wrinkled with fierce concentration. "I don't know if I can…" she started. "Oh, yes, of course I can." She made up her mind. "Thank you, James. I'll be there."

(She was and we did.)

I wondered just how much I was going to tell her; not too much probably. "I'm going to the Staff College next week," I said, just for something to say really.

"You'll do well there," she decided, expressing a confidence I was far from feeling myself.

We walked into the church and found a pew near the back. The coffin was there already and so was Freddie, sitting stony-faced in the front pew. There were some servants from Highworth sitting just behind us. I spoke to those I knew. They were all in tears. They'd loved Sally. Carlo, who I knew best, wiped his eyes and said "Oh sir, I loved her so. She was such a good lady." I just nodded. I couldn't speak. I was afraid I might start crying too.

The service passed for me in a sort of dream. Although I had seen Sally lying dead in my bed only a few days before, I found it very difficult to believe that she was actually inside the flower-covered coffin at the top of the nave.

After it was all over we filed out into the churchyard again and followed the coffin to the waiting grave. I didn't realise it then but I discovered years later that she was buried next to her parents.

I lurked about near the back of the crowd. I was numb inside and felt very little at the time except a sensation of irritation at Freddie's attitude of saint-like bravery in the face of the great tragedy that he bore with such fortitude, that it almost concealed the fact that his heart was broken. I noticed several people nudging one another and indicating the grieving widower.

After it was over he gathered up just those that he wanted to return to Highworth. He appeared not to see me at all. He accepted Anne's few words with grace but without an invitation.

When she moved away and Freddie was by himself I saw my opportunity and, taking my courage in both hands, went over to him. He saw me coming and glared at me. I looked down at him. He knew all about me then. As Sally's next-of-kin he had come to my flat with the undertakers' people to collect her body.

"I am sorry for you," I said. I meant it.

"Sorry for yourself, you mean," he sneered.

"No, not just me. For both of us. We have just lost the most wonderful and beautiful woman that either of us has known or ever will."

He said nothing more. He just glared at me. I turned and walked away. I found Anne and we returned to my car and drove back to London.

In the car Anne was at first rather cross not to have been invited to the house but she soon forgot about it and talked mostly of Peter with whom she was by now besotted. As he seemed to have everything she wanted in a man, it did not greatly surprise me when I returned to London from Shrivenham some weeks later to find letters from both of them telling me of their forthcoming nuptials and, in Peter's, a request that I be his best man.

The wedding date was carefully chosen to suit my convenience, being fixed for early January, at the end of my Christmas leave and before I had to report to the Staff College at Camberley.

The wedding reception was at the Hyde Park Hotel where so many receptions were held in the fifties and sixties. I can still clearly remember the day. It was crisp and very cold and Anne looked pretty and surprisingly virginal in white. I hadn't spotted Freddie in the Guards' Chapel and I didn't know that he had been invited until I saw him at the reception. It was just before the end. The happy pair were changing preparatory to leaving for their honeymoon which I knew was to consist of a night at Claridge's followed by three weeks in Jamaica.

I took Peter's suitcase down to put it in my car. It contained his wedding clothes which he would not be needing in Jamaica. The stairs were crowded with people waiting to see them off. On the landing at the top of the stairs, standing by himself, I found Freddie. I almost bumped into him.

"Hello," I said surprised.

He looked at me with a fish-like stare. "I shall never forget what you have done to me," he said levelly. "I shall have my revenge one day."

I was quite unable to think of a rejoinder. Before I could say anything he turned and walked away and I continued my journey with Peter's suitcase.

I often thought about his remark later and wondered what he intended to do. I don't remember being especially perturbed by it. I could clearly recall everything he had said to Sally when he had almost caught us together in their flat. Perhaps he had decided that there was no point in doing anything like that now. There was now nothing to be gained by getting me sent away somewhere, and no real possibility that he could have me kicked out of the Army. Our paths never crossed again. When he became a junior minister in the Ministry of Defence it occurred to me that he might one day be in a position to do me a bit of no good, but fortunately for me it seemed that he adhered to the view that revenge was a dish best served cold and he died before he was in a position to taste it.

There was a mild flurry of publicity when his father died and he renounced his earldom.

About a year after Anne and Peter were married, when

I had just left the Staff College and started an interesting Grade Two staff job in the Ministry of Defence, I went to a cocktail party and met Felicity Fanshawe again. She was if anything even prettier than she had been when I had last seen her nearly two years earlier and she was as slender and elegant as ever. Her hair was done quite differently and I didn't recognise her at first.

"Hello, James," she said cheerfully. We had come face to face in a corner of the very crowded drawing room on the first floor of a house in St Leonard's Terrace overlooking the cricket ground of Burton Court and the mellow bricks of the Royal Hospital beyond the smooth grass.

"Hello," I said brightly, wondering who she was. I wasn't a good enough actor to fool her.

"You don't remember me, do you?" she reproached me.

"Of course I do," I said, trying to bluff my way. "I can't remember where we last met though."

She looked rather hurt. "We have only met once. It was well over a year ago and even if you don't recognise me now I'm sure you won't have forgotten the occasion." She paused and smiled at me. It was a sweet and very pretty smile and I noticed her dazzlingly white teeth between the full soft lips and I couldn't understand how I could have forgotten her.

"What was the occasion?" I asked, imagining she referred to some splendid social event.

"It was the night you killed Quintin Frensham," she said casually.

I gulped. "Of course," I said. "You're... er..."

"Felicity Fanshawe."

"Ah, yes. I remember you very well now." I had a sudden picture in my mind of her sitting nude at her dressing table massaging her pretty little breasts and, perhaps because there had been no one since Sally, I felt a surge of physical desire for her.

I looked into her big brown eyes and saw a flicker that I imagined (correctly as it turned out) was a favourable response to the message that I was unconsciously signalling to her.

"I've had enough of this party," I announced abruptly. "Come and have some dinner with me. I have a feeling we should have a talk."

She didn't reply directly. "I asked you to ring me up when you got back to London but you never did," she accused me. "I suppose you were too busy with that lovely girl I saw you with that night – the one in the those rather riveting photographs of Quintin's."

"No," I said slowly. "She died of leukaemia a week or so later. Since then I've been getting on with my military career."

She stared at me. "She died? How dreadful. She looked so healthy. Was it very sudden?" She sounded genuinely amazed and horrified.

"Yes. Very sudden. Almost unbelievably so. I'm still not quite used to the idea, even now."

"You poor thing." She spoke softly.

"Will you have dinner with me?"

She nodded and her dark hair swayed about her cheeks. "I'd love to. I'll just ditch the man I came with. He won't mind."

A few minutes later I drove her up to the King's Road and along to one of my favourite restaurants of those days Au Pere de Nico, where we sat at a corner table and talked and talked over quenelles de brochet and slices of lamb cooked in rosemary.

I asked her why she had been so pleased when she found

that Quintin was dead. Her explanation was interesting. Quintin had behaved cruelly to her but the circumstances reflected no discredit to her and need not trouble us now.

In a few days we were lovers and because the sex was so good we jointly decided we were in love and we were married that summer.

It was almost a carbon copy of Peter's wedding to Anne, only this time I was the groom and he was the best man. Felicity was a stunning sight as she walked down the broad aisle of the Guards' Chapel and arguably even more ravishing in a superb suit and hat when we left the Hyde Park for the Savoy after the reception.

I was excited and happy and I wasn't troubled by Sally's ghost. I don't remember thinking of her at all that day, but that night, lying awake in our enormous bed in the Savoy, I looked back on the events of the day, my wedding day, and suddenly recalled what Sally had said to me the night she died.

"You'll find someone nice, someone to be happy with."

I looked at Felicity in the dim light. She was a nice and good person. Perhaps I should be happy with her. But oh, how I wished at that moment that it was Sally's golden hair on the pillow beside me and not Felicity's dark locks.

She slept peacefully, exhausted by the excitement and by the vigorous and prolonged consummation of our union that had recently come to a most satisfying conclusion. I lay beside her, physically satiated and therefore able to think clearly, and recognised the pathetic truth. I was still in love with Sally; in love with someone who had been dead for over two years; in love with someone I should never see again.

Although some people might be able to feel themselves in love with more than one person at a time I was certainly not one of them. I recognised that that meant that I was not, could not be and never had been in love with Felicity. It was a depressing moment of understanding; to realise with such perfect clarity on my wedding night that I was not in love with my wife. I gave myself up to self-pity as I thought of what might have been and I felt hot tears run down my face.

I indulged myself for a while with memories of Sally until I felt so thoroughly miserable that I was on the point of sobbing aloud. I rolled over and pressed my face into the pillow and tried to control myself.

When I trusted myself to do so I raised my head and looked at Felicity. She still slept. Her long black eyelashes lay thickly on her cheeks. I thought, 'This is what I have. There's no point in crying for the past, for the unattainable. I must make the most of what I have and soldier on without whingeing about what I have lost.'

That, on the whole, was what I did in the years that followed. I was never in love with Felicity and I wasn't faithful to her, but as the years passed I grew fonder and fonder of her and we went through quite a lot together. Sometimes the vicissitudes of life threatened to drive us apart, but we clung on and in the end I reached a state which, if it could not be called real happiness, was at least a very comfortable and pleasant feeling of contentment.

Several years before I met the grown-up Lord Coniston I had come to the somewhat surprising conclusion that I had a better marriage than most of my friends.

I went on gently mourning Sally for a long time. I stopped suddenly on a day that I can actually put a date to. After my staff job at the Ministry of Defence I went back to Regimental duty, first as a Company Commander and then as Second-in-Command of our Second Battalion.

During that time Felicity had our first baby and we sold the flat on Chelsea Embankment and bought a house.

After two years I went back on the staff, promoted to Lieutenant Colonel, to Headquarters United Kingdom Land Forces at Wilton in Wiltshire. Felicity was pregnant again and as our first child had been a boy we hoped this time for a girl.

The baby when it was born turned out to be a girl all right, but she was born dead. It was no one's fault. I got some leave to be with Felicity for a few days, although we were snowed under with work at the time. My immediate boss, a Colonel GS, was a most charming and understanding Grenadier officer and never once suggested that I should return to work.

However, there was little that I could do at home and my sense of duty forced me to return within a reasonable time. A few days after the birth I took Felicity to convalesce with her parents. I delivered her, the au pair girl and my small son at their house immediately after breakfast and set off to drive to Wilton via Aldershot.

"If you wouldn't mind calling on Two PARA on your way back, James," my Colonel had said to me on the telephone the night before when I rang to announce my return, "I should be eternally grateful and so, I think, will be the Commanding Officer of Two PARA. He's got all sorts of problems about Exercise Snow Drop and if you go to see him I'm sure you'll be able to sort things out for him."

I agreed, of course. Exercise Snow Drop was a winter warfare exercise that I was writing for the following January.

I finished my business in Aldershot shortly after twelve and, declining an invitation to lunch in the Officers' Mess I set off for Wilton. I was in no particular hurry but I was temporarily totally ungregarious. I felt the need for solitude and a chance to examine my misery at the death of the tiny daughter who now I should never know.

I set off along the A31 towards Winchester. It was a road I hadn't been down for years. I always used the A30 to go to Wilton.

After I had passed Alton I came to a bit of road that I recognised and a moment later I saw the turning for Highworth. It came up quickly, and I had no time for thought. As though impelled to do so, I turned off the main road and drove carefully along the narrow lane.

I came first to the gates of the house itself and I slowed almost to a stop. I saw the house through the trees. There were two cars parked there. I imagined that one might belong to Freddie so I kept going. It all looked very much as it had.

I drove on into the village and past the Rectory. I stopped outside the church next door. As I did so I realised why I had come. It was of course to visit Sally's grave. It was the first and so far the only visit I have made.

I got out of my car and locked it. There was no one in sight and no traffic to be seen except a van parked outside the village shop. I walked in through the lychgate and turned in the direction I could remember from the funeral. It was a fine summer's day with a light breeze whispering in the leaves of the great trees in and around the churchyard. Otherwise there was no sound save the birds. It was the most peaceful graveyard that one could imagine.

I strolled slowly along a gravel path which took me around the church itself, and right at the back of the churchyard I found a little row of graves set slightly apart from the others. I knew from the comparative freshness of the gravestones that the furthest was Sally's and I paused deliberately at the two older ones, as though saving Sally's as a special treat until last.

The first and by far the oldest grave was her mother's. 'Sarah,' I read and I remembered then what Sally had told me that day by the Thames after our narrow escape from drowning. She was described as the beloved wife of the Rector, Sally's father, who lay in the next grave, the headstone of which was only marginally older than the third. He had died, I noticed, less than a year before his daughter, thereby giving her, I now recalled, the freedom to take a lover.

Last I came to Sally. 'Sarah, Viscountess Frensham, beloved wife of Viscount Frensham, MP, mother of Timothy' the inscription started. It gave her dates of birth and death, the first being the same as her mother's death I saw. She was described also as the daughter of the Rector.

I put out a hand and touched the top of the stone. It felt rough and hot from the sun. I looked carefully around me... There was still no one in sight. I sat down on the grass beside the grave itself. It was neatly kept, as were those of her parents. I wished I had some flowers to put on Sally's but I had none. I felt confident that she would understand.

I studied the inscription on her stone. She had died seven years earlier, or at least it would be seven years in September. I had been married for four and a half years. I thought back over that time and wondered what my life would now be like if Sally had lived and we had married. Just the thought of the happiness I had missed so aggravated the sadness I already felt about my little dead daughter that I almost broke down. My life seemed blighted. My heart literally ached with anguish for all that I had lost.

"Oh, Sally," I said aloud. "I still love you so much." I was close to tears. I thought back to the night she had died and to the things she had said.

It had been a long time before but the memory of that night was so sharp and clear that it might have been only a few days earlier. The savage, almost fatal, wound was as fresh as it had ever been. I had a feeling that I was not going to be able to bear it any longer; that although I had gone on for almost seven years, bound by the promise I had made to Sally, this new tragedy was the final stroke of fate, the last straw.

I lay down with my face on the soft grass of her grave and gave myself up to misery.

And then a strange thing happened. The feeling of indescribable sadness gradually faded away and was replaced by a sensation of warmth and lightness which spread throughout my body. The misery was lifted from me just as though it was a blanket which someone had gently removed, exposing me to a golden healing light.

I felt at peace. I was happy. I sat up, wondering if I had died and been transported suddenly to heaven. The churchyard was exactly the same. The same sun shone hotly on my head and shoulders. The birds still sang in the gently waving trees. I was not dead. I was certain of that. What *had* happened to me? For a moment I was puzzled. Then suddenly I knew with perfect clarity and understanding.

Sally was with me.

I remembered how she had calmed me just before she died. She had put her arms around me and I had felt very similar to the way I felt now.

"I prayed for you, darling," she had said. "You'll be brave now."

I couldn't see her but I *knew* she was with me now. I could hear her words inside my head.

"Don't worry about your little baby," she told me. "She's with me now. I'll look after her. You'll have other children I know.

"You mustn't be unhappy any more, Jimmy. I'll always be with you. Go on with your life. Do your best. Be a good husband to that nice girl you married. She's even more unhappy about the baby than you are, you know."

I stood up. So powerful was the feeling of her presence all around me that I was amazed that I could not actually see her.

"Sally," I said. "You really are here, aren't you?"

"Yes, my love. I'm always with you."

"I wish I could see you."

"You will. One day."

"The day I die?" I guessed.

"I'll be there to welcome you."

"Will we be together after that?"

"Oh, yes, my love. We'll always be together."

I drew a deep breath and stood up straight, as though on parade, head up, shoulders back, stomach in. I felt fine.

"You'll be all right now, my darling," said Sally softly.

The sun suddenly went behind a cloud and a shadow fell over the graveyard and I knew that Sally had gone. But she had not gone very far from me. She would never be very far away. And when I died we would be together for Eternity. It was a wonderfully comforting feeling giving me great confidence but, rather surprisingly, no desire to commit suicide.

In the years that followed my strange mystical experience in the Highworth churchyard I sometimes wondered whether I had dreamed the whole thing. But whether I dreamed it or not did not actually matter. The result was the same. I had no fear of death.

I knew now that life was a sort of assault course and I had to get over the obstacles in the best way I could. At the end of it all was the perfect bliss of reunion with Sally. At night sometimes, when I was unable to sleep, I used to imagine we were together, walking hand-in-hand through Elysian Fields. I still do it to this day. It is a great comfort.

And now she was surely with me and her son in the Wellington Barracks office of the Regimental Lieutenant Colonel of the Musketeers. He was a fine-looking young man and as we talked I kept seeing in him glimpses of his mother. His nose wrinkled when he smiled, just like hers. It had given me a very nasty shock when I first realised who he was but I was getting used to the idea now, indeed I was loath to let him go.

I looked down at the form in front of me. It was satisfactorily completed. My Adjutant had been right. Any other officer sitting in my chair would have taken the same view of him. If Sally had somehow twitched a magical string so that Timothy should receive a sympathetic reception she need not have bothered, though I was glad it had worked out as it had. Perhaps she had done it for *me*.

Just to keep the conversation going a little while longer I asked him about his hopes and ambitions in the Army.

"Well, sir," he said cautiously, "I rather hope that after a few years in the Regiment I might manage to get into the SAS."

"Why not?" I said equably. "There are lots of Guardsmen in the SAS, officers and soldiers. If you've got what it takes you'll find it very exciting."

He nodded enthusiastically. "I certainly should like to try."

I looked at my watch. "It's time for lunch," I said. "Have you any plans?"

"No, sir."

"Would you like to come to the Club with me? The food's not bad."

"Thank you, sir. I should like that."

I stood up. "We can continue our conversation there," I said, feeling cheered.

I picked up my hat and umbrella and opened the door to the next-door office.

"I'm going to the Club for lunch now, Michael," I said to my Adjutant. "I'll be back this afternoon."

"What about the candidate, sir?"

"I've done all the bumf," I told him. "I'm taking him to lunch with me."

He smiled smoothly. "I see, sir. I imagine that means we're accepting him."

"It does," I grinned back at him. "You're not surprised, Michael." It was not a question.

"No, sir, I'm not. I'll arrange for him to join the next Brigade Squad."

I nodded. "He'll do very well, I think. I expect he'll be the Lieutenant Colonel one day."

"You never know, sir." He looked thoughtful. "Colonel The Earl of Coniston sounds rather splendid."

"So it does, Michael. So it does."

I shut the door and ushered young Timothy out of my other door into the passage. We walked down the stairs, passing the portraits of all the Colonels of the Musketeers since the Regiment was formed in the seventeenth century. I noticed Timothy looking at them with interest.

We left the building and crossed The Square to the gate into Birdcage Walk. We walked past Buckingham Palace where the sentries on the other side of the Forecourt spotted me amongst the now-thinning groups of tourists and saluted. I removed my bowler hat in acknowledgement. Some of the tourists stared at me, no doubt wondering who I was. Several took photographs of me. It was quite like old times.

As we crossed Green Park Timothy, rather daringly I thought, said, "I couldn't help hearing what you were saying to the Regimental Adjutant, sir."

"About you?"

He blushed slightly. "Yes, sir. It's quite a thought that one day I might have your job."

"It is, isn't it?" I agreed. "You'll be surprised how quickly the time will pass." I felt very middle-aged. "If you keep your nose clean you'll go far."

"Keep my nose clean?"

"Just behave properly. Don't have an affair with another man's wife… if you can avoid it," I said vaguely.

He nodded, looking rather shocked.

"There's no reason why you shouldn't get to the top of the Army if you want to." I was thinking of his remarkably impressive examination results which I had discovered during the interview. "Of course you'll need a lot of luck. As Napoleon observed, luck is the most important asset for a soldier."

"What's your next job, sir?" he asked after a pause.

"I'm going to Germany to be a Brigadier."

We walked in silence for a while. Then I said, "Your mother once told me that I ought to be a General, and I'm doing my best to please her."

He laughed. He thought I was joking.

He said, "It's awfully nice to be able to talk to someone about my mother. I don't know anyone who knew her except Anne. I'd like to know what she was like. Anne said she was very pretty, but she *was* her best friend. She suggested I should ask you about her. She said she had introduced you to her."

"I remember that," I said, wishing that Anne had forgotten it. "I was asked to take her to Highworth where your parents were giving a dinner party for a deb dance somewhere. That was the first time I went there. I can remember you as a small boy. I actually bought you your toy Musketeer and I taught you how to salute. Your mother adored you, she would have made a wonderful mother to you if she'd lived."

He stared at me.

I decided to change the subject. "'Pretty', Anne said, did she? That was an understatement. Your mother's face could have launched a thousand ships any day."

"Sir?" He looked puzzled.

I tried again. "She was the most beautiful woman I ever met. She was also a very nice person. She was charming and good and kind. Everyone loved her," especially me, I almost added. "Of course she knew she was beautiful but she wasn't in the least conceited, and she had a lovely smile."

He looked delighted. "That's wonderful," he said after a moment. "Thank you, sir."

I smiled at him. He was a nice young man and a credit to his mother. "The servants all thought she was an angel." I laughed lightly. "Perhaps they were right." I asked about Freddie. "Didn't your father talk to you about her?"

"He didn't, no. He never did. I imagine it was too painful for him."

Of course he'd found her memory painful, but not for the reason young Timothy imagined.

We crossed Piccadilly in a break in the traffic and walked up the steps of the Cavalry and Guards Club.

A few minutes later I took Sally's son into the bar for a drink before lunch.

A NOTE ON LOCATION

The house in Jamaica where our hero and heroine stay is not an invention. The location is loosely based on Ian Fleming's house, called Goldeneye. I was there in 1963. He wasn't there then. I think he was in England. He died the following year. The house was a fairly simple bungalow. The table where Fleming typed his books was deliberately placed so that if he looked up from his typewriter he saw only a blank wall. He was therefore not distracted by any view. Near the table was a shelf containing a few books, one of which was entitled *Birds of the West Indies* by James Bond, the name he chose for his hero as a dull name for a very exciting character. I discovered years later that James Bond (the author) was an American who was educated in England at Harrow School. For the building itself I borrowed another house, which was a few miles along the coast, and transplanted it to the site. It was blissfully comfortable and had a delightful swimming pool immediately outside the bedrooms. I expect the beach I describe is more or less unchanged. The big black rock at the water's edge will still be there.